Neurogenesis

A novel by Helen Collins

Published by SpeculativeFictionReview.com

www.speculativefictionreview.com

ISBN 0-9785232-4-5

Cover Art by Peter Dingus

Praise for Ms. Collins book *Mutagenesis*

"The book has a strong intellectual and emotional focus, but it is neither as tidy nor as pat as I first feared it might be. I think that it is talking to itself, rather than lecturing us, and that makes for a lively discussion"—Russell Letson, Locus Dec '92.

"…The biological speculation is rather interesting, the characters much more real than the setting, and Collins manages to use their viewpoints and relationships as a vehicle for some interesting meditations on…gender roles and the artistic personality..." — Norman Spinrad, Asimov's Magazine,'93

"There is plenty of adventure and scientific puzzle, but particularly interesting is Collins' use of language. The story points up how language shapes people's thinking—overall the novel's language has an unusual feel: intuitive, playful, lumpy, engaging. It makes the people eccentric and real. Collins is a welcome new voice." —Martha Soukup, The Washington Post 2/28/93. She recommended the book for a Nebula.

Neurogenesis

www.speculativefictionreview.com

To Nancy

Chapter One

Attempted Murder on a Windy Planet

Telem
2/21/3550oe
High Garda, Arine Archipelago
Zalterius II

"She's coming back."

Tel drops the horn audio, skins on the video, and stares at the screen. "She's coming back," he says again.

He swivels around, opens his mouth to say it once more, but the only other occupant of his study is little Pen, his youngest son.

Tel looks at the child for a second blankly, then rises from his chair and bounds toward the door. "Father!" he calls, "Father, she's coming back. My . . . your . . . my mother. Father!"

Tel's second wife, Dorey, runs toward him along the long hallway. "What is it? Is something—"

"Get my father," he says and turns again to the screen, flat set, glowing on the horn table. The message is there, of course. In written letters. He reads it again.

TO
Telem Allain
High Garda
2/20/3550oe
FROM
Pentente Mission Direction
Plateau Office
Arine Archipelago

Concerning: regulations governing dispersal/disposal mission returnees

Description: Mission 707—Quivera Project, Procne (departure 3519, projected return date 3645—55, actual return 3550); seven original members; six survivors—three former inhabitants of Arine Archipelago

Directive:
(1) Allain family will prepare to accept survivors Diana Rise Allain and Fron Maces to Allaincroft estate, High Garda Island. (Inclusion of subject Maces is a temporary, non-regulation arrangement, subject's descendent line being discontinuous and his original home island, Angel, Archipelago Nord, no longer residential; subject expressed resistance to placement on Corse or elsewhere in Archipelago Nord.)
(2) Michalis family will prepare to accept Gisonne Michalis to Laurel House, High Garda Island.

"But who is it, father? Who is coming?" Tel's son asks.
"My mother."
"Why is she coming?"
"She is my mother. This is her home." Tel answers without taking his eyes from the screen.
"I don't know her," little Pen says.
"I know you don't," Tel says. "She's been gone for
... thirty years. I don't know her either."
But then he looks up at a blank place on his worn and tattered study wall and almost remembers. There was something there, long long ago, a painting, her special painting. He tries to see it. Was it a bird? Yes, an off-world bird. White. He recalls the image: white feathered arcs of wings, narrow legs, a strange background, flatland, still water, tall grasses.
But he was little more than a baby when she left them. Abandoned him—them, all of them. No, died. Just the same as

dead. He had always refused to imagine her alive somewhere. What did it matter? She would not—could not—return in his or his children's or great grandchildren's lifetime.

But yet here she is—returned! Already on The Plateau. To arrive on High Garda tomorrow.

It must be wrong, Tel thinks. A mistake. But no. The Allaincroft OS system is sorely in need of repair, but the message came direct and is the same on audio and video in letters on screen.

"Gods drown it! Who needs her?" he says aloud, loud enough to drown the bird painting, the smell of linell flower that seems to have invaded the room, the image of an old fashioned, white silk shirt, of blond hair loosely tied. Most of all Tel wants to shout away the memory of his mother's face before it emerges from that lost time. "Pontus drown her anyway."

"Who? What is it, Telem?" Tel's father, Blake Allain Rise, shuffles cautiously into the room, long neck turning over his threadbare collars and stooped shoulders as he peers about from side to side.

"My grandmother is coming back," little Pen tells his grandfather.

"What! What is the child saying, Telem?"

"Your first wife, my mother, Diana Rise Allain, The Allain, will arrive here on High Garda tomorrow." Tel waits with almost cruel anticipation for his father's reaction.

But Old Blake says nothing, shows no emotion, then shakes his head and almost smiles. Tel is impatient. Does his father smile because he is pleased?

"No, she isn't," Blake finally says.

"Yes, she is. Just come and look at the message."

"No, Telem, it's not possible." Blake speaks as though Tel were still a child, unable to comprehend. "They were programmed for a planet so distant that they cannot return within two centuries. They never told us before departure. We thought it would be two years. Not just us, the Michalises too. They thought Gisonne would return—"

"Father, stop rambling and look at the message." Tel magnifies the screen and pulls his father, almost roughly, to stand with him before it.

Blake frowns as he tries to read, shakes his head slowly, and starts again at the top. Impatiently Tel skins up the sound as though Blake's ears are as weak as his eyes.

Old Blake is not as old as he acts and looks. The poor vision and vague peering result from eye trouble—once easily correctible by Malaacan surgery—surgery no longer accessible to inhabitants of z2. He has had the stoop since Tel can remember, since in the old, rich days it was considered a courtly bow, sign of grace and breeding. And the hesitant walk, Tel believes, is not due to arthritis but to tentativity and lack of decision.

And now, eyes wide in wonder, he looks to his son for meaning.

Tel, not Blake, has been The Allain and head of the Allain family since his maternal grandfather's death twenty years ago. It has been Tel, Blake's younger son, who has had to fight to hold together their estate and remaining possessions in the face of deprivation and Pentente penalties, to protect wider groups of relatives and dependents, to deal with the off-worlders, to live down and compensate for the ruined family reputation.

Yet now there is nothing Tel can say to his father. For all their differences, for once they are as one in bewilderment. They turn away from the screen and look in silence through the study window, down over a half-mile slope of sidelawn, a precipitous dark strand, and below it, to the ocean. Tide is almost all the way down, exposing the long artificial pilings of the zoid dock on which Tel's crippled cousin Jevry sits huddled in his new, used wheeler. Even as they watch, a cloud shadow races across the lawn, and the wind suddenly whips up from the sea, pressing the bent grasses and shrubs flat and rattling the small, square gloid panes. First the horizon, then Zeig Island, and finally Jevry disappear in blowing fog.

Jevry

And, as always, the winds blow the fog away as quickly as it came and the sun leaps out almost painfully bright on water and land. Unaware of, or perhaps indifferent to, his uncle and cousin watching him from the house on the cliff above, Jevry Alfred Allain tilts his sun hat and keys a shift in his wheeler to ease the ache in the bad leg. The new angle does nothing to reduce the glare from the water. He considers dimming his goggles but decides that the loss of brilliance won't be worth the slight increase in comfort. Such questions become more and more important as time goes by. "Do I dare to eat a peach?" he asks. But he will never "walk upon the beach"...or anywhere else.

Jevry hears someone above them hurrying down over the lawns toward the beach. Even though they've gotten the old generator working again, Tel's new wife, Dorey, always prefers to walk and run rather than take the lift and use up any of their scant power. Yet she is not wearing her wind suit.

Jevry pulls his own worn, wind wrap tighter, hunches his shoulders, and sets his face to stare morosely at the waves until she reaches him. When she arrives he pretends not to notice and then to be surprised, mildly annoyed. He shrugs to let her know that he has been content in his reverie—alone.

But this time she is not solicitous; she doesn't coax him or coddle his attitude.

"You knew Diana Allain, didn't you?" she asks, still breathless. "'The Allain'? A long time ago?"

"What? My aunt? My aunt Diana? Long dead. Why?"

"Not dead."

He shakes his head and waves an arm in dismissal. "Same as dead. Both of them. Gone."

"She's coming here tomorrow."

"Who?"

"Diana Allain."

Jevry waits for the sound of her words to make some kind of sense.

"Cousin Jevry," Dorey says. "Do you understand me? The mission she was on has somehow . . . somehow returned to z2. I don't understand it, but it's true. They are on The Plateau now. Tomorrow—"

Still Jevry does not speak. Dorey squints into his face, curious. Jevry is always grouchy, always pessimistic, but this is different. His face is dead blank, unreadable.

"Thirty years ago," she says, "you were . . . you must have been . . . young—I mean younger. Thirteen or fourteen? You must have known her—her and another one from this island, one of our neighbor dynes, those Michalises, a Gisonne from that generation?"

Jevry doesn't speak, move, or change expression yet his head seems to hunch more deeply into his shoulders, his features grow sharper and older.

"Jevry? Are you all right?" Dorey asks.

"Gisonne Michalis," he says finally.

"What?"

"Gisonne. Gisonne Michalis is the other one."

For a long time he stares down the strand. He seems to have forgotten Dorey completely.

A figure appears in the distance walking down the beach, toward them. It is Troi, Tel's older son, fourteen years old, beautiful, strong, and golden in the sun's slanting rays. He bends over and pokes through the sand. Looking for shells. There were few to be found even when Jevry was his age.

Troi straightens up, shakes hands with himself, and grins at Jevry and Dorey. He kicks sand out behind him like a male dog and sprints to the dock. He deep bends his long strong legs, jumps high, and lands lightly in front of the wheeler. Jevrey's own crabbed legs twitch in response. He presses a key randomly and the wheeler jerks back.

"Sorry, cousin Jevry," Troi says as if he had actually bumped him.

"Never mind. It's fine. It's fine."

"Look. I found a crab leg."

Jevry snorts. "In my day we found whole crabs. Fiddlers. So what? It didn't mean anything then either. Dropped by a Malaacan bird. Bird's gone too. Long gone."

"Look, Jev . . . Cousin Jevry," Dorey went on, "I thought you'd be the one to ask all these questions. I didn't know you would be upset. I . . . I'm sorry. But why is it so important? Why are Tel and Blake all—all shaken? I mean people do come back from other times. Usually no one we ever really know or . . . What was she like?"

"Which one?"

"Your aunt, of course."

"Oh, her. Aunt Diana was perfect," he says. "Gisonne was not."

Dorey laughs, thinking he is, as always, ironic.

Troi begins to listen. He sits on the dock, feet dangling.

"Troi," Dorey says, "your grandmother is coming home tomorrow."

"What grandmother?"

"Diana, grandfather Blake's wife."

"The one who went away forever?"

No one answers him. Jevry continues to watch the rising sea and Dorey watches Jevry.

"I heard about her," Troi says. "She was on a mission. She can't come back."

"Well she is back," Dorey says. "Now she's being 'replaced' with—with us. She will have been gone over thirty years."

"Diana really was perfect," Jevry says. "In all things."

"She was a lousy parent. Leaving her babies! For what?"

"No. She was a perfect mother," he insists. "And a perfect wife."

"I never heard Tel ever mention her. And wife? How did old Blake take it? How could he have let her go?"

"Let her go? He had nothing to say about it. She was an Allain—The Allain. Just as Tel is . . . thinks he is now."

Jevry shrugs against the back of his wheeler and keys an angle change. Dorey puts a hand on the arm as if to help, but there is nothing he and his chair can't manage.

"Why? Why did she go?" Dorey persists. "Why did she abandon her family and her planet just before the bad times?"

"No. You've got it wrong. All you young people. Nasty rumors. She died for the family and z2. Anyway she didn't explain to me. And neither did Gisonne. To her—to both of them in different ways—I was only a kid."

"And she was thirty-four," Dorey says.

"And Gisonne was twenty-two . . . Pontus, Pontus—this can't really be true!"

"I—I think so. I know! It came on the horn. They are coming here tomorrow."

"Gisonne," he says. "Gisonne, too?"

"Yes, if she's the Michalis woman."

"Gisonne," Jevry says and stares in silence out toward z2's close horizon, his eyes tearing in its blinding brilliance. He decides to dim his gloid goggles afterall and fusses with the controls.

Troi frowns and then decides to reduce the importance of what he cannot fathom. "So what? That's nothing," he says. "A friend of mine from school lives on the same island with a family dyne whose great, great, very great uncle or something came home. He was so old nobody had ever met him—not even heard of him. PMD just probably figured out who his descendants were and—"

"No, no, boy!" Jevry shouts. "You don't know what you're . . . ." His fingers are white on the arms of the wheeler.

Troi looks helplessly at Dorey, who pats his shoulder. Both watch Jevry as his breath slows and his face calms. Finally he turns to look at them, almost smiling.

"Home is where when you go there they have to take you in," he says, laughs, and then adds: "Diana is not going to like this world. . . . But Gisonne might."

Dyll Breff

2/20/3550oe
Nordport
Archipelago Nord

In the embassy on Nord, Dyll Breff, Pentente Grand Viceroy, stares at his horn with an astonished frown. The message is from PMD officials at the port on The Plateau in the Arine Archipelago. A SPEED ship has landed there. A certain mission has returned early, two centuries early as a matter of fact. Inexplicable, unpredicted, unprecedented, unprogrammed, impossible.

He casts his eyes down the Quivera Mission 707 roster. Yes. He remembers these names. After thirty years he remembers them all. Not only the names but some details of the biographies, details both personal and professional.

He shouts at the horn: "Perl! Perl, listen. You've got a job." Breff stares again at the crew list.

She is back.

Diana

2/22/3550oe
High Garda

The next day the winds are more erratic than usual. A sudden blow up, strong enough to knock unripe fruit off the crooked trees, is followed by a dead calm and sun so steady and warm that the small family group, climbing the steep hillside behind and above the main house, unbind their wind suits and dim their goggles. But then, only a few seconds later, they are leaning forward into another whipping, breathless gale.

Troi is eager to see the new floater, designed on Malaaca thirty years earlier especially for the fierce air currents and steep terrain of z2, to replace the old island hoppers, but withheld until now by the Pentente. Troi doesn't care that it promises to eliminate some of the treacheries of local air and sea travel, that people may no longer have to take tractor buses over the steep, sharp roads from small and dangerous air fields or climb or be lifted up from the sea, or that it is being given to z2 more for the comfort of the increasing numbers of Pentente off-worlders than for the natives. He wants only to see the wonderful invention in action.

The others are making a big deal over the grandmother thing. Troi's father Tel, Troi's new stepmother, Dorey, his little brother Pen, and most unlikely, even old cousin Jevry in his wheeler have climbed the steep lane to the clearing among the upper orchards, where the floater is to drop its "anchor." Nimee Michalis from Laurel House, around the mountain, mother of a great span of children, the youngest of whom are Troi's friends, has joined them because some relative of hers has come back to z2 on the same vessel. Only Grandfather Blake was not well enough to come out.

When the floater finally appears, Troi is not disappointed. It is a beautiful thing—much better than the old island hoppers—

and much larger than he expected, coming in low and straight from the west. Then it slows to hover above the small field.

It seems to drift randomly and slowly. Troi is glad when a sudden small tempest blows up. He wants to see the craft do its work, adapt flexibly to the worst.

It bends more. Is it supposed to fold upon itself that way? No! It is collapsing, toppling, falling! My god, they all cry. Falling!

They stand, expressionless, gaping, as the white, mothwinged thing spins, rotates, tumbles down from the sky to break apart, almost slowly, on the grassy hill above them. It splits open and spills its innards, while pieces of itself detach and roll down toward the watchers almost gracefully.

But the cries are not graceful.

Cousin Jevry is the first to move, but his wheeler is defective, has no risers and was not designed for bumpy, steep terrain. The rest, who reacted seconds later, pass him by and race up across the open space among the fruit trees.

Troi and his father get there first; Tel bends over one still figure in a pilot's uniform, while Troi tries to pull a large piece of metal off another, a lady in her mid or late thirties, sort of pretty but with a sharp scar on her right temple—and a large white bird. The animal is alive and chattering, the woman very still.

"This man is dead," Tel says and leaves that body to run over and help Troi with the woman. At the same time Nimee Michalis, a little heavy, encumbered in her very old, tattered but voluminous wind cloak, reaches them, calling, "Is it my sister? Is it Gisonne?"

Tel doesn't answer. Nimee moves up next to him and together in silence they stare down at the pale woman. Both her light hair and the animal's white curls twist and flatten in the again rising wind, but her face seems to be made of stone.

And then Troi's father says a weird thing in a tone of voice Troi has never heard him use before. "Mommy," he says. "Mama."

"Gisonne? Is Gisonne there?" cousin Jevry calls loudly from where he has been left behind alone.

"It's not Gisonne," Nimee Michalis finally shouts back to him. "It's Diana."

"Then where is she? Where is Gisonne?"

Gisonne

2/22/3550oe
The Plateau, Arine Archipelago

It is not windy but warm, bright, and still in the midafternoon sun on the campus of the Arine branch of Zalterius II's single university. The extensive grounds are overgrown, unkempt. The few buildings, which vary in style, expressing the changing attitudes and visions of diverse ages, are alike only in their strength, illusion of height, and, most of all, utter shabbiness and neglect.

The medical and research area is exceptionally quiet. Few people now-a-days walk the lanes or sit on the benches. Broken wheelers and rusty walkers slump empty above motionless ramps. It is one of the few places on the island, and, indeed, on the whole planet, that the ubiquitious beating and breathing of the ocean cannot reach. Nor, from this high interior plain, can one hear the noise of The Plateau's circle of markets directly above the cliffs. The only sound is the occasional hum and broken clatter of the hospital venting system.

A figure appears from a cluster of rectangular buildings and moves across a wide expanse of faded, patchy green toward a tall, double fronted, stone edifice at the far end of the compound. It is a woman stalking, rather than walking, with uncomfortable, unlikely strides.

She appears to be in her mid or late twenties; her short, loose dark hair has a sharp white streak on the right side, and a narrow scar across the left temple. Her forehead is broad and the rest of the face far too narrow, especially the nose which is just too pointed to be delicate. The lips and chin are delicate though, or would be were it not for a fierce tightness of expression. She is wearing some kind of loose uniform, not the garb of the usual hospital patient, nor the normal dress for the outside world. An old patient watching her idly from his cracked window might have recognized it as a fashion from his youth, the old wind-cloak style common thirty years earlier. Is it a young woman, gone mad, dressed in her grandmother's clothes?

As she approaches and bypasses the first entrance, she looks up at its worn lettering, frowns, and slows her steps. The words "Allain Institute of Human . . . " are worn. Whatever once followed has been hidden under a bold white and dark green sign announcing "Malaacan College of Neurobiology and Psycholinguistics." The woman stops, stares like one extremely near-sighted or illiterate, shrugs, and continues on her way.

She turns a corner and, without hesitating, enters a small unmarked doorway. She moves quickly down an empty corridor with shabby, peeling walls, turns right into a small alcove, and stops. The door will not yield to her grasp. She whirls about, retraces her steps through the deadly quiet to the larger corridor, continues to its end where she turns right again and climbs three flights of a stairway. The corridors on that floor are busier. Men in laboratory suits pass her, some glancing curiously, but it is no one's job to stop her. Women running machines in offices with open dutch doors glance but she passes too quickly for them to really see.

Finally she stops before a dark green board, an index of offices. She brushes back the dark hair, moves her face close to the raised letters, squints deeply. She turns about to look purposely down each of the corridors. Then, with a quirk of her tight, thin lips, she abruptly starts toward a hallway on her left. Here she moves deliberately with the same strong strides with which she had crossed the lawns. At last she stops before a wide doubledoor, ignores the small print on its gloid pane, and pushes through.

There are two people in lab wear, conferring over a chart or perhaps only gossiping. Their heads rise at the sound.

"Do you want some—" one begins but the woman is already inside the next area.

It is more an office than a laboratory, but equipped with various machines and viewers. An elderly man is sitting by one of the viewers. A shaft of very beautiful, silk white hair hangs rather dramatically over his forehead; in spite of his large head and crooked profile, his face is gentle, bemused; he is absently fingering some kind of instrument, smiling at a young, off-world man on the other side of the room.

They turn as one toward the woman bursting into their space, both startled. Then the face of the elderly man changes. The frown deepens between the white brows. The thin lips stretch open. A smile and a grimace at once.

For a second the intruder stops moving. She looks from the old man to the young and back again. And then there is no more hesitation. Her eyes fix and hold the older man and she strides across the room and pushes him backwards hard with both hands against his chest. Her expression never changes. His chair tilts but hits the table top and does not fall. She has both hands around the narrow wrinkled throat and strangles and shakes at the same time, banging his head on the table.

His young colleague starts to call out, starts to move, does neither and then does both at once, but too late.

With her right hand, the woman has pulled a knife from her jacket pocket.

"Gisonne," the old man says. "No, Gisonne."

"Old man," she says.

Chapter Two

Dynasphere

Dynasphere/group—sori, a sphere (in certain circumstances a circle)
TL—task leader—Lapin, roughly equivalent to director of activities, often but not always group center
CN—central negative, voice of opposition—orck, a wind spirit or demon, the source of wind power, gale against the wall
SeL—social-emotional leader, sometimes group center
TR—tension releaser—sann, one who lifts with the right hand (thought to be related to the left hemisphere of the brain)
IP—information provider—jav, bearer of knowledge, bard
SO—silent observer—dark watcher, lull in a storm—dangerous, misleading
ScF—self-centered follower
R—recorder—bard, teller, historian, often also IP
Cell—connects to outside
NC—new comer, outsider in process of adaptation

6/23/3519oe
The Plateau

In 3519 the grass on The Plateau campus had been a brighter and happier green. It lay broadly carpeting this one flat place in all the Arine Archipelago. A few more buildings stood then and they were not shabby or crumbling. Ancient but shining with love and money, antique cornices and trim were proudly and deeply stained in veritcal lines the old way—contrasting narrow moldings pulling the eye ever upward to the mountain top.

Gisonne Michalis swung her light wind cloak as she walked, breathing deliberately and deeply of the high, thinner air—so much better than the damp, organic, thick odors of Estuary. Gisonne did not like closed-in places.

Her task on Estuary, adjusting a malfunctioning dynashere, was almost done. It had been her first professional test, and her success had been in some doubt. It was always a challenge for a natural Tension Releaser to function alone in mending a group. The very characteristics that made a good TR were sometimes obstacles to direct intervention: the need and ability to please, to make others feel good, to prevent social discomfort, to placate, to prevent antagonism and hostility, to mitigate distress, to joke. In a way the job was harder because results had to come through indirection and suggestion. Yet the adjustment was coming along nicely after a slow beginning; the unhappy, disintegrating ornithology group was becoming a fully functional dyne. One more trip back to Estuary should do it. As of now, Gisonne was no longer an intern.

She resisted the urge to skip, and instead tossed her head, enjoying the swing of her straight, black hair, and walked faster to the meeting of the newly-official Zalterian Dynasphere, ZD, organizaton.

She had always been a good Tension Releaser, an important role in any dyne, circle, or other designed or undesigned group, not in spite of but because of her shyness. She loved the work, if not all the members—dynamates, but that was as it should be in a well-functioning group. And ZD had to function well, since its function was the study of dynes.

Inside the Allain Institute of Human Studies people argued and laughed aloud in the corridors. Gisonne walked through the old great hall study dynes and more professional task dynes, all of which revolved and overlapped. Pairs and triads occupied the central benches, while undyned students and researchers burrowed into stalls and carrels carved into the old stone outer walls.

ZD met in one of the newer wings, whose space was more sensibly divided into small lecture halls and even smaller

meeting rooms, and which housed the new softer sciences, both home-grown and off-world. ZD was the newest
social science although, ironically, its subject was the oldest: the nature, history, and functions of Zalterian groups, circles and spheres whose origins predated the first settlers and the Octente itself.

The members sat around a circular table. (The ideal group, dyne, is a circle although some are 'y's or 'x's by necessity.)

"We have a new project," Evan, both center and TL, Task Leader, said.

"We are too heavily committed to tasks now," Cly, CN, Central Negative, said. (CNs and Sc-fs, Self-centered followers, are critical roles; "a good group maintains a two to one ratio between positive and negative comments.")

"This one might be most important. It might be the chance we need."

"What is it?" they asked.

"We get to design a group—a superior dyne if we're really good—and lucky."

"We do that all the time," Cly said.

"Not really," Aj, IP, Information Provider, said. "We study existing structures, we tinker with and try to adjust dysfunctional groups—when they let us, and we form and reform test circles out of volunteers in the lab, but we never create the pattern and choose the members for—"

"Right, Aj, right. We know what we do. But, Evan, what is it?"

"A project of Doctor Cres Trjol. Some new kind of horn. Actually the Operating System of a SPEED ship."

Since they all worked in the large Allain Institute building, Gisonne had seen Trjol before but knew only that he had once studied off world—on Malaaca—and was supposed to be a distinguished neuroscientist.

"I don't get it," Cly said. Others murmured with him. "You mean Trjol—the big brain guy in the other wing? That Trjol?

He's a neural something, Malaacan science. Trained on Malaaca. What's Zalterian ZD theory to him?" Cly, of course, addressed the question to Aj.

"I can't recall any connection," Aj said. In that case, they all knew, there wasn't any and never had been.

"We'll find out," Evan said. "I know only that it has something to do with designing a mission crew."

"The dyne will be a crew?"

"A crew is always a dyne," Cly said, "but a dyne is not always a crew."

One or two of them moaned politely. Gisonne wondered if he was stealing her role and if she should do something. Compete? Joke? Too late. Too shy.

"Seems so," Evan said. "We're meeting with him today."

"Excuse me, Evan, but I have to go back to Estuary," Gisonne said. "The ornithology circle I've been advising needs more—"

"Delay it. This could be more important."

About goals and business Evan was usually right, a good Task Leader; but about persons and methods not always effective, not a SeL, Social-emotional Leader, which he tried to be from time to time. He was older than other ZD members, having had a career in some kind of government diplomacy earlier. He had a broad Asian face, pleasant smiling eyes, and a mouth that almost but never quite smiled. Gisonne sometimes wondered if that was why his diplomatic years had been brief.

Right from the beginning Gisonne found Doctor Cres Trjol generally unpleasant—in both manner and looks.

The meeting took place in his space, a large discussion room next to his laboratories. He sat at what had to be the "head" of the room on top of a desk, presenting himself as not only TL but Leader of the temporary circle ZD and his few people formed together. Was he aware of group terms and concepts and what his physical position meant?

Gisonne looked around to see if others—especially

18

members of ZD—were thinking the same thing. Cly shrugged and shook his head at her. Aj was nodding knowingly.

Trjol started without introducing himself—no need, he assumed?—and without greeting his listeners: "The mind is not a machine. In spite of all attempts for fifteen oe decades no OS has ever been designed with a mind. You all know that, of course."

Cly stirred and several other ZD members frowned.

"Now that for the last 500 years we have a particular bacteria which, with out quiveron, we can try again. But we will not try to design a mind. A mind can only be produced through evolution, natural selection. The selection is based on the reality around it, its environment. We can design its environment, its human environment. That is what you will do."

Trjol's people clapped warmly and he bowed slightly.

More applause was joined by some confused ZD people.

"Horns, OS's, are, have always had minds," Cly said.

"No," Trjol almost shouted, turning his head slowly to stare at Cly. He waited a second and dropped his voice to an almost inaudible, dramatic whisper. "I say the OS, the horn, has no relationship to mind. An OS is designed, built. Even when it goes on to further design itself beyond what we could do, it is not evolved."

"Anyway what has designing horns got to do with us?" Cly asked, this time deliberately misunderstanding.

"I have already told you. Once again—a mind is not a single unit but a community. It is an analogue of reality. The new mind—I call it the 'edel' in honor of the great historical neuroscientist, Gerald M. Edelman—will be evolved, an analogue. But an analogue of what? Of a dyne, a group of human beings."

Obnoxious, Gisonne thought. But then she saw that Aj was laughing, and even Cly smiling.

"I still don't understand," another member of ZD said.

"You don't have to. You group people, ZD you call yourselves . . ." He glanced at his memo as if checking the name. " . . . are not qualified to design a mind and a mind cannot, as I have said, be designed. ZD will design a dynasphere. With your latest techniques, you ZD people will select the members. And your carefully constructed dyne will then become our edel's outer reality. The edel will, by trial and error, evolve into a living analogue of the group mind."

Gisonne found the man presumptious, theatrical and arrogant, and the plan reductuve and wasteful of ZD's abilities. Evan must not have understood what he was getting them into when he accepted the invitation for ZD to join this symposium.

"We do not think in terms of a 'group mind'," Cly said.

"But of course you do," Trjol said, warm this time, benign, gentle. "You may not use the accurate term. My people have reported to me on your research and theories."

Patronizing, Gisonne added to the list of the man's personal and social defects.

"Then you know there is no such thing as a dyne mind," Cly said. This time other members of ZD raised their voices in agreement.

Trjol looked from one to the other slowly. When he came to Gisonne she felt herself grow warm with embarrassment. She could not bear to speak aloud in anything larger than a small circle and doubly hated to argue in any situation (except within her family circle). Her role was to release tension, not add to it.

"And you?" he asked her directly.

"The concept of group mind is contrary to our basic principles, the importance of the contribution, growth, and well-being of the individual," Gisonne said, as her face burned.

A woman wearing Octente insignia on her collar turned fully about in her seat and squinted at Gisonne as at a peculiar form of scum from the sea.

Trjol nodded. His eyes, half hidden under the heavy brows, were fierce with anger.

One of those natural emotional, autocratic leaders with fawning followers, Gisonne added to her list.

"Wait," Evan looked back at her from the the front—right up there with the cheer leaders. Did he have to add to her embarrassment? "I agree with you, Gisonne, of course, but let's find out more about what Doctor Trjol proposes."

Evan was playing both TL and IP for ZD. And apparently Lieutenant for Trjol at the same time! Cell. Playing too many roles. Playing fast and loose.

"Design an optimal group for me," Trjol said, sarcasm evaporated, tones gentle, humble, wooing ZD. He let his head drop and looked up from under the fine, silk black brows like a little boy fearing punishment, needing protection. The Octente woman smiled up at him and nodded.

There was no reply from any member of ZD, but Trjol went on as if there had been: "Timing will be everything. Creation takes place in time." He stopped and looked down at a note. "'Dyning' I beleve is your term. That is why we need ZD's expertise in determining the necessary components and choosing group members from among our applicants."

Gisonne had to admit he was good. His charisma consisted not only of alternating between emotional deprivation and reward of his audience, but of a genuine, contagious passion for his subject. For a second she almost understood his "groupies."

And she disliked him even more.

"Yes. Now—the project. Here it is. This is Braitt Jones, liaison between us and the Octente Mission Direction."

Gisonne watched in disgust as the Octente buro female from the front row stood and walked to the podium, smiled sidewise and up at Trjol, and turned a serious face to the audience. Braitt Jones was actually attractive, not beautiful, but piquant, with small, pointed features except for extremely large moist eyes.

"One of Octente Mission's briefest and most frequent missions. Destination Quivera. Not quite a regular shuttle. SPEED but short. Two years oe, two seasons SPEED time."

Unlike Trjol's long circumlocutions, the woman spoke in abrupt little blips. "A short stop at Agricula on the return."

They didn't get it.

"You'll pick the crew," she said. "From OMD's pool of applicants. OMD can't afford experimental junkets—even for someone as respected as Doctor Trjol—just to study its personnel or an experimental Operating System. The flight will fullfill its regular functions. The mission will be one that would have taken place anyway."

Braitt Jones stopped speaking as abruptly as she started. She stood staring, glaring rather, around at the audience. Trjol seemed not quite to realize that she had finished. He touched her elbow inquiringly, and she glanced quickly up, blushing. Love, Gisonne thought, poor thing. She should be his group lieutenant instead of OMD liaison for the Octente.

"As Braitt said you'll pick the crew. All but one that is. You'll have to choose the rest around that one," Trjol said. "I'm going. Me."

"We can't afford not to do it," Evan said back in their own quarters. "Not just financially. Working on such a project will give us prestige, recognition, validation—all of which we need. Financial backing which we need even more."

"This Trjol is a egomaniac," Gisonne said.

"Maybe a monomaniac," Evan said. "Monomaniacs get things done. And for ZD there may never again be such an opportunity. All variables so completely within our control, choices of individuals so wide, potential combinations astronomical, timing so defined."

"But do we want it done?" Cly asked. "Is it a worthy goal? No. Maybe dangerous. Counter human. Robot brains. Yech."

"I think," Evan said, "that for us the mind thing doesn't really matter. The conditions make it a perfect experiment. As the ship's crew, the group will have an ulterior function, some purposes other than the behaviors we are specifically studying.

"Also isolation is good. A completely closed system. Avoiding dilution and loosening of group cohesion. And as the great man said, this is a one-time chance to design a group almost from scratch. We don't have to adapt our design to preexisting conditions—except the inclusion of Trjol in the system."

"It's almost too good to be true," someone else said. "We can design the total system, create any group ecology we want. The only disadvantage is we can't watch its phasic development. But maybe that's for the best. With all the control, we'll be able to compare input and output. The mission return will be a fascinating study."

"Wait a minute! If we decide to do it, what about control groups?" someone else asked.

"Members of past missions? We can survey all kinds of crews," said Aj, always a good IP.

"Great idea, Aj," Evan said. "Past crews as control groups. Will you and Gisonne be a subgroup whose task is identification, location, and description of suitable returnees? Mission Direction should happily supply all the information, given the friendliness of Braitt Jones to the whole project."

"Are you sure the 'friendliness' isn't only to the wonderful genius, Trjol?" Cly asked.

"All right but I . . . I am going back to Estuary first," Gisonne said.

"Yes. So that's it?" Evan asked. "We're taking on Trjol's project?"

People nodded or grunted assent.

"This whole project makes me nervous," Cly said.

Chapter Three

Estuary

7/3/3519 oe
Estuary

Jevry sometimes wanted to become a climber, not just of the island tops of z2, but other places, Zipag in the Tryllium system where the mountains were twice Earth's Himilayas or Anu where one climbed down and then up rather than up and down. At other times he planned to be a games coach or a"legal swimmer." Never, never would he become a politician—even though he was an Allain—or perhaps because he was an Allain.

On the other hand, there was Jevry's best friend, Denny. Even though he was good at everything, zoology, OS tech stuff, and swimming and climbing, he had always known exactly what he would be someday, a geoshysicist.

Gisonne Michalis, Denny's older sister, invited them to visit Estuary where she had been working with some kind of dyne. Gisonne had a profession that Jevry sometimes understood and sometimes thought was stupid. Everybody was in dynes and groups naturally but Gison's work dyne studied other dynes! Now Gisonne had been working all on her own fixing a "malfunctioning" group.

Denny was happy but Jevry shuddered. Enclosed swamps were not for him. But he said yes. Because with Denny it could be fun. Because it would be in the fall, when he could take a break from his school and other task dynes on The Plateau. Because it would please his grandfather, Xaviour Allain, who thought Jevry should take some interest in Zalterius II beyond running wild all over their home island, High Garda. But most of all because it was Gisonne who asked.

Jevry stood in front of her, close, but he carefully didn't look at her. Next to him Denny leaned dangerously over the rail of the lookout platform, head almost upside down. The platform was the end of a raised walk way built on steeloid piles, extending out from a natural promontory, the high spine of the low island called Estuary. From this height they could see several salt ponds whose passages were so narrow they were almost stagnant, the entire bay and its wide mouth, the short expanse of outer water, and then the wall of tall barrier islands protecting Estuary from high seas and winds. To Jevry there was something unnatural about it. Flat, smelly, still. All enclosed. It was stiffling, like living in the bottom of a used soup cup. One didn't need a windcloak.

The inner bodies of water were banked, not by vertical rock walls or steep slopes as on other islands, but by flatlands as level and low as their own surface, waiting for the tides to cover and soak, recede and bare. Some had reeds and other sparse bright green grasses; most were mudflats through which ran the precious, rare, tidal streams.

From somewhere around the bluff, out of sight, came the thin warning whistle, then long seconds of silence, a double bang of explosion, silence again, the cracking, smashing and splashing of falling rocks, another, briefer moment of silence, and last and longest, rolling claps of thunder as water crashed its way into the new pocket ripped out of the land.

The teacher stood near them with an dyne of small schoolchildren. He had his back to the sea and waited for the noise of the detonation work to decrease.

"This is the lowest and softest shoreline in the Arines," he said finally. "Estuary is the only island with the right topography. To create estuaries and marshland—with slow flowing streams, and productive bays—the engineers need a flat place. This one island already had wide underwater shelves, so this shallow bay is partially natural. At the far end, see." He pointed to a channel cutting into the shoreline on the right.

"That's the entrance to Estuary's oldest artificial estuary that works. The movement of the currents is creating tidal wetlands. With help, of course. On its own—if it survived flooding and storms—it would take 14,000 years.

"These are the only tidal marshes on our planet and they are still too young to support a productive food chain. Too young. Too few."

Jevry paid little attention to the guide's words. He concentrated on the unusual, not quite pleasant, sensations Estuary offered: the rumble of the still broiling waters, the strange whistle of the osprey—first of the large water fowl to be introduced—and the warm, rank odor of marsh. And on Gisonne standing directly behind him, close.

"It is almost low tide now," the guide was saying, "but just imagine that with very high tides all the wetlands you see before you are under water. The whole thing, marshes, streams, and ponds, becomes one great lake or bay. But it is never very deep and it never lasts long. For us to create a 'natural' food chain, sunlight must penetrate to the basin floor, get to rooted plants, worms, clams, oysters, shrimp."

The warning whistle blew again.

"A hydrosphere is a closed system," the guide went on oblivious to th sound. "Saltwater wetlands and their tideflat species are necessary for an autonomous food chain on Zalterius II."

The explosion blotted him out and all other sound. In spite of the warning whistle, it shocked the total person, body and soul. It was louder and seemed closer this time. Jevrey and Denny embarassed themselves by jumping back from the railing. The platform shook under foot and the distant flatland trembled.

When the noise stopped, the teacher began to describe the techniques of introducing off-world flora and fauna, adapting them to the planet system, of inducing mutations.

Jevry felt Gisonne stirring around behind him.

"A stupid waste," someone said. Jevry turned to see a tall man with black hair hanging in his face. He seemed to be talking to Gisonne but she was just looking at him like she didn't know who he was, staring at his face. She looked miserable.

"Hello, Gisonne Michalis," the man said. Jevry didn't like him. He shrugged and turned back to the view.

"This is my brother," Gisonne said. She snapped Denny's suspender—hard. But Denny paid no attention.

"And Jevry Allain," she added. Jevry turned. No choice now. What a pain in the neck. "This is . . . Doctor Trjol."

Before Jevry could respond, Trjol said, "Allain? Really." Only for a second did he take his eyes off Gison's face.

Jevry turned his back again—abruptly—and leaned with Denny over the railing. Trjol was not insulted. He didn't even notice. He talked on to Gisonne.

"Gisonne Michalis, since our previous meeting, I have learned about you," he said. "your particular contributions. You wrote a paper on role repetition in task oriented groups. You handled the restructuring of a dysfunctional group here on Estuary almost by yourself—ornithologists, I believe ."

It didn't sound like a compliment to Jevry. Trjol spoke in a dry, indifferent monotone and stood too close to Gisonne.

"Are you interested in . . . in this work?" she asked.

"Oh, no. No. I have no interest in swamps," he said.

What a dumb conversation, Jevry thought.

This time there was no warning whistle, no sign of any kind, just the explosion. They were deaf and felt rather than heard the rumbling and groaning of the rocks. But it was wrong. Not in the distance, not coming to a new stillness, but underfoot and growing. Surely it was an earthquake, the beginning of a catastrophic tectonic upheaval, a quake to end the planet. Pontus shaking with laughter from his watery core.

No, not an earthquake. The platform began to sway. The quaking and noise of explosion stopped and was replaced by an ear-splitting cracking as pilings collapsed and plastoids ripped.

And then, very slowly and very silently, the nearest part of the raised walkway just behind them fell into the marsh below.

People must have been screaming, but they were all deaf and could not hear one another.

Jevry and Denny backed fast away from the edge; Trjol, Gisonne, teacher and pupils moved in toward the safer center area. Yet even here their weight threatened to crack off this broken lip of the platform.

One child darted back toward the edge in panic and Gisonne leaped after him. Denny shouted at her. Jevry reached to pull her back.

"Stay back. You're too heavy," she said.

There was a new cracking sound.

"Stop moving!" someone shouted.

Jevry caught Gison's wrist and elbow, and pulled her and the child. And then Trjol was there too, and they were all pulling themselves back into the center, squeezed, a tiny, tight and pathetic crowd, isolated in space, huddled on the unstable platform until, much later, with help from both sides, the gap was spanned with steeloid and planks.

"The misplaced detonation was no accident," Denny said as they walked back to the workers' station.

"Of course, it was," Trjol said, addressing Gisonne rather than Denny. "Just evidence of how inept the engineering is. The whole Estuary project is wrong headed."

Without another word, he turned abruptly and walked away.

"Who was that guy?" Denny whispered to Jevry.

"Just some old man coming on to Gisonne," Jevry said.

Chapter Four

Mission Direction

7/31/3519 oe
The Plateau

    "Just read this," Gisonne said, pointing to the fifth flat-set screen on her end of the horn table. She and Aj were in the bowels of the OMD section of the government building on The Plateau, searching for records of old returned crews, good examples of "natural" groups, ideal controls for ZD's latest project, to design Trjol's task-oriented crew. It had promised to be a simple and satisfying bit of research but instead involved them in a morass of inconsistently applied policies and fragmented historical records.

    While there were hundreds of individual records in varying states of disorder, locating a complete group, crew of any one single mission, all still alive and on z2, was not easy. Followup records on past crews were incomplete or missing.

    The most frequent destination of missions between 3300 and 3450 had been some station called Agnese—sometimes spelled Agnice unless that was another place altogether—on some satelite, a moon of some planet, in some system beyond the Tryllium.

    "It looks like some of the earliest arrivals left last and later ones returned sooner. Here's the record of someone born in 3195 on Ipag; he leaves z2 in 3466, so he must have been on other missions before. Anyway he comes back with a crew from that Agnese satelite in 3475, but there's this other person," Gisonne said, pointing at a name near the bottom of the screen, "same crew list, but who seems to have left here in 3370."

    "So they needn't have gone back and forth with the same ship mates," Aj said.

"But what did they do there for a hundred oe years? They couldn't live that long. There had to have been other trips, side trips, but I can't find any record. And look at this other very early one. A two person mission. She left years later than her partner—came back earlier."

"Same destination?" Aj asked.

"I don't think so. Some kind of accidents in space? Anyway all the records on these periods are a mess. How can we find a 'group' out of any of it?"

"Does that account say if any of these people are alive and on z2 now?" Aj asked.

"No. There's not even a cross reference. But most of them must have died of old age if they didn't go out at SPEED again and if so they'd be on the later missions you've been looking up. Maybe we should cross check the names and birthdates."

"These newer records are just as bad in a different way. To tell you the truth I can't understand some of the buro jargon and it's not all together here either. Some placement locations are given; some aren't. The cases of the missing returnees."

"Then why don't we start from the other end instead first," Gisonne said. "Let's ask for the placement records of all returnees known to be on z2 now."

But when they asked, the records custodian directed them to OMD on Styxx.

"We want to know the whereabouts of returnees on z2, not Styxx," Aj said, "and we can't go to Styxx or communicate with anyone on Styxx. We're working on this project this decade."

"We've been given permission by Braitt Jones," Gisonne added.

The man suggested then that they take a lift to the next floor and get the material from her since that's where it was.

"Very funny," Aj said, as they walked down the hall to an OMD branch office. "His little power place! You can tell he's had no dyne experience, stupid little Octente buro. Spends most of his life here and never makes any attempt to relate to or recognize our customs or values. He needs a therapy dyne as well as a kick in . . . "

"Here's something else even funnier," Gisonne said as they came into Jones' reception area. "Evan is here."

"But this was our task," Aj whispered.

"Enter," Braitt Jones said. That greeting and the desk she sat behind were anachronistic and off worldish. Gisonne wondered if they were deliberate affronts especially to members of dyne. Or would Braitt Jones even be conscious of dyne values or care enough, if she were, to offend?

But Evan seemed not at all offended. He sat with legs casually crossed, not in front of but at the side of Jones' desk. He smiled at Gisonne and Aj as if it were not strange or improper for a dyne TL to become involved in the task of a subdyne without notice.

"I'm going to give your superior here all the material I have," Jones said. "I am reluctant. Much of it relates indirectly to Octente internal matters. But Doctor Trjol has assured me that your access to it is necessary. For his project. And he assured me that you will not infer the significance of or abuse its more sensitive information."

Since Evan only smiled at these remarks, Gisonne decided to ignore the insults. Temporarily.

But Aj said, "Evan is our group center, not superior. That is a decadent concept and usage."

Jones blipped a short snort.

"It's all right, Aj," Evan said. "B. Jones follows the charming customs of her world. And in spite of our differences, she is enabling ZD to further the knowledge of human behavior."

"My purpose," Jones said, "is not to encourage nonsense but to help a great man like Cres Trjol in any way I can." She tossed her head back in a quick movement just as Trjol did to get the hank of black hair off his face. But her hair was short, brown, and tufted.

A few days later ZD met again in its regular quarters in the Allain Institute.

"So it's a mess." Aj addressed all the members—after she and Gisonne had shown them samples of the older records on screen and given some accounts of the data. "But look at some of the information B. Jones gave us access to." She rolled over masses of material.

"There is very little psychological or social assessment overall," Gisonne said. "Even now replacement practice depends on very little theory. And that is more conjecture than science."

"For example," Aj said, "in several places the buros contend that 'the correlation between departure date and return date is not an invariable indicator of the success of reassimilation.' But as Gisonne says, their evidence is anecdotal rather than quantitative. They give cases—the man who, two centuries oe out of his original time period, adapted quickly and perfectly, became a leading citizen, contributed to society, etcetera. This was on Malaaca or Ipag or somewhere. Not here."

"But how old was he?" Cly asked. "That must make a tremendous difference. I mean if he had been personally old as well, adjustment would be harder."

"Some reports completely contradict others," Gisonne said. "One says it's bad when returnees have been gone too long. Too long and they can't function. There's language loss, concepts impossible to grasp, assumptions unassumable. Most often they never catch up. In the last century some have returned that the government, even the Octente, have never heard of. 'Mariners' they call themselves, pontus help us."

"Yet," Aj laughed, "one Octente memo to the local OMD stated 'It is easier for returnees completely out of their own time; nothing is misleadingly familiar.' What are we supposed to believe then—it is best to have been gone very long, but not too long—whatever that is? Ridiculous."

"Maybe not," Gisonne said, "'misleadingly familiar' makes sense, I think. It must be like a betrayal. You trust when you should mistrust. What seems is not what is."

"All very interesting," Cly said, "but, as usual with our subdyne reports, irrelevant to our higher goals."

"Perhaps if you centered a subgroup yourself, Cly," Evan said, "and showed us how it should be done . . . " Evan, Gisonne often noted, was a good TL but less effective as SeL.

"The trouble is," Aj went on, "there are too many variables and the anecdotal evidence does not consider their complex interconnections. A returnee who went crazy, another who could not deal with a particular social change—women as leaders or the disappearance of same sex spouses on Ipag—there is no consistency in ages, sex, length of absence, time per—"

"Don't forget," Evan said, "the whole problem was only a by product of SPEED."

"Are you saying, Aj," someone asked, "that we have no crew dynes, groups alive or even sufficiently documented, to use as controls?"

"Maybe," Gisonne answered instead. "Individual returnees were sometimes let loose and sometimes sent home—when there was such a place. In later times some have been located in a government compound with other returnees."

"In a way those places are group homes," Aj said, "dynes separated from society. They must have formed their own groups, dyned themselves naturally."

"Nonsense," Cly said. "Except for crews coming in together both from the same period of origin and from a flight of the same destination and duration—which you have shown we don't have—what they have in common is that they have nothing in common. Less than the rest of us—who share at least the same time and space."

Several dyne members began to speak at once, all rebutting Cly.

"Well," Gisonne said, "OMD seems to agree with him. They now mandate that each returnee be returned to his home, family home that is. Even if the subject's been gone for centuries."

"We all know this," Cly said. "People say they make up the family connections—just to get rid of the problem."

"You can't have it both ways, Cly. Either they go home, each to his own, or they are grouped. Dyned by necessity."

"Or they are just lost," Gisonne said, but it was only a mumble.

"Or—as sensible, healthy Zalterians—they don't SPEED in the first place," Cly said.

"In spite or our being a powerful member of the Octente," one of the oldest ZD members said, "we are a small, out of the way, 'backwater' planet—deliberately of course. Exclusive. Very few SPEED missions originate and return here compared to the numbers on Malaaca and Styxx and a few other commercial/tech/industrial places of that nature."

"Anyway," Aj said, "the point is that there are returnees here on z2, some may be from the same crews, but in any case, whether because they were original 'natural' dynes or newly formed groups with disparate temporal backgrounds' they're there, and we might as well take a look at them. No one else has."

"A waste of time," Cly said.

Chapter Five

Party

8/5/3519 oe
High Garda

The Octente ambassador said, "It may look beautiful but it's no utopia. I've never gotten in shape for Zalterius II." He stopped in front of the large, but simple portico of the Allaincroft main house and looked back down the steep stone-paved path he and his younger companion had just climbed.

"How can you say that, your honor?" the new Octente delegate to z2—a young Stycian, Dyll Breff asked. "We weigh a third less here than on Styxx and only a little more than on Malaaca."

"But here I have to drag the weight up and brake my way down. This is a place for fish and eagles."

"And yet, sir, they have very little of either."

"Ssh. Don't start. It's a dangerous subject." But the older man laughed. "Their damned ecosystem is the last thing we want to get into tonight—especially after the near-disaster on Estuary. You must promise to discuss only safe subjects at this gathering—safe like the weather. Ah no, I forget—even the weather is dangerous, very dangerous, on this world!"

"I'm not sure it is a world with these mad winds. Surely not a world for humans—if these people are human with their mad groups. I hardly followed it all in my briefings."

In the dusk close by Jevry Allain was listening. Not spying, of course, and not exactly hiding, but just waiting around for the party to begin. If he was beneath the notice of self-important politicians, on or off-world, it wasn't his fault. He kept listening.

"It should take more than a briefing to prepare a delegate for a society like . . . " The old ambassador's voice sounded disapproving and he stopped himself, changed his tone. "Yes, it is wonderful. Circles within circles, small tighter circles, circles circling around larger, looser circles—two dimensional, three dimensional. They call them dynaspheres, or just dynes, spheres, balls, globes."

"Committees. Just committees with pretentious names," Breff said.

"Hah! No, not the same. Every activity, task, and plan is by dyne, multi-dimensional circle."

"So they are like members of a hive—"

"No, they are individuals. Very much so . . . perhaps too much so. They move in and out of groups; each belongs to many groups, small and large, depending on purpose and activity."

"But there are leaders! The social structure is obviously hierarchical. These Allains dominate—"

"Bad word. There are centers, hubs, cores—task leaders. It depends on which angle you're looking from."

"Foolishness and wanton waste. They brought that estuary disaster upon themselves with their expensive, useless project. Autonomous ecology! They did not produce the wealth autonomously. We supply the means for all their wild experiments. We should declare the whole planet uninhabitable and move them all off."

The older man turned fully about, again solemn, worried; he looked into Breff's narrow face with its sharp Stycian features. "You're serious, aren't you? I hope you are speaking just for yourself."

"I . . . Not yet. Just wait. We—"

"We? We who?"

"We the Octente," Breff said.

"The Zalterians too are the Octente. Their ancestors created the league before there were eight worlds. And they own the quiveron. They pay for everything they import. Actually, they are their own suppliers. As individuals most of the Nord political leaders and the Arine family centers are the richest in the

Octente. However foolishly they wish to spend their income, transform the topography of this damned planet, it is theirs."

"Is it?" Breff snorted and stirred to move on, but the ambassador, still breathless from the unaccustomed exercise, gestured to restrain him.

"Their ancestors created the Octente. They discovered, settled, exploited Quivera with its quiveron. Quiveron is one half of all quod, and you know—without that power we would all still be struggling, isolate little colonies. On some worlds human beings wouldn't have survived at all. It has all but eliminated the need to terreform inhospitable—"

"I don't know. I am not a technologist, . . . sir. Nor a historian. These things are irrelevant."

"But you do see that Zalterius II was their resort, a vacation paradise, then a suburb."

"Only a deranged people would deliberately choose these rocks and winds," Breff grunted and shook his head, and with a gesture, urged the ambassador to move on into the house.

"Again, Breff, with quod any planet is habitable. Terreforming is unnecessary," the ambassador went on, not moving. "However it is true that they are eccentric. For all their concentricity!" He laughed at his own joke. Breff did not join him.

"And, in spite of its geography and infernal wind, this planet is the most beautiful."

Breff was silent.

"There is something you're not telling me, Breff. I've been on z2 as Octente delegate and then ambassador for longer than I care to remember, and you've been here only an oe month. As much as I complain, I know these people. Some of them are my friends. I have a right—"

"I'll tell you one thing, Ambassador," Breff said, "Allain power will be history, an anachronism."

"I don't understand. This Allain family has holdings on Malaaca, the mine on Quivera, and property on Corynn itself. On z2 they have held power for generations."

"The Octente is changing," Breff said. This time he omitted the "sir." "You will see. Why are we standing here? Let's go in and join the party."

Jevry watched the two men, the new one from Styxx tall, narrow, and dark, a sharp contrast to the familiar ambassador, older, shorter, and fatter. Next those two foreign turds would be falling all over Diana and grandfather—bowing low and saying how delighted and privileged they were to be invited. Most adults were hypocrites and liars, anyway. Except his group therapy leader Piro Tren, Jevry guessed. And except Gisonne Michalis. But then Gisonne hadn't been an adult long enough to grow stupid.

Where in pontus were the Michalises anyway? Their Laurel House was the nearest large estate on the island. Usually they divided up when they came over to Allaincroft, some of them walking, others, the older ones, riding a tractorvan, but this time they'd probably all arrive together since this party was so important; conservatives from Nord, off-worlders, and Arine families were to dine and drink together.

The day had not been bright, and the dark gathered in even, drab grays. Mountain above and water below had disappeared well before nightfall, leaving the front of Allaincroft a small spot in the vast dark, like a brightly lit stage suspended over an invisible and silent audience. And the evening was so unusually calm—mid Summer—that most of the guests carried their windcloaks, so that as they passed Jevry and approached the open doorway, light from within glinted on off-world jewels and real worm silks, brightness and luxury that contrasted with the stone facade and stern, country style of the house.

Guests began arriving in bunches all at once it seemed— professionals from The Plateau, who must have all flown over on the same island hopper, and prominent families from various of the nearer Arine islands. The Larens from Zeig Island, and right behind them, the powerful delaCours from Double Nef, Jean and Emil, male spouses, accompanied by a large number of relatives and followers—all dark-skinned, large, and handsome, especially the women. There was still no sign of Michalises.

Not long after the delaCours had passed into the house, an odd figure appeared out of the dark below. An old man whose slow steps and bent head suggested struggle, as if he walked against a heavy wind—a wind which tonight was just not there. He kept his worn wind cloak, winter black, wrapped tightly about him and as he slowly climbed past him, Jevry saw that it was a government garment. As the man entered the house the light from the open door showed his ancient face. He was not an off-worlder, definitely a native of z2, but wrong somehow.

There was laughter then, at the end of the walk, out of Jevry's sight. A large group. He knew the voices. Michalises.

Now Jevry could start enjoying himself; things would be great.

"Hey, Denny, you're late!"

Denny waved back as he appeared round the turn among his brothers and cousins. Even some of the older people smiled at Jevry. No one asked why he was alone outside when his family was hosting so grandly within. The Michalises were not like that. They didn't bother you the way the adult Allains were always after him.

Denny's mother motioned that he should join them.

As Jevry strolled—very casually—toward them down over the lawn, Denny's sister Nimee appeared, guiding their great aunt in her wheeler. And that was all. They were the last.

"Where . . . I thought—"

"Gisonne?" Denny asked without looking at Jevry.

"Yeh."

"She's coming. Soon. She flew over from The Plateau with . . . a couple of her dyne people."

"Oh—" What good was dignity with no one there to see it? Jevry faked a blow to Denny's gut. "Hey, some of the guys from our old sport dyne went in before. Let's go find them."

Denny feigned a jab to the jaw, feinted to the right, and took off in a sprint to a side door, Jevry racing behind.

"They looked so grown up a minute ago," Denny's mother said.

"Such energy—and strength," the great aunt said from her wheeler.

* * *

Stark, Gisonne thought. In all the years she had never seen Allaincroft this way. Perhaps she had never really seen it any way at all. Yet she knew the halls and walls as well as her own Laurel House. Was it that she had grown up, gone away and come back again that made her resee the familiar? Or was it the presence of newcomers? She was seeing through the eyes of Evan, and the other ZDs, Braitt Jones, and especially Cres Trjol.

Yes it was stark. The candelabra, the sconces, the real fires and the swelling, glittering crowd could not hide or warm the bare simplicity of the huge rooms. The house had been kept faithful—in spirit and appearance, at least—to the primitive style and native materials used by the first off-worlders to settle on the Arine Archipelago. The few pieces of furniture were also primitive, almost crude, made of native wood. The walls were bare except for a few hand-painted portraits, very old, as old as the first generation of Allains on Zalterius II; a few, strange in style and background, and others, most of odd birds and other flying creatures, were even older.

"I thought it would be more . . . opulent." Here was that Trjol again, standing beside Gisonne, whispering in her ear. His breath was as warm as she remembered.

Obviously, he was blind to the subtlety and beauty of the art and artifice right before his eyes. The zoid floors were so perfectly imperfect that one couldn't tell where they began and the remnants of ancient, real wood left off. The subtle satin finish of the wide boards contrasted with the few hand-woven rugs, whose deep colors were dimmed and drabbed with time and wear—or with a careful, costly, off-world simulation of time and wear.

"It is opulent," Gisonne said. Too hostile to a person who had pulled her back from death on Estuary.

"This house must have been crude," he said. "When it was built, I mean. What kind of people were their ancestors?"

"Like all our ancestors," Gisonne said, surprised to hear the question. "And yours." As he had said, he had no interest in history, politics, swamps, dynes, or anything besides "brains." "We all lit on the cliffs and built from native materials. Unlike you Norders, we Arines know enough to preserve the past."

"I am not a Norder! Do I look like a Norder?"

Gisonne had to admit he did not. His features were not flat like the Norders. He was darker—especially eyes and hair.

"My original island belongs to neither of your political molehills," he said, looking around disdainfully at the hall. "Is this . . . this arena the oldest?"

"The great hall, yes, almost . . . there are some even more ancient areas."

"Show me."

Trjol followed her through a long side hall, down three steps, round about a cupboard area, and into a slate-crooked nook, the neck of a place. Dark and stoney. The only light was from from Diana Grande coming through lattice onto sloping floor tiles.

"These must be servant areas," he said.

"Servant? Arine families have househelp dynes, not servants! You sound more like an off-worlder than a Zalterian."

"I was educated partly on Malaaca," he said. "And my family never was . . . provincial."

Gisonne ignored the remark and led him to one of the tiny windows. He leaned close to peer through.

"Look at the glass, not through it," she said. "This is glass as ancient as any you can find on z2. And sashes that were never replaced in all the centuries. See the marks on the lintels—codes of some kind. Icons."

But he was looking at her instead.

"These markings," she said, "came from somewhere else like the portraits in the hall."

He wasn't smiling anymore. He looked angry somehow. He touched her still bruised cheek with light fingertips.

"At Laurel House we have nothing this old save the foundations."

"Old," he said. "Am I too old for you?"

His hand was down, moving over her throat. She felt his arm hard on her back, pulling her against him. And those too thin lips were shockingly soft and strong on her mouth, chasing a sudden tingling thread of pleasure down to her breasts.

No. This was not her script, not any one of her possible scripts.

When she tried to pull free, he let go and stepped back away from her.

"I'm hurting you. I'm sorry."

"No. Yes," she said and ran back the crooked way they had come without looking back.

* * *

Diana Rise Allain stood in the center of a small group of guests. She was dressed as always in white, a geometric soft suit—simple like Allaincroft itself. Trjol, Gisonne thought, was probably disappointed again. She tried again to see him as a fool, but this time it didn't work.

And then, it seemed all at once, Allains appeared: Diana's father through the rows of long wooden food tables leading a small procession of formidable guests, including not two but three off-worlders; swelling the progress was Blake Allain-Rise, Diana's husband. Although taller than his father-in-law, he was always bent in a slight bow, the better to listen to smaller people. Gisonne had always admired his grace and courtliness. People called him the prince consort.

And on the other side were Diana's children, brought into the hall by a member of the househelp dyne. They stood side by side, gentle and upright like pictures of the martyred princes. Hentor, almost but not quite a teenager, looked at the floor while little Telem's eyes darted from stranger to friend and back to stranger—until they found, stopped, and stayed on his mother.

Shy Hentor, who had once lived with the Michalises for two seasons, at last looked up, saw Gisonne, and smiled.

"Hentor!" she called but was cut off by the crowd. Groups converged, merged, and regrouped. All over the hall voices and laughter grew louder.

Diana's father Xaviour was suddenly next to Gisonne. "This is one of the Michalises, our neighbors and very old friends. And Persy Perl, our new friend," he said patting the shoulder of a young man Gisonne had not seen before, but he was so ordinary, so forgetable, such a gray person that she couldn't be sure.

The ambassador bowed. "And this is my new colleague Dyll Breff," he said.

"More assistant than colleague," the younger man said, making an even deeper bow. "Thank you for the honor, Ambassador."

This new off-world delegate, Gisonne thought, was definitely not gray, definitely unforgetable. For all his "humility," a part of off-world manners, there was a cold arrogance in the eyes and a hardness in the mouth that frightened her.

At Diana's approach he bowed again. "Mistress Allain," he said, "I greet you again—"

"Yes, yes," the ambassador muttered. "Our hosts do not use these honorifics, remember. When in Rome."

"We understand," Diana said. "Dyll is new to z2. And welcome."

Strange, Gisonne thought, that an ambassador would not be better trained in protocol. Or is he deliberately polite to be impolite?

From the other end of the long table Jevry caught her eye, grinned—and bowed deeply, pliet, mocking the off-world manner. She looked away not to laugh—focused on the faces and voices close around.

Breff lapsed into silence, while the old ambassador, who had learned local customs, assumed the noddings and greetings as various persons were presented. The new "friend," Perl or something, tried to insinuate himself into the discussion but was ignored all around.

An old politician from Nord identified himself gruffly to Diana and almost turned his back on her as he moved forward to remind the elder ambassador that they were old acquaintances.

Diana showed no sign of having noticed the slight. She asked Emil delaCour, the quieter spouse, about the soil problem on Double Nef.

"Utopia has to have swamps!" A familiar voice was raised from among a group of young people sitting around the next table. It was surely Denny already arguing with dyne mates about his favorite topics.

"Impractical," the Nord politician said, turning to locate the speaker, his flat face as expressionless as his tone of voice. "Terreforming is outdated, egocentric, ruinously expensive, and—with quod—unnecessary. Redundant. Duplication. We own everything we are missing right next door on Agricula, Zalterius III—assuming you can successfully create these stinking, ugly swamps. They are contrary to the nature of Zalterius II and—its beauty."

Denny seemed startled to have been noticed by such an important personage but went on bravely. "Nature doesn't work by itself on z2," he said. "Imported animal life disappears from the wild in two generations at best."

"And so we'll import more, as we always have done."

"And what about bacterial products for our own technolgy?" a dynemate of Denny's asked.

Gisonne saw the new assistant ambassador nudge the older one. Neither spoke but they watched each speaker carefully.

"And SPEED ships, even our local airboats, are not manufactured here," someone else in Denny's circle added. "No hardware is produced on z2. We have no means of independent survival."

"Our ancestors knew that when they came here. That was part of the attraction—a vacation land, breathtakingly beautiful—not meant to be sullied with industry. Z2 is a garden, not a farm or a factory," the Nord man continued, the angry words conflicting with the tonelessness of his voice.

"He's right." It was Trjol, to Gison's annoyance. But why should she care what he said? Did he remember that Denny was her brother? "We inhabit a sector of a unit. The Octente itself is a system with a multiplicity of interwoven ecological subsystems, each complementing, fulfilling the needs of the other. You are not inhabitants of a single, small world. That is provincial, devisive. Only with cooperation, pooling all resources, will we make the great discoveries in science, discoveries just around the corner."

Same old pretentious speechmaking, Gisonne thought. Whose side was he on!

"Surely it is impolite to have a family argument in front of guests," Diana said to the ambassadors. "Forgive us for boring you with our trivial disagreements."

"Z2's affairs are mine," the older ambassador began. "I care as—"

"Not bored," Dyll Breff said. "Puzzled perhaps. I do not quite understand how one affords to live in a garden."

There was stunned silence. The ambassador blushed. The Nord politician's mouth hung open. Even Trjol frowned.

Xaviour Allain spoke first. "Your joke, Ambassador, is not quite clear. Perhaps a cultural mis—"

"Toiling in mines, working in factories, growing foodstuffs, developing the industries, the technologies, the medicines, the means of exchange and transfer of goods keep the Octente flourishing. How can the Octente afford an Eden? How can we allow—"

"Your rudeness to my father may be off-world manners. Your lies are not to be overlooked." Diana's tone was low, her face expressionless, but Gisonne saw the ice in both.

"Lies, Mistress? The cost to keep you is intollerable."

"Breff. Breff, what are you doing?" The older ambassador took Breff's arm.

"Keep us!" Jean delaCour shouted from the center of a dyne of relatives. His spouse Emil stood beside him, protective and proud. "We Zalterians are the center of the Octente. Our ancestors created it and our possesions maintain it. We keep you."

"I see nothing here, nothing but luxuries borrowed from other planets. Your ancestors left the center when they chose to perch on these barren crags."

"Quiveron!" the Nord politician sputtered. "Our quiveron and . . . and our gems. The gems of all the worlds come from our mines. And you don't feed us. We feed ourselves. Our Agricula is more than sufficient food basket."

"Your? How? Not our Agricula? Not the Octente's Agricula?"

* * *

After the two ambassadors left, the party broke into noisy natural dynes, all temporary and fluid. Gisonne watched roles form and dissolve as people moved about looking for answers and listeners. Groping for IPs and leaders, they turned again and again to recognized centers, Diana and Xaviour, Jean delaCour, and the Nord politician. The Norder fumed and orated, but finally said nothing.

"Amazing that the Octente would send such a rude lout."

"Absolute ignorance of history."

"What is going on on Corynn? All standards of behaviour lowered to this? That they would send us someone from Styxx!"

"Perhaps he should be taught a lesson. They need quiveron more than ever. Let them know we won't tolerate—"

Diana said very little but maintained her central position.

Most of the non-Arine guests departed at the same time, still in a flurry of anger and confusion, traveling in one large island hopper to The Plateau. There was a sense of relief, almost intimacy among the rest, even those who had never or barely known one another before. The only remaining off-worlder was Braitt Jones who would stay as long as Trjol did. The others were mostly students, young friends who were to stay at Allaincroft and Laurel House, and other members of the hosts' various dynes.

Still discussing the new envoy's behavior, they gathered in a smaller, friendlier room, a library full of bound volumes—all of the operating system hidden behind books and tapestries or concealed in primitive wooden desks and tables.

Jevry Allain was somehow sitting near Gisonne while Trjol had chosen to stand against the fire place on the far side of the room with a small circle of university students from the Arine Branch sitting and standing around him, listening eagerly to the great man's words. Gisonne had to admit that he cut an attractive figure—spoiled only by a hovering Braitt Jones.

"I heard those Pontus scum talking about us," Jevry whispered to Gisonne.

"Who? The ambassadors?" Denny asked, dropping himself onto the floor at their feet.

"Yeh. Well, the new one, he isn't really ambassador—not yet. He's the real bird turd. A Stycian—mean like all of them. They didn't know I was there."

Jevry was telling Gisonne and Denny what he had heard when a stranger, a very old man, came into the room. He followed a straight path to one person, a young student guest, obviously chosen arbitrarily.

"Where is my family?" he asked.

Confused and embarrassed, the young man looked to Diana, to his companions, but encountered no sympathetic eye.

"I have been within the great leviathan for many of your lifetimes. And it has thrown me out back to the land and shores of my people. And my people are not here. Where are my people?"

Again the young man looked around for help. His companions looked away, glad they were not the one selected.

"Can't someone get him out of here?" the nondescript Perl said.

"I saw him come in earlier," Jevry said.

"Have you driven away my people? Murdered my race?" the old man asked without taking his eyes off the boy's face.

"Me?" the boy stammered.

"He's crazy," Perl said. "This is ridiculous."

But no one responded; there was something hypnotic about the old man. Everone in the room stared in silence. Only Trjol and a couple of students stopped listening, more interested in their discussion.

"I came home, but I am not home. I cannot find it," the man continued.

"Who are you, old man?" Diana asked.

"I am Jonah, woman," he said. He never took his eyes off the boy.

"I know this man," Braitt Jones said. "He's a returnee. An old one."

"Is he one of that crew we heard about a couple of years ago?" someone asked. "One of the first crews out at SPEED and one of the last back. OMD Circles couldn't find any record of the mission."

"There was no OMD when they left," Braitt Jones said.

"I returned to this strange place. My towns and my father and my children are gone." For the first time Jonah looked around at the other faces, stopping at each for a long second before going on.

"No, we are your people," Xaviour Allain said. "You have been gone a long time. Things have changed. It has been a long, long time. But we are your race, your people's descendants."

Jonah wept.

"It's all right," Diana said, "Jevry will find a place for you to rest."

"Of course, he's crazy. I told you so," Perl said after Jevry had led Jonah out of the library.

"And is it any wonder?" Gisonne's mother asked. "Look what the man has been through. How many personal years in space? To come back to find his—"

"But why is he loose?" someone asked. "He might be dangerous. He . . . he needs care. Isn't there a place for . . . for displaced persons?"

"He has done nothing wrong," Gisonne's great aunt spoke up. "He has a right to be free on his own planet. After being encased in some miserable antique craft for most of his lifetime, for generations of our history."

"We do have homes for them," Braitt Jones said, "the ones who have no families or willing descendants. But they come from such different eras—"

The thought sickened Gisonne. Claustrophobia was natural to many of the people of z2 but for her especially, home and family and High Garda, wide open and familiar, were as necessary to life as oxygen.

Chapter Six

Corse

8/20/3519 oe
The Plateau

"Where are you going and why do you have to go there?"
Trjol's light touch above Gisonne's elbow was strong enough to
draw her back from the other ZD members arguing their way out
of his office after one of their regular sessions.

"To Corse. To aid and abet your project."

"Me? I never told you to go there. I want you here."

"To visit the returnee home there. To talk to them. To ask
about their crews, their experiences as members of natural
uncontrolled groups during long periods of isolation and—"

"Don't go."

" . . . and to try to reconstruct what the individual group
member's role actually was."

"Retroactive name calling."

8/22/3519
Corse

The OMD compound where the largest number of z2
returnees was housed had been originally built for all kinds of
Mission personel—retired local technicians and off-world
workers permanently unable or unwilling to make a trip home. It
was located on the campus of the Corsican branch of the
university away from active Octente and local government
centers on Nord and Nord Port. In fact, Corse was not
geographically or politically part of Archipelago Nord, but an
island by itself in an empty part of the Nord Sea.

Like the rest of the island, the campus had been maintained
as part of the rough natural environment. Some of the buildings

were hard to distinguish from the rocky cliffs and crags, while the quads were wild fields, almost barren except for the early fall yellow daisies, black-eyed susans, coreopsis, and linell flowers everywhere.

The path winding and zigzagging up through an uncut hay field was actually the main access to the whole complex. It had debouched from a narrow dirt road that itself was just a branch of the main road from the island's landing fields.

A handful of people climbed steeply, wrapped in light wind cloaks against the gusts whipping up from the dark green sea below. Although it was warmer, the wind was just as strong on Corse. It bent the few trees and scrub bushes, flattened the hay and wild flowers around the travelers.

After a seven-hour flight—half way around z2 from The Arine Archipelago—to Nord Port to refuel and pick up odd government people and students, another two hours to landing fields on Corse, and a three-hour ride in a tractorvan—over narrow roads etched into vertical mountainsides, roads without rails to guard or signs to warn of the immense drop to the black stone beaches, Gisonne and Aj and several of the other passengers had chosen to walk this last crooked leg of their trip.

As they approached the campus, the high ground became open, sweeping fields—different from the gray crags and sharp profiles of High Garda and The Plateau but, most of all, from Estuary. Gisonne ran off the path to pick an unfamiliar purple flower.

"This is great," she shouted back to Aj as a sudden gust blew their cloaks into a frenzy. "I believe in Estuary, but I didn't like it. Adjusting that ornithology group took most of Spring."

"Have you ever seen such green water? And look at the buildings—so primitive!" Aj waved toward the nearest of the narrow, dark stone structures.

* * *

"My reality, my sense of self, my identity are all a function of those people, that life, that place. Here—now—I have no existence. I'm not real. I can't see myself. There is no mirror. I'm a vampire."

The young man's accent was so heavy that Aj and Gisonne missed some of his words and others were meaningless to them. Resting on his nose and hooked awkwardly with wires over his ears, were binocles made of real glass and far too small to be wind goggles. Was he deliberately rejecting Malaacan surgery or simply clinging to an old identity? The people of his time would have known what those ancient "eye glasses" stood for; Gisonne did not.

"I have no one to fight with, no one to prove wrong. Shared history, shared experiences, people who hit off the same backdrop, even enemies share reality. If I do something wonderful—or bad—I need my mother, my friend, sister, a baseline person to react. I'm not just now; I'm a process; I take place in time."

"Jake's a philosopher," the other young man said. "In his day he was a professor, weren't you, pal?"

The two young men had been the first group presented to Gisonne and Aj. A pair is not a dyne. And these were a mismatched pair in everything but personal age.

The first speaker was as different as possible from a present day z2 native. He had been gone a very long time, centuries, though not as long as Jonah, yet, in a way, he was stranger to them than Jonah because of his very youth. One expected— illogically of course—a person from an ancient period to be old.

The contrast with his "pal" was startling. The second young man was at first glance completely contemporary; his clothing, speech, manners and carriage were all so familiar to Gisonne and Aj that they had thought for a second that he was not a returnee.

"Oh, I have a home," he said. "Yes I do, pals. On Bavaria."

"And why don't you go there?"

"I did. I did. I was there for a while. OMD flew me over right after the debriefing."

"But you didn't stay. Didn't they—your family—?"

"My great nephews? They were all right. Took me in."

"Took you in? But you must own part of it?"

"Own all of it, pal. All of it."

"So why—?"

"I didn't like it."

"Was it so changed then? You haven't been gone long compared—"

"No, it was the same. My own room—just like it was. That was the trouble. My maman and . . . my friends—all gone."

"Misleadingly familiar," Gisonne remembered one buro report said. "But wait," she said. "Your friends would still be alive. Most of them must be."

"Yes. Just about alive, the old fossils. They won't move. All they talk about is how bad the young generation is. And they're right. My great great nephews are an arrogant bunch. Think they're smart with their slang, words I don't know even though I'm only a couple of years older than they are. They make jokes I don't get. Laugh at me. They say I talk and think like their grandparents, that I'm weird.

"The grandparents are nasty old men, too! Worse than the young ones. When I first got back we talked about the old days, but, you know, they don't remember it right. And they got mad at me—for nothing."

Gisonne and Aj said no more. For them, too, it was odd, uncomfortable. He was about their age and talked like their grandfathers. A twenty-five year old whose values and language belong to the elderly. It must be mind-bending for him. He didn't belong to either generation.

When the two young men wandered away, arm in arm, Gisonne thought of Cly's contention that no bonding could form among these disparate individuals.

During the whole of that afternoon they interviewed one other group, a foursome, a fragment of an original seven, the crew of a mission to a place called Isola in 3310. Two had joined a side expedition, supposedly for two years but never came back to Isola. They were only able to replace one of them, with a man from a small obscure planet in the Tryllium system, so for the return trip to z2 they were six. Half way back another member had died. And just last season the fifth remaining original member had taken the shuttle to Agricula.

The present four then actually composed a young group, a new dyne, but with a historical pattern complicating its ecology. Yet it could be studied by direct observation as well as questioning, interaction studies, and process analysis. The earlier groups of which these four had been a part could possibly be reconstructed from intensive and extensive study of their responses and memories—a difficult but interesting challenge.

In fact, as Gisonne said to Aj on the way back across the fields to the campus guest "chalet," the history of each crew deserved years of study by group theorists, beyond their immediate use as controls for the composition of Trjol's crew. They were not only natural dynes that had functioned in isolation for long periods but had undergone various long and short term changes in make up. Role constancy and the universality of basic group structure was Gisonne's greatest interest and the most difficult to pursue in one lifetime.

As crews were organized in the 34'th century, function seemed not to dictate status, except for captain. The roles of the original group members had emerged naturally and reemerged in interesting ways. It looked like the two who disappeared had been leader, TL, and Tension Releaser. These remaining members all spoke of that original TR with affection, humor, and regret for his disappearance. Yet one of those four today had acted obviously as leader and another had made the tension relieving jokes. So their roles had been filled from among the followers—as always happens: the group had unconsciously attempted to reconstruct its ecology.

"Where did they say they went anyway?" Aj asked.

"But it doesn't matter," Gisonne said. "It is incredible how the results of the displacement accurately reflect the artificial lab studies. We construct a dyne of ten, give them a false task, and automatically someone is either selected or emerges as leader and someone else as lieutenant or secretary. Then we go back and say 'Oops, we made a mistake, sorry' and take the leader and lieutenant away and tell the rest to resume the work. Another leader and lieutenant emerge from among the eight followers. Then we do it again until it's down to three and still . . . "

"I know," Aj said. "It's always amazing. Keep going and the second shyest follower becomes leader—but I just wonder what happened to them."

"To whom?"

"The ones who never came back."

* * *

The long bright day on dark Corse ended with an even brighter sunset. Sharp blinding, yellow-white rays shot in an arc across half the visible sky from blood red roots at the horizon, their reflected image flattened in gold streaks across the surface of the sea, a sea wet-black. The rough greys and browns and drab greens of Corse's daylight surfaces, of its mountain turf, sparse almost treeless countryside, rocks and more rocks, dry fields and meadows sliding toward the cliff edge, and the perpendicular drop to the green/black ocean below, all had grown brilliant for a second and darkened and disappeared in black shadow. Only the ghostly glow of reflection of the lost sun identified the configuration of the mountains, the buildings, and human faces.

And Gisonne suddenly recognized one of those faces. Walking toward them across the Chalet garden was Cres Trjol. He had followed her halfway round z2 to Corse!

Within moments the night grew densely, evenly, and, to Gisonne, dangerously black. Aj disappeared into the chalet without apology, leaving Gisonne and Trjol alone, standing side by side, hands on a crooked, wood fence rail, feeling and hearing waves hurling themselves at the sheer mountain wall somewhere below.

"The young Allain man?" Trjol said. "Is he a . . . a particular friend of yours?"

"Man? Friend? You mean Jevry . . . oh, no! He's just a kid. My brother's friend. I'm much older!"

"You don't seem old at all to me," he said. "I am the one who is old, too old." They had been through this before. This time she let him wait. She would be SO. It was not easy because as SeL and TR she usually prevented long uncomfortable silences in ZD.

"Are you angry with me, Gisonne?" he asked. "I can't see your face. Your wide beautiful brow and an exquisitely delicate mouth."

She said nothing. There was nothing to say.

At that moment the blackness paled, as, over the ocean's edge, Diana Grande began to rise. Her rim alone made them visible to each other. Then as she cleared the horizon, Corse and everything on it grew grey, silver, then white. Dazzling, colorless brightness.

Moonrise was beautiful everywhere on Zalterius II, and moonlight always white, but it brought this sudden and startling transformation of reality only on those few nights of the year when Diana Grande appeared at least an hour after complete sunset and before Diana Petite made an entrance.

"Young," he said again, staring amazed at her open face. "I'm so old."

"No," she lied. Was it the SeL lying or everywoman in the moonlight? She thought he was old. That was the truth.

But the white light sharpened his features. A dark shock of hair had fallen over his forehead and into his eyes, eyes that were

only black shadows under the heavy brow line, and his white
shirt had opened widely at the throat.

"Special," he said, touching her brow.

"You," Gisonne said, "you're the one who's special." Foolish
words. She couldn't think what to say that he needed to hear.
"Your work, your control, your—" She wanted to say
"monomania," monomania as a good thing, but he wouldn't
understand. "Your vision."

His eyes were fierce. A muscle moved close to the pressed
thin lips. She saw him swallow before he began to speak.

"Gisonne, I . . . I think you are the only one who understands
who . . . I mean what I am. Even though neuroscience isn't your
field, you seem to know more about what I'm trying to do—my
dreams and goals —than . . . "

She mumbled something negative as he pulled her close.

But she knew that she did understand him. She knew how
vulnerable he was, how insecure in spite of his brilliance and
showmanship, how much he needed her.

"I want you, Gisonne," he whispered, voice almost
indistinguishable from the sound of the ocean.

He didn't kiss her or touch her body with his hands, but held
her lightly, as if she were a loose bunch of coreopsis, protecting
her from the wind rising over the sea. He raised his head and
stared out over the cliff. Stone profile. Curious that she had not
noticed before how rather magnificent it was.

Only after a minute did he turn again and pull her hard
against the length of his body. "I need you," he said. She felt the
sound of the words where her temple rested against his chest, felt
his lips moving on her forehead, smelled his peculiar warm
sweet breath.

They walked in silence back to his room in the chalet.

Chapter Seven

Blocking

8/27/3519
High Garda

For the first time in his life, Jevry saw members of the Allain family lose their control. Even when his own parents had been killed, Grandfather and Aunt Diana had not let the loss affect their dignity and serenity. But the news on the horn from Nordport knocked them all over.

A SPEED ship was in orbit—not the long-awaited, much-needed supply shuttle from Agricula, but a Stycian vessel. It sent no greeting, no messages at all besides communications with Nordport necessary to the business of landing.

And worse, when it did land, it was still silent. Even its crew, unloading and making repairs, were strangely quiet, not joking, gossiping, or sharing news with z2 dock dynes and local Mission technicians. The only information came at the end of that first day and was not official. Xaviour Allain's network of people in Nord reported that all the ship's records they had gotten hold of, even simple invoices, told of a change in Octente authority. Corynn imprimatur appeared on everything, even goods from Ipag.

"The dominion of Corynn presides now over The Octente" was the meaning.

The adults talked, the Arine family centers, Allains, delaCours, Larens, Joneses, Michalises, Rises.

"But Corynn has been official capital of the Octente for years—in actuality."

"Now it PRESIDES."

"Let them call themselves what they will, give themselves titles. What is it to us?"

"It means Styxx and Malaaca are controlling the Octente."

"Didn't that Breff say things about reorganizing trade routes—things about efficiency and more centralized management?"

"Styxx is far away and Malaaca farther."

"What can they do to us?"

"They need us. Their companies depend on quiveron."

"They can't touch our properties. Legally—"

"Distance won't protect us."

"From what? An attack? The Octente attack one of its own! Attack itself?"

"From starvation."

They repeated these things to one another over the horn for days as they waited for information.

Jevry tried to dismiss it all as just politics. It would all work out. The Octente marketing traditions were inviolate. Because of the huge time lapses in transporting goods, interplanetary trade and marketing contracts had to be sacred. One's grandfathers' promises were never broken.

Jevry wondered if the ship had brought goods of interest to him—the new power ski lifts, the latest Malaacan horns and other equipment for the university science labs on Corse and The Plateau. And books, horns and hornwriters, vids, the newest plots and latest music from Myll on Corynn and from Ipag. Art and animals from Anu.

But that brought him right back. He knew well that most luxuries and necessities were paid for by quiveron mined on Allain and other family properties on Quivera. And he remembered the words of that obsequious, patronizing Dyll Breff. Breff must have known this takeover was going to happen before he left Styxx—that is if it hadn't already happened— especially with the SPEED distortion, however small.

The official announcement was delivered the several days later as a minor item in an otherwise inconsequential report:

Personal absences of more than fifty oe years shall presume neglect, desertion, and abandonment of possessions by proprietors resulting in forfeiture of such appurtenances to the Octente. Title to such properties and the feality of any local inhabitants are expressed, conveyed, assigned, or transferred to the Octente. In addition to relinguishment and forfeiture of said properties, former proprietors will be fined and assessed payment of damages and the costs to the Octente for transfer of titles and management and maintenance of said properties and persons and goods thereon.

"Why not just say you have to live on your property? No absentee landlords."

"They'd screw most of themselves that way. They all, the top people on Malaaca, Styxx and Ipag, own other planets and parcels of more. But they are closer and they, unlike us, like SPEEDing."

"They won't really confiscate our—"

"No," Xaviour Allain said, "we'll be there when they get there. At least one of us will."

9/2/3519oe
To The Plateau

It was easier to fly all the way around z2 than to island hop in the Arines. Schedules were impossible to plan or keep—especially when Diana Petite was in the wrong hemisphere. Sudden tempests forced unplanned landings, long stays, or instant rerouting.

An unusual number of people were leaving High Garda in the middle of the fall season. Several students were starting new courses at the Branch, Jevry among them, Denny's great aunt had an appointment at the university hospital, Denny himself was making a changeover for Bavaria, and Diana Rise Allain had undisclosed business on The Plateau.

The flight was wild as the small craft met rough gusts above high seas. The gusts gathered to become a tempest whose impossible thermal air currents prevented picking up passengers on Double Nef.

"The Malaacans are working on a new safer kind of hopper, designing it especially for z2," a student said as they rose and dropped.

"Yeh. It's supposed to float and lift. It has some kind of forces that make it in . . . "

"We'll never see it," Denny said.

Instead of the exuberant discussion and arguing that would usually follow such a comment, the younger people fell into an uncomfortable silence. Diana's presence could do that.

Jevry glanced at her across the aisle. She seemed to take no notice of other persons or of their conversation. Her head was turned toward the front. Her pale face and strong profile gave her a hardcarved look, not softened by the pulled back light hair, or the stiff, high narrow shirt collar rising to her chin. As always she was dressed in shades of white, except, of course, for her fall gray wind cloak neatly hung on the back of the seat.

Jevry's own wind cloak was roughly rolled into a pillow behind his head. He sighed and slouched down in his seat, legs bent almost in two, knees sticking up above the seatback in front of him, a posture breaking all turbulence rules and irritating both the girl in that seat and Denny whose view of the ocean he was blocking.

But then the sky grew darker as they approached The Plateau and there was nothing to see anyway. The wind lashed rain against the windows and slapped the ploid hull like a flat angry hand. They seemed breathlessly held up and back, unmoving, above the island.

And then suddenly it was clear and the wind let them go, and down they headed in fast relief. As the landing field grew larger, the pilot made a noise, cursed and they hard jolted, almost a stop, and rose again sharply, moving up away from the field.

Only then did Jevry see the other craft, a large Nord plane, coming in, already below them, but just below—inches.

Their pilot was cursing again, shouting at the comm horn: "Pontus-drowned Nord pilot!"

When they finally landed, Jevry saw passengers walking away from the Nord plane. Among them was Gisonne. Although still hiding the shakes from the near miss, he grinned and started to sprint across the field. It was too late to stop when he saw Trjol with her.

And Denny, instead of following, was doing the right thing, helping his great aunt off the plane. So alone, Jevry strode forward. Gisonne saw him and looked equally unglad. She looked embarrassed, in fact.

"Hey, Jev," she said.

"Hey," he said.

"You know my friend Aj?" Gisonne pointed to a woman coming along from the plane. "And . . . and Doctor Trjol?"

"Yeah, sure," Jevry said. "Good afternoon, Professor."

Trjol nodded.

They stood for a while. Trjol touched Gison's elbow, just a gesture, meant nothing at all, meant everything. Jevry looked away.

"Isn't that Diana getting out of your plane?" Gisonne said suddenly. "Why did she come in now? Octente problems, right?"

"Yeah. Yes," Jevry said, glad to have something harmless to talk about. Harmless? Hah. Whole planet starved by the Octente was easier to take than looking at these two. "Everybody's all excited. Where have you been?"

"We . . . I . . Aj and I have been on Corse. Working."

"Oh. Well."

"Well. I'll see you, Jevry."

"Yeah," Jevry said. "See you."

But he never saw her again—for thirty years.

Chapter Eight

Interchange

9/2/3519 oe
The Plateau

"Let me go. I have to go over now. They're waiting."

"No, no, Not yet." Trjol said.

He kissed her nose tip and her broad forehead.

"I—have to go now."

"Me, too," he said.

"No, you really don't," she said, struggling to pull herself upright. She brushed her hair back. "They'll . . . we'll get more done without you."

"No," he said. "I have to make clear exactly what is wanted. There must be specific direction."

"You have told us already. Often. We understand as much as we will ever understand and as much as we need to understand in order to do our part. Telling us again will only hold us up."

He looked hurt now. A scolded boy. Always dramatic, always changing.

"Look," she said, just as if he were a little boy, "our part is separate. We have to discuss all sorts of group things that you find dull and tedious. Even more tedious is our going through every vitae of every member of the mission pool. You would find persons eligible and qualities attractive that are not relevant to our needs for a particular group ecology. And, you know, it's especially difficult with you as one of the components. We have to discuss you and assess your person—objectively! Without you there." She tugged at his hanging lock of black hair, pretending to use it to pull herself to her feet.

"If you insist upon being part of the mission," she said. "You can change your mind. It will be better if you change your mind."

If Trjol goes, he will be too dominant. They cannot select a CN strong enough to counteract him. She had tried to explain it to him often.

"No, no—I won't be leader!"

"You think not?"

Of course, he would be leader. He would emerge as leader sooner rather than later no matter what person they designated leader ahead of time. That showed how little he understood of dyne ecology. Or of himself.

"You can come, too, and keep me in my place," he said.

"That's not how it works. And don't joke. I could never go. I hate travelling and I have always had a horror of being confined. And besides I don't want to lose part of my life."

"That's ridiculous. You'll gain time. Be younger. I traveled to Malaaca. I was younger than my peers when I came back. By a small amount. It hardly mattered actually."

"Hah! You probably did it just for that!" And seeing him CRESfallen, she added, "I don't mean it. Seriously, hadn't your colleagues gained a competitive edge while you were at SPEED?"

"No. My time on Malaaca gave me far more advantage. The greatest contributions have been made by those scientists and scholars who have traveled, researched, taught and learned on other planets—the chemist Wilte Laren in the 34'th century and Louis Dubois, exobiologist and renowned anthropologist of the 33'rd. As I keep arguing with you isolationists, z2 can not be autonomous. Right now on Malaaca—"

"I'm not an isolationist. I don't care who goes anywhere as long as it's not me. I'm going over now. Bye." Gisonne dashed out of Trjol's little apartment in the rear wing of the Allain building and strode through corridors and down and up stairs to ZD's main offices and labs.

They were all there. Cly glared.

"Where's Trjol?" he asked.

"How should I know?" They all knew and she knew they knew, yet she sounded like a sullen teenager. Had she changed into ScF, Self-centered Follower?

"Okay, let's go back to Task Leader," Evan said. "We all agree then that we'll need a very powerful lieutenant because of Trjol's limits. But with a strong but flawed TL and an expert lieutenant, the balancing power of the CN becomes crucially important. I'm still not satisfied with the three candidates for emergent Negative."

"The limitations are only in Doctor Trjol's training as a crew captain, Gisonne," Aj said. "We don't mean—"

So with Gisonne present they were not free to deal with the Trjol element in their construction of the crew dyne. She had to be "handled." Her relationship with Trjol was destroying her role in ZD. How could she continue to function as SeL, Social-emotional Leader or TR if she had become part of the task? If only he would decide to withdraw! Stubborn old buzzard. But she smiled with pleasure at the thought of him.

"It's all right," she said. They would see that Gisonne could be as objective and professional as the next person. "We know Trjol will emerge quickly first as Social-emotional Leader and then as Task Leader. Right away, during the primary tension. The rest of the crew will believe and then pretend to believe that someone else is leader until that person—probably a first phase Information Provider—becomes too obvious a Trjol follower or turns in anger into a Central Negative, possibly destructive."

"But even if we can find another equally strong leader, the group may fragment—if not in earlier phases, during secondary tension," Evan said. "Interesting to us perhaps, but dangerous for a space crew, and useless in programming Trjol's edel."

"Don't let him hear you use that word, 'programming,'" someone said. Several people smiled and did not look at Gisonne.

"It's his own fault that we have the problem," Cly said. "He is undermining the formation of the dyne by including himself. Sorry, Gisonne."

"As I said earlier," Evan said, "let's not put in another strong leader. Let's find a weak Lieutenant and a strong, healthy CN, but not a CN who wants to be a leader. A natural CN."

"Like Cly!" Gisonne said, trying to be TR again.

"Emil delaCour will become Lieutenant surely," Aj said. "His place in his family circle, the quiet partner in a dyad—"

"Trjol will absorb any Lieutenant," another member said.

"That's all right, too. We'll choose risk-prone, dominant communicators as other members, especially TR and IP. We can prevent an overly cohesive ecology and still avoid disintegration," Evan said. "It'll take a lot more research and careful planning. Let's see that last batch of lab results again."

"It will be ironic if the whole mission is cancelled because of the Octente changes, after we go through all this," Cly said.

They worked for the rest of the day correlating the results of weeks of sub dyne research, individual histories, trait and attitude assessment studies, compatibility scores, general psychological profiles, and hours of interviews.

And they continued to work day after day for weeks. They created, dissolved, and recreated real, but necessarily short-term, dynes, observing and coding individual interchanges, microverbal exchanges, allegiances and blocking, participation and directivity, status and role constancy. More often, since there was so little time, they only hypothesized groups of these real individuals, projecting and comparing likely macrocommunication patterns, degrees of cohesion, status hierarchies, possible growth of sentiment and, most important, behavior and attitudes of individuals in member-centered and leader-centered structures. They designed these descriptive models with experimental frameworks, circles, chains, stars and 'y's.

The applicant pool was reduced in stages. Since "influence is closely related to possession of information," it was hard to find IPs who were dominant communicators yet would not compete for complete leadership. They had seven possible IPs finally and five potential TRs, individuals in "role ruts." Others were less constant; they could emerge potentially into one of several roles depending on the composition of the rest of the group. Both types were necessary to a dynamic, productive dyne, a functioning system.

The missing element in the structure would be the "outsider." First of all the members would be all outsiders, unknown to each other before hand, although all were self-selected in that they were willing to travel. Then the very long-term isolation that would keep the dyne uncontaminated also precluded the gradual assimilation of an Outsider, a newcomer, important to a later phase in a group's evolution. The original members both exclude and try to win over and impress or even warn the newcomer at the same time. The new perspective and judgment feeds their sense of themselves as a group.

Sometimes at night Gisonne tried to explain it all to Trjol, but he was impatient. "I don't understand," he said, "why you can't just pick some good people with complementary skills and experience, no ax murderers, people who can work with me, and that's it."

"See?" she said. "Work with you! You'll be emergent leader, both task and 'social-emotional.'"

"There you go with your jargon and labels. You talk about individual freedom but once you name the 'roles,' the labels become selffulfilling."

"It's descriptive, not prescriptive."

"Only in theory. All labels, names, become prescriptive forces. Controls."

Gisonne said nothing then, but thought he might— sometimes—be right.

"Why did you ask ZD's help then since you think dyne theory is nonsense?" she asked instead.

"To be with you," he said and reached to pull her down into his bed.

"Let's go outside," she said. "Let's go down to the water."

It had been a long time since Gisonne had been on the beach or bluffs. Except for some meals in the commensary, she had lived and worked inside this one building, the Allain. And this part of The Plateau was a high but small interior plain, out of view and sound of the ocean.

Reluctantly he agreed and they dressed in bathing clothes under their wind cloaks—just in case she could get him under a waterfall or into a stream.

"Since I'm doing this trek with you," he said, walking down the narrow path ahead of her, "you have to come with me on mine."

"You never stop, do you? I can't go. I will never leave z2. Even on a regular flight to Agricula—never mind SPEED. I hate traveling. I'm even homesick here on The Plateau just being away from the cliffs. I was miserable on Estuary."

"But don't you care how much I need you?" he asked.

"Then don't go. Stay with me," she said.

The descent grew steeper and they held the railing and watched their feet. Below the ocean was a joy in the late sunlight. Gisonne realized how much her reality had been doubly dominated: ZD and Trjol. All inside work. She took a free breath and wished he'd move a little faster.

At the bottom finally, they walked along the narrow stony strand toward a jetty, part natural, part university built. Students passed them by, skipping and running, calling out to one another. Two boys beyond the jetty dashed in and out of the surf, daring killer waves to crash over them. One might have been Jevry.

Hey, boy with legs so brown, so shaped, Gisonne thought madly. Trjol walked ahead of her on his hairy, pale limbs—not unshaped but so naked.

They sat on a flat rock by the jetty and Trjol talked again about his dreams for the edel. Gisonne felt spray, so fine it was almost a mist, with each breaking wave.

"It should be unique, not a human being and not an OS."

"An OS times ten," Gisonne said.

"No," he said, "not by multiples but by nature . . . Oh. You're joking." But he went on anyway. "It will be a larger, deeper, more complex mind and, I believe, I hope, a different mind from any before. That's why I have to go on the mission. I can't wait for the return. Don't you understand? No, no, you don't."

He touched her chin to turn her face to him and frowned. It was wet. Her eyelashes glistened. He laughed. He and she were both wet, lightly, perfectly sprayed. He hadn't noticed.

He kissed her, pushed her back onto the rock, ran his palm up over her damp, naked thigh. She thought of the students, but they were gone, or far up the beach.

His fingers touched, moved away, and when she made a small sound, back again.

"But you see," he said, not stopping his slow probing, "I can't go without you."

She moved her hands along his arm, grasping his elbow to encourage his fingers, then up to hold tight to his shoulders.

"It will be for such a short time, just two seasons for us, two years on z2."

"But I can't," she said, pulling away from him, trying to sit up. "I saw those returnees. My reality is here, my center."

"I'm your reality," he said. "I'm your center." He slid down to the ground beside the jetty and lay on his back, and she came down onto him.

They didn't see the sunset, but then it is not as astonishing on The Plateau as on Corse.

Chapter Nine

Risky Shift

10/25/3519 oe
The Plateau

"NO! No, no!" Cly shouted. "Diana Rise Allain is going along on our mission! Be a member of our dyne?"

"No," Aj cried. "It's not fair. After all our work. We'll have to start from scratch and there isn't time." Aj, so dependably reasonable, serene, informative, was standing, waving her arms, wildly out of role.

"Not from scratch," Evan said. "All the preliminary work still stands. Even some of our short list—"

"We can't do it. I won't do it," Cly kept shouting. "Two conditions are too many. We can't build a viable group around two. One was bad enough."

"She has no qualifications," someone said.

"Just influence where it counts," someone else said. "Diana Rise Allain will wreck the whole thing."

"Why? Why?" Aj asked.

"Can't Trjol use his own influence to stop her?" someone else, an SO who rarely spoke, asked.

"He wouldn't understand why he should," Gisonne said. "He still doesn't appreciate sociometrics."

"Listen, everybody," Evan said. "We have no choice about this."

"I say we all quit." Cly's voice was low this time, almost deadly. "You're bending to Allain pressure, Evan."

Evan's face reddened, but he responded without other outward urgency or anger. "The goal is more important than our project. The mission goes to Quivera." Did he believe what he was saying? Gisonne wasn't sure.

"How is Diana Allain's going to Quivera or Agricula or any place else going to accomplish anything? The Octente—"

"A new Octente property law. Personal presence, as I understand it—"

"Pontus." Cly waved a dismissal. "Protecting Allain interests, Allain money. No matter how bountiful these families are, the money is finally theirs. And why weren't we told sooner—before we did all this work?"

"Wait a minute," Gisonne started to say, "my family—" But no one was listening. She felt angry but did not want to excite the group more.

"They couldn't let it out before the Stycian ship left. And it's not just Allain money," Evan said. "I've been informed that most of the families in the Arines, many from Nord, individuals and corporations, have turned over all their off-world property to her. She is now the official owner of most of z2's quiveron mines; she is the richest person in The Octente—and will be until she comes home and gives it all back two years from now."

"All the families?" Aj asked. "Mine? I never heard of it."

"Your family and mine," Evan said.

"Then how can it possibly be a secret?" Cly asked.

"Was a secret. The Stycian ship is gone now so it doesn't matter. Diana Allain has to get to Quivera to confound the new absentee owner policy."

"But Malaaca and/or Styxx forced Corynn to make those rules just to confound us. I don't think the Octente would ever really apply—"

"It doesn't matter what we think. No more discussion. Let's go to work."

This time it was worse. With any new element the old structure promised to collapse. And though the informal consensus was that Diana would emerge as Task but not Social-emotional leader, she presented a possible role conflict with Trjol who was both a Task and SeL. But someone noted that Trjol had become a leader as an individual, while Diana had

partially inherited her position and it was built on family and
other dyne and circle constructs, especially her father Xaviour. If
there were open competition, Trjol would probably win. If the
struggle between them was latent, no one could predict the
outcome since Diana's manipulative skills were unknown.
However if she lost either way, would she then become Central
Negative?

In dyne terms, she was an unknown, uncontrollable
variable. Even if she were willing, there was no time for ZD to
do a complete workup, and certainly no time for trial groups.

"Sloppy," Cly said. "Guesswork. Dangerous."

They looked up her biography, the history of her dynes and
looser circles: government, family, therapy. Sent confidential
questionaires to associates. But who would tell the truth about
The Allain? And they questioned Gisonne.

Gisonne was amazed at how much she didn't know. Surely
there was no one else, outside her immediate family dyne, whom
she had known longer or seen as often. Hentor, Diana's son, had
lived with the Michalises for two z2 years. Gisonne had roamed
through Allaincroft as freely as Laurel House. Jevry Allain was
her brother's closest friend. But Diana? Who was she?

"She's strong. She has high ideals. She works hard. She . . .
she's beautiful," Gisonne told them.

ZD was not satisfied. They knew all this.

"I guess I was never part of her private life," Gisonne said.
She did not say maybe there is no private Diana. What you see is
all there is.

They suggested their bringing Jevry in, especially since he
was within quick reach at the Branch, but Gisonne discouraged
it. He could add nothing, she told them. Actually she knew he
would hate it and go through emotional contortions. Jev was a
great person, full of energy, humorous, ecstatically alive, even
after fighting through the pain of his parents' death; sometimes
he seem to live on a thin, superficial plane, shallow,
thoughtlessly physical but Denny and Gisonne knew that equally

often he was hypersensitive, too introspective, too hard on himself.

10/26/19

Trjol refused to be surprised about "Diana's Quest" or even much interested. Gisonne tried to explain to him how her presence on the mission would complicate the crew/dyne, but he had recently become emeshed in breakthrough work on neuro-regeneration or longevity being done on Malaaca, reports of which had come in on the same ship with the bad Octente news.

"They're wrong," he said. "Those Malaacan geniuses! But they have discovered one very interesting thing—about the material base for the lower synapses. I would love to examine—"

"Cres! Are you going to talk about brains now? Can't you see? All our work—"

"You're right. I don't see. It's all sociological mumbo jumbo. Diana Allain should be fine. Her status will add to the project's prestige, bring in more money for future work. And she's used to working with people. The crew will work together. . . . Maybe the Allain family will put some money into edel—"

"I can't believe you!" she shouted. They were having their first fight since they stopped fighting. "And by the way, don't say anything about her going. It isn't a real secret anymore but—"

"Why? My work is no secret."

"Not your work. Her work. It has nothing to do with your work—or mine. The Octente—"

"Local politics again! These little games are going to interfere with some of the most exciting scientific achievements in human history—just ahead of us. We have to cooperate. Malaaca has so much. Just look at this report. Even their mistakes—"

"Politics! z2 is threatened and you—"

"Ridiculous. Scare tactics of local petty politicians. Braitt Jones says—"

"Braitt Jones? When were you talking to that . . . off worlder?"

"You know I work with her. She's Octente Missions—"

"What were you doing on Estuary?"

"Why? Looking at it."

"You don't believe in swamps. Braitt Jones was there."

"Braitt Jones is dedicated, an idealist. And that was a long time ago. Before you and I—"

"Dedicated to you. Patronizes everyone else. Doesn't have the courtesy of respecting our customs and manners."

"They are only symbols. These things change with fashion. Just social games. Braitt is just showing her independence and separateness from z2. It's hard to be an off worlder—I know from my time on Malaaca. I never told you but some parts were painful. Braitt's just trying to protect her authority as a Octente agent. She is a lovely person. And very lonely."

"She is not a lovely person. She's a snob, a throw back. And if she is lonely, it's because she's isolate, selfish—" Gisonne stopped there. Cres could be kind, sensitive in unexpected ways. There were so many hidden parts to him. Gisonne herself would not be less humane. Braitt Jones probably was lonely, living most of her life among aliens. The Joneses of Mount Desert, some kind of cousins, were her only relatives on z2. Family was important to Gisonne.

"Well, can I attack that other off-worlder, that humble little Breff? Obsequious."

"I didn't really notice him. Gisonne, leave all this to the people who love it. Love me instead."

"Yes," she said.

They skipped their evening meal at the commensary. There was a new urgency in his love making, as if he were trying to quench a need beyond lust or love. And she was bolder and more open than she had been before. Perhaps because he was not perfect, because he was needy, because he worshipped her, she was free to love him and take him. To move and demand physically. To satisfy her own lust. Or perhaps it was because they had argued.

In the morning he got out of bed and walked over to the mirror. He looked closely into the glass, touched the furrow between his thick brows, but didn't notice it deepen as he leaned in even closer to examine the individual hairs just above his right ear.

"Stop frowning," Gisonne said. "You're very young."

11/1/19

Nimee horned to tell Gisonne that the she had a spouse and that she was already pregnant. Gisonne felt glad—and sad, a pang of homesickness.

"Come home then!" Nimee said. "That project must be done. The mission leaves . . . in two weeks, doesn't it? It's interesting that Diana—"

"Oh, you know that she's going? It's supposed to be a state secret."

"Yes, so everyone says. No one's supposed to mention it. Well, better her than us."

"Yes," Gisonne said. "You sound so happy, Nimee."

"What about you? Trjol?"

"Well . . . yes."

"Uh oh. Not a brief obsession?"

"Oh, Nimee, he's wonderful. I really do love him."

"Oh, dear," Nimee said and was silent for a while. "You're going to miss him—but it's for only two years."

Two years, Gisonne thought. Two years without him. How could she bear it? And then what about him? He needed her. His life and work would fall apart without her. And his work was so important. Her greatest contribution could be as partner and as a kind of personal SeL and TR. How could she be so selfish as to reject his pleas?

11/23/3519
The Plateau

ZD were not happy with their final choices. There was
much information on Emil delaCour—for example, his spouse
had been family speaker—but he was less known qualitatively
since he had been one of a pair since late childhood. His
acceptance of the mission was evidence of his loyalty and
obedience. He would have to recover from the personal
fragmentation the separation would cause. As the weaker of the
spouses, he had probably been lieutenant.

Diana's roles were even more uncertain.

Fron Maces, an astronomer from a small island in
Archipelago Nord, should emerge as a strong Information
Provider, strong enough to prevent group fragmentation. He had
some OS training, navigation experience, and was risk prone
enough to be a dominant communicator, yet was unlikely to
compete for leadership.

The only veteran SPEEDERS, Lonney and Bram, were the
necessary Silent Observers. Bram showed signs of being a Self-
centered Follower, but Lonney was a constant Silent Observer.
Both were followers.

The weakest points in their network were lieutenant and
Tension Releaser. None of the candidates exhibited the exact
right traits.

"I do," Gisonne said. "I am a strong TR, and I can be Trjol's
lieutenant without being devoured. I want to go on the mission."

Except for Aj, their objections were not as violent as she
had expected. The project was already in ruins as far as most of
them were concerned. Cly laughed and slapped his thigh.

As they talked the idea seemed to take hold and then to
appeal. It might be interesting to have one of their own observe
the phasic development of the group—as an insider. While
including an ZD member in any dyne was completely against

group policy, this case changed the rules. After all there was no other way to study its evolutionary phases.

And, Evan urged, Gison's relationship with Trjol might be turned to advantage since they could never become a dyad powerful enough to dominate or dissolve the rest of the group. She would be a strong Tension Releaser but too submissive to Trjol and emotionally supportive of the dyne to be lieutenant.

Only Aj persisted in arguing against it, and her motive seemed personal, having more to do with Gison's well being than the project.

SHIP'S COMPANY roster

TL   Cres Trjol (Diana Rise Allain)
CN   Diana Rise Allain (Cres Trjol)
SeL   Cres Trjol
TR   Gisonne Michalis
Lieutenant Emil delaCour (Gisonne Michalis)
IP   Fron Maces
Cell (not functional) Fron Maces
ScF   Lonney (dyad Bram)
SO   Bram (dyad Jonney)
SO   Emil delaCour
R   Unknown
O

Chapter Ten

Critical Mass

11/25/3519 oe
Nordport

The presence of such a large number of people, including Arines, Norders, and off worlders, on Nordport at any one time was unusual and excited curiosity and rumor among the dockworkers, technicians, and some of the guests themselves. Unlike Estuary, The Plateau, or Corse, Nordport rarely attracted visitors beyond the infrequent travelers leaving or arriving and, less often, their friends or associates.

The Nord way was to crouch against the wind. The structures for storage of goods and equipment, OMD buro offices, and the housing of personel and guests were almost identical: thick-walled, single-storied, and made of the same black stone as the sheer, naked, almost vertical, dark mountainside against which they huddled.

This "village" and the landing platforms were on the same horizontal plain, a black, a half-mile-wide rock shelf, projected almost at right angles from the mountain just above sea level. Over the centuries its surface had been leveled with explosives and smoothed with use, storms, and extreme high tides.

Except for the ubiquitous sound of the ocean, the protective shapes of the mountains, and the horizontal surface so rare on z2, two ports could not be more different. The landing field on the Arine Plateau was smaller and lay high above the sea, open to the sun, bordered with green vegetation; Nordport's mountain was blackly massed above, hovering over the landing fields, further diminishing the human structures, and blocking them from sun as well as wind.

Yet those structures usually provided more than sufficient housing since the few dockworkers and some of the technicians belonged to more than one work dyne. They spent most of the lives in their home villages, farther inland, tightly fitted into the bottoms of the crotches and deepest valleys of Nordport Island.

Ironically, local planetary craft and Nord island hoppers took more of the work dynes' time and attention than the interstellar and interplanetary SPEEDships and shuttles, which arrived so seldom—and yet had momentous effect on Zalterian lives.

But, other than the small SPEED shuttle, Procne, being prepared for departure, there were no off-world ships in port. The only other vessels were a handful of Nord hoppers and several larger Arine craft, which had brought the unusal number of "visitors." Local people were doubled up and tripled in sleep quarters, and large dynes—some wealthy and important Arine families—were crowded into tiny suites.

Gisonne and Aj, who was always at her side since ZD had left The Plateau, sneaked a break from ZD work to walk the Nordport's single road, separating the buildings from the landing fields.

It was interesting to see so many broad Nord faces. Arine's traditional ancient rivals seemed much less strange in this strange setting. Stranger was the Stycian Dyll Breff. It was impressive that the Embassy had sent the new envoy. That meant the off-worlders had learned that The Allain was going to Quivera. Lucky the Stycian ship had left earlier. How frustrating for them not to be able to report to the Octente until the next SPEED ship came in!

Breff stood in a doorway—hardly inconspicuous—with Braitt Jones, deep in conversation. Standing near them, perhaps with them, perhaps not, was that little man who had been staying at Allaincroft, the one Jevry hated so much. He was inconspicuous! Gisonne couldn't think of his name. Something ridiculous. Persy?

Aj said that several of the central Allain family had accompanied Diana but Gisonne never got to see them.

Her own family would not be told she had left until after take off. She told herself it was to spare them pain and futile arguing. The truth was that seeing them would hurt too much and Gisonne was afraid she'd weaken. But afterall it was for only two years!

But there, as she and Aj were on the way back to the crowded ZD quarters, she saw a teenaged boy in the distance and thought for a moment it was Denny and she knew that two years are a long time—crucial time in a young person's life and Gisonne would miss them.

ZD members insisted on testing and retesting her, claiming she had joined so late they had no time. Again she resented it, even though she would do the same—eagerly—to someone else. Her heart wasn't in it; it was elsewhere—wherever Trjol was.

And then when she thought herself free at last, there were more foolish OMD regulations, questionaires, medical checks— overkill for such a small expedition. It showed how little of importance these buros had to do, Gisonne told Aj. They had to make themselves important with busy work, trivia, instead of doing what they should be doing—dealing with the problem of returnees.

11/29/3519 oe
SPEED

The restraints had not been released or the cubicle hoods swung back until the ship was in SPEED. Gisonne slid off her bunk, pushed too hard, and almost swept herself through her q door. She reached for a rail to slow herself, missed, and bumped the opposite wall lightly. The second time she moved slowly and cautiously. She was one of the few on the mission for whom weightlessness was a new experience.

By the time she reached the end of the narrow q corridor, she could hear voices already ahead of her in the central cabin.

She could not hear Trjol's among them. In spite of her need to see him, she had to move herself gingerly.

To enter central was to be immediately and closely among the others. As Gisonne tried to pull herself into the area unobtrusively, she saw that Trjol was not one of the three already gathered.

As part of ZD's plan, the crew had not met as a group until now and were awkward and formal, almost denying the intimacy that must follow; two to three oe months of "togetherness" in extremely small quarters meant total interdependency. And it was a dyne from which no one could resign and go home; they could not vote to dissolve and disperse. So they were all polite.

Diana came a few seconds after Gisonne—making them five.

And then—suddenly—there were six. A tall man came in head first from the navigation cabin opposite the q entrance. Gisonne recognized him. She knew all of them; she had selected most. But it was different on horn, on screen, in the lab. Here was a flat-featured Norder addressing them all without preliminaries, in the irritating, toneless Nord manner. Fron Maces.

"The charts," he said. "Our destination's been changed. The course—"

"A malfunction?" someone asked.

"No. The course plan has been altered," Fron said.

"Well, can't we change it back?"

"No, of course not. The OS has been set. Ineluctably. Permanently. Forever changed."

"What is the change? Where are we going?"

"Waldseemuller."

No one had ever heard of it.

"Where is it?" Diana asked.

Fron shook his head slowly. "Very far," he said. "According to the OS, the transit time from Zalterius to Waldseemuller is 110 oe years planet time, 11 or 12 SPEED."

"Doctor Trjol," Gisonne said. "Cres Trjol will—"

"I'm afraid not." The seventh member of the group, a young man Gisonne had never seen before, spoke softly as he came into the central. "I am Doctor Trjol's replacement. Doctor Trjol changed his mind about participating in this mission. He is not on board."

Chapter Eleven

Necrology

2 mo's SPEED
8/15/3521

They had gone through the stages of dying: disbelief, anger, compromise, depression, and now, after one and a half oe months in SPEED, most had reached resignation—acceptance. All the stages of dying—all but the last—death. They didn't die. But then they had been dead from the beginning—if death is being out of life.

DENIAL

First they just didn't "get it." What is incomprehensible is not real. Several had laughed furiously. They said it simply wasn't true. They disbelieved first the human and then the machine. Fron Maces was joking. He was lying. Or he was ill trained and incompetent and had misread the horn.

Fron himself wanted them to be right, to prove him wrong.

They—including the ones who knew nothing of horns or piloting—had to see for themselves. They saw.

Then they examined the horn's written displays in several languages. They listened to its vocal communication—audio alone. The flat, typical horn voice repeated the words, "Destination Waldseemuller."

Fron's reading was accurate. The course was not what they had signed up for, one year to Quivera, a short stop on Agricula, another year back to z2. They were instead bound straight outward for one hundred planetary oe years.

So change the course back? What was the problem? Fron told them what the veteran travelers among them already knew:

The navigation programs of an operating system on a ship at SPEED cannot be altered in any way. And for some reason, Fron had discovered, this particular OS was more than usually inaccessible.

Lonney decided that the course change was a horrible practical joke. One of the more immature technicians must have falsified the horn output to scare them. They were actually following the original course. Only time would tell if she was right.

Fron Maces suggested the whole thing was a plot, cooked up by ZD. The other Zalterians had only vague notions of what ZD was or did, and Lonney and Bram had never heard of it, but they all listened eagerly. They turned, as one, on Gisonne, glad to feel the relief of anger. Her very presence was evidence, Maces said. Obviously a born information provider, he explained that ZD people did not become members of the dynes they managed! They demanded she tell them the truth—they were being tested. As a group? As individuals? Was she on board to secretly observe their reactions and subsequent interactions in the face of catastrophe?

Gisonne was dumbfounded. Surely she would not send herself into nowhere for two hundred years—twenty years of her own life—just to study group dynamics! Then when she understood what they meant, she almost laughed. They were accusing her of simulating the catastrophe in order to study them. Their route hadn't really been changed. Sociological and psychological types were always doing things like that. Again there was no way to prove them wrong—yet.

It was Diana Allain who first suggested that the horn's external displays were malfunctioning, that communication functions were somehow defective, but the Operating System itself fine. They liked that explanation and Diana had authority.

But again only time would tell.

And too soon it did. Fron again delivered bad news. The ship's direction and acceleration were matching the horn reading;

their destination could no longer be doubted. They were indeed bound for Waldseemuller.

ANGER

It was almost impossible to tell what Diana or Bram believed but the rest no longer denied their fate. Instead they looked for someone responsible to blame and then one by one, separately at first, they began to curse, to condemn, to rage.

Those who understood the reason for Diana's presence, again the Zalterians, Emil delaCour, Fron Maces, Calib Lendari, and Gisonne, blamed the new rulers of the Octente in general. The Stycian envoy Dyll Breff in particular. Only he and the offworld buros close to him could have learned about Diana's mission to Quivera. It was obvious; there could be no other explanation. Some inwardly, others aloud, they cursed the Stycian and all Stycians.

Calib Lendari attacked Diana. "It is your pontus-damned 'mission' that did this to us, Allain of Arine!" he shouted. "Of all the foolish, childish projects, as infantile, romantic, useless, impractical—"

Then looking at Diana, cool, apparently indifferent or perhaps deaf to his words, he stopped, and, almost sheepishly, turned away.

They wanted a reachable object for their rage and looked again and again at one another. Someone, a Zalterian, must have worked with the off-worlders. Neither Breff nor one of his lackeys could walk into Nord navigation areas and openly tamper with the ship's OS.

Gisonne found herself looking at Fron Maces' flat Norder profile and for the thousandth time wondering if he were not the only one of them capable of tampering with the course before takeoff.

But why would it be he or any one of them? As Gisonne herself had asked when they first accused her and ZD, for what momentous cause would anyone be willing to travel ten or a hundred years to nowhere?

Besides she had her own object of hate and rage and he was not a member of the crew.

In frustration, their anger went from the particular to the general. Fate. Gods. Pontus himself.   It was not fair. It had never happened to other travellers. Why them? What sin had they committed?

COMPROMISE

They would be good. They regretted past mistakes. They talked aloud about the gods. Someone—anyone—to make a deal with. Some prayed.

DEPRESSION

But there was no answer. Gradually they stopped talking and stared at nothing, each alone. Most ate nothing. Bram and Emil began to sleep most of the time. Gisonne and Lonney never slept. The others fell in and out of consciousness.

And then somehow at some point, "Why me?" became "Why us?"

For a short time, two and sometimes three of them started to share their depression. They understood one another as no one outside their little coffin ever could.

They talked about death and fear and hope and childhood needs, and long-gone loved ones. They still could not imagine that gone only yesterday was gone forever.   They grieved together for their dead lives, their lost identities. Isn't identity one's reflection in the eyes of others? Sister, brother, center, cn, father, student, even male and female, who are we without out roles? Is all meaning relational?

RESIGNATION

So it was finally together they accepted the end of their lives. But they didn't die because, of course, they had already died. Yet still they sat and waited.

Amazingly, they continued to breathe, to sleep, to dream, and then to wake, eat, and then again to talk to one another. Some were surprised, others disappointed perhaps. But this new life went on, in this narrow reality of seven living human bodies entombed in a capsule in emptiness.

It was not their persons, but their lives that had died; everything they had known outside of themselves was forever gone. They were dead to that world, and it was dead to them.

4/1/3521 oe
Zalterius II

The old ambassador from the Octente to Zalterius II, suffering physical and mental problems, probably due to a lifetime on a planet hostile geographically and culturally, was relieved of his ambsassadorial duties and, being too ill for SPEED, placed in retirement in OMB facilities on Corse. His assistant, the envoy Dyll Breff, assumed his functions but was given broader powers.

Professor Cres Trjol discovered distinct phasic levels in the neurodegeneration of the human brain in the aging process. He is attempting to improve certain Malaacan neurosurgical techniques in order to combat the deterioration. However, Malaacan medical procedures are being phased out on z2.

Chapter Twelve

Emergence

3 1/2 mo's SPEED
11/29/22 oe

In SPEED the only thing to see in the port is your own reflection, and Gisonne didn't like hers. The face of a fool, the eyes of a fool. The eyes looked back with contempt to match her own. The eyes knew more than she did. Where had they been when she needed them? She laughed and watched her face change. But the shape was unfamiliar; the contour was wrong. It bore the nasty grin of a stranger.

She looked beyond her own bitter and ugly image, over its shoulder, at the others mirrored in the panel. And there they were as always, squatting, floating, huddling in the common area, the ship "center," one little hunk of a catacomb. As in any crypt, there was eternal sameness, same gray, narrow walls, same slow time, same bodies. The only difference was these corpses moved, but the motions were constricted, repeated, redundant, in two months already predictable.

Except for Emil delaCour, lying as usual in his sleep cubicle—q, they were all there. Lonney and Bram, veteran SPEEDERS, leaning together over some kind of horn game— different in age, sex, physical type, but becoming a dyad as ZD had predicted. And the Norder, Fron Maces, Information provider, full of knowledge and advice, all useless now—ZD had been right about him too. ZD!

Every time Gisonne forgot for even a second, another after-shockwave of the same memory washed over her, as crushing and suffocating as the first time she heard the news: her world was gone. There would be no ZD in 200 years! No ZD. No Nimee, Jevry, Blake. No mother! And no damn, pontus-damned Cres Trjol!

10 SPEED years out, 10 back. Gisonne woud be forty-six. All right—she could take that. But even ten years seemed like a long, long time. It was almost funny. Permanent changelessness while the outside universe changed with the SPEED of light.

And would they get back? What was Waldseemuller? A name for a rock. How could they turn and return?

And if they did—supposing the person who had done this murder had set the program for return—return to what? Zalterius II would be a world as alien as any other way out there—more so. Home is a place in time. Home is gone.   This time Gisonne caught herself from falling into the black pit of rage and grief. Think—think about other things.

Dark head always bent closely over his horn terminal, Calib Lendari, Trjol's replacement, "sat" in a different spacial plane from the rest, refusing to share their arbitrarily chosen up and down.

Tall, serene, always silent, Diana sat with them. One could look at the lovely face but not into it. No sign that she was sorry for bringing this horror upon them.

Again reality hit Gisonne—like a sharp pain that can never be ignored and never loses its force or ceases to surprise.

Gisonne turned not only away but inward, avoiding the never-ending after-shocks with her last defense—fantasies of revenge.

5 mo's SPEED
2/27/3524

Diana sat in the ship center, horn in hand unused, Fron Maces leaning over her, whispering in a voice that was both urgent and monotone at the same time. His tall, narrow frame, curly head, and flat features had become as familiar in five months ship time as the seams and colors of the cabin itself— dull, dull, deadly dull. Had someone once said that boredom was a kind of anger? Or the reverse? Gisonne couldn't remember.

Something from her ZD training. It didn't matter. Nothing did. Why should it? For what?

Diana shook her head, not looking at Fron or at anything. Her white-gold hair had grown much longer but its shape held and it shone as her head moved, swinging clean, beautiful, perfect. Fron raised his voice.

"You must do something. Organize a plan. Direct me to make schedules."

Diana finally looked in his direction but not quite at him. She said nothing. He sighed heavily.

"I've been studying crew functions. There are things we have to do. Bram knows—Lonney, you too. You've both been on OMD missions before."

Bram stared at him blankly. Lonney nodded, smiled. "It was slave labor." Then she looked toward the corridor in the direction of Emil's q. "He hasn't eaten," she said to no one in particular, especially not Gisonne, who had also rejected her overtures with consistent coldness. Bram squirmed and frowned when Lonney straightened up and pulled herself out into the corridor. He moved the game pieces about aimlessly, then slammed the system out, a petulant child. Or a demanding but helpless old man.

Lonney came back into the center towing delaCour behind her, his beautiful brown face empty—blank.

Gisonne thought she heard Calib sneer, but he did not raise his head from the horn.

"Diana," Fron persisted, "what do you think about—?"

Gisonne laughed aloud. ZD had known Fron would be no threat to leadership. A good IP, efficient Lieutenant, but always a spoke attached to a strong hub. Now he was hubless, headless. Gisonne was amused, distracted for a moment and then more angry than ever—at herself—at them—at Trjol.

"Forget it, Fron," she said to his reflection in the port panel. "It won't work. You can't force her into TL." Although Fron knew about dyne study—as he did most things, he did not know details like that term, anymore than he knew he was IP. Gisonne went on anyway, testing the fit and feel of her new role, CN— Central Negative. "Face it. There is no purpose. We won't work. We're broken. Malfunctioning ZD."

"The Stycian ship has reached Malaaca," Diana said. "I am not yet on Quivera. z2 will lose all its possessions."

Except for Emil they all stared at her. Pontus, Gisonne thought. Diana is still Task Leader but TL in another reality.

That explained her refusal to join anyone in the only topic which had recurred in every phase they went through and never wore out no matter how hard they chewed at it: who did it?

And now again.

"She . . . is she mad?" Lonney asked.

"Heroic," Fron said.

"Heroic madness," Calib added, "and you Norders are worse. Historically you should have learned better."

"You talk? You who have allegiance to nothing. Not even z2."

Calib's dark face reddened, thick brows merging. "I told you," he said, "again and again. My family, my mother, my loyalty has been to them. You, a Norder, are incapable of understanding real loyalty. I had to volunteer—for their sake. They would have lost everything. Bah—it's none of your business."

He had told this much several times before but no more. He said again he had not been one of the original pool. Later, after some family financial misfortune, he had applied but heard nothing. He said he had almost forgotten the project when, just one or two days before takeoff, he received urgent acceptance from OMD and an extraordinary incentive—immediate help for his family.

That might explain why Gisonne did not remember him, but it raised other questions. Why hadn't she known about such a change, such an emergency? Had someone—Evan?—added Calib to the roster, without telling Gisonne? Why?

And there was something else about him, beyond his very presence, beyond his hostility and general nastiness, something oddly familiar and strange at the same time.

Lonney asked Fron again if it were possible that the course had been changed by accident. And he said as he often had. "I am not an OS technician; I'm a navigator and astronomer."

"You're the only one who could have done it," Bram said—as he often had. "You fooled with the horn; you're always fooling with the horn."

Fron shrugged. "Why? Why would I?"

No, it could not be Fron Maces, or Calib, or anyone on board, Gisonne thought—as she often had. Unless he or she was mad?

And then it must have been to get rid of one of the crew permanently. Who? "Not me." Gisonne's family—never! Besides they didn't know she was going. No one knew but ZD and the OMD buros—and Trjol. And Brait Jones. Who in ZD? Aj? Ridiculous. Was Cly negative enough to destroy the experiment? Evan had been very friendly with Brait Jones, but that seemed unconnected. And Braitt Jones herself might want to send Gisonne out of the world if she knew Trjol wasn't going too. But did she know? And if so, it still wouldn't be worth getting rid of Gisonne to spoil his project and ruin one of OMD's missions. Unless she was also working with Breff to stop Diana.

Braitt or no Braitt, it was obvious. The Octente must have had the course changed to prevent Diana from getting to Quivera and saving z2. But again surely their instrument of execution must have been someone who remained on z2—certainly not a member of Procne's crew.

"Diana, tell us who was in on it? Who had connections to the ambassador or that Breff? Who . . . no. The question is absurd. Everyone knew. But when? Was it after the Stycian ship had departed or—"

"I cannot speak on this subject," Diana said.

They stared at her—wondering.

"She refuses to speak 'on this subject,'" Gisonne said. "The Allain has to keep her mission a state secret lest one of us leak it to the enemy!"

6 mo's SPEED
12/13/3524 oe

Lonney and Bram were reflected in the port in their usual positions, leaning close over some kind of horn game in a hand-held holobox just behind Gisonne. Bram frowned as Lonney's quick fingers flashed a move and then he nodded slowly, never smiling but approving as always of everything she did—everything that had to do with him.

The two had become a very tight pair, but not quite as ZD had planned because of Lonney's unpredicted, extreme role change from SO to TR. Gisonne remembered very little about Lonney's history and test results except that she was a fixed Silent Observer; nothing in her past crew or other group behavior had indicated she could possibly become Tension Releaser. Had she been sucked into the role, into the vacuum Gisonne had created with her own change? Or did overwhelming disaster shape-change the personality? Shake individuals out of their customary relational patterns?
Gisonne didn't know. It was certainly an interesting new variable.

Bram didn't know yet that he was becoming half a unit; Gisonne almost smiled. But the dyad was not sexual, more parent/child—with Bram the child though much the elder—how old it was hard to tell. They would be a turbulent pair. Lonney was compelled to feel for the others, others plural. To comfort, empathize, support—to mother. To seduce?

Gisonne saw Lonney's reflection begin to move. She glanced at Calib—as she always did, but he, as always, was unapproachable. Gisonne knew the behaviour pattern well but strangely—for the first time in her life—felt no desire or need to "play the role" herself. Her kind of anger left no room for "releasing" anyone's tension. Cres Trjol!

Think—think about other things. Sanity meant facing reality as well as escaping it and reality was this unchangeable here-and-now with these seven people in it. And in the same way that they were trying to lose themselves in attacking one another, fighting, sleeping, horn and daydream fictions, Gisonne tried to distract herself in studying them—plying her trade.

For example the Norder, Fron Maces had seemed to reach a level of resignation sooner than the others and had become more and more preoccuppied with his journals and the ship's OS and the OS hardware—preparing himself for his IP role—if he could get anyone to want information. He repeatedly asked that Diana join him in the navigation cabin to "consult." She never agreed, most often not acknowledging the request.

She, once important Zalterian center, erstwhile Task Leader, spent most of her time going from horn program to horn game to horn fiction to horn music, stopping at none.

Emil delaCour, who had begun spending more time in the center on his own, watched Fron and Diana without expression. ZD's research and testing had indicated that Emil had no talent or desire for leadership—one reason he had been selected for the mission. He had never been a functional center, even though nominally half of the spousal pair that led the large and powerful delaCour family. But now he seemed even less, less than a follower, less than a person, a fragment.

Calib Lendari worked intensely at his chosen diversions. Still sitting in his own "up and down," he seemed completely absorbed, even while he ate, avoiding them all, shutting them out.

All in together again, Gisonne thought. Ship's complement complete!

The only escape from the population sink in the center was the navigation cabin, which could hold three—very uncomfortably—or their individual coffin-sized sleep cubicles, their q's. They had staggered their sleep times somewhat, but it had not helped. There were never fewer than four persons in central at any one time and no way to be alone with anyone else—if one should ever want to be.

All present and accounted for, counted again and again in the mirror of the port, the port that Gisonne herself faced, always, choosing to "stand" with her back to the others.

Others! Other whats? Two zombies, a Tension Releaser who creates tension, a great big, old, little boy, a preoccupied, droning Norder, a contempuous dark horse, and Diana Rise Allain, a beautiful icy zero. A group without a task, without a purpose or theme. A dyne with no center, no outside dyne or world to interface with. She hated them all, was sick to death of them all, and they had not yet been out half an oe year.

7 mo's SPEED
8/30/3525 oe

Another month—how many years on z2? Years gone forever.

"We're still in Octente space," Fron said.

And still in ship space, Gisonne thought, standing in her usual spot, facing the blind port, its panel permanently, eternally, reflecting their little cave; the illusion did not double its apparant size but underscored its finiteness.

Although they had every life support, health, cosmetic facility, they had begun to look like strays—except for Fron and Diana. Lonney's short hair had never been shiney, but now it was grubby, thick-stranded, lank. She scratched at her head nervously even while she maintained her helpful, sympathetic smile.

Calib Lendari put out the horn holo carefully and turned about to listen. His hair was longer, his face thinner, eyes sunken and darker. Something about his face still attracted Gisonne but was haunting, frightening at the same time.

"Four oe years," Diana said, as if she heard Gisonne's thought.

"Later we go through the Tryllium system—missing its major worlds," Fron said. "We'll pass within a lightyear one of the farthest out planets in . . . in three months. It's called Isola."

"It's now 12/'24 on z2," Diana said. "What will it be on z2 then?"

"I . . . I didn't figure it out," Fron said. "Do you want me to?"

"Stop!" Gisonne cried. "Don't you see what you're doing? It doesn't matter. It has nothing to do with us. It will be 3620 when we get to Waldseemuller."

"The Octente wants Quivera," Diana said, "and the Octente is Malaaca and Styxx. I must—"

"Oh, Diana," Gisonne turned around and pushed hard toward Diana. She was trembling and heard her voice, ragged, shouting as if it belonged to someone else. "There is no Octente! Let it go."

A strong dark arm reached around her shoulders, pulling her back away from Diana. Gisonne turned to look into Emil delaCour's benign face and then just next to him was Calib. She stared into his fierce eyes. Terrible eyes—not benign. She forced her own away and saw that Fron had moved in front of Diana, blocking her from Gisonne. Three heros defending a snow queen.

"It's all right," Gisonne said, still loudly, breathing too hard. Then deliberately she didn't move for a few seconds, and finally laughed. She had once been a fine tension releaser, TR, afterall—a long, long time ago. "I'm not physically violent. I am now just very, very Negative."

"I wonder what the weather's like on Waldseemuller," Lonney said. Perhaps physical violence was all right after all, Gisonne thought.

9/28/3525

Conflicts were growing more frequent and more violent.

"Floor of pontus!!" It was a growl. Calib had tried to jump to his feet, at the same time shoving Lonney away from him. She rolled—almost gracefully in a free fall somersault—hitting the opposite wall with a slow, fulsome crunch. The blood that rose from the back of her head curled with equal grace, bounced on the same wall, and splattered like weightless rain on all of them.

They watched. Calib slowly ended his own reactive backward fall, face dark red.

"Pontus' excrement!" he cried. Only a true Zalterian would use that expletive, Gisonne noted.

Fron looked to Diana for direction. Emil alone acted, awkwardly looming large and dark in the center of the space. Gisonne saw that he was looking at her, wanting something.

"I've had enough of her touching me," Calib said.

No one moved to help Lonney. Calib breathed heavily, shrugged, and turned away from them as though none of it had happened.

"Lonney?" Bram whined. He started, finally, to go to her.

"Help her, Fron," Gisonne said, cursing all of them. Cursing their fate and hers. Their fate, their doom, was blind chance; hers was Cres Trjol. Whichever—it could only get worse for all of them.

Fron looked at Diana, who paid no attention, and then at Gisonne. He picked Lonney up and took care of her wounds.

It was not only Lonney's and Gisonne's but all their roles were warping as they became exaggerated, empty of purpose.

Fron's IP-Lieutancy was becoming, more and more, a bizzarre caricature, a mockery. He grew repetitive and querulous rather than informative. He continued to advise an indifferent Diana, told them all facts about the ship, astronomy, the weather, tried to carry out orders never given.

Diana, Task Leader, led nothing. Nor did she follow. Yet Gisonne did not believe she was really crazy. She knew the truth literally but her imagination couldn't yet accept it. She just couldn't shake herself of the old reality. She still fought the battles of the past.

Bram's intelligence level seemed low and dropping. Gisonne tried to remember him from the pool of volunteers. Surely neither ZD nor the OMD would recruit a mentally limited or defective crew member even as simple follower.

While the rest deteriorated, Emil delaCour started to improve. Although he never spoke, he did seem to listen—Silent Observor by default. Gisonne had seen him often in the past at their family gatherings, but she assumed he did not recognize her. She was wrong.

"Michalis," he said later that day or night or some other time soon. "When" didn't matter anymore.

Gisonne started, looking up from some indifferent holofiction she was staring into, not sure who had spoken.

"Michalis," Emil repeated. He was looking directly into Gisonne's face.

"Yes. Michalis . . . Gisonne," she said. There was a time when she would have smiled, welcomed him back to the world.

He only nodded.

With everyone else it continued to grow worse—and worse.

Most of the confrontations, of course, were the result of repeated accusations of responsibilty for their fate, some more bizarre than others, hurled at Diana, at Gisonne and ZD, at Fron simply for being a Norder, at Lonney for not being an authentic Zalterian, at Calib for nastiness and secretiveness. Most were verbal; a few became physical.

Oddly, Gisonne found herself barking the commands that ended most of them. And oddest of all, most of the others listened.

The final violent rupture took place in the navigation area. From center Gisonne heard the banging and the voices and ignored them—until Emil rose and said "Michalis." When she refused to move, he touched her shoulder.

"Bastard of Pontus!" Fron was yelling at someone—Calib. Calib was not in the center. Neither was Diana.

"Turd." Calib's voice was muffled, a distant croak.

Gisonne pulled herself after Emil through the narrow passage and peered over his shoulder. Fron sat on Calib's thrashing body, throttling him and bashing his head against the base of the horn bench. Calib's face was already swollen, lips and tongue ugly red blooms.

The area was so small that Diana, who sat calmly on the bench itself, was only inches above the men, beautiful face staring without expression through the port at nothing.

Gisonne hesitated. There were choices. Die. Let them kill each other this way, and/or rot and starve slowly from neglect and waste. But—two—if they were all to die, surely it would be better to commit suicide—neatly, cleanly, painlessly.

But, third, if life was better than death, even this life, then they should try to live it.

"Stop him, Emil," she said.

Gisonne stood again—and for the last time—facing her blank port. She made plans. They had to have something real to do, a task of interest and value—in itself and then maybe—to all life beyond their own narrow point of reference, transcending their original place in space and time. And what might that be? There was only one, the very task they had been selected for— pontus-damned Trjol's pontus-miserable edel. Grow a mind. The others actually looked around when Gisonne laughed aloud.

But how in pontus was she going to know how? It wasn't her field. She had paid little attention to Trjol's explanations. Could Fron help? He'd been fooling around with navigation and—Bram was right—worked extensively with the ship Operating System, OS, the main horn. Of course, they all had indirectly.

There was no sign at all that this OS, this computingmachine, differed in any way from all other old tried-and-true horns that, as Trjol said, only processed information—no matter how clever they seemed. But Trjol had insisted that this one was more, an edel, and would evolve in response to the group "mind."

And here reflected in the port was the group—waiting, Bram for Lonney to return her attention to him, Lonney for Calib to pay attention to her, Fron for Diana to need him, Diana to arrive at Quivera, Gisonne for what?

She laughed again. They—these miserable seven inmates—were the outside world, "reality" as far as the edel was concerned. What did it know, poor thing! And what a rotten mind it must become!

10/3/3525 oe
Zalterius II

Dyll Breff has been granted the Octente title: Viceroy.

Persol Perl is first representative from the Arines to serve on the new Zalterian senate in Nordport, a cell organization functioning to optimize and expedite relations between Zalterius II and the Octente and to advise and assist the Viceroy, and to clarify his executive decisions to the populace.

Only a single Agricula food shuttle and four of the expected eight SPEED supply ships arrived since 6/1/3522. Three of these had distant origins and had been in SPEED since before 3520.

A medical supply ship arrived and departed without off loading.

All Malaacan medical procedures have been eliminated on z2.

Xavior Allain, accused by the Viceroy's office of crimes against the Octente committed by him and his daughter Diana, died of cardio failure in his home, Allaincroft.

Chapter Thirteen

Punctuated Equilibrium

7 1/2 mo's SPEED
3/29/26 oe

"It's going to be hot in here," Gisonne said.

Emil nodded. Calib whipped his head up, frowning deeply. The other three just looked at her.

"Hot! Why?" Calib asked. "Something gone wrong . . . or another one of your insane experiments?"

"We agreed, Calib," Gisonne said. "We're going ahead with the project."

"I never agreed," Calib shouted. "And you never made it clear that you were going to risk our lives, threaten life support. What happened with that sound augmentation thing you did a few days ago?"

"Wait, Lendari," Emil said, "Michalis told us what would happen."

"Yes, blast us out with our own voices."

"And heartbeats," Lonney said. "I liked it."

"You can't deafen a pontus-damned-drowned horn, but you can deafen us. And what did it accomplish?"

"So far—nothing. Nothing we can see."

But Gisonne was lying. Something had been accomplished in the last two SPEED weeks but not to the OS. Since Gisonne had become center and TL and given them a collaborative task, they had stopped trying to rape and kill and blame one another. And, she noted, their physical positions and movements had begun to change. Calib had actually glanced at Gisonne as she came into central and turned away again with annoyance rather than disgust. Bram and Lonney were together as usual but both the games they played and their attitudes toward them had changed. Their attention was studied; they looked to each other for responses.

Lonney's hair, while still growing out jaggedly, seemed lighter and softer, Bram's round face was less petulant. However, whenever Lonney turned her attention away from him, he still sulked.

Diana had changed in two ways: she now concentrated on one activity, creating delicate, precise floral and bird drawings through a horn program and she had finally begun to talk—if only to Emil.

Otherwise she was the same. She took no notice of anyone but Emil and carried her shoulders as broadly and her head as high as she had in the halls of Allaincroft, denying or defying the hideous narrowness of their environment.

And even before the heat experiment they had begun to discard or pull back their cloaks, letting the colors of their shirts and leggings relieve the ubiquitous gray.

Gisonne did not tell them that Trjol had been adamant when he said that there should be and could be no conscious, delberate attempt to pattern or control in any way the evolving edel mind. Too bad, old man! One had to have some goal, some reward, to keep going. Screwing up the edel would be some satisfaction though an incomplete revenge; Trjol would be a hundred and fifty oe years dead by the time it was accomplished.

The cabin was growing warmer. Maybe Diana would react now.

"Attach this connector to your horn, Calib," Gisonne said.

"This place is crawling with wires. I feel like I'm in a snake pit. Get the thing away from me."

"That's temporary; I'm working on the remotes," Fron said coming in with more hardware.

"If this what's-his-name—Treejaw—really planned this absurd project, if it's not some mad idea of Gisonne's—she seems to be the only one who knows anything about it—wouldn't he have everthing set up ahead of time? Wouldn't the pontus horn have been totally linked to us from the beginning?"

"Gisonne has said she doesn't know," Fron said. Drops of sweat glowed on his forhead. It was growing hotter. "I'll find out as much as I can as soon as I have time. I'm hunting through the System for Trjol's papers. But just in case, we're going to create as many links as we can now."

"I don't see how there can be more links or whatever than there already are, always are with horns," Lonney said. "On every mission I've been on—"

"Right," Bram said.

"True," Fron said. "We are always connected to the Operating System. We tap into it to use its programs. And it has access to our input, visual, auditory, to maintain life supposrt but those contacts are only partial and arbitrary and functionally different. Now we've been giving it total access to us."

Lonney laughed and shook her head. "I don't know if I want it to have access to everything!"

"Everything," Gisonne said. What a heavy, humorless Task Leader she had become. That was funny.

As the heat continued to rise from uncomfortable to miserable to intollerable, Gisonne wondered if this were her first and last mistake—on this project. Maybe she was driving the group back to barbarianisn, their hearts of darkness.

"It's too hot," Bram said. "Lonney, tell them to turn it off."

Calib studied his horn vid, his back turned as usual, but Gisonne could see streams of sweat running down the back of his neck.

Fron lowered his voice, speaking only to Gisonne. "I still don't understand why we are creating random links? Emile's q? Bram's cardiovascular—"

"Every contact on every level, through every port."

"I'm afraid of dissolution, Gisonne. Irrelevancies introduced with unpredictable effects . . . we have no control. There could be contamination of programs. Remember some of them are self correcting, 'fuzzy'?" Fron stared at the various horn hardware around the center, beads of prespiration falling onto his shirt. Gisonne tried not to show her own misery.

"It's too hot," Bram said again. Lonney patted him and said something about the puzzle they were playing.

Diana wiped a hand across her forehead. "My father Xaviour," she said, "expects the Octente position will revert to normal. Our complying with the ruling will not be seen as acceptance of its legality but merely a delay until natural order reasserts itself. The federation is in a state of imbalance now. The instability will be temporary."

As always since she had been speaking to anyone at all, Diana directed these comments only to Emil, Gisonne guessed it was because, he was a center of a central family, an important dyne.

Emil listened and nodded, glancing sideways at Gisonne. She smiled and shrugged one shoulder.

"I still don't get what we're doing," Lonney said, looking up at Gisonne from her game. "The horn does anything we need now. Solves any problem. It already thinks. It sure outthinks us!"

"I believe Trjol" (Gisonne hesitated in pronouncing the name aloud) "would say that what you take for thinking is processing, computing and reporting information."

Calib laughed aloud, but it might have been at something he was watching.

Lonney frowned, sweat flowing through the crease and into her eyes. "But isn't that what . . . "

"No, that isn't thinking." Gisonne couldn't believe herself. She had once thought Trjol's distinctions esoteric, irrelevant to reality, as precious and arcane as group theory was to him.

The cabin was growing oven-hot.

"I'm too warm, Nimee," Diana said, without looking away from her flower art.

Nimee! Nimee? Gisonne's younger sister? Gisonne wanted to shake Diana. Throttle The Allain! She, Gisonne, had been giving orders for two weeks—doing Diana's job—and Diana didn't know who she was.

Gisonne grabbed a contact from Fron and held it between her and Diana—all without losing the sharp edge of her anger.

For the first time since the news of their banishment Diana showed a reaction to something in the here and now. Eyes widened, face grew stiff; she actually looked at Gisonne—and seemed to see her.

"You're not even a Silent Observer," Gisonne said. "You . . . " *You're the Outsider!* she thought. *The Newcomer. The one who can't fit, the one mother cat will throw away—or eat. Or the one who will cause the dyne to recognize, know, and recreate itself.*

"Michalis," Diana said.

"Yes. Gisonne Michalis, Gisonne, not Nimee."

Emil and Lonney had moved up to them, Lonney touching Gisonne's arm lightly, trying to distract, Emil simply waiting, ready to prevent harm. "What's in a name?" Lonney asked.

"Nimee was my younger sister," Gisonne told Diana cruelly. "Now she's my older sister. And your son Hentor—"

"No." Diana put her hands over her ears.

"—is . . . let's see . . . seventeen! And your father—"

"Michalis, what are you doing?" Emil pulled at Gisonne's elbow.

"Stop," Diana said at the same time.

Now Calib was looking up at them. Although the heat had turned off, sweat was pouring down his face, running over and into a tight grin, whether a grimace of pain or smile at a secret joke Gisonne could not tell.

8 mo's SPEED
9/1/26 oe

It was up to Fron from now on as Gisonne's lieutenant and the group's IP to study the horn. Since they began the project he had been searching for Trjol's studies, notes, plans, anything to help them understand his "edel" theory. Fron looked for access codes, references of any kind. Either they were extemely, deliberately, well hidden or Trjol had never really planned to be on the mission. But he had, Gisonne thought. Or had he? When exactly had he changed his mind? She flushed, again mind-blind with anger and shock. Would it never quiet? The pain never dull? Time doesn't heal; it scars.

Fron had no success and Gisonne didn't mind. Maybe it was better not to know, better to go on the way they had been, even if in ignorance. Keep convincing the crew that they were working on a vital "mission for humankind," for all intelligent life, so important a project that it would matter still in one hundred or two hundred years.

Gisonne didn't know what behaviors and events were supposed to precipitate what if anything in the edel. Trjol had said one could not know. Gisonne did not tell the others that either.

They tried many things, some more foolish—Gisonne secretly thought—than others. The heat plan failed because it would turn off before harming them or the hardware. Life support systems were always highly protected. Other attempts to upset the environment—increasing sound levels, then playing early music, eliminating light, then spotlighting areas and people randomly, seemed to affect only the human beings. But then wasn't that the point—if they were reality to the edel.

So they had to expose every area of their persons, personalities, interrelationships. Gisonne and Fron enabled it to observe everything. Gisonne's own angry confrontation with Diana was only a beginning. The shame she felt afterward, Diana's subsequent change in behavior, Calib's tight anger and contempt, Fron's behavior as frustrated IP, Jonney's attempts to be tender, all were "life experience" for the edel.   "It's supposed to be mind, intelligence that is evolving," Lonney said later. "Why are you feeding it all this emotional stuff?"

Gisonne didn't know. The question was too big. Trjol had never in all his talk and lectures said anything about a relationship between emotions and mind. Horn people for centuries argued about intellect creating feeling as they tried and tried, and always failed, to create artificial intelligence. But perhaps it was the opposite. Could emotion come first and somehow precipitate the development of intelligence?

She said these things to Fron but not to Lonney or the others. Calib might understand but would never let her know; he would laugh with contempt. Emil would do anything not obviously harmful that she or the majority of the group decided on. Bram understood nothing. To Lonney she explained that it was a first step, that the next phase would be more abstract. And besides "we've got to do something."

Sex, Gisonne thought. Maybe it was necessary for the edel to have an experience to balance the fighting and hostility. Should it be sex? Maybe its generative values, maybe oppositional forces, their coming together and apart, the uniting of disparate elements, maybe . . . maybe Gisonne was fooling herself.

But in any case, who, with whom? Never Diana with anyone. What would happen with Bram if Lonney slept with one of the other men? Or with Gisonne? That left Gisonne. Emil would be easiest—she prefered him, actually simply liked him best, but first of all he was more homosexual than bisexual, second he was not physically attractive to her (although she would not let that alone stop her, of course), and most important, she and the dyne needed him as follower. If they had a sexual relationship, either he would become abject, a dependent lover, jealous of her attention, whining "yes, dear," or go the other way, struggle for leadership—domination in their relationship and possibly concomittently of the whole group.

The idea of Bram as lover was not tolerable—for any purpose, and, like Emil, Fron's role might be jeapardized.

Besides there was something about Fron—although he was always "there," he was actually less accessible than Calib.

Calib? Gisonne looked at him hunched in his regular place, ignoring them all, playing some kind of intellectual horn game or reading pontus knew what. What was there about Calib? Though he was very young, he was not handsome in a youthful way. There was a groove of anger between his rich black brows, and the eyes hiding beneath them glinted fiercely with the same anger when he looked suddenly up. He aroused some kind of strong feeling in Gisonne, almost physical, but she wasn't sure what it was. Somehow, she felt, he could help obliterate Trjol.

Could be. It couldn't hurt. Afterall he already hated her.

9/1/3526 oe
Zalterius II

No supply ships, SPEED or local, have arrived on Zalterius II.

Ships sent to Agricula have not returned.

Science, technology, and medical students sent after 3519 to Malaaca for training have not returned.

An Octente SPEED ship arrived from Corynn with Stycian troops rather than goods.

Speaker for The Viceroy's office, Persol Perl, is in charge of the rationing of food supplies. Perl warned Arine families and Norders to prepare for severe consequences for their refusal to pay fines levelled against them.

Jean delaCour has taken a new spouse, his young second cousin, Henree delaCour.

Tel Allain was given permisssion to marry Adriana Rise.

Chapter Fourteen

Neural Networks

8 1/2 mo's SPEED
11/5/26 oe

An image of Jevry Allain came to Gisonne, Jevry swinging himself from an overhanging tree, catching a jutting rock with both legs, and pulling himself up onto a grassy precipice next to her. And all around them the wind blew, wildly whipping their hair and their clothes.

How old was Jevry now?

8 3/4 SPEED
1/10/27 oe

Experiments continued.

"How will you know?" Emil asked, as they all had often, even Gisonne herself. "How will we know if any of these things work?"

"It will tell us," Gisonne said.

But, of course, through the linguistics programs they all talked to it and it—those various constructs—"talked" back to them all the time, as did any horn. And they could not resist asking if it were changing. It answered that all programs—when on line—were functioning as usual, etc.

9 mo's SPEED
6/6/28 oe

"No sign of consciousness," Calib said after yet another try at disconnecting programs. "Neuralactivity zero. None of our little quiveron neurons got married." He smiled almost sympathetically. Gisonne shrugged and Fron went back to restore the systems.

Later after most of them had retired, leaving Fron and Bram watching some kind of Stycian play, Gisonne made her way to her own cubicle. She had raised her hand to the sensor when she felt rather than heard a sound at the far end of the passage and turned in time to see Diana letting Lonney into her cubicle.

Gisonne lay in her bunk, trying to think what it meant—in group terms, role terms, gender terms, any terms, but gave up, laughed, shrugged, felt lonely, and shivered. "I'm cold," she said aloud but made no move to the controls. She worked herself into her hammock and lay for awhile thinking nothing. Then came the warmth. Gentle heat began to fill her space.

10 1/2 mo's SPEED
8/29/28

"This is it. It has a mind!"

Lonney had been running a fuzzy educational program designed to redefine its own internal settings as the lessons proceded. The instructional method included socratic questioning and incremental repetition, graduating, selective responses to the learner.

Fron addressed the personna, asked it questions, which it rephrased and asked back.

"What is mind?" Fron asked.

"Mind is a concept. What is a concept?" it answered.

"Are you intelligent?"

"You must not avoid the question. Try again. What is a concept?"

"Are you intelligent?" Fron persisted.

"I am a concept," it said.

"Nobody's home," Fron said.

The false alarms grew more frequent. Most, like Lonney's, were a result of the deceptive flexibility of some programs—especially audio.

Gisonne began to realize that they were all confusing mind with personality or humanness. When she tried to explain, they—and she—could not say why the present horn was not a mind—pure intelligence without emotion, without humor, without the ability to respond to beauty.

It finally happened when she wasn't looking.

Flan appeared with Lonney's tea. Of all their foods, both rehydrated and recycled, Lonney liked that one sweet and sometimes ordered it with her largest meal, but not this time—or so she claimed. Gisonne guessed Lonney's fingers had skinned it out of sheer habit.

But the flan appeared again with Lonney's next meal. And the next. Gisonne remembered the heat coming on in her q. This might be it.

Before celebrating, Gisonne said they must find—or provoke—more evidence. First she tried exclaiming aloud and smiling over rehydrated onions. No onions appeared on their own. When she shivered and complained of the cold in the navigation cabin, the temperature stayed where it was.

There was also no sign of life in the relationship between Diana and Lonney. Or Gisonne simply missed it. Maybe the clandestine visit to Diana's sleep q had not been what it seemed. Perhaps it was something else . . . no, there was no room in their bunks for anything else.

But it made no sense given either of the two persons involved. Diana's whole life had been public, well-known, simple. She had the perfect spouse. Together they were an ideal matched pair—princess and her prince. They even looked alike. There was never rumor of an outside liaison for either of them, male or female. And in all their almost eight months in SPEED Gisonne had never seen Diana speak to Lonney. She had assumed she found her as tiresome as Gisonne had at first—if she noted her existence at all.

And Lonney? Gisonne wished she had the ZD records. Had she been so obsessed with Trjol that she saw nothing else when ZD studied the volunteers?

Lonney still touched people, the men, but it was like a mother cat grooming and petting her kittens. What Gisonne had seen as a kind of flirtation, a needy sensuality, was perhaps nurturing. Her touch was restorative not seductive.

How could Lonney be the mother in the family configuration? Should Gisonne then, and not Diana, be Lonney's lover? Mother and father. Or did it really mean that Diana was true TL afterall and Gisonne only her lieutenant, her spokesperson?

And Calib? No sign of life there either. In fact, for the last week he and Gisonne had not looked at each other.

10 3/4 mo's SPEED
12/1/28 oe

"Pontus!"

When Diana swore, everyone listened.

"My drawing," she said. "It's gone again."

Calib glanced at her screen. "Some glitch," he said.

"I didn't make this thing," Diana said. "Someone fix the program. Fron?"

Gisonne leaned over to look just as Fron reached to touch delete on the screen skin. "Fron, wait." Instead of Diana's neat, elaborate and symetrical flowers, there was a crude drawing; it might have been a human figure.

"It's been getting worse and worse for hours," Diana said. "It's either this thing or nothing. Empty space."

It was Gisonne's turn to shout "Pontus!"

It took three ship days of trying; in dyads and triads, they took turns linking through the art program, drawing cartoon-like figures, simple human faces, complicated astrocharts, before an "answer" appeared—two answers if one counted the second screen that always accompanied the first, turning on but remaining blank. It seemed to be the same figure but with slight alterations showing it had been redone. The face was a blank place but there were no features. Another had arms but no legs, just a flat extension of the lower torso, and there appeared a big cartoon face, again without eyes, mouth or nose, but this time it had large ears.

Bram insisted he could not draw. He cheated, implanting a stock icon of a human figure from the program instead of doing a freehand. As usual, Lonney defended him, the others moaned or scolded, and Calib laughed. They went on with the project, each arguing the case for his own type of art, but now there was no answer at all; nothing appeared on either screen for days again.

When the next answer did come, it was an icon too, similar to the one Bram had chosen but not the same one. Again a second screen lit, but contained nothing. Fron brought up both images from the program stock to compare. They all understood. The edel had "learned" first to access one of the horn programs and to use it to link to the outside world, and now—second—to borrow and use the objects the program offered. Two steps! It would only be a matter of time before it also learned to use the word processing programs—or so Gisonne thought.

They continued with the stylized characters, inserting first more of the human and human-like figures. Gisonne enlarged the eyes disproportionately on several of them. Erratically, similar figures appeared on the screen—always accompanied by a second blank screen, but there were still no eyes or mouth, but when Fron chose flowers, nothing came back.

Calib played chess with a games program, losing as usual. They turned off the program, keeping, of course, its icons. There was no response to any of his moves. They simplified the holoboard to two dimensions and tried again. Calib moved a piece. Waited. Moved another. Then slowly an opposing knight moved diagonally. Calib moved again, and again an icon moved. Then another and another, faster and faster, all over and off and above the board, and the queen fell on her back and Calib's men began to tremble and they all fell down.

Lonney patiently experimented with simpler games from children's learning programs. Gisonne almost expected her to put her arms around some part of the horn, or pat the wall encouragingly. The edel did respond in various ways but none showed any comprehension of the game as game. And finally there was no response at all.

Could it be tired, confused? Lonney suggested they had pushed it too hard.

Gisonne explained once more that it was consciousness, mind, intelligence. Purely. Its physical parts could not tire. Or could they? Was it a life form?

She couldn't help feeling it was Trjol's child.

They were all in the center. Gisonne was studying yet another human language history when she felt Calib caress her ankle. The hairs on her nape and arms rose. Fear? Sensual arousal? Chill? Repulsion? Yes.As she looked sideways and down, moving eyes only, she felt the hand move away. There it was, resting on his own knee, dark fingers curled loosely, relaxed.

Gison's body remained frozen and her mind began to race. Speak. Act. Don't act. If she showed anger, took offense, the others would react; Fron or Emil might attack. She would be compromised as rational, as father, as TL; it could be a usurpation, an invitation to chaos, a destruction of their fragile order. She must prevent dissolution—but—but maybe not. Perhaps the equilibrium must again be punctuated for the edel intelligence to grow, to evolve further.

But the disruption must be something else, something tremendous and threatening. But about this ankle matter she decided to keep quiet. And maybe it hadn't happened.

11 1/2 mos SPEED
7/5/29 oe

They had kept trying for days without success. Fron had sent a diagram of life spaces on the ship, a blueprint of the whole ship, a picture of the horn—its various external images, and charts of all kinds—including the astronomical route to Waldseemuller.

Then, when they had stopped to replan, the edel resumed sending with double screens, one with the incomprehensble abstractions, two and three dimensional geometries, complex and simple, black and white and in colors—all far more sophisticated than before—and then again the human-like figures—now with eyes, eyes with accurate anatomical detail, showing the artist understood their function.

This time the second screen was no longer blank though it certainly looked blank to Gisonne. Fron said it was a projection of space ahead of the ship as it appeared at SPEED.

A human ear appeared on the first screen and simultaniously there was sound, musical but not music, violin sounds, drums, and then amazingly, humanlike "voices" from the various programs, sometimes male in timber, sometimes female, tones—no words. Just as, with the visuals it had "learned" to use the pictographic stock rather than "freehand," it had now gone on to a second stage, using the audio programs

At this step, Gisonne was disappointed and puzzled. The edel had accessed and used the stock and then the methods of a number of programs but not language.

She continued talking to it.

And a few cycles later Calib, too, began not a monologue but half a dialogue with the edel. He "chatted" with it, somehow, in a childlike way—as if he assumed it understood and could respond. This behavior was so unlike Calib's usual personality that they all wondered.

"Good idea, Calib," Gisonne forced herself to say, though she meant it.

"Oh, you approve? Pontus! You know nothing." He flung himself abruptly away from the link and withdrew to his q.

And once again the edel stopped all communication, this time for several days. Child of Trjol. Willful child—withholding. Gisonne decided—with anger—that it chose to withhold.

Then there suddenly appeared, completely filling the wall screen, a huge, projected scan of Lonney's face—close up, peering straight into the video link. The other wall—same size—continued to present the SPEED-distorted space ahead.

The next image was a small figure with a grotesquely long narrow penis and ape-like arms.

"What in pontus does that mean?" Calib asked.

"It's a man," Bram said.

"In most human mythologies," Fron said, "the enlarged sexual organ symbolizes fertility and in males—"

"What does it know about—?"

"Well, if the ear meant sound . . . ?"

"It's figuring out all our functions!"

Later Fron started routine geometry lessons. He said he would some day "talk" to the edel with symbols—almost hieroglyphics, pictographs, ideographics, the way communication is initiated with aliens.

Gisonne tried to include spoken language in every project. She and Diana sent back the edel's own drawings, carefully pronouncing identifying words. Gisonne pulled children's language lessons out of the horn library stock.

The lessons went on and on. The edel began responding correctly, but always with a picture, never a word.

Until one day it—she—said "no." The voice was female.

Gisonne had been asleep in her q when Fron shouted her awake. She fumbled her way down the corridor and into the center. Fron was staring at a horn speaker, Lonney grinning, and Calib laughing.

"What? What had you done?" Gisonne asked.

"We showed it . . . her . . . a picture of itself, of the physical horn, I mean," Lonney said.

"I've shown it a thousand diagrams of every horn, operating system, computing machine and cyborg that ever existed," Fron said. "There was never anything. Oh, sometimes it sent prints back, but meaningless, childish copies or imitations of mine. Now this!"

"Do it again!" Gisonne cried.

Fron turned the vid on those parts of the horn that physically existed in the navigation area.

"It has seen every inch of itself and everything else on the ship since we left," Fron said again. "All sensors are—"

"Yes," Calib said, grinning, "but this time you told it what it was."

"I did," Lonney said. "I said this is you, horn. I mean, edel."

12 1/2 mo's SPEED
6/2/30 oe

Another month. Almost another year at home. Fron told them—almost proudly—"We have just passed the farthest defined boundary of the Octente."

"And we have only another nine years to go," Calib said, "about ninety planet time!"

Lonney reached to comfort him (did the woman never learn? Gisonne wondered) but this time he only shrugged her off indifferently.

"Why is this link to the edel closed?" Fron asked. He frowned at Lonney as he reached to touch it on. Lonney burst into tears.

"Laahnny," the edel said.

They jerked about in astonishment and froze, waiting for more. What would be the best way to reply? Gisonne turned to coach Lonney, but before she could give an order, Lonney said, "Hello, edel."

Pontus, how stupid, Gisonne thought. She saw the same opinion in Calib's smirk, and Fron's deepening frown. Even Diana smiled. Fron coughed and tried to signal Lonney, shaking his head. But Lonney ignored them all. She looked at the nearest audio terminal dot as if into the eyes of a friend and waited.

"Are you there, edel?" she added after a while.

Calib groaned audibly and Fron stared at him fiercely. Gisonne waved at Lonney and and mouthed "no."

"Lah . . . Laahnie," the edel said.

"Yes," Lonney said.

"Quodlibet," the edel said.

Lonney turned, helpless, to Gisonne. Gisonne shrugged.

Fron touched on a program, pointed to its menu, opened an item. A medley of ancient earth music filled the ship.

13 mo's SPEED
12/1/30 oe

Lonney read from the horn dramatically: "Our relationships will vibrate like a tuning fork; with repetition a pattern will emerge from disorder and—"

Fron, Calib, and Gisonne looked at her in amazement. "Where did you get all that?"

"Just something in a horn file Bram and I were playing with."

"Trjol's material!" Fron said.

6/2/30 oe
Zalterius II

The Octente is now the Pentente.

Dynes of Zalterian youth from both the Nord and the Arine archipilagos attempted to seize the Stycians occupying Nordport and the Branch on The Plateau, but the Stycians had been forewarned and withdrew into their ships and fled into orbit.

There was a catastrophic implosion on Estuary, destroying all flats and estuaries and killing many people. Among the dead were Hentor Allain, scion of the Allain family, son of escaped Octente traitor, Diana Allain, and Denny Michalis of the Michalis family. Jevry Allain was severely injured.

Tel Allain, now The Allain, has been married a second time. His present wife is Marian delaCour.

Chapter Fifteen

Quodlibet

13 1/2 mo's SPEED
3/25/31 oe

Gisonne dreamed she was home, home on High Garda, in her room up under the eaves of Laurel House. She heard her mother's voice somewhere far below talking to the children, chiding one of them affectionately. Gisonne smiled and curled her toes with pleasure and then stretched, reaching long with feet, legs, arms over her head—and met in every direction the tight walls of her prison—her q, narrow coffin within an iron vault. And she wept.

But the voice was real. A woman's voice, but not her mother's. It was Lonney, Lonney talking to the child that was the edel. Daughter of Trjol. For a second Gisonne hated it again, as if it were the cause of their loss and not the potential savior of their humanity and sanity.

She shed that feeling in turn as quickly as the dream had fallen away. She moved through the cleansers, picked red for her shirt, and went into central. They were all there.

"She told me she is isolated," Lonney said. "She wants us to—"

"Nonsense," Calib said. He turned toward Gisonne for the first time since she had come in. "It doesn't know the word 'isolated.' As always it doesn't say anything."

Lonney was outraged. "Of course it . . . she does. She meant isolated. She uses sounds and whistles to tell me things. And her Zalterian vocabulary increases incredibly. No child—"

"Nouns," Calib said. "Only nouns. And it uses them in weird ways."

"It describes," Diana said, at work again on her drawings. "That is saying something."

Gisonne was surprised that Diana spoke at all. It must be the issue that drew her interest, description, adjectives—and so drawing.

They were working themselves up into an angry circle. For the first time Gisonne saw the other two women draw together—in public. Emil moved toward the middle and Bram to the rear of the cabin. No, it was not a circle, but a skull.

And Fron, all flat verbosity and conscience, frowned down on them all and began to talk: "The women are right: it's still learning. But more important than making random sounds, it's learning to use the computing systems of the OS, just as we did as children. But it's dependant on some of them as we are not since we have our own eyes, ears, and voice boxes."

"How many times do I have to hear that, Maces? It's stupid. The old Tree is a failure."

"No, no," Lonney said. "She's still young. And her sounds are not random."

"She? Anthropomorphism! Right. So let's say it has the level of a dog. It recognizes a certain number of words. Except that it can almost repeat them and the dog can't. Or we could say it's only a piece of a mind, an amorphus growth—like a tissue culture, cells with incomplete DNA, a malformed human head. Yes—human. Autistic."

"Enough," Gisonne said, "We need more information. Research."

"Search!" Fron said. "In the two weeks since we found them, I have studied all of Dr. Trjol's records of his work on this mind, of its evolution. In none of it is there anything about—"

"Pontus damn Trjol," Gisonne said. "He started something he didn't understand himself."

She noticed that Calib had turned to look at her curiously.

Lonney said, "Perhaps . . . what's his name? Dr. Teebol? . . . perhaps he failed in its physical structure. Maybe there's something like a blockage?" She tried to whisper to Gisonne but Calib heard and laughed loudly.

"Listen, Lonney," Gisonne said. "Trjol didn't design the edel—or so he said. He put in the regular horn elements, protein and quiveron, uh . . . and some other bacterium—individually. They were left to colonize, form their own connections— linkages. Evolve into . . . Who knows . . . "

Fron was shaking his head. "That is a fanciful description. Bacteriorhodopsin and lipid components are plated out on surfaces—"

"Never mind," Lonney said.

"But there is much more," Fron said. "Self-organization—"

"Never mind for now, Fron," Gisonne said .

A few days later, during one of Fron's sleep cycles, Calib followed Gisonne into navigation.

"I have things to say to you and things to ask you," he said.

She nodded. He didn't look angry, he didn't look afraid, and he didn't look controllable. But he was almost polite, waiting for her to say something. She didn't.

"You must have remarked what a sexless bunch we've all been?" he said.

"Yes, outwardly anyway."

"I have to ask," Calib said. "It's the past—yours and mine. Trjol." Calib pronounced the name accurately. "How did you know him?"

Gisonne was first startled. And then she stumbled over her own rage and humiliation—never far from the surface. Anyone who knew about her relationship with Trjol—Nimee, Aj, perhaps Jevry—was back on z2 and for them it was an old story, more than a decade in their past. This crew luckily knew nothing of it. They shared their common fate, they shared their present pain, but not their pasts. Why? She immediately answered her own question. Self protection in close quarters—such gates opened could never be closed again.

If she confided in anyone it could not be a CN. And also there was something about Calib's interest that warned her to keep still.

"I told you ZD worked with him on this mission," she said as flatly as she could. "You know he was supposed to have been on it."

"Of course, I know. I'm here in his place."

Calib moved very close to her, traced a strand of her very straight, dark hair with a finger tip.

"Michalis," he said. "Gisonne. You drive me crazy. You're a mad woman. So cold and so strong. So stubborn! And then sometimes I see another person, warm—" He kissed her. "Warm."

The immediate surprise for Gisonne was not that they were in each other's arms but that it felt so good and the way it felt good. To be held, to feel the touch, the affection of another human being—Gisonne had not known how much she missed human touch. Not just—perhaps least—Trjol's. Her family, Nimee, her mother and aunt, the little children. Cuddling, nuzzling.

Then it changed and she wasn't so sure. He moved against her harder. She felt his excitement. She began to be aroused and and pulled her head back a little to look at him, into his eyes. She saw only the heavy brows, the dark hair falling over the forhead. And jumped back in horror and rage. Trjol!

Now she saw his whole face—offended, red, confused, surprised, and not Trjol. Not at all like Trjol. What was the matter with her?

"Michalis," Emil said from the navigation entrance, "are you all right?"

Gisonne realized she must have let out a cry. In fact, she could still hear the sound or its memory.

"Yes, yes. It was nothing." She looked back over her shoulder as she moved toward the entrance. "I'm sorry, Calib."

His face was stone.

9/14/33 oe

The edel continued to whistle and produce flurries of notes and say actual words to Lonney and sometimes to others. It knew their names and sometimes pronounced them with matching views of their faces, three times life size on the wall screen—and strange, struggling faces they seemed to be from its point of view.

If it were an animal, as Calib had suggested, they could reward it with food, Gisonne thought. With what could one reward a mind? Information? Ideas? It had all of those at its own command.

But maybe that was it. Take away its material.

"Shut down the music programs, Fron."

For the first time since the second stage of dying Lonney showed anger. "This is monstrous," she cried. "She . . . he wants to hear music. What else does he have? He is isolated, alone, afraid."

Gisonne shook her head.

"Give him the music! You . . . sadist. The poor b . . . boy—"

"OH, Pontus below us!" Calib shouted. He had behaved outwardly as always since Gisonne's rejection, jibes part humor, part contempt. But Gisonne sensed, or imagined, a difference: it was a performance now, a charade covering something else, something worse than Negative. "Shut the female up! A b . . . b . . . boy now. The drowned machine is a male child! Anthropomorphism."

Lonney's face reddened. Tears threatened but she lunged for Gisonne instead, not Calib. When Emil blocked her way, she screamed and pounded his chest. Calib reached for her from his odd angle.

Before Bram could join the fray, suddenly from everywhere in central came a painful, ear-shattering boom, heavy bass and cutting shriek at the same time. They all stopped in mid-motion, palms to ears. And onto the pain came solid darkness, not only the lights but all horn signals off.

Bram grabbed at instruments, shutting audio, but the noise continued, unendurably. They could only wait.

The lights came back on first. Calib had slumped into his "corner." Emil had backed away from Lonney but still stood between her and Gisonne. The noise stopped a second later.

"We are going to dismantle the drowned thing," Calib said.

Fron shook his head. "It was a glitch in the OS. Some wave—"

It was Lonney who laughed ironically—another first for her.

"We are not a mob," Gisonne said. "We'll leave it alone until we have a meeting, a dyne meeting."

Diana sat in her usual place, working on her latest drawing—as if uninterrupted by noise or dark. What kind of a person, Gisonne wondered, sits unmoved and apparently indifferent as her lover is attacked physically a foot away?

14 1/2 mo's SPEED
12/29/31 oe

The only other person—unusually—in the center was Bram. Although he never paid attention to whatever she was doing, Gisonne turned away from him as she worked out the dates with the ship's computations. Drown the years! Jevry and Denny must be twenty-six . . . her mother, more than fifty and . . . Trjol—

"Gisonne," Fron said from the navigation doorway, "shall I try the port to Diana Allain's sleep cubicle?"

"What?"

"Shall I investigate? There may be a problem?"

"I don't get . . . why?"

"She is not here in central," Fron said.

"Why should she be?"

"Diana is always in central well before this point in the cycle."

Gisonne was amazed. She had never seen their time as anything but roughly and arbitrarily compartmentalized, hardly cyclic.

"But no one's here now. Just me—and Bram."

"Emil is always half way through his sleep period now. Calib's absence or presence is not noteworthy. His routine is always erratic."

So, Gisonne thought, Calib skews the rythm of the dyne's time as well as space.

"You know all this?" she asked Fron.

"Of course." Fron seemed puzzled at the question, Fron, the IP, assuming her perception of reality was his. "I think we should investigate," he added.

"Call her then."

"I did. There was no response."

Gisonne was already pushing off into the sleep corridor. In two seconds she reached Diana's q, touched its tab, then pulled at its bar.

"Release through the horn," she called back to Fron—vocally, loudly. The bar moved, the panel slid around, and Gison's breath and then body were sucked inside—into a near vacuum.

"Fraaah . . . !" she tried to shout, but gasped and choked.

It didn't matter. He was there already, grabbing her leg and then elbow, dragging her out backwards. And at the same time it became easier as air from the corridor was pulled into the q.

"What is it?" Lonney's voice was muffled with sleep as she came out of her own q at the far end of the passage. No one else emerged although Fron had opened all q's at once.

Gisonne dove to her waist back into Diana's q as Fron darted toward Emil's. "Get Calib!" he was shouting, not to Lonney who was cut off by Gisonne as she dragged Diana out into the narrow corridor, but to Bram, who had made his way at last to peer in at them from central.

Three inert bodies were finally tugged and floated into central. Gisonne was gripped in silent panic when at first only Diana stirred. She leaned close to listen for Emil's breath. It was there—faint, perhaps fading.

"Oxygen," Fron said, skinning OS access. Nothing happened.

Diana began to gasp and choke. Lonney was forcing her breath into Calib's mouth.

"Tell it, Lonney!" Gisonne said.

Lonney turned to her, panting, face blank.

"Fast! Tell the drowned monster to give us oxygen or whatever it takes."

"Me? I . . . Oh. Edel," Lonney said, raising her voice, turning needlessly, as she always did, to face an audio port, "fix the air."

There was no change, no response. Lonney's face reddened.

"Edel," she cried, "I want you to make Diana better." She started to cry. "And Emil and Calib. Edel, I need them."

"Laaahny," the edel said—voice male. There was a loud whoosh and strong odors, odd and unpleasant, the temperature in the cabin dropped, Gisonne was suddenly dizzy, and Bram threw up. But Calib and Emil began to breathe.

"It's a pontus puking murderer," Calib said. His face was distorted, twisted, as if suffocation had warped it. But Gisonne thought it was more; there seemed to be a deeper change, one that began when she left him in navigation

"Then we are a murderer," Gisonne said. "Edel is this crew."

"He saved you," Lonney said to Calib.

"Attempted murder," Fron said, looking at Gisonne.

"Turn it off," Calib said.

"We can't turn it off; it isn't a horn."

"Then kill it."

"He's too young," Lonney said.

"But don't you see? It has the capacity to alter the basic structure of OS programing!"

"To destroy us?"

"Suicide," Gisonne said.

The outworn tale—the machine gone wild and turning on its creators? No. Edel was no machine. Then a monster myth? All as old and tired as blood-sucking flying animals. Legends out of time, pre-expansion stories to scare children and inform the dreams of the mad? (Was Trjol one of those? Was he still alive? Gisonne hoped so. He would hate being old.)

But ritual comes before theory, story. Groups are first mythological and only second a sociological science. But what myth will work? The Zalterian sphere? ZD had understood only part, the lesser part. And their ancestors, the first Zalterian settlers, had known more of dynaspheres than all their new theory. Degeneration?

If Gisonne was right, if all the old arts she had been discovering had validity, the edel is both the whole group and, at the same time, only one more member of it. As newcomer, last born, it has to fit in to ensure its own survival. Why does it destroy Diana's drawing? Does it know Diana and Lonney are lovers? Or is it simple oedipal jealousy—a term from yet another antique paradigm? Does intelligence have an unconscious mind? Does a dyne have an unconscious mind?

The dangerously powerful infant, the "it" without an "over I"? Gisonne wondered again how to control it? Withhold its music? Hurt Lonney? Yes. Punctuate—puncture the dyne's equilibrium? Yes.

So Gisonne insisted on the official meeting: a "structured" meeting, she told them. Calib sighed in disgust. As always, Diana sat where she was, drawing leafy, vined borders around a flower—maybe she had joined the meeting and maybe not. One never knew. Lonney pulled Bram to attention, Emil was already waiting at attention, and Fron came in from navigation, information ready. Fron alone had been coached by Gisonne, and that only partially. She knew his own personality and role would do the rest.

Gisonne put herself in a squat, dead center and instead of anxiety-provoking silence, used speech. She said vile things about Calib, hinted at disgusting practices, acccused him of incest. He had lived with his mother?

Calib was first astonished rather than angry. Then Gisonne's suggestions grew more obscene. She described his activities graphically.

Nervous laughter stopped. The others tried to calm Gisonne, fearing for her sanity, Calib's rage, and their fate without her. She worked on the fear.

When she added patricide, Calib lost the boundaries that had always defined his show of hostility. No jokes and light mean wit now. He shouted, raged, bellowed, trying to blow her down, to destroy all of them with his breath since Emil blocked physical assault.

Fron's control was verbal, not motor. His body was motionless, in a vertical stance just to Gison's left, as Gisonne had planned, he talked, talked, and talked—to Gisonne, to Calib—reasoning, sermonizing, explaining symbolic logic, pouring encyclopedic astromomical information onto them.

On the right Diana sat, her drawing still visible but forgotten. She watched.

Behind them were Lonney and Bram, she in tears, choking and trembling, he pushing at switches, touching controls, apparantly involuntarily, changing air balances, trying to close down the blower which seemed to have suddenly activated itself, lowering the cabin temperature, raising the light. His actions were so automatic that Gisonne thought later they must have been part of his task on some other voyage—or on many, many voyages.

Gisonne continued to talk, now challenging Diana and Lonney, the women. She began on Diana's motherhood, sex life with Blake and then with Lonney. She made ugly gestures. Diana stared, grew white and tight. Lonney's eyes widened and filled but she didn't cry. They came together and moved to Gison's right. Or seemed to do so. The cabin was small, again a skull too narrow for its contents.

"You were a mother who never mothered," Gisonne added. "You were a father, not a mother."

"I was my father's daughter," Diana said, as though in some way that answered it.

While she talked, Gisonne heard Fron, his reasoning, the flow of information, wisdom and morality, that came from him to her. Even this material she turned into ugliness and irrationality.

Quodlibet, Gisonne thought. Now the edel has its quodlibet. With counterpoint.

She and Fron continued talking, each saying something else, not different languages, but different realities, different ways of knowing. She inched to the left, making the separation between them wider.

Gisonne attacked Bram's age and past, said he was not what he seemed, accused him of beastiality on other planets, of canabalism. Bram bellowed louder than Calib.

As Gisonne moved farther left, Calib was facing Bram, opposite and below him.

Gisonne told Emil that his family's sexual and marriage practices were barbaric, his brother a pedophile, his children abused and corrupted. She persisted until his solidity crumbled.

The dyne was breaking apart in the force of the gale, a tempest, vectors clashing, whirling.

And then there was another, stronger wind, physical, coming from the air controls. Bram was not doing it. In fact, Bram began to beat at the controls he had touched before but now with no effect. The wind howled and they were knocked against the bulkheads. And the air grew cold, very cold. The sweat of their angers froze, icing their hair and clothes. Gisonne tried to crawl back toward the middle but the wind and ice held her.

Her eyes were freezing shut. The air seemed thin as well as cold. Had something broken the ship open? Was . . . . Gisonne knew she was losing consciousness. Dying . . . again?

12/29/31
Zalterius II

Two Stycian and one Ipagan ship landed within four oe weeks at Nordport. Troops were off loaded.

Cres Trjol received an Award for Contributions of Distinction to the Octente. He will continue his work at the Malacaan College of Neurobiology and Psycholinguistics, formerly the Allain Institute of Human Studies.

Chapter Sixteen

Interruptions

14 1/2 mo's SPEED
1/1/32 oe

Silence. Once again they were not dead. Broken, not totally dead. Anger gone, fear gone. All gone but exhaustion. They lay about, without pattern, floating, turned away from one another in a clutter of fetal curls. Horn time said they had been out for more than a day. Edel said nothing. The ship's systems were again operating soundlessly.

They began to stir. And then straighten "up." Silently Fron moved into navigation and Diana took up her drawing while the others were still stretching and scratching.

The first one to speak was Diana, hours later. "Look at this. This is a new one." There were two large circles; in one were a group of tiny stick figures, human. In the other was, as usual, nothing—nothing but the emptiness that lay before them.

Gisonne saw the frown line that divided Diana's once perfect forehead deepen. When had it first appeared? Gisonne realized she had been seeing it for a long time but had not noted it. She glanced at herself in the port reflection. Hers were smaller wrinkles, about the eyes, laugh lines. Not likely. Squint lines probably from trying to figure everything out.

"Let me—"

"Oh!" Diana recoiled, a jerk away from Gisonne.

Pontus below, Gisonne thought, she's afraid of me! The Diana Allain, The Allain who never lost her mystery and presence, trembling before Gisonne Michalis. Suddenly she understood. More than anger and rejection, it was fear. They were all afraid of her.

"I thought you all understood, it was deliberate," Gisonne said. "We had to shake it loose. Punctuate its, that is our equilibrium."

Fron mumbled something through the navigation port, Lonney looked stricken, Emil apologetic, and Bram plain afraid. Diana turned away. Calib was stone again.

Let them be afraid; as long as she knew it, Gisonne could control it and maybe them.

She certainly couldn't control their destination or the edel.

After that no one ever referred to the horrible things she had said. Yet for half a month no one looked at her directly. They moved themselves around, ate, played games separately and silently, and spoke when necessary. Lonney and Diana remained farther apart than ever in central. Calib stared at yet another of the "challenging" mental horn games. Fron spent most of his wake time in navigation.

Until one day he peered into the center and said: "The course has been changed."

No one answered.

"The course has been changed," he repeated.

Slowly each head turned.

"We are no longer headed for Waldseemuller."

They all yelled at once. Even Emil.

"Home?"

"We've turned back?"

"It must have been a hidden command all along."

"We haven't turned back. Not to Zalterius, not the Octente," Fron said. "Not even within the Tryllium system. It's—"

"Are you crazy?" Calib muttered, almost unintelligibly, never looking away from his horn. "Then there is no change! You are hallucinating, you Nord dropping."

"Where then? Where?" Lonney asked.

"A system beyond the Tryllium. On the navigation charts it isn't identified but, on one of the earlier Mission Control maps, it seems to be called DeMaiollo ."

"What?" Calib asked. "Another rock?"

"Well, we're really not aimed at . . . anything," Fron said. "Or it's so small that we can't tell yet."

But anything—even nothing—was preferable now to Waldseemuller. And if there had been one change, there could be another

"How long?" It was everyone's question.

"It's calculated on the charts themselves. Four and a half months SPEED. Almost another four years oe. And now another four—"

As individuals they were confused, hopeful, angry, or bemused. As a broken, reanimated dyne they shrugged.

And then it was back to "normal" for good and for bad, Gisonne observed. The course change had done it, broken the trance. Roles reassumed. Activities resumed. Except for Calib. Something was very wrong with him.

For almost another month they speculated while the Procne continued on its new course, which formed an acute angle with the old. "As 'the crow flies' we are getting closer to z2," Fron said.

"What does that mean?" Lonney asked.

"It means our new destination is closer to the Zalterian system than where we are now."

"I meant what does 'crow flies' mean?"

Fron shrugged. No information.

"There's still time," Diana said a day later. "The Octente, Styxx and Malaaca cannot have acted."

They were embarrassed.

"What about their travel times, Fron?" she went on. "From Malaaca to the Zalterian sytem must be—"
we—z2—has resisted them! Empty threats. My father . . ."

Still denying, or again denying, Gisonne thought. Could Diana not see that it would be Hentor, if anyone, fighting, centering? Now already, Hentor was a young man—twenty-one. And Jevry? Twenty-four!

"Diana, even if our new course were for z2, it would be another ten years. That is without stopping at Quivera to enforce our claims." It was Emil who spoke, gently, apologetically.

Calib said, "We're off on a side trip. Getting more for our money." The old Calib's words, the changed Calib's expression.

Gisonne remembered the name DeMaiollo. It was somehow related to a distant and early Octente trade station, something she and Aj had encountered.

"I know I've heard of the system," she said. "Fron, let's look again at the early maps. Even the ancient inaccurate—"

"I'll do it," Fron said.

A few days later there was another kind of sound, loud a blare or squawk. They had heard nothing like it before. Lonney insisted it was not one of the edel's "speaking" sounds although it emanated from the horn.

Later a painful screech filled every space—and did not let up. Was the OS coming apart? Was the ship disintegrating? They scrambled for the controls or clapped hands over ears.

Before Fron could push himself into navigation, the noise stopped.

Later it began again, changed, somewhat muted, less painful but still irritating. It stopped again.

Days later they heard the screech but it was brief and softer, and became finally one of a series, not only of screeches, but creeks and cracks, and odd notes. This time it went on for hours, unpleasant but not nerve destroying.

They were able to talk over it and about it. Fron tried to find mathematical patterns—meaningful spacing or repetition. He used horn programs, horn cipher games. And there was patterning, many kinds of repetition within the variation but of no meaning to Fron or the os.

"The dropping has found new ways to torture us," Calib said.

"It's a song," Diana said a day later, looking up from a drawing above her right hand. For a moment Gisonne thought she meant the holo. The sounds had been on for so long and so frequently that she no longer heard them.

"There a rhythm—and now tune! Hear it?" Gisonne didn't.

"I think I do," Lonney said. "Da da duup. Isn't that it?"

Diana did not respond. She and Lonney had resumed taking their their cycles together in Diana's q. Yet, even after the tension had been relieved by the change in course and Gisonne's accusations "forgotten," they never touched and rarely spoke to or looked at each other in "public."

Large figures began again appearing on the wall: circles and side ways v's.

They poured over the horn stock for the patterns.

"I don't know what your picture is, edel," Lonney said to the scan.

"It's a bird," Diana said. "Some kind of fowl. In profile."

Gisonne was amazed.

And later there were circles again, a single one on each screen. For the first time the second screen held something other than the SPEED space ahead.

"Fil," the edel said in its male voice.

"Who is it?" Gisonne added, slowly and loudly, waving a warning arm at Calib.

"Fil," the edel said again.

"He . . . it talks better in the female voice," Lonney said.

Gisonne jumped at her. "Of course!" she cried, patting her shoulder. "Lonney, you're a wonder."

Lonney flinched. Gisonne was offended and then cold.

"Can you make it switch voices? Try." It was an order. Gisonne glared another order at Calib. No insane interference right now.

"Hello, edel. I'm glad you're back," Lonney said. "Speak from the other way."

Gisonne waved down the others who had started to moan, shake heads, or correct Lonney.

There was nothing for a few moments and then the female voice said, "Edel . . . Edel + Fil. 1 + 1. Family. Corvi."

"Ask it whose family?" Fron, IP, could not control himself.

"Edel dysphere," edel said.

"Edel, where are we going?" Fron asked.

"Fil . . . Fil house," edel said.

They continued asking it for information in their various ways, Fron through his charts, Diana and Bram drawings, and Lonney and Gisonne talk, human talk.

At first it—or something—responded only to Fron: a wall holomap appeared. It was almost the same as the chart showing their change of route. More detailed models followed and with it all, masses of astronomical mathematical information. The materials were clear and straightforward; they were heading for DeMaiollo.

Why? Why? Why? Maps don't tell you why.

16 mo's SPEED
4/28/33 oe

Edel talked to Lonney and sometimes to Gisonne, but its speech improved very little. The male voice was even less articulate.

It sent some of the old stock figure drawings from time to time when Diana was working on her own. Eyes and feet were featured heavily but Gisonne could see no significance in any of them.

For all the activity nothing much changed; nothing was added to their knowledge. They could only wait.

"Wait and see," Lonney said to Bram. But she was really talking to herself or indirectly to the edel—if it was listening—assuring it that they trusted it. Bram was waiting, but only for the next game or next meal.

7/10/33 oe
Zalterius II

Severe penalties for noncompliance with Pentente regulations have been again exacted from the Arine estates. Travel on the planet has been limited to small air shuttle to close islands. Those attending school or working on The Plateau are required to pay an extra Pentente tax and to obtain passes.

Food supplies are to be further cut back.

Chapter Seventeen

Parliament

24 1/2 mo's SPEED
5/24/40 oe

As they approached the DeMaiollon system, the ship's OS was able to project clearer and more detailed charts and holomaps. They strained forward, stared, looked to Fron for explanations, which he gladly, if flatly, gave. How long? Where? In another half month they would be in orbit around the very small, fourth planet, still nameless on the charts.

"Another rock," Calib said.

"No," Fron was able to tell them later. "Rich atmosphere, vegetation, plains and low mountains."

And then later he said, "Inhabited . . . ."

And again, when the Procne came out of SPEED and made the first parabolic loop around the planet, " . . . but the structures are not Octente, not humanoid." Now they all strained to see for themselves; the ports were no longer mirrors.

They had been in orbit for one fourth month when a human voice came over the com.

"Greetings, sirs. Corvi greet you."

The message was barely intelligible. The dialect was an old form of preOctente Zalterian and the voice, male, creaked, whether with disuse or with age they could not tell. They heard a wheezing as if the speaker struggled for breath.

"Who are you?"

"The lander will dock with your craft in five. You will enter—some flock first and remainder flock second."

There followed more gasping and another sound, a kind of squeak. "We are corvi," the speaker added. There was no more.

139

The "lander" was small, smaller than z2's island hoppers and unlike Octente landers in every way including its fit with their airlock. Its mouth was far too wide but the Procne port slid open anyway. They could see the gap.

"We can't risk it," Fron said.

Gisonne was already pushing into the lander—out of the Procne! She would have leapt into a hole in the ocean to escape.

Diana and Emil were behind her. And they were packed against each other. What Gisonne had assumed was a foyer was the entire craft, except for navigation—wherever that was. This "cabin" was a round hole. The floor consisted of a grid of smooth poles over three more feet of space, the stinking bottom of the hole and it stunk—horribly. There were no benches, no furniture of any kind. The three of them stood, pressed together, trying to balance on the round poles.

And then Bram exploded into the space, hitting them hard, knocking them over in a heap. But Gisonne saw, between and above bellies and shoulders and legs, Calib's face looking at them from Procne. He had pushed Bram through the lock!

The airlock closed, Bram cursing, all four of them gasping for air, disgusting as it was. They finally managed to sit a breath apart from each other, finding room for their legs between the poles. A small wrench and they were swept away from the Procne.

Miserably uncomfortable as they were, it grew worse later with the return of gravity. The poles were as cruel on behinds as the rungs of a ladder on bare feet. Their own weight, less than on z2 they learned later, was still an unpleasant surprise.

Whoever and wherever the navigator was, Gisonne decided he was good at his job. It felt as though they didn't just drop vertically, but glided and flew, veering as if on wind currents.

Suddenly the currents bolted; the craft was whacked out of its own path with tremendous force. It was not a crash landing; they were still airborne, but wobbling and falling—fast. There would have to be a deadly crash.

However, their falling speed decreased gradually, as if they were braking or a parachute had opened above them. Was this the way these people always landed their aircraft?

Then they were obviously, solidly, on ground. But the port did not open. The air inside was dead and hot and the smell grew worse. Sickening. Gisonne was nauseous. There were beads of sweat on Diana's too-white face and Bram was gagging. If he vomited!

There was a banging on the airlock. The frail craft was shaking, being rocked by someone trying to pull the door open physically. This was followed by loud crashes and then a cracking. And then there was air.

They crawled toward the ragged opening, one behind the other. Gisonne, first aboard, was last out. Just as she turned her face upward to light and air, both disappeared in smothering heavy black. Some kind of thick covering had been dropped over her head and down to her knees. She was pushed onto her back and someone or something was tying the blanket around her waist.

Gisonne first struggled wildly, shouting as she tried to tear the material apart and then to punch holes in it with her fists. She kicked as hard as she could and felt her foot sink into something soft, a belly with lots of give. Her only satisfaction was a weird screech from whoever was holding her. The only other result of all her fighting was depletion of air.

When she shut up, she could hear Bram's rumbling curses. There was no sound from Diana or Emil.

The people who had captured them said very little to one another and that was unintelligible. Squawks and beeps. Maybe code signals to keep the prisoners from understanding.

Gisonne heard Diana's voice making some kind of objection and then she herself was hoisted up and onto something. The something turned out to be alive and moving. Gisonne had seen horses only in vids but she guessed it must be one.

The trek that followed was hot and painful. Gisonne was lying sideways over the animal's back, torturing her own back and sending blood to her head. Only the air improved when someone tore a hole in her covering.

As they moved along, Gisonne's "mount" wobbled from side to side, shifting her weight with nauseating regularity. The covering muffled most outside sound so that she couldn't hear foot or hoof steps or any voice sounds. Once in a while she heard chirping. She tried several times to call out to Emil or Diana but there was no response. Her captors said nothing but did not try to stop her shouts.

There was finally all around squawking and whistling, overlapping as the animal came to a stop. Gisonne was pulled off and tossed, with a bounce, into what felt like some kind of hammock. And then, after a piercing whistle, she was rising—rising. She felt the pull of gravity and the tug of air causing hammock to swing as it rose. Below—far below—she heard another shrill whistle and later another and another.

The journey ended with a jolting drop. Gisonne heard and felt nothing more for awhile. She struggled again to free herself from the miserable blanket but it was impossible to untie it from the inside. She had just managed to tear at and widen the air hole someone had made for her, when there was a thump beside her. Someone else had roughly landed.

"Diana? Emil?"

"Muff," one of them answered.

There was another bump and another. Gisonne felt someone untying her and pulling off the cover. Air! And Emil!

"I was able to tear the thing apart as we rode," he said, already working on Diana's knots. Diana was very still and too cold—shock, Gisonne thought.

Gisonne fumbled with the ropes around the bulk that had to be Bram. Bram had been sick and swallowed some of his own vomit. His smell was the final insult to Gisonne's own stomach and she too threw up—not onto herself but down through openings between the poles that formed the floor, a slatted grid like the one in the lander. Where the vomit went, she did not ask herself.

When she could, Gisonne checked Diana—stirring—and their new prison. They had been dumped into a small, cup-shaped, roofless room. Its rounded walls had panels which might have been short wide doors. She almost laughed. What an escape they had made!

And now for another escape, but to what? From what? From whom?

She turned to Emil but wished for Fron. Emil was dependable lieutenant, never only silent observor, sometimes disobeying to protect her from herself, but he was not an information provider. He would do whatever Gisonne or this bleeding fragment of a group decided. And Gisonne did not want to decide. There was no information. Without information there is no power.

She looked around at the others. Diana and Emil were watching her.

"Well, Michalis?" Diana said. She was still extremely pale, beads of sweat stood out on her forhead, and she shivered at the same time. Yet she was her calm self, not hostile, but waiting, almost trusting that Gisonne would lead.

The only way out seemed to be the open roof, high above. The light coming from there was dim, green, and probably natural though it looked very unnatural to Gisonne—so different from z2's sunlight. Yet after more than a year of ship light, it made her doubly sick with longing to be home.

They looked around again at the seamed walls, hopelessly. Emil staggered over the dangerous, uncomfortable floor to test and prod the panels.

Bram was still staring upward when an unpleasant, cracked squawk hit them from above. Incredibly, Bram squawked back. He raised his arm and pointed to something on top of the wall.

Looking down at them was the ugliest head Gisonne had ever seen—shiny black with one even shinier black eye. It disappeared immediately.

"Corvi," Bram said, turning to Gisonne.

Diana and Emil were no help when it came to speculation or handling Bram. Gisonne needed Fron and Lonney.

"What are Corvi? What do you know? Bram!"

Bram looked back at Gisonne, puzzled, either at her ignorance or at how to respond to her. With maddening slowness he turned to the others for help that wasn't there.

"Just tell us what you said to me. Was that thing Corvi?"

Bram nodded and pointed upward. "Corvi," he said and squawked harshly again.

"Well, what is it?" Diana said.

"Do you know where we are?" Gisonne asked.

"No," Bram muttered. "I saw one corvi on Agnece. My crew, long gone circle, we spoke. One old one showed us how to talk to it. It was a long time ago."

"Can you talk to it for us?" Gisonne asked.

"He can hardly talk to us," Emil said. He shrugged and for the first time Gisonne saw impatience and anger on his face. Amazing and wondrous how roles changed when a group changed. Was Emil to become Central Negative?

Gisonne forced herself to pat Bram, to be Lonney. "You'll try, Bram? And tell us what they say?"

Bram nodded.

"The edel said something about Corvi—Corvi house," Diana said.

"Drown the edel," Emil said.

There was nothing more to do. The walls were unmovable. They lay miserably, blunting the painful floor poles somewhat with their heavy coverings. There was nothing else in their prison. No water and no food. The only toilet was the spaces between the poles.

9/11/31 oe

When the black eye next appeared, Bram turned his face up
to it, opened his mouth and throat as one, and squawked
painfully, loud, repeated cries.

The eye disappeared but in a short while a basket of dry
food was dumped over them from above the wall.

Bram, the same Bram who had whined to Lonney that it
was too hot, squawked again and again. He poked Emil and
gestured that he too should cry out.

Gisonne was so dehydrated that she could hardly stretch
her mouth, but she managed a few shrill squeeks. Diana refused
to consider it.

And then Gisonne saw the horrible eye again and an ugly,
scrawny, long-fingered hand lowered a bucket of water on a
rope. The rest of the body was out of sight behind and below the
rim of their prison wall.

They scooped water into their hands and drank.

Later there were more squawks and screeches and a new
one, very loud, "awk." The voices or calls seemed to overlap,
interrupt one another in a cacaphony of rage. For a while there
seemed to be a large number of individuals crackling all at once,
and then there was a silence, a couple of softer clucks and what
must have been a dialogue, a somewhat quieter debate between
two.

Gisonne demanded Bram translate. He knew one of the
sounds—and tried to imitate it. "A warning," Bram said. "Bad
things will happen."

"So they don't talk," Gisonne said. "They signal danger—
like many animals."

"They talk," Bram said.

Hours or days later—their timepieces measured oe only and
this planet was unknown to them, especially without their IP—
another head appeared and another. The first one moved higher
and she saw it was wearing some kind of a bizarre mask, a beak.

And as it seemed to pull itself up higher on the wall, she saw more of its warped body, all torso, horrible thin arms growing out from the middle of its fat belly, ugly hands and long horny fingers. Its legs were out of sight, probably hanging down the other side of the wall. And it wore a gray-green vest with long, full, shiney black sleeves.

"Pontus!" Diana said.

"Some . . . some fool thing made on Anu," Gisonne said. Suppress the panic, TL.

"Corvi," Bram said and squawked again.

The thing's head jerked and turned 180%; now its other eye stared down at them. They were fixed in its sharp single view and held.

When it began squawking and chattering again, Gisonne was sure it was addressing them or answering Bram. Other calls could be heard from out of sight beyond their prison wall, but it kept its eye only on them.

And then she realized! Of course, its other eye was looking in the opposite direction. Why that awareness came as such a meaningful revelation she didn't know. But it was crucially important.

Pontus the drowner, she missed Fron! How can one function without an IP?

There was a louder harrassing shrill squawking which grew more and more painful and shrill as it seemed to come nearer. The corvi on their wall shifted, seemed to quake and, horribly, the empty sleeves raised and fanned out away from its torso and then whipped about its head like opaque black wind.

There was a sudden whistle of wind invisible speed and and an explosion where the huge corvi had been. But it was still there, two corvi struggling, two great heads, many wings, a giant whirlwind, a tornedo, blackening the sky above the enclosure. Long black feathers gracefully, softly, and slowly floated down upon the humans.

They knew that the outcome would be their fate. Why? How? Which winner meant what fortune?

Gisonne tugged the nearest elbow, Diana's, and they crawled to the wall and pressed themselves against it. Emil and Bram moved but too late. One Corvi seemed to fall back, give up, but as the winner let go and wheeled upward, the loser dove straight down. Its huge, sharp beak stabbed into Bram's back while a claw grasped Emil's calf. Blood spurted in a circle. The beak opened wide to get a better hold—no, a better bite!

They are going to eat us, Gisonne thought. It was too absurd to be true. There was nothing left, no hope, but why not try?

She opened her own mouth to cry for help. Next to her Diana was shouting upward. Bram was squawking louder than ever. Emil had turned to curl himself in agony around the creature's ankle, its nails still deep in his flesh. But he too was fighting, struggling, and crying upward.

Grubs and worms do not open their beaks and scream for help—or food.

Another corvi descended into the space. And more followed. It was suffocatingly black and airless; large bodies struggled heavily. It was far different from the fight in the air above. Gisonne was pushed harder into the wall, smothering under the pressure of hot, dense, feathered bulk, the back or front—she couldn't tell—of a huge torso.

And then it was suddenly over. The great bodies ascended in a rush of air and the humans were left alone.

Gisonne stared up blankly, beyond relief, at stars appearing among the leaves overhead. She couldn't, and didn't want to, turn her head to see how the others were.

Some of the stars dissappeared. Corvi back on the wall blocking the sky. A rope was again let down but this time with a platform instead of a bucket. On it stood an old human woman.

"You are welcomed," she said, in an ancient Octente dialect.

5/24/40 oe
Zalterius II

Nimee Michalis assumed unofficial centrality of the
Michalis family after the disabling illness of her mother, the
deaths of her aunts, and the imprisonment of her father and
uncles for withholding maintenance and life support payments
and for other crimes against the Pentente.

Chapter Eighteen

Encircled

6/3/40 oe

"They would eat us," Bram groaned.

"They looked at you with the wrong eye," the woman said. "They do not yet look with both eyes."

Gisonne could barely follow either of them.

"Who . . . what are they?" she asked.

The woman shook her head and gestured that Gisonne should step onto the platform.

"But who are you?"

The woman only repeated the gesture.

When Bram repeated Gisonne's question in the old language, the woman said, "Sene."

Then, in spite of the pain raging in his back and buttocks, Bram crawled aboard and Gisonne shrugged and followed. Two by two they were hauled up, over and down the other side of their prison wall. They could hear Corvi voices in the distance and the rustle of leaves overhead. Except for a few stars they were in total darkness until Sene lit a small artifical light.

Gisonne had expected to see whatever beasts of burden had carried them here but she was relieved to see instead a strange van with an open flat bed—and the same wretched poles for flooring. This one, however, had wide boards covering some of the area, enough for two or three human beings to sit on.

In the lower gravity, Diana, Gisonne, and Sene were easily able to hoist Bram and help Emil onto the back of the truck. Diana climbed on too and Sene motioned for Gisonne to join her in the cab.

It was not wildly different from a Zalterian tractorvan. There was a steering stick and a human-shaped zoid seat for the driver. A kind of treadle, obviously made for human feet, controlled whatever powered the thing.

It ran quietly and smoothly, as if cushioned by the universal Malaacan magnetic risers that made life on z2 possible.

Gisonne set her mind to remembering all she could of earlier languages spoken by some of the returnees. She thought of Jonah's dialect, somewhere in the evolution of Octente/Zalterian, halfway between Sene's and contemporary speech.

Slowly and clearly, Gisonne asked again, "Who are they?"

"Corvilla," Sene said.

"And why were they attacking us?"

"They are unpaired, immature—you see?"

Gisonne did not see.

"They roam far, test themselves in severe and primitive northern climes."

"And that makes it all right for them to . . . to harm people?" Gisonne could not bring herself to say "eat."

"They must rebel. They must be angry with the Ravelian flocks. If they are not . . . bad, they will not mature."

Gisonne was not sure whether it was the concepts, the language or both that were incomprehensible.

"The rest of our crew? Were they hurt?"

Sene seemed not to understand this question at all. She began to talk of what she did know: she had received a message from "Rave" to come and get these four and bring them to the city/air/village/flock.

Wait and see. Gisonne could see very little in front of them. The little light showed nothing more than a flat, grassy surface moving fast beneath the truck. Once in a while there appeared a rut, large tree root, or rock, but the risers eased them over unnoticeably.

In a short time Sene stopped next to another structure or vehicle, impossible to assess in the dark. But the inside was similar to the lander that had brought them down from orbit. It was a bit larger and mats were strewn here and there on the poled floor.

Sene produced some kind of food, dry and nutty, and water-like liquid. They ate, drank, and stretched out on the mats. As the car lifted, flying somewhere, Gisonne fell asleep, woke, guessed they had been drugged, fell asleep.

At least they hadn't been eaten—yet.

Most of Gisonne's dreams in the last year had been set on z2—so waking was always painful. Only a few dreams involved the Procne or its crew and they had been the nightmares. But when she woke the next "morning," it was not a sad shock, but a joy to see Lonney's face just above her own.

It was like someone from home, lost but found again. Lonney—such a good Tension Releaser that Gisonne cried.

Lonney stroked her head with a wet cloth and murmured kindnesses.

Gisonne noticed that Lonney looked good, healthy, and clean. She was wearing a black cape, not over the regular OMD shirt and leggings, a bright tunic with simple lines, —a narrow old mother hubbard.

"They didn't hurt you then? Pontus be forgiven."

"Hurt us? Who?"

"Corvilla?"

"What is that? Are you all right, Gisonne? When your lander crashed, you must have—"

"Crashed! It was caught . . . by them. Corvilla."

"I don't understand you. What's—"

"Listen! I hear them now!"

There was a squawking and crackling from somewhere out of Gisonne's sight.

"Oh, Gisonne, it's all right. Those are the birds, wonderful things. I wish they could live in the wild on z2 as they do here."

"Is she awake? Is she all right?" Fron's expression was almost warm.

"Yes. Yes, she's fine" Lonney said, patting Gisonne, reassuring. "She's had bad dreams, that's all. Understandable after such an accident."

"Not dreams," Gisonne said. "This is a primitive, horrible place. We were—"

"Gisonne, you've had a shock," Fron said. "Look around. This world is a technological marvel. It Operating Systems, its very furnishings—"

Gisonne did look and it was true. The instrumentation, the wall screens, the very bed she was on that moved to her shifting position, made the round, rough prison they had been rudely dumped into the nightmare of fever.

"Tell us about the crash," Fron said. "Soon the reality will all restore itself in your mind. The mariners have excellent methods of care. I checked all of their medical knowledge myself. Just wait."

"And see," Gisonne said. "No. I am not hallucinating. You know me better than that. There was no crash—or if that is what it was, it was no accident. Those things captured us . . . Where is Diana? Emil? They know."

"Bram and Emil needed more intensive medical treatment. They're in another facility. I'm not sure where Diana is."

"I can't believe you're so gullible, Fron." Gisonne was growing angrier, now at Fron. And Lonney too looked a lot less lovable at the moment.

Lonney and Fron looked at each other in sympathy—what a switch—and the cackles and squawks grew louder—and closer.

"There!" Gisonne sat up.

Two large fowl came into the area, one waddling awkwardly, the other lifting feet high, a slow prance. The first was green and red, a parrot, Gisonne recognized easily. The Allains had imported one once. The second, the thin preener, was shiney black—a small corvi!

A young girl came in behind them, leash in hand, long voluminous black cape flowing dramatically from her shoulders.

Sene followed, calling out unintelligibly. The girl stopped and responded in a strange tongue. Gisonne recognized a few familiar terms from the old Zalterian but many more were new. Even stranger were the squawks and raucus caws blended comfortably into the natural rythm of their speech. But it was clear that Sene was reprimanding and the girl arguing.

"Sene!" Gisonne cried out. "Tell my friends about Corvilla—what happened to us. That is a corvi infant?" Gisonne pointed to the black bird.

Lonney tried to press her back against the cushions. "It's all right, Gisonne."

Sene laughed, stopped and laughed again. "That is a pet, our pets," she said slowly and clearly in pure old tongue, and again laughed. She added something in the other language to the girl who also began to laugh.

"Stop, Sene. Where are the corvi? Where are we now? Where is my dynemate Diana? Tell Fron what has happened. Wait. Stop!" But Sene was already out of the room, pulling the girl and birds behind her.

"Hush, Gisonne. The woman cannot understand our language; it has evolved far beyond hers," Fron said. "I'll explain everything to you when you're calm. I've already been working on learning more of the old tongue. If only I had studied it. If only I had access to the Procne OS! If—"

"Fron, no more."

"I'll bring you food, Gisonne," Lonney said. Just wait."

"I'm thirsty," Gisonne said. "We were imprisoned without food or water for so long and last night the food was dry. I think it was drugged."

Again Fron and Lonney looked to each other sadly. Fron shook his head and Lonney pointed across the room at a gentle waterfall built into the wall.

The room was strangely lovely, large and circular with small, oval, latticed windows every few feet. A steep stairway led to a round balcony, and continued to the ceiling. Built-in shelves served as bunks, seats, or tables, depending on height from the floor, depth, and cushioning. The floor was thickly carpeted. All the materials were brightly colored, dazzling when the light struck through the windows.

Gisonne lay back and looked up at the ceiling—and realized it was one large trap door, a removable roof. The stairs led, not to an upper story, but outside. She turned to point it out to Fron, but changed her mind.

Lonney brought food, dry and grainy, and a cup of water from the little stream. She patted Gisonne's head and tried to feed her.

"How much of this place have you seen?" Gisonne asked them. "How many people? What do you think you know? How did you land? Who was there? Where's Calib?"

"There's a lot to learn: the technology is as advanced as Octente, in some ways more sophisticated, and is similar in its basic functioning, but . . . but the machines and tools differ in looks," Fron said, "as if based on the same principles, scientific discoveries, inventions, etc. but adapted in form to—"

"Or perhaps our technology was adapted to form," Gisonne said.

"Calib wouldn't get into the second lander," Lonney said. "It was terrible what he did to Bram. He wouldn't say why. He was angry."

"He is insane," Fron said. "We have to face it. I have studied—"

"But would Bram have moved fast enough to get into a q or grab an air mask?" Gisonne asked. "Maybe Calib was—"

"Anyway," Fron interrupted back, "the lander looks nothing like ours inside or out. The interior was unpleasantly small and poorly designed, but the exterior was sleeker, smoother, lighter than—"

"The inside of the one I was in was horrid, too, squinched, a stinking mess. I never saw the outside," Gisonne said. "But how was your landing? Who was there?"

"These same people and they are really nice," Lonney said. "There were three of them outside, not Sene. She didn't come until last dark with you. They talk a little bit like Bram."

"It was an ordinary descent for such extraordinary circumstances" From said. "The port opened. Our hosts were waiting and brought us up here. We've been here ever since. The language problem has made it difficult to get more information. I'm extremely curious about the elevation devices. On z2 in the Arines, you have no choice. Here they seem to arbitrarily choose difficult—"

"Difficult for humans," Gisonne interrupted.

By their faces she saw that Fron and Lonney thought again that she was still suffering delusions.

It took several dark/light cycles—shorter than z2's—for the new half/dyne to begin to adjust to the rythm. They couldn't be arbitrary or follow individual sleep patterns as they could on ship because with the first lighting of the sky before each rise of DeMaiola, there was a burst of sound coming from everywhere at once, close and far, high and low, music and cacaphoney. On fauna-bare z2 imported birds survived only on Estuary or in captivity as pets, farm animals—chickens and ducks, or zoological exhibits. Gisonne had never heard wild mixed-species choruses—multiple singing. Piercing, beautiful, ugly, trilling and thrilling, sometimes counterpuntal, call and response, love offered, love rejected, territories conquered, cries of agony as nests were lost to raiding armies.

The Zalterians tried to explore but found themselves limited to three round rooms, two identical, the third a storage kitchen with chutes, open and closed, through which goods, foodstuffs, wrapped and contained materials, perishables dropped daily. Gisonne realized that the preponderance of dry food their hosts offered, and ate themselves, was choice, not necessity. They liked it.

When Fron, through Gisonne, asked for more information or to be shown more of the "house" or the outside world, their hosts could not understand. Sene shook her head or patted her lower lip, apparently an idiomatic gesture. Pressed she said, "Later. After you rest." Another time she said, "Rave, the Ravel, will let us know when it is time."

Ironically, Gisonne had, by sheer persistance or force of authority, just about convinced Lonney and Fron that her story was true when the roof slid open and Bram and Emil descended the stairs, accompanied by one old man.

Both had changed. Emil, limping, infirm, and bent, seemed smaller and older. And Bram looked cheerful—almost jovial! He waved across the room at them as he reached the bottom step.

The man just behind him was also smiling. Bram pointed at Lonney, said something over his shoulder, and both laughed.

And Bram actually showed some civilized manners by attempting to introduce them to the man, Gape. The two were old dyne/crewmates from 3410—3475 oe enjoying a surprise reunion.

Gape's clothing was exactly like Sene's and the other "hosts": a colorful simple tunic under the long black cape. He was grizzled and wrinkled, much older than Bram. Yet they had been the same age as crewmates a century earlier.

"Bram, ask Gape to tell us about this place," Fron said.

Bram looked annoyed, shrugged his shoulders, did not ask Gape anything, but Gape must have understood a bit. He looked a question at Bram and Bram shrugged again. Obviously Bram himself had learned nothing from Gape and was not about to try again in front of them.

Gisonne tried. She took Gape's hand, smiled, and said slowly: "Of course, you understand how frightened and confused we are. Why are we here? What is this place? When are we to leave?"

"Does he understand what Gisonne is saying?" Lonney asked Bram. "Tell him what she says, Bram."

Bram resumed his old stupid, stubborn look and Gape looked sadly at Gisonne, apologetic. He started to say something and then looked over her shoulder and stopped.

Gisonne turned quickly enough to catch Sene's warning frown and lip touch.

And so it continued for several cycles. Gape talked and talked; Bram chuckled appreciating the memories but said little. They learned about century-old crew life, the drugs to be had at ancient ports, the songs sung then, and the scandals of long dead people, but little of the navigational maps, the politics, the history and nothing at all about the planet they were on. But even after they knew they would gain no information, Fron and Gisonne listened to every word to learn the language.

Chapter Nineteen

Rave, the Ravel

6/6/40 oe

"These 'mariners' are only people, human, related to our ancestors. They could well be our ancestors—yes, biologically! Why should they harm us?" Gisonne said. "They saved us from those monsters so their intentions are benign. We have to force them to—"

"To what?" Emil asked. "To let us go back up to the Procne and then where? Waldseemuller? Some other—"

"You sound like Calib," Lonney said.

"They may have means of reprograming our OS. Technologically they are at the level, more or less, of Malaaca. The differences make it hard to tell. On the other hand, there are some things that make me believe they have—or once had— some familiarity with hardware of the Octente worlds."

"Of course, these mariners are here, aren't they?"

"No, I mean much earlier. Not just a few centuries ago."

Gisonne, Lonney, Emil, and Fron were huddled in a corner of the cornerless room. For once all their hosts were absent. Gisonne noticed how good the others looked; Lonney in a gold tunic and Fron in deep green both looked vibrant, younger. Emil's tangerine tunic made his black skin seem to glow with health in spite of his injuries. No matter how technically perfect, ship illumination could not compete with a sun's light, even indoors, cut by small, latticed windows into brilliant geometric patterns on carpets, coverlets, tunics and faces. The dark of unlit spaces and of their voluminous, black capes was deepened in contrast. So different from the monochromatic "calming" uniformity of the ship.

"And where is Diana? Emil, we have to find out. We're going to do it," Gisonne said. "Fron, I'm sure, has studied their habits."

Fron nodded and began a recitation: "Gape is here from just before dawn until evening. Sene is in this room and the next from late afternoon until—"

"Don't go through it all! The other women and the girl are completely silent or unintelligible and I think Sene may be most controllable. When is she alone with us?"

"Often—not always—late evening. The other women come in around midnight."

"Tonight then. As soon as she is alone and in this room."

"Good," Fron said. "I think communication instruments are limited to the 'kitchen.'"

"But you don't know," Emil said.

It was so easy that Gisonne felt foolish that they had not tried it sooner. Sene had come when Lonney beckoned. Gisonne and Emil—still against his better judgment—came up behind her and took hold of her arms. Gisonne had experienced the strength of this woman and expected a struggle but Sene gave in immediately.

They did not need to force her into a seat and bind her with her cape as they had planned. She sat herself and waited.

"Now you must tell us what we want. We will not hesitate to—"

"Yes," Sene said. "What is it?"

"All right. First, where is our groupmate, Diana?"

"It stays with the Rave."

"She. She. Diana is female. Have you lost your senses? We want to see her—now."

"Yes, you must." Sene nodded. Must what? Gisonne wondered.

"Who is the authority here?"

"Rave. I told you."

"Then . . . " Gisonne wasn't ready. She had been prepared to repeat her demands.

"You will take us to him." Fron did not hesitate.

"It. Yes," Sene said. "Rave said to bring you to it tonight. Follow."

Rave, the Ravel, was five feet tall, fat-bellied, glossy black, and extremely ugly. It stood on its lower gnarled foot/hands, curved in a tight clasp around a floor pole, and held its upper arms tight against its sides. If it had tiny upper hands, they were hidden under the black, feathered cape that flowed down from where its shoulders should have been.

They stood before it, staring at a profile and being stared at by one eye, a shiny, black ball. Fixed by a predator? Welcomed by a host?

"'Flock guests,' it says. It invites you to flock/village/house." Then Sene added as an aside, "right eye."

Gisonne had seen immediately that the black bird "pet" could not possibly be a child corvi. They were no more like than were a capuchin monkey and an Earth-evolved human being—perhaps less. The humanoid and a monkey were obviously both primate. One could not say that Rave the Ravel was avian. Saurian at all? Earth-evolved?

"It says you are to visit flock/house."

"Tell him—it—that we want to leave soon. Tell him we need help with our ship."

Sene squawked briefly and Rave seemed to shriek back, feathers ruffling, head jerking.

"Rave says ship needs help," Sene said.

It made no sense. Sene must have confused Gisonne's meaning. Or Rave's. Gisonne reworded the same request.

Sene made more Corvi sounds but there was no way to tell if she repeated Gisonne's statement. Then Rave, more calmly, squawked and chirped back at great length. It was distracting and disconcerting to see the beak move in "talk" pointed in another direction while the one eye stared. It seemed to be looking at them sideways and talking to the wall.

The room they were in was also round and windowed, but larger, and had the miserable poled floor, with the spaces between wide enough catch a human foot. Where platforms, built in bunks had been in the human quarters were more poled recesses—perches. The place smelled evilly.

"It says you, Gisonne, will come to its flock house. Emil and Fron visit Nil's flock house."

"What kind of answer is that?" Emil asked.

"We must have information," Fron said. "What is a flock house? Who is Rave? Is he a center? Of what? What about those things that attacked Gisonne and Emil?"

"We will not be separated," Gisonne said.

Sene moved closer to her and said, as another aside, "It is not comfortable to include large numbers of primates in any one village/house/flock. If you do not separate, you will remain in first rooms always."

Her words were loud and clear. Did that mean that the Rave creature could not understand human speech at all?

"You can't hold us prisoner," Emil said. He straightened up in spite of the wounded leg and his features widened into a stone mask.

Rave obviouly understood some human body language. It seemed to grow larger—or fatter—and its head began to turn, slowly.

Sene said something to it in its own squawks and clucks and its head turned back to its original position.

"Are you its guests or its slaves?" Gisonne asked.

"Yes. Neither," Sene said. "Do what Rave asks. It is better. It is not a real separation. Corvi need to see flock/groups with both eyes. I will explain to your two dynemates at Nil house/village/flock."

Gisonne said, "Tell him we accept his invitation."

Sene croaked something, Rave stood taller—tip toe if those were toes—and its great cape fluttered, ballooned, and began to flap. Not a cape, wings. Noisily, awkwardly, it flew up and out. They had not seen the roof slide open.

Even above and in the air, wings spread against a brightening morning sky, it was an ugly warped person to Gisonne. Everything about its body was a distortion of good form; its motion ungraceful; and most horrible, incredible to civilized eyes, disgusting, it had defecated as it rose. Its feces fell to the floor and disappeared down between the poles.

They left, not the way they had come, directly from their rooms through a wide sliding connecting door, but the way Rave had gone, up and out. They climbed the stairs to the top of the wall and stared in dumb surprise at the outside unnamed world. Before and below them spread a meaningless pattern of green. Leaves! Millions of leaves. Trees. They were looking down at a forest! The first Gisonne had ever seen. With a sweep of delight mixed with homesickness, she realized they were on a great height, not a notch in the rocky, naked verticals of z2, but a plateau.

At the bottom of the stairs Emil and Fron went with Sene to the same van that had brought them, while Gisonne followed one of the young women on a footpath along the side of the building they had just left. It turned out to be a series of connected, flat-roofed circular rooms—a crooked chain of topless rotunda. The path was unpaved, rough and rarely used, yet the walls of the "house," were obviously machine-made. Then Gisonne realized that this "house," or string of rooms, was in turn connected in turn to another and another similar cluster, each on its own level.

The girl led Gisonne to what appeared to be a major entrance, yet another technological marvel, a series of metal but fluid darts from ground to roof, each capable of sliding apart separately or as a unit. Next to it were several riser platforms—elevators, lifts—both open and enclosed.

Just inside the ground level entrance, Diana waited.

The difference between a lean-to shed and the main Octente Malaccaan-designed Embassy building on Nordport was not greater than that between that horrible, round prison and this part of the village/house/flock. Yet in no way was this place like the embassy except in being the product of a high culture and technology. There was no floor, just the same round rods or poles stretching across the empty space below. The round wall was niched and balconied; angled poles crossed from one part to another creating corners and "places" of various size; platforms or goods elevators rose and lowered with an almost inaudible hum. Platforms, large and small, poled and solid, swung from wall brackets. Everything was up and down, above or below.

Horizontally things did not begin and end at the same places. There was no vertical line where one could say the room was divided into two sides, no "natural" divisions. What appeared to be aesthetic design alone—one could not be certain about the function of anything—were horizontal stripes in vivid colors circling the room at various heights. These varied in width as well as color. Some flowed in graceful sweeps while others were geometric lines. A top turned inside out. Dizzying from the human point of view, two eyes at once.

And there were corvi here and there, at different heights above Diana and Gisonne looking up from below. Gisonne panicked. These must be more Corvila! She turned back to the entrance. Diana too was moving swiftly, but she was pulling Gisonne to the side, close to the wall. And Gisonne saw why! Urine and fecal matter fell casually, unpredictably, and ineluctably here and there from above.

Gisonne gaped in horror. This was it. The ultimate degradation and humiliation.

Diana poked at her and she turned to see a smile, rare for Diana. Diana was laughing.

And Gisonne understood. No insult intended. This was their way. Gisonne and Diana stood close together, leaning against the wall, laughing helplessly.

Gisonne was introduced to the "household," indirectly—through Diana through a man named Jarl, whose dialect was old but not as ancient as the others' and sounded more Zalterian than general Octente. Jarl said he was not a mariner but a "trader." Gisonne recognized the word from the old records and guessed 33'rd century oe. Jarl thought she was right, but there had been so many trips and so many planet rests that he wasn't sure when was when. He knew he had returned to Zalterius II more than once. He remembered his most recent trip "home," only a hundred years ago—perhaps. He had spent most of his relatively young life aboard ship, and it was hard not to confuse SPEED time and oe time. Also he had stayed at the port—Nordport?—only two weeks. The language had already changed so much that he had had a hard time understanding.

"Why didn't you stay? z2 was . . . is your home." Gisonne asked the question herself and repeated it with help from Diana. It was the only way to learn.

"I didn't belong there," he said. He had learned to enunciate sharply and speak very slowly in order to do his job, communicate with and teach Diana. "It was all changed, spoiled, strange. Not like the old days."

"And this place isn't strange!" Gisonne spoke too quickly for Jarl to understand. When Diana started to paraphrase, Gisonne stopped her.

Reluctantly Gisonne repressed her almost overwhelming impulse to see everthing at once, to examine if not come to understand the technology, to demand answers of anyone and everyone, human or corvi, in authority. At first she had been annoyed that Diana had not done any of it in the oe weeks she had been here. But, of course, it was and would have been foolish—and dangerous, and not even possible. Fron was right: information is power and right now they had so little they were weaker than helpless.

A good TL knows when to "lie low" and "wait and see," Gisonne told herself. And laughed. Some Task Leader she had been! Her crew had not turned the Procne around, could not communicate with or control the edel, had followed her blindly into the corvi lander, had failed to get themselves out of the corvila prison, and had been unable to persuade or force the inhabitants, corvi or human, to help them.

Jarl was tall, slender and fair. In fact, he looked something like Blake—not only in manner, dignified, gentle, and, to Gisonne, princely in the off-world sense of royal—but in his features like the Rise family, long allied with and intermarrying the Allains. Had he remained on z2 a hundred oe years ago, the OMD would have returned him to the family. He could have been some great, great uncle of Diana and Jevry. Silly thought. The OMD had not been as strong then and placing returnees with family of origin had not been its policy until recently.

Recently. Gisonne's recent was not recent anymore on z2.

Jarl clarified Sene's comments about the corvilla. Gisonne and Diana understood the words but the subject remained incomprehensible. The corvilla were the young, unmated adults. They left the family/village/house, some voluntarily, others driven away. About a third remained—or were allowed to remain. These cared for the hatches/incubator, the nurseries, helped the "workers" outside sometimes, and continued training and schooling if they chose. Some with specific talents were guided into professions/roles/right-eye work.

"The males leave and the females stay?" Gisonne asked.

Jarl's expression was something between puzzlement, shock, and repulsion. He didn't answer.

Diana repeated the question, thinking he had misunderstood.

"No," he said. "They are all the same."

"Until what age," Diana asked.

"Always," he said.

"How can that be possible?" Gisonne asked. "You don't understand. They are male or female, even though it is not obvious as it is with us. I can't tell which is which and probably you can't, Jarl, but they know. So the ones who leave home must be—"

"They do not know. Only old flock mates who have flown together in mating flight remember but they never mention it. It is not . . . not polite."

Gisonne was sure Jarl misunderstood. She would wait and see.

"Why did they capture us? One tried to kill."

"That I don't know," Jarl said. "There must be something happening. Some seasons the corvila join Dubwa and turn against the villages/flocks/houses. I don't know much about all that—only what I overhear in their language and that I understand more than most, but poorly."

And we, Gisonne thought, understand you but poorly.

For the first several of the quick planet cycles they were ignored by the corvi. They went through various areas unquestioned. Each room—level—was so enigmatic—some busy, some quiet that Gisonne had to ask Jarl what the function was. When she saw corvi eating, she assumed it was the dining room or kitchen. But she was wrong again. They ate wherever and whenever—just as they performed certain other bodily functions, almost unaware. Eating was like breathing, almost involuntary, and not a ritual or social activity.

Sleeping was another matter. Jarl said that each corvi and each older pair had its own sleep place—sacrosanct and the only open hostility among them was in guarding its possession and privacy. A severe punishment was to lose one's bed and be given a sleep place more public and lower on the wall.

The corvi went about their business or just stood/sat/perched. Gisonne found they paid no attention to her rude stares; staring was what they did all the time—when their right eyes were open. The left seemed usually out of sight from Gisonne's angle. If not, it was shut or patched.

So she studied them freely and found them still physically ugly, repulsive, and smelly.

One large room had machinery—electronic, clearly—up and down the wall with platforms and swings usually occupied. In that laboratory/office the noise was as painful to Gisonne and Diana as the smell. A thousand lines of screeching, creeking, crackling, squawking voices smashed against each other from every direction.

In another building there were visuals—on the bottom where a floor should be. The roundness of the room was functional here. There were tiers of seats all the way up, a theater in the round but the "stage" or "screen" on the bottom. The corvi viewers looked straight down from above. The only lifts, constantly moving, were the very small dumb waiters taking food to the corvi watching from each level. Diana and Gisonne found no way to get higher than the lowest balcony. From there they had to crane their necks and the angle was still not good. Also it was even more dangerous here than elsewhere with all those corvi above.

From a low angled ladder-like structure the floor pictures was much made some visual sense: geometries of flocks; some flying creatures; icons. They all seemed at times chaotic and at others designs of unity and unbelievable beauty. None of it was of help in gaining information.

There were no other senses communicated. Who could smell anything anyway with the stink of the personel?

Chapter Twenty

Points of View

6/9/40 oe

"Rave wants to see/look at/meet you," Jarl said.

"I met Rave," Gisonne said.

Rave was on a raised platform on the flat house top, roof to Gisonne, lid to corvi. It was holding a monocular in one clawed foot/hand, standing on the other and looking out into the distance. Other corvi stood by, one on a lower platform, the rest on the roof itself, lower place, lower status. Less power? Gisonne had no idea of the political structure and Jarl did not know either or was unable to explain it.

Except for the constant automatic, quiet eating and deficating, the corvi were unusually still and silent.   Rave's head turned 180 degrees until its right eye stared into Gisonne's two eyes. The rest of its body had not moved. It squawked.

"Its child won first in the field contest," Jarl said. "You are to watch 'two eye' return."

"Its name is 'two eye'?" Gisonne asked.

"No. It was named Eap after its first flight. The contest is conducted with both eyes. The offspring finds its own parent by song alone," Diana said. "I saw it last time—before you arrived."

"You never said you had been intro . . . presented to Rave or any other corvi."

Diana said nothing, looked cooly out at the tops of the nearest trees. The black cape suited her in pattern but paled her skin. Underneath, of course, her tunic was white. How she had managed that Gisonne couldn't guess but was not surprised. With her pale hair and straight posture she looked quite dramatic, a royal queen upon the parapets in some child's holovid. Jarl made a perfect escort, though not the aristocratic match Blake had been.

The corvi were fatter and uglier out here in the bright Demaiollon light. Only their odor was less obnoxious.

Rave clucked and hopped down from its platform with a short wing flap. The others followed it. Ugly black barnyard chickens, Gisonne thought.

More corvi joined them and they all shuffled around, and then formed a straight line behind a low rail a few feet back from the roof rim. On the edge in front of them were obvious landing places, poles for upper hand holds and foot/hand holds.

Gisonne looked for Rave and realized she didn't know which one it was. They were all identical—to a human anyway. Apparantly not to corvi. Two more approached the line up with bright blue sacks and placed one over each head and upper torso. Gisonne thought of the heavy covering she had been trapped in. Corvi must like that sort of thing, but for them at least their foot/hands were free; she had been helpless.

Beaks appeared all the way down the line through a small hole. What a foolish sight the whole thing was! Gisonne looked to Diana to share her amusement but Diana was again staring off into the distance expectant, enthralled.

There was a blast of song that these corvi never made, a host of tiny yellow birds were let loose to fly up against the blue sky, and from farther away came the unpleasant cawing of a great group of corvi. And then over the edge of the tallest distant trees appeared a flock of fledglings.

Gisonne would never call them beautiful certainly. They flapped wings with noisy difficulty. The open mouths spoiled the head shapes. But it was still a wondrous transformation. The horrid little legs were out of sight.
Necks were arrow straight. They flew low above the trees and then the ground. They did not soar. One could see it all took heavy effort.

The flock moved right, then left apparantly without signals. They landed simultaneously, darkening instantly the branches of two trees and then in a rush of air rose up and forward toward the house roof.

Then each parent in the line up began to iterate a series of two or three notes. If there were differences Gisonne could not tell. Perhaps the speed or timber varied.

As the mass came closer, Gisonne was amazed to see how large each fledgling was—more than two-thirds the size of the parent.

And then they seemed to be coming right at her! Flying at the roof. Attacking! Gisonne ducked automatically.

It looked like chaos; fledlings collided in air and others landed on top of each other on the roof. The parents stood still and kept calling their own notes.

Suddenly there were clucks and caws of approval from the bystanders including Jarl—and Diana! One fledgling had found its parent way ahead of the rest and was already tapping its parent's beak.

"Rave has won," Diana said.

Elsewhere on the line there was still confusion. Here and there two or more had chosen the same parent, who squawked loudly until the mistaken ones flew off, while the remaining child tapped happily at the protruding beak. One parent remained alone until a straggler, smaller than the others, flapped awkwardly, tired, down the line to find it.

"Once again, Rave's prime fledge has known its parent's song before the others," Jarl said.

"How can you know?" Gisonne asked. "They are identical. Unless . . . unless you can distinguish the calls?"

"Somewhat. I can guess somewhat. Also I can tell by the reaction of the people," Jarl said.

"The people! And the 'people' are rooting for Rave? Why her?"

"Rave is center," Diana said. "The Ravel."

Would Diana never cease to astound? She was identifying with an ugly, egomaniacal, avian matriarch. But Gisonne corrected herself. They were not so ugly when one looked at them for what they were. The fledglings had had a kind of beauty in the air, both of movement and of body.

Before the next short day, Rave sent for Gisonne. She followed Jarl to one of the busier cylinders and then up to an enclosed platform. Rave was already there, perched on a swing while another corvi stood on foothands with its back to them. It seemed to be handling some kind of unrecognizable equipment.

Rave began to squawk after a very brief nod. Jarl frowned, cleared his throat, frowned again. "It speaks about your . . . flying person/OS/carrier . . . no, bearer. It says it cannot understand how you came by such a . . . creature/captive/being."

Hopeless, impossible Gisonne thought. How to explain through such a poor interpreter things that she couldn't explain in her own language—things she didn't understand herself? Before she could attempt an answer, Rave was talking again, gesturing toward the second corvi.

"This person is . . . a teacher/learner of . . . ." Jarl hesitated. "There is no word for its profession . . . one who studies living beings."

There probably was a fine Octente word but Jarl didn't know it, Gisonne thought.

"Professor," Gisonne said.

When suddenly she heard sound, chirping and screeching as well as some electronic buzzing and bleeping, coming from a dark oval on a post, Gisonne realized she was looking at instrumentation for a system of communication. The language seemed to be Corvi but the "voice" was wrong. Wrong but familiar—the edel.

"Edel!" Gisonne cried out—in spite of herself.

"Gisonne," the edel peeped in its female voice. "Lahnny?"

The second corvi, the "professor," Gisonne guessed, tapped something and the communication stopped. It did not turn its head to look at her with either eye.

Rave spoke and Jarl gave a corvi nod. "Rave says this . . . studier, professor—his name is Deetch—will talk with you by me."

Oh, pontus, Gisonne thought.

Deetch then began a rather gutteral chirping, turning around finally to look at them only in the middle of its very long speech. Jarl's translation seemed far too short.

"It says you used corvi tissue to make edel."

"What?"

Deetch must have perceived Gisonne's confusion. It muttered again for a while.

"Nestling germ," Jarl said.

"You mean genetic material from . . . ? No. No, just basic bacteria. I'm not a biologist."

Again a long more low keyed chirping and squawking came from Deetch. Its head, and so its eye, never moved. Gisonne could not tell if it meant to address Jarl or her directly.

"You either lie or are in ignorance; the patterns of the being's mind/seeing/position are saurian," Jarl said finally.

Gisonne bore the insult, not sure of the validity of Jarl's translation.

"Tell him absolutely not. It's ridiculous. Trjol's whole purpose would be defeated, his theories meaningless," she said. She could only hope Jarl himself understood her. But he spoke so briefly in Corvi that it seemed unlikely.

"Deetch says in all kinds of language and attitude/positioning/seeing edel is saurian. It now believes itself to be saurian." Jarl stopped for a long second. "Maybe your own avian pets—"

"Our birds are not intelligent."

Yet again Jarl spoke Corvi, and Deetch gave such a long answer that Gisonne's anger was diffused.

"On one of your old worlds, Anu, it might be possible to have spliced saurian fetal tissue and some human . . . DNA? I think DNA," Jarl interrupted himself. "Together—"

"Nonsense," Gisonne squawked and screeched so that both corvi would know her feelings independently of Jarl. "That would make the edel simply a product of genetic engineering and not evolution." When she stopped all three watched her in silence.

"Tell him, Jarl," she shouted. "Tell him exactly what I said. And add that I want to talk to the edel again."

Jarl said something and Rave said something and Deetch untapped whatever it had tapped. Gisonne heard the familiar sounds of the Procne interior, OS sounds.

"Edel," she said. "It's Gisonne again. Can you hear me?"

"I hear, I see, right eye," it said, female voice again.

It is insane, Gisonne thought. Calib was right.

"Is Calib there in . . . with you?"

"Calib. Calib," it said.

"Jarl, ask Deetch how well the edel speaks Corvi. No, ask the edel if it speaks Corvi. No, talk to it in Corvi for me."

Jarl looked to Rave and then spoke briefly. The edel answered in Corvi.

"Yes," Jarl said. "Not very well, I think."

"Tell it . . . ask it—" Before Gisonne could form the question, the edel began speaking.

"It says it is lonesome. Its new family doesn't visit/meet/talk. There is only a piece of you there, Calib. Calib is bad."

Deetch snapped the system off again and, through Jarl, said, "It speaks our language better and better. It is becoming a complete person. A fledgling becoming an adult."

And finally Rave spoke. "It brought you here," Jarl translated. "It could have eliminated you altogether."

As it talked, it rose on foot/hands and then lept up to a handhold above, clucking something more back at them.

"It wants you to come to its home balconey," Jarl said.

Gisonne followed him again, this time back to the largest central circular structure where they were elevated to the highest balcony apartment with a view of all the levels below. Rave's apartment was no more luxurious or colorful than others, but larger, higher, more prominent and, at the same time, more private. The poled floor, the bright, tight but soft cushions which curved from raised sleeping platforms up the walls, the beautiful shell, water fountain and fall, and the bowls and dishes of food, never empty with "silent butlers" constantly rising, shooting on wires around the walls, serving other corvi, descending.

Rave pushed a bowl of food toward Gisonne with a foot/hand, clucking softly, addressing her. The 'butler' arrived with a human cup and Rave gestured with a wing/hand to the fountain.

It was time to be TR now and definitely not TL. Gisonne nodded the way she had seen the corvi do to one another, filled the cup with water, and drank.

They ate in silence for awhile. Rave jerked its head slightly now and then, fixing Gisonne with its right eye for a few seconds each time.

Finally it prodded the silent Jarl with a upper hand finger and began to speak.

"It asks if you are a parent?"

"No."

Jarl made some noise—heavier than the corvi's—and Rave peeped on, without the loud squawks.

"It says you have seen its beautiful cherished smart one. You admired the best fledge, its Eap."

"Yes. How many fledges does she have? Or do I just ask for this season, Jarl? Say whatever is acceptable."

"It—not she—has two," Jarl translated. "Both are good. It . . . loves both."

"Tell her that I admire her children. I want children too. I must go back to my family, my home."

Jarl hesitated. "I'll try." He went on, at far greater length this time, stopping for long pauses.

Rave squawked then and began the peeping.

"It says it always has difficulty understanding my . . . my words. It says that is why it will teach Diana to speak."

"What? Teach her? How long—"

"Wait. I'm trying to follow it."

Rave went on, loud and soft, squawks and peeps.

"But it says your sound is better for its ears than Diana's. It wants you to try to speak now."

"Is she crazy?"

"It knows you have been trying to learn to understand and speak language," Jarl said.

"Not to stay here as a Greek slave!" Gisonne opened her mouth in wide mockery and anger and squawked. She hoped the thing would get her meaning.

It lifted its foot/hand and offered her the plate of food again! Wrong cues!

Diana took the news that she was in training as translator so cooly that Gisonne could not tell if it was new information.

"It means they intend to keep us here indefinitely—forever," Gisonne said. "Don't you understand?"

"Of course I do," Diana said.

"Unless they send us into the future," Jarl said, as his head and then shoulders appeared as the lift raised him to their level.

In the Ravel house/village/flock/city/whatever—Gisonne wished the human interpreters would give the corvi term instead of these clumsy equivalencies—the three humans shared a balcony, which had been adapted somewhat to their physiology and habits. There was even an enclosed compartment with a fountain/bath—and with holes in the floor. Each person had a private sleep q, small but much larger than on the Procne.

They also enjoyed a raised ploid table with actual chairs designed for the human shape. Diana and Gisonne sat there now drinking something like tea. Gisonne wore a deep green tunic and had defied custom by removing her black cape. Diana kept hers on, but pushed back like a cloak blown by the winds of z2, and, as always, her tunic was white.

Jarl was as placid and courtly as ever, bowing to them corvi-fashion as he stepped off the riser.

"Into the future?" What a choice! "We are already in our own futures!" Gisonne said.

"Human persons and some corvi mariners come and go and come back," Jarl said. "I believe they plan it for the time changes, unlike the Octente missions. Your people find it an unfortunate side effect. Corvi use it."

"For what?" Gisonne asked. "And why haven't they shown up on any of the Octente worlds?"

The second time Gisonne visited Rave, Jarl was not along. Rave led Gisonne down to a balcony just beneath its own. Its private space was even larger than Gisonne first thought. Two or more stories, at least, for this small dyne/flock within the Ravel flock?

The two fledges were in the inner room, one perched on a swing, the other rolling on a cushioned bed. There were feathers flying, pillows rolling, and loud notes, up and down a recognizable scale, and shrieking squawks. Two other corvi stood by with food, washing materials, and some unfamiliar wormlike objects. Toys? Were the two servants? Then Gisonne remembered—corvilla, the young but full-grown unpaired who had not left home as temporary criminals but chose to remain within the larger flock to nurture and serve the infants of older, mated corvi.

The "children" froze when Rave came in. It looked at them with its left eye. The two caretakers—Gisonne thought of them as handmaids—stood back and turned their heads so neither eye watched.

Suddenly Rave's wings spread wide and it peeped. The fledge on the swing leaped/flew down to it and the other flipped onto its foot/hands and in the corvi-awkward walk joined its sibling in the parent hug. Wings wrapped the two very big little ones and beaks tap tapped all around.

When Rave turned back to Gisonne and opened its wings proudly there was no need for a translator and Gisonne smiled in spite of herself—and then almost wept because the pontus-drowned bunch of them reminded her of home.

On Gisonne's third visit, Jarl was again with them. This time they talked.

It was Rave who questioned Gisonne.

"It wants to know what you . . . no, why, why you desire to leave its house. It says your flock mates are here. You can have nestlings here." Jarl lowered his voice, as if Rave could understand, and added: "It never asked me or Diana anything like that."

"Tell her my family/flock/dyne is not here. My . . . my mother is not here. She should understand that. I miss my mother as Eap would miss her."

"I can't do the subjunctive," Jarl complained. He looked at Gisonne silently.

She wondered, as she had earlier, if he had been translating her meanings accurately. "Just say it so you make the point."

"Also I can't translate 'mother,'" he said.

"Oh, pontus! Female parent then!"

Jarl shook his head but went on haltingly in the corvi language.

Rave squawked briefly and sharply.

"It says you insult your parent," Jarl translated.

"I love my mother. Go ahead—tell her that."

"Look, Gisonne, you can't say 'her' either. They don't do that."

"Do what? Explain. You were raised on z2; it doesn't matter if it was two hundred years ago. For you it was only a few years ago. What's this about sex?'

"It is not the sex act, though that is private—"

"Unlike other functions."

"Yes. For corvi one's sex—gender—is very private. It is no one's business. Curiosity is a violation. It would be like one of us being naked in public."

"But they are naked—" Gisonne said

"But you can't tell, can you?" So there! Jarl seemed to say.

Gisonne wanted to laugh. Do corvi have any behavior analogous to laughing?

"But surely they can tell!"

"No, they can't. I told you that before."

Through all this, Rave had been watching each speaker in turn with small jerks of the head since corvi cannot move their eyeballs. Gisonne wondered if it could pick up any of the words.

"All right," she said, "tell IT I love my parent as Eap loves IT." She deliberately peeped in a high tone when she pronounced 'Eap' and had the satisfaction of seeing Rave flutter at the sound.

Jarl translated and Rave nodded at Gisonne.

They talked then about the corvilla. Gisonne asked if Eap would join them when he . . . it was first grown. Rave said it would if it remained unmated. No doubt Eap would join them; it was not the kind to remain in house/flock to learn.

Gisonne could not tell if this was good or bad to Rave. Jarl thought it was said proudly.

"Will you not miss it terribly?" Gisonne asked.

"'Yes, oh yes,'" Jarl translated the answer. "But it will be best, for it will 'grow strong and bold and be a proud flock/center when it returns and is forgiven for wicked acts.' And besides," Jarl added on his own, "Rave's nestlings will be fledges by that time."

Gisonne pictured the corvilla attack, one stabbing deep into Bram's back and ripping Emil's leg. Surely Rave would say that was not so easily forgiven.

"But look what the corvilla did to my flock/mates," she cried, pitching her voice high, trying to shriek and squawk.

At first Jarl refused to translate or paraphrase, but Rave itself squawked at him, obviously demanding to know what Gisonne had said. He complied, accurately Gisonne hoped.

For the first time Gisonne thought she recognized expression on a corvi face, or half face. The eye's nictating membrane slowly closed, and then the upper and lower lids came together in the center. The head lowered almost imperceptibly until the beak pointed downward.

Jarl's face was easy to read; he was afraid of Rave and angry at Gisonne.

After long seconds Rave's eye flashed open and its head jerked upright and turned toward Jarl. It peeped and chucked.

"It asks why you know nothing of their enemies. It says I should have told you about Lichel and Dubwa, about corvilla who learn to see only with left eye and who are destroyed by Lichel and follow it."

"And why haven't you?" Gisonne asked.

Rave said something more to Jarl and he nodded.

"I thought you knew; everyone does. You were actually in a corvilla camp until the Ravels rescued you. If your being . . . edel . . . had not called to Ravels, those corvillas would probably have taken you to Lichel and Dubwa."

"Are they corvi? Likell and Dubwa?" Gisonne tried to say the names the way Jarl did, with corvi sounds.

"Lichel is corvi. Dubwa is human. They say Lichel can speak Octente—"

Rave interrupted Jarl. Gisonne recognized the name Lichel in its speech.

"It wants to be sure I'm telling you how bad they are and how fortunate that your flock was rescued by Ravels. I'm to say that those two are trying to destroy corvi life everywhere. They take advantage of the unpaired young who envy the paired and older persons. They entice them into the north and teach them to see with the left eye."

"What does that mean?"

"We are grub to the left eye. Food. That's why a confused young one attacked. It looked at you with only the left eye."

Back on their own balcony Gisonne pressed Jarl for more information about corvi eyes, but he knew no more than he had told her. It seemed to him obvious, simple fact.

Next she asked about 'nestlings,' infant corvi. How many did Rave have? Where were they?

All corvis in each village/house were hatched, nurtured and kept warm in one large incubator. They were fed constantly by unpaired young adults.

"I would think a person like Rave would want to be with her babies."

Jarl shrugged. Gisonne could see that the subject was not interesting to him and he was tired of explaining all these things. He smiled when Diana appeared from her q. The two of them went down on the riser to parade about the village/house together.

Chapter Twenty-One

Siblings

6/13/40 oe

There seemed to be some interesting machinery operating across the "floor" in one part of a living structure. Gisonne stood under a low balcony wishing she could examine it up close, but being uprotected out in the open was too disgusting to bear.

She hoped Fron was gleaning more information than she was, besides language. She wanted to know how labor was divided, how individuals were trained or educated to function in what she saw more and more was a sophisticated society. Were there schools? For all she knew she could be watching schooling going on right in front of her and not known what she was seeing. And where were the persons—corvi or not—who operated the space flights and designed the operating systems for village/house/flocks and spacecraft?

Jarl seemed to know none of these things or didn't have words to explain them. Was there something about old time mariners—like him and Bram and Bram's old buddy Gape that made them inarticulate? Had SPEED slowed them down mentally?

What a thought! Gisonne made a mental note to take up the question with the OMD, Braitt Jones or . . . Would she never truly accept reality!

Gisonne became aware that the din of voices had increased on the balconies above. Corvi seemed to be calling to one another across the open.

"Gisonne." Gisonne was startled by Jarl's human voice next to her.

"A sad thing has happened," he went on. "Three of the Ravel fledges were killed this morning. A predator. They flew too far and grew tired—"

"Eap?" Gisonne cried. "Rave's Eap was one of them?"

Jarl nodded.

Gisonne ran to the lift and rode it up to Rave's balcony. It was as terrible as she had dreaded. Two corvi were there leaning on each other side to side, mewling shrill thin notes, beaks pointed downward. Gisonne didn't know which was Rave but approached their huddle with her hands opened. One wing of four raised itself and enveloped her.

Rave made it possible for Gisonne to meet with Fron. She followed a silent corvi outside and across a glorious glade with a small brook filled with fish. Her guide stopped on the bank, dipped its beak deep, came up with a small gold fish, and swallowed it as they continued over a little human bridge to a human bench where Fron was waiting. His corvi guide was above on a tree branch eating fruit—luckily not directly overhead. Gisonne's guide leaped/flapped up to join it.

Gisonne found she was pleased to see Fron's flat face and more pleased that he seemed eager, almost in physical need, to pour information over her.

"Their 'speech,'" he began, "is so unlike any we know that I'm not sure linguists would call it language. It has no grammatical basis whose logic we can recognize."

"How can you know all this, Fron? Yes, I remember that you have two or three languages in addition to the Octente dialects, but—"

"Research and logic," Fron said with an edge of huffiness."

"But without the Procne OS libraries and—"

"Primary research. The corvi have light hollow beaks and no jaws."

"Anyone can see that," Gisonne said.

"And," Fron continued, "they have no larynx and 'speak' by vibrating the syrinx, the lower end of the windpipe."

"Oh."

"And—most of them can use several chords at once. And each chord has its own complexity of meanings."

"And they think I and Diana can learn it!"

"A human woman's voice can imitate some of their sounds, but sounds belonging to only one of their several systems of communication—aural systems, that is."

"What else? This is interesting, but how can it help us leave?"

"They can't really fly. They make 'flights'—the young fairly easily—with a great flapping of wings. The adults can raise themselves just above the ground and cover short distances. They are much better at straight vertical moves. They spring, using feet and wings, up to a high place, balcony or roof."

"And yet they walk so awkwardly—waddle! Anyway how can it help us? What have you learned about the space technology? They are communicating with the Procne in orbit, with the edel but where are their spaceports? How did they interfere with us?"

"I'm not sure they did." For the first time Fron looked puzzled. "Have you actually seen the operating and communication systems in the Ravel house?"

"One part of it," Gisonne said. "And there was a whole room of visuals only—on the floor. I'm never sure what I'm looking at."

"You actually heard them in contact with the Procne? Calib?"

"No, edel. The edel talks with them in corvi."

"Oh, you mean the OS telecommunication program. The edel can barely speak Octente-Zalterian. What could it know or tell them—"

"The edel brought us here. It saved us from the corvilla. It thinks it's one of them."

"It cannot be. Perhaps the difficulty of understanding them has misled you, Gisonne."

There was not point in arguing. Fron, the rational, would not be moved without empirical evidence.

"I think we may be dealing with two species," he went on after a while, glancing at Gisonne and waiting for the reaction.

"Two?! As far as I can tell they are all identical—the adults and the juniors except for size and that is very little. They could be clones! Have you other types in . . . wherever you're staying?"

"Nil house/village," Fron said. "No. It's that the others are somewhere else altogether, or we have two different species that . . . that look alike and live in the same abodes. I know . . . "

"That's absurd. Ridiculous. Unless one is . . . some kind of slave race? Genetically manipulated to have no intell—"

"No, no. Not that. Just different. Look—the communications. I think that there are two libraries—totally different in symbology, iconography, signs, everything, even in the physical structures of the equipment, the tools."

"Are you sure? Maybe as you said to me their systems—all right both systems, if you will—are so unfamiliar that you—"

"No, of course I'm not sure. Maybe when we get in closer communication with corvi individuals, we can simply ask. Sene is a problem for me. She seems to block rather that facilitate sharing of knowledge. How about you? What kind of human intermediate are you dealing through?"

Gisonne thought of Jarl and smiled.

"Not very helpful but I think he simply doesn't know much." Now was not the time to go on about her theories about mariners. "But I have formed a relationship with Rave, herself. She has feelings I recognize. I'm trying to—"

"She? You can't know such a thing." Fron sounded as scandalized as Jarl. "And when and if they understand you, they will be offended."

"Ridiculous. Rave must be female. She adores her young, knows each one's personality in fine detail—"

"These judgments are unlike you, Gisonne. If these traits indicated gender, all the corvi would know. As it is only the pair mates know which is which. Unless you were on their first mating flight—"

"All right, all right." Gisonne glanced up at their two guides, who were hopping around and in the trees, eating, as always, and leaving fecal droppings beneath them everywhere, as always. Ironically, she certainly couldn't tell their sex by looking at them.

"By the way," Fron said as their paths parted, "are corvis from your house participating in the 'mobbing'"?

"What's that?"

"A young, strong flock is gathering to mob a hawk. It seems it killed some of the fledglings."

This last bit of information was all that interested Diana. She wanted to see the flock.

Jarl claimed to know nothing about a new flocking or mobbing or that a hawk had been Eap's killer, but he accompanied Diana and Gisonne to visit Rave.

When they ascended to Rave's top balcony, Gisonne, for some reason, knew at once that the corvi there was not Rave. It may have been her pair mate, the one who mourned with her for Eap.

"Ask him where Rave is," Gisonne said.

"It," Jarl said. He squawked quietly at the corvi and the corvi gave a brief snort and beep.

"It is Rave," Jarl said.

"You misunderstand," Gisonne said. "He probably said he is Rave's mate."

"I may miss most of their meanings but I do know it said it was Rave and it is Rave. It is Rave and it is Rave's mate. Both are Rave."

"What?" Suddenly Gisonne understood. This was the first Rave, the one who met them in the human rooms. Rave, the mother, was the one she had grown close to.

"I want to view the flocking," Diana said. "Where is it?"

"Where is my Rave?" Gisonne asked.

The answers were the same: on the roof—to which all four found their separate ways and arrived in time to see a hundred corvi flying in formation, a two-dimensional vee, like a boomerang hurled at the quickly sinking sun. The greens of tree tops and distant grasses glowed with emerald light for a few seconds before the night rushed up from behind the watchers, over the trees, and enveloped them, the house/village/flock, and the corvi world.

Automatic lights recreated the roof and a line of corvi watchers. Gisonne saw Rave move away from the others and come toward her. Somehow she was beginning to distinguish individual corvi, Rave most easily. What the cues were, she did not know.

Rave raised a wing and touched Gisonne's shoulder with delicate upper hand fingers. It said something to Jarl.

"It says the flock will find the hawk and destroy it in spite of the mad ones protecting it."

Gisonne suspected that Rave had said much more—all those message systems Fron had learned about—much more than Jarl had understood or could or would translate into Octente.

"Ask her . . . it how they learn their formations? How does each know the rules for his own role? Which is the leader or center?" Gisonne was still dyne student!

"I can't ask that?" Jarl said. "I can't even understand it."

Gisonne insisted he try and he did squawk something, and Rave struck some chords in return. Jarl sighed hopelessly.

"Each corvi knows rules. Its rules. All rules are the same."

Now Gisonne sighed. "Ask it about the hawk? Is it intelligent? Who protects it?"

Jarl said something again and seemed to be answered.

"The hawk is a fierce predator. The mad ones say it must live. Uh . . . Dubwa and Lichel are . . . something. They are 'in argument with corvi peace.' That's enough. If it wanted you to know these things it would send you to class—or tell you."

"Did she . . . it say this?!"

"No. I am saying it."

"Ask it if there is a class where I can study flocking."

"Why? You don't need—"

"Jarl, I am not asking your opinion or your permission. You are an intermediary, not an authority. Do it!"

Jarl compressed his lips and remained silent.

Instead of pleading or commanding, Gisonne again went above his head. She began squawking and peeping, staring at Rave with sad bent head. Rave in turn, squawked at Jarl. Gisonne began then to understand some ancillary corvi meanings.

Jarl responded to it, listened, and paraphrased: "'there was once a class/ecole analyzing flock behavior led/centered by Dabwa. It was unnecessary and weakening'—something about right eye/left eye confusion. 'Dabwa researched to weaken and destroy through knowledge. The Ravel corvi had to . . . exile it.' Look, Gisonne, I missed most of it but this is the best I can do."

The next day Gisonne and Diana prowled around together— not their usual habit. They came by accident upon something that Gisonne had wanted to see for a long time, the incubator, combination hatch rooms and infant nurseries.

It had been there all along, filling the lower third of the second largest cylinder/room, a room Gisonne assumed was only for the manufacture and preparation of foodstuffs. They must have passed the sturcture often and not seen it for what it was. It consisted two silos, one tall and narrow attached by tracts, wide hoses, and tubes at various heights to the wall of the other, squat and much wider. While most corvi machinery operated as silently as Octente OS's, a gentle hum emanated from this compound.

Diana and Gisonne inched along the edge of the room, and as they passed an open entry to the shorter silo on their level, they heard another sound: thin cries, generally unpleasant, peeps and screeches. They moved carefully across the precarious floor, looking down to watch their steps from pole to pole and looking up to watch for corvi over head. Luckily there were more machines than workers in the higher spaces of this cylinder.

Inside the air was extremely warm and the smell was very bad but different, fetid, stuffy, somewhat rotten. Gisonne fought her urgent need to back out. But even as she heard Diana gagging beside her, she reminded herself that the other smells had grown tolerable with time. Diana swallowed, nodded at Gisonne, and the two went forward.

It was easy but disappointing to identfy the egg rooms: great containers with huge padded lids and on the floor in front, ribbons of color and miniature icons that Gisonne had been seeing everywhere, probably some kind of electronic scans, information about the condition of the egg or eggs within. Unmated corvi paroled the area, stopping to examine the scans with right eyes. Their left eyes wore patches. Once in a while one would stop and make an adjustment to what must have been controls—regulating temperature? It was like cooking something in an oven. No corvi mothers sat on these eggs.

As they turned toward the source of multiple cheeps and cries—also the source of the worst smells—Jarl came hurrying in.

"Uggh!" he said. "What are you doing here?"

Gisonne and Diana went on to the nursery, and he trailed behind, gagging.

"Stop," he choked. "They don't even come in here themselves. Rave told me to—"

"Look!" Gisonne cried.

There at last were hatchlings—and horrible things they were. Wide open throats, beaks so obscenely parted that one could see both the inside and outside of the ugly necks at the same time. The rest was skin, naked, blotched in painful colors, covering bone but no flesh.

Water ran from pipes down through grooves and out through a hole beneath the mesh bottom of the funnel shaped 'crib' but did little to remove the debris of rotted food, urin, feces. The infants rested in folds of synthetic cushioning.

Food was brought by corvi workers, who stopped before each crib, raised a container with a foot/hand and dumped its contents into the widest throat. Rather unfairly, Gisonne noticed, some got fed more than others.

The whole thing was inexplicable. Why this sloppy, disgusting system when everywhere else in the Ravel village/house/flock all systems from laundry, medicine, to food serving were efficient, comfortable, if not clean? Obviously the food here was perfectly formulated for the needs of the hatchling, water flowed at the right temperature, pressure, and angle, and corvi aides kept overall watch. But where were the parents? It all seemed such a contradiction to the intense attachments of parent and child Gisonne had seen so far.

Maybe this crib held exceptional offspring or the offspring of an exceptional subfamily—criminals? Social outcasts?

Across the aisle was another 'crib,' with four hatchlings. One of them was not only smaller, obviously undernourished, but a different color, no color, pale skin, traces of white down, tiny half-open beak pink.

"Albino?" Gisonne said to Diana. Diana shrugged, and Gisonne wandered off by herself to check other cribs.   "Let's get out of here," Jarl said, coming up behind her. "What are you looking for?"

Gisonne moved aside to let a corvi aide pour food into the open mouths. But, she noticed, shocked, only two of the three hatchlings got any. The third, far the smallest, was left unfed, its mouth open. The first two resumed their shrill cries.

"Oh, pontus!" Gisonne cried. "Doesn't she see she's not feeding that one? But maybe she's rotating! Maybe that little one is a runt. Jarl, what family are these? We have to tell—"

"These are Rave's hatchlings," Jarl said.

An automatic feed shute opened near the top of the crib. The two larger corvi infants stretched up to catch the pouring dry food into their open throats; the third was pushed down under them and again got nothing.

"Let's go," Diana said from across the room.

"No, wait!" Gisonne said, turning to watch the corvi aide approach. She pointed at the starving little one.

The aide again dumped the grub/mush into the larger siblings, paying no attention or not seeing the meaning of Gisonne's signal.

"Jarl! Tell her! Tell it."

Jarl said something to the corvi. It only clucked once in return and went on to other cribs.

"What did it say? Why is it starving the little one?"

"It does the care taking duties," Jarl said. "Now let us go out of here!"

Gisonne followed him and Diana, ranting all the way.

The air outside seemed fresh and cool, but Gisonne hardly noticed. She headed for Rave's balcony, while Diana returned silently to theirs.

Jarl too at first refused to come with Gisonne until she threatened to tell lies about him to the corvi.

To her misery neither Rave was there. Could the baby live much longer?

Back on their own balcony she cried about it to Diana. Diana nodded but said nothing.

"It would be terrible for Rave to lose two children in such a short time," Gisonne said.

Again Diana nodded. "I saw a corvi working some kind of operation machine yesterday," she said. "I might be able to adopt it for drawing, my kind of drawings."

Gisonne stared at Diana. "I'm talking about dying infants," she said.

Diana looked at her and then away, out at all the other balconies, as if studying them one by one.

190

"You have never had a feeling in your life," Gisonne said. "What ever did you do with Lonney in bed?"

Diana continued to examine the distance. "And your feelings have kept you from saving us," she said to Gisonne after a while. "And so because of you z2 is lost."

Chapter Twenty-Two

Strange Attractors

6/23/40 oe

Rave's wings lifted a few inches from its side and fluttered. Its head tilted or dipped at a new angle as its left eye fixed on Gisonne.

"Don't you see? Someone is trying to murder your infant through neglect." Gisonne was shouting and pulling at Jarl's arm, urging him to translate, at the same time. "Are you saying what I am saying?" She pressed her fingers into his flesh painfully.

Jarl flinched, tried to tear his arm out of her grasp, but did squawk and cluck to Rave. Gisonne found her inability to speak for herself unbearable.

Rave began to cluck and pipe more than squawk, not a good sign Gisonne already knew. It seemed also to dance, moving its weight from one hand/foot to another. Gisonne found the immobile eye threatening now, the way the corvilla had looked at them before attacking. But it was Rave's right eye—thank pontus.

"Let's go down from here, Gisonne," Jarl said. "It cannot understand/tolerate your . . . violations. The basic . . . the rudiments of decency—"

Gisonne saw all at once that she had made a great error— though not what it was. It mattered only now that she had projected her categories of reality upon the corvi. Yes, it was her great error; however, she could not forgive them their reality.

It was time to back away.

Besides the hatchling was surely dead already.

For several days Gisonne remained mostly in her cubicle to avoid Diana and Jarl. Rave avoided her.

"Gisonne, come out," Diana said on a late afternoon. Gisonne wondered if finally she wanted to talk about real things. But no. Sene was there on their balcony, waiting.

Gisonne was back to her wait-and-see mode. She sat and said nothing. Sene stood with more than her usual stillness, her cape so completely wrapped around her that the mauve rose of her tunic barely showed at the neck. Diana too remained standing, but her cape was thrown back, as always, as if blown in a Zalterian wind. The three women seemed posed and composed for a still life painting. Gisonne did not ask for what or whom they were were waiting.

A corvi dropped onto the rail of the balcony and flapped a bit for balance. It was not either Rave. It wasn't Deetch. In fact, Gisonne was fairly certain she had not seen it before. Its feathers were sparse and, when it spoke, its cawing sounded rougher in timber than most of the others.

"Humans," it said. Or seemed to say.

"Riik and I together will tell you lessons of living here," Sene said. "Riik speaks our tongue. I see you are surprised and delighted."

The only truth in the statement was Gisonne's surprise. Diana didn't look interested, hardly surprised. To say that this Riik spoke Octente or any human language was a grand overstatement, and Gisonne was far from delighted.

Riik gave a brief version of the corvi nod and began squawking unevenly. Every once in a while Gisonne thought she heard a human word. When it seemed to finish, she looked to Sene curiously.

"And I must add," Sene began, "since once I was human, I understand your mistake. A human person begins to be with birth. It then acquires its name. Corvi begin to be with flight from cribs."

"That's ridiculous!" Gisonne's words were so explosive that both Diana and Riik started. "We saw those infant individuals, free of any egg or womb."

"Not grown, but growths." Sene seemed to think for a minute. "When we grow a tree, we wait to see which is the stronger branch before we prune. Or if there are two or three saplings growing too close together, we wait before we cut out the weaker. The smaller make the stronger grow faster, taller to reach the sun."

Sene was watching Gisonne's face for signs. Of approval? Of agreement? Perhaps only understanding? Gisonne wondered if Sene really cared what she felt.

What had Diana said about emotions? Gisonne said no more. Other things needed to be done.

"Rave loved her . . . its fledge, the one that was killed, Eap. If Eap had lived and remained unmated after the first mating flight, he . . . it, it would have joined the wild, young adults and lived as an outlaw." Gisonne spoke very slowly, loudly, and precisely to Riik. It said something she didn't understand at all and then something else to Sene.

"Yes," Sene said, "that is true."

"Why? Why are they not learning? How will they work or have professions if they return?"

Sene talked to Riik—obviously it didn't understand human language any better than it spoke it—and Riik responded at length.

"They have been trained and schooled before they are adults! Of course!" Gisonne couldn't tell if the shock at her ignorance was Riik's or Sene's own. "Most return."

"And the ones who don't?" Gisonne persisted.

Riik squawked loudly and again there was an interchange between it and Sene.

"Some die or are killed because they lead lives of danger," Sene said. "Those who return are strong and strengthen our world, and they make reparation and are forgiven for their criminal acts."

"But what about those who choose to remain away? What do they do? Who are Dabwa and Lichel?" Gisonne pronounced the names as distinctly as she could and was pleased to see Riik's agitated fluttering.

"Traitors," Riik screeched.

"Traitors," Sene added.

Riik made some kind of speech, not long, not long enough anyway to account for all that Sene seemed to translate and paraphrase. She must have known the story all along and was deferring to Riik. It listened to her in apparant approval—as if it really understood much of what she said.

According to Sene, many, many years ago, Lichel had been a precocious fledgling, not only a rare flyer but an excellent student (some of Sene's terms Gisonne was forced to update in her own mind), a natural research scientist. When it failed to mate on its first mating flight, to the great disappointment of its mentors, it left with the other young adults. Its exploits as a corvilla were the subject of rumors and wonder stories. It was said that it was wounded in a dramatic battle and recovered but could no longer fly. That was no great matter to its family/flock since, except for great athletes, most corvi could make only leaps and ground dashes when they grew into middle age. Everyone awaited its return and its contrition eagerly.

But Lichel never returned to the corvi village/house/flocks.

Dabwa was also from an early time. He had traveled at SPEED for long periods of time even before coming to the corvis. He claimed to have met corvi ancestors on other worlds in the old time when corvis allowed other peoples to know of their existence.

Gisonne hid the wave of agitation that fell over her at this information. She glanced at Diana, saw no response on her face, but then felt a quick pinch on her wrist.

Sene continued: Dabwa lived among the corvi as had a few other human beings before him and many more in later times. He stayed and left to travel at SPEED several times so he is still alive now.

But Dabwa changed during these times of travel and became an enemy of the corvi—especially those who flock around the Rave centers.

An example of his hate was his persuading Lichel to stay an outlaw and remain with him and other renegade corvi and humans.

The form and diction of this explanation convinced Gisonne that it was a familiar, often repeated narrative, probably used by corvi and humans for the teaching of children—more than newcomers. It might serve as a warning to future corvilla.

Before she left, Sene touched Gisonne's shoulder. "Growths," she said. "Only growths."

When it was over and both Riik and Sene were gone, Gisonne felt she had been let out of school.

"Well, what do you think of all that?" she asked Diana, not really expecting much of an answer. She got none. Diana had leaped up and run into her cubicle. And stranger still was the sound that came from there—a thin squawk, a hatchling cry. Gisonne moved quietly to the door.

Diana stood beside her cot, putting food into the gaping beak of the albino infant.

"Oh, pontus, the drowner, you've kidnapped one of their babies!" Gisonne whispered.

"They don't want it," Diana said.

Gisonne believed that there was to be a fete or grand party of some kind. It was hard to tell. First there was preening and public washing and what might have been a visit to a beauty parlor.

And during this preparation, for the first time, Gisonne saw signs of social ranking beyond the literal housing hierarchy or the dominance she had ascribed to personal qualities—Rave's, of course. Two or three corvi—not the help corvilla—arrived with cloths and gems, which they lay before the residents of certain balconies with corvi nods. In the bath cylinder certain corvi allowed others to bathe, rinse and sprinkle them at length.

Gisonne alone followed Rave and its suddenly acquired corvi entourage to the "beauty parlor." There, Rave first, they were all given pedicure/manicures, beak shines, and feather oiling. When Rave eyed Gisonne's hands and hair, and clucked at the corvi "beautician," Gisonne left quickly.

Rave sent for Gisonne often during these times, as if wanting her to see and appreciate or learn, as if Gisonne were a fledgling, a child rather than a social inferior like the other corvi. Sometimes Jarl was told to accompany her, more often not.

Gisonne listened to Rave and its remaining fledge practice their recognition song—over and over. She assumed that the contest, or some form of it, would be held at the upcoming celebrations/ceremony/party. At first Gisonne couldn't distinguish Rave's notes from other parents' call-and-response she heard here and there from the living balconies and training on the roof, but gradually she began to know it and then to hear it in her head. Jarl had explained what he could to her and Diana about the songs' vocabulary meaning. There wasn't much in their terms: "Go. Go. Go. My Parent, I come. Come. Come. Where? Where? Where? I am here. Here. Here." Variations of these were repeated endlessly.

Much more beautiful song with instumentation began to be heard in the Ravel village/house/flock cylinders. In addition to the pet song birds which were always there, large visitors arrived, singing their way in, singing as they descended from the open roof and then rose again into the air, far more gracefully than their hosts, and wheeled high in the open centers of the cylinders, notes flowing out behind them. Animals or persons? Guests or paid performers? Trained slaves? Gisonne didn't know and Jarl didn't understand the question—or pretended he didn't.

The roofs remained open for long periods of time as outside corvi began to arrive, more and more each day. Some were indistinguishable from the Ravel flocks, but other groups were shorter, stockier, and seem to have coarser voices. These were assigned to the lowest balconies.

Nil house/village/flock arrived. From Rave's balcony Gisonne spied Fron, Emil, looking entirely healed, and Sene. And Lonney? Where had she been living? Gisonne realized how much she missed her own "flock"!

There was a huge, poled platform, so large that it formed a balcony extending halfway across one of the cylinders. Corvi from different Ravel families spent time together there often, with much squawking and cawing. Gisonne called it the "picnic table," and Diana said it was a public meeting room or maybe a "parliament" hall. The fact that the corvi ate, drank, and, of course, deficated there in no way signaled its function.

Gisonne headed toward this central meeting place, hoping to find Fron and Emil; as she tried to skirt the crowds of newcomers on the lower levels, she heard loud, cackling, and screeching—the loudest caws and squawking yet.

There a few Ravel corvi, including her Rave, stood almost in a line facing a flock of the short visitors. Their horrid cawing accounted for some of the noise, but it was clear that there was a great dispute going on not only from the loudness of the calls, but the confrontational stances and other body language that Gisonne had learned to read.

When a corvi next to Rave started to squawk, the others on both sides were suddenly quiet. Gisonne recognized Riik. It went on for a while and then was obviously interrupted by a screech/caw from one of the short visitors. There followed an overlapping of many voices on both sides, creating a din so loud that it hurt human ears. Gisonne was frightened that there might be physical violence. Perhaps this big festival was really to be some kind of official battle! How could anyone tell? She was afraid for herself, her crew, and Rave.

As the "debate" continued the participants grew quieter and Gisonne made her way back to her own balcony. She ignored the tiny cheeping coming from Diana's cubicle and found her own cot.

"Ask it what the argument was about," Gisonne said to Jarl.

Jarl said something that Rave seemed not to understand. He tried again and again and scowled at Gisonne as if it were her fault.

"Say, 'Riik,'" Gisonne said.

This time Rave answered.

"Rave said it is about predators. The awds want to exterminate them."

"And the corvi don't?" Gisonne cried. "After what happened to Eap!"

Rave did not wait but began clucking and sounding notes at the same time.

When Jarl could not translate, Gisonne pushed him, not good behavior for a TL but she didn't care.

"The Ravel corvi want to destroy the predators but they don't or can't act against the agreement with . . . the . . . with Dabwa and Lichel."

"They have an agreement with the evil enemy? I don't get it."

"That's the best I can do," Jarl said. "Leave me alone. Learn to talk to it yourself."

"I'll get Sene," Gisonne said.

"Hah, Sene is worse than I am," Jarl said. "I am lazy and inept—an aristocrat, Diana says—but Sene is a liar. She has been here and SPEEDED with them a very long time, and she is female; she belongs to them."

"You insult females? Rave is female."

"You insult Rave, not I."

Rave's head twitched back and forth to watch as each one talked. It squawked something to Jarl and he shook his head.

"Sene!" Gisonne said to Rave, saying the name with the squawk she had heard.

Rave raised its head and called out to someone somewhere. Not long after Sene appeared on the riser and Jarl was dismissed. Rave looked at Gisonne and waited. Gisonne told Sene what they had argued. Sene did not need to ask Gisonne if she would never learn decent behavior; her face said it all.

She said something to Rave, head down apologetically. After a brief but heavy silence, Rave clucked—and clucked.

"It says—" Sene stopped as if she could not bear to go on. "It says you are part of its flock and—"

"Oh, does it—"

"—and it will forgive you. It will answer your questions— things it would not say even to a favorite fledge."

"Oh. She somehow brings back my mother's—"

Sene laughed aloud, clucked innocently to Rave."

Rave burst out in loud staccato squawks. It raised a wing and waved Sene away. When she had gone, it waddled close to Gisonne—who did not back away.

"No eggs," it said.

"Well, is it a hetero or homosexual affair you are having?" Diana asked when Gisonne returned to their balcony.

"What! An affair with . . . ?"

"All right then. An affair of the mind—of the heart. Is it heterosexual or homosexual?"

"I don't know," Gisonne said. "I think it's heterosexual."

For the second time in their life-long acquaintance Diana and Gisonne laughed.

Chapter Twenty-Three

Driving Force

7/8/40

Gisonne assumed the festival/ceremony/celebration/
holiday/war/Olympic contests had not officially begun since
more and more guests kept arriving—among whom were human
beings, some with corvi flocks, some coming in through lower
doors in small bunches by themselves. Gisonne studied them
carefully from a distance, trying to place their original time
periods and home worlds. But because they all wore identical
long black capes and she wasn't close enough to hear them
speak, all she could guess were their subjective ages.

One small group of humans passing below their balcony
ranged from a man of perhaps 90 oe to a teenage girl walking
arm in arm with a young light-haired woman. And the young
woman must be . . . was!

"Lonney!" Gisonne called, leaning far over the railing.

Lonney looked up at that moment though it was impossible
she could have heard with all the corvi ear-breaking din. She
waved and pulled her companion toward the nearest riser. As
they ascended Gisonne identified the girl as the one from the
three human-friendly rooms they had lived in first. Trust Lonney
to have befriended her. Who was whose caretaker now?

As they stepped off the riser, Gisonne heard a small peep
from Diana's cubicle, but Lonney was already crying a greeting
and throwing her arms around her and hadn't noticed. Gisonne
glanced over Lonney's shoulder at the girl's face but saw only
sullen resentment. Just wait till she saw Diana! Bram's
possessiveness all over again?

Then Gisonne realized that Lonney and Diana had not seen
each other since they left the Procne. Interesting.

She was not disappointed. Neither was prepared and it showed. Diana stopped dead in her cubicle entrance and Lonney froze mid-sentence, arms in air.

Gisonne and the girl were almost as still—watching.

Then Diana tossed her head, threw back her cape, strode across the balcony, and put her arms around Lonney. Lonney inhaled audibly and hugged Diana. They held each other for a moment and that was that.

The girl and Lonney sat at the human table with Gisonne and Diana and, like corvi, ate and drank steadily as they talked.

"I ran into Fron . . . somewhere," Lonney said. "This huge place is confusing. Just a while ago. He said he knew how to locate your balcony. But look, I've found you first!"

"So have you and Bram stayed all this time in the human rooms?" Gisonne asked.

"Yes, except for some trips. I saw some farms—I'm fairly sure they were farms. Lots of things were growing and there was weird machinery, like back hoes with beaks instead of blades and spades. And there was a sea—"

"A lake," the girl said. Her accent was less difficult either because Gisonne had grown used to early Octente or it had changed with Lonney's constant company.

"—with fish, live fish, all kinds, big and little. And in another water place there were shell fish. The corvi caught tons of them in huge scoops, scoops shaped like beaks. And all the time they worked they ate."

A beautiful, glowing, brown human face appeared, followed by the whole, very erect body, rising toward them on the lift. Emil! And behind him was Fron.

They were all on the flight roof, Gisonne, Diana, Lonney, Fron, and Emil. The girl was no longer with them. She had disappeared, unfortunately not soon enough for them to talk openly or to hear some private news Emil promised in a whisper. But there would be time.

There were so many corvi that Gisonne feared for the cylinder. Fron, of course, had learned all about corvi construction methods and materials and assured her it would take a lot more weight to collapse it. He also started to explain to all of them about flocking and the contests and exercises they might witness.

"Collectives," he said. "What it shows is what I've suspected all along. While they have evolved abstract intelligence, unlike humans they retained some or all of their 'instinctual' behaviors. This flocking is an example of complex, collective instinctual, behavior, 'inherent knowledge."

"I don't think so," Gisonne said.

Even in the open air the corvi noise was overwhelming. Bunches, not groups or flocks, gathered, dissolved, tightened, grew, or simply split. There were two types, the short guests and the familiar tall corvi, some gathered separately, others politely "mingling." Individuals of both types were drawn, magnetically, to larger groups, which achieving some unspecified number, broke apart into two, three, and four small bunches, and they, in turn, sucked in dyads, singles, and grew and grew until again reaching a critical mass. In a flash, Gisonne saw the "party" in the huge hall of Allaincroft, the knots and clots of persons—natives, off-worlders, Nords, Arines, central family members, outsiders, adults, children, Allains, Michalises, motion, the fluid masses, the individuals drawn and repelled.

But beyond the corvi audience, nearer to the takeoff platform were the athletes—flyers in perfect formation. Perfection. Pattern: "ready," "get set," but not yet "go."

Fron was again explaining. "Instinct takes over. The individual gives up reason and becomes an element in a larger unit. Only one corvi—the leader—retains control but in it, too, instinct—"

"No," Gisonne said, turning to Fron's blank Nord face. The rust tunic under the ubiquitous black cape suited him, as if corvi helpers knew what they were doing.

"There is no other possibility," he said. "Such 'complex collective behavior' as flocking demands an equally complex mechanism—"

"Like optimally functioning dynes?" Gisonne asked.

"Of course not!"

"And what about your theory of two kinds or a subspecies of corvi? Have you found more evidence?"

A sudden blare of an instrument—Gisonne would be hard pressed to call it musical—"played" by a large green guest with a manacled hand/foot vanquished all other sound and was followed by bird song, real music, as clouds of tiny yellow warblers were loosed into the air.

The demonstration/performance/sporting event/air ballet/ game or contest that followed was marvelous and beautiful to any intelligent species with vision. It was hard to imagine Fron was not right. Such synchronicity, deceptive spontaneity, and rythm must be orchestrated. Fifty corvi flew forward, turned, reversed, always shifting pattern at the same time. Gisonne tried to keep the corvi at the vee point, the vertex, in sight but it was impossible. But again impossible that the same corvi could still lead when the vee became a straight line flying in another direction and then an X, a Y and suddenly a circle.

Amazingly the flock formed three dimensional geometric forms, a diamond, a cube, a sphere and the figure kept moving and changing direction without pause. And finally the sphere began to spin and it rolled across the sky above them.

"And I called them ugly," Gisonne said.

"We have to get out of here," Emil said.

"I know," Gisonne said. "Sometime. We aren't prepared yet. We need—"

"Information, more information," Fron said. "There is no way we can manage now."

"They have the edel," Emil said.

They were back again, home, Diana and Gisonne's balcony. Diana stood in the entrance to her cubicle. Lonney had removed her cape and looked naked in her yellow tunic—like a pet animal without its collar. Fron and Gisonne sat again at the human table and Emil stood, back to the railing, more an eminence than he had ever been, even as family center on z2.

"Wait," Gisonne said. "What do you mean 'have'? The edel is in orbit. They do communicate with it. I talked to it briefly myself."

Lonney cried out excitedly, Fron looked skeptical, and Emil simply shook his head.

"Not in orbit," he said. "Not any more anyway. It's been brought down."

"Where?"

"How do you know?"

"Is edel all right?"

"No. Much of it is non-functional, they say. Some parts were destroyed by their not knowing how to move it and more because of us! Supposedly we abused the systems. The OS itself caused some of the harm. To itself!"

"I have no such knowledge and I've been with you in the Nil village/house/flock." Fron scowled.

"Is Calib there?"

"What corvi flock has them?"

Emil answered only the last: "Nil, under Ravel."

"Where?"

"I don't know. But there is more. When you hear you will have to agree. We have to get out. Right away."

"I have to leave," Diana said.

"But no one is a prisoner here—or seems to be," Lonney said. "Sene says her life is far better than it was on Styxx. And Gape too—"

"Not here!" The solemn, supportive lieutenant Emil was shouting. "At SPEED. Yes, at SPEED again. Some distant destination of their own devising for their own purposes. We are to be prisoners again. Soon. Right after this affair—maybe as part of it."

The others were finally silenced.

"How did you learn this?" Gisonne asked finally.

"Listening. Not Sene. She's too careful. Other guides. I make no show of understanding either language."

"No," Fron said. "You must have misunderstood. It contradicts other information. We know that mariners have come and gone from here for centuries."

"Voluntarily?"

"Look," Fron went on, "I too have learned some of the language, and I'm becoming familiar with the politics. These . . . people are civilized, relatively benign. We will be able to deal with them eventually. And most of all we need the help of their technologists—the ones who are studying our OS in order to—"

"To find out how they could have controlled the Procne's OS when we couldn't?" Emil asked—like Calib.

"They may not be either," Gisonne said. "The edel has been controlling itself. But Emil may be right." She told them all she had gathered from Jarl, Sene, and Riik—and some very old OMB records back on z2.

"Are the corvi a monolithic political organization? Planet-wide?" Gisonne directed the question to Fron to restore him his role.

"Yes," he said. "No other group or nation is ever mentioned."

Gisonne was sure he was right. The shorter awds were disgruntled social inferiors, not a separate organization.

"Except the renegade corvilla," she said. "With Lichel and Dubwa. We have to get to them—eventually. But right now let's get out of here."

The plan was simple: kidnap one of the human guides and steal one of the human-adapted vans parked among the many ground vehicles outside the first Ravel cylinder and go. Sene was too clever so the guide had to be Jarl. He was fairly ignorant and might be less helpful, but Diana could control him. It was up to her to lead him to the van.

Jarl had already said there would soon be another grand air competition that day. They stuffed food and other goods under their capes and waited for the mass movement of corvi to the roofs. Diana paraded about openly, as she often had, with Jarl, while the rest milled about where crowds were thickest.

Time out was over, Gisonne told herself. It was time to act, to be TL again, without the emotional weakness Diana had accused her of.

But while they waited for the right moment, she had something to do. It would be unremarked since she had done it so often before.

She moved along the wall to the rise and ascended to Rave's platform. Rave, her Rave, was alone, studying some kind of shiny metal jewelry—choosing which to wear to the event, Gisonne guessed. Its followers must have retired to their own balconies for the same purpose.

Gisonne gave the quick corvi nod when Rave looked around and it nodded in return. They looked at each other, two eyes to one eye. There was no guide to translate.

Gisonne sang: "I am here. Here. Here."

Rave stared; its feathers ruffled. Then it responded: "Where? Where? Where?"

"Here. Here. Here."

"Fledgling, come. Come. Come."

And then without planning it, Gisonne changed the order.

"I go. Go. Go." She looked up then at the roof: "MY parent. My parent. Parent." Without looking back at Rave she walked over the familiar poles to the riser and descended.

Emil took Jarl's elbows from behind and hoisted him into the van in one movement. Gisonne was in the driver's seat, feet testing the treadle function, one hand on the steering stick. She had watched Sene as closely as possible but one rarely drove any kind of vehicle on z2. In a way that might help. There was nothing to unlearn.

Fron, of course, was next to her, carefully examining the controls, and the others had propped themselves against the sides of the open flat bed, feet wedged for balance on the poles of the flooring. Emil plopped Jarl down in the same position between him and Diana. Jarl looked at Diana, back to Emil. He said nothing. He didn't get it.

There were small aircraft weaving about overhead, perhaps in complimentary imitation of the personal flying to follow but these soon disappeared as they always did when the show began.

The crowd noises too stopped, leaving a strange silence in the strange green afternoon light.

And Gisonne started the strange machine. It didn't lurch but leaped forward, scraped another vehicle, raced off the bare parking area, lifted and flew just above the tall grasses, aimed at the cliff edge. Gisonne stopped it on time but with an explosive noise, loud enough certainly to be heard on the cylinder roof.

They waited, hushed, too visible out in the open on a sunny afternoon. A weak cheeping broke the silence. Diana had brought the hatchling! It stopped and there was nothing. Gisonne thought she heard, very faintly, the recognition songs but perhaps it was a trick of memory.

They all stirred then. Gisonne figured out reverse. Diana explained to Jarl that Rave wanted Gisonne to learn the land vehicle as Sene had. Fron figured out and carefully explained the steering stick. Lonney asked Emil if he thought the corvi would harm edel.

Finally Gisonne drove the van away along the road that followed the edge of the ravine. It didn't matter where they were going, only to get far enough away from the corvi village/flock/houses before they were missed. Or perhaps distance was not as important as terrain. They had to find hiding places—places where they would not be spotted by keen corvi eyes searching from above. For Gisonne had to stay on the road in order not to leave tell-tale tracks.

"Where does this road go?" they asked Jarl. He had no answer.

"Well, how do we find the thickest covering?"

"The forest," he said.

Gisonne felt a faint panic. There were trees here and there on the shallow soil of z2's rock islands but nothing that could be called a forest. And here they had seen miles of forest but only from above. How would it be to be under all that folliage? A new kind of claustrophobia—like estuary—like tales of drowning beneath the weight of pontus' ocean—but better than locked alive again in a coffin buried in infinite, empty space.

So keep going. It had seemed from the cylinder roofs that forests covered the planet in almost every direction. Surely chances were that this road led to one.

Except for certain kinds of workers and farm hands, corvi rarely used ground roads. Life was lived on high. At home treetop bridges crossed ravines and connected village/houses, and they traveled any distance away in aircraft. Roads to corvi were only ostrich paths, a source of certain kinds of food, a place under the world.

Gisonne had the awful fantasy that the planet's surface, especially in the valleys, was to corvi what the ocean bottom was to humans, especially Zalterians—cold hell, the horrid domain ruled by Pontus.

But the road was everthing to this chartless, guideless group and when it disappeared they were lost.

"We came this way to the farms," Lonney said.

"But there's no road," Fron said.

"It just doesn't show right here."

"But how can anyone, even corvi workers, know where—"

"Corvis are usually dropped into places, like farms and ponds," Jarl said. "They don't crawl around in the weeds and mud like grubs. Turn around now. We've been away long enough."

They continued on, and the road appeared again and disappeared again. When it seemed to fork, they bore left because Lonney was sure the right led to the huge farm complex she had been shown. Sometimes it was so rough that the risers came on. And gradually the incline grew steeper and the road curved more and more sharply as it wove its way down the cliff or mountain side.

Fron pointed out how very high the plateau really was. The Ravel, Nil and several other village/house/flocks were cities in the air. Gisonne only cared that they would reach bottom before dark.

After suggesting once or twice that they go back, Jarl remained passive. Was he so accustomed to obeying that it had become automatic? Was he in love with Diana? Was he slow enough to still believe that both Gisonne and Fron were learning to drive?

When Fron and Gisonne changed seats, Jarl made no comment.

The road forked several times but they always picked the one that continued downward. It was difficult to guess how deep the valley was because of the constant twisting. Sometimes it felt like they had gone around 360 degrees and would be climbing, but it never happened.

It grew darker as they went on and down; the trees were so close together that there was hardly a road at all, and the leaves intwined overhead. But dense as it was, the shadows were dark green and it was still day.

They planned to leave the road before real dark swallowed them without warning, as it did on this planet. Once they were missed, every road would be traced from above—easily in the day, perhaps electronically by spotlight or some kind of sonar or radar at night.

Fron turned off into one of the few places that the van could fit between the trees, but very shortly the opening narrowed and began to disappear. The only choice was a sharp right and suddenly the van plunged downward at a terrifying angle. Those in back clung to the railing, Diana almost strangling the hatchling, Emil trying to hold onto all of them.

And then the van plowed into a thick underbrush edging a stream and came to a dead stop. Dead silence was followed immediately by dead dark.

Chapter Twenty-Four

Local Interactions

7/10/40

Emil kept the first watch. The others slept beside the van, glad of their capes. Diana wrapped herself loosely around the hatchling; Lonney lay next to her and Jarl on her other side. Gisonne and Fron, who had stayed awake longest talking and trying to plan, fell asleep side-by-side a small distance away.

Gisonne woke later—hearing things. No birds sang in the dark. And there were none of the anonymous hums or metalic echos of the Procne, nor the howling winds and crashing waves of z2. For the first time in her life Gisonne was listening to small animal life in the brush around them. Rustling. Tiny cries. Hoots. Skittering.

Gisonne awoke the second time in a green wash of light. She stared up at the leaves and felt something good, something she couldn't identify at first. Freedom. She was not locked in something. The trees were not at all oppressive as she had feared. They were tall, stately and protective.

But not protective enough. As the fugitives began to move and stretch sore muscles, shadows passed over them, quickly one after another, traveling in different directions. Things were passing between the trees tops and the sun. The quiet corvi aircraft were already searching.

For two short days and nights they waited. They ate all the food they had brought and drank water from the stream whose lip had stopped the van. And when the air search seemed to have stopped, they waited another night and half a day.

Without risers the van could not have been moved. Once Fron had backed it up onto more level ground, he just managed to turn it around and the others climbed in. They had left so many gouges and broken branches that it was easy to follow their tracks back to the road.

Those in the back strained to watch the sky—even on the road leaves almost met overhead—and listened for the nearly soundless aircraft. After several hours Gisonne and Fron changed places.

Lonney heard the sound first and then they all did. It was a machine hum, on the surface somewhere behind them. Gisonne tried to accelerate but it was difficult with all the twists and turns. The sound grew louder. Obviously the other vehicle was not having as much trouble—or had a more experienced driver.

There were no forks, no side clearings. On one sharp turn, the van veered off the road and Gisonne just avoided smashing into a tree. She had to slow down.

And at that moment they heard additional sounds, the distant faint murmur of aircraft.

"When I stop the van, jump out fast. And run," Gisonne said.

"But what about you?" Lonney asked.

"I'll be right behind you. First I'll pull off the road as close to the trees as I can. Get off. Hurry."

A second later Fron jumped out on his side and after Gisonne heard the others landing on the ground behind him, she jerked the van into motion. But she didn't pull over—not then. She drove straight ahead, fast, leaving the others shouting after her, and kept going until she heard the other ground vehicle getting closer. That meant the others hadn't been seen. It must have gone right by them.

Gisonne pulled the steering stick hard to the right, the van swerved off the road and scrunched its side against the trees. Before it came to a dead stop, she was out and running, first straight ahead on the road and then off, this time to the left, and into the woods.

And someone was running behind her! After her!

But it was human feet and then a voice calling: "Gisonne!" Emil.

He caught up with her and they ran along together until the trees and underbrush were too thick. Then he took the lead, protecting her from ruts and branches. And she was very glad and called him lieutenant.

They slowed after a while and made their way more carefully, trying to avoid leaving tracks. And recalling old off-world vids, they changed direction several times and walked in a stream. Gisonne could only hope they had covered a great distance. Two Zalterians, who had never seen a forest before and whose only hiking had been up and down rocky, naked mountain sides, were unlikely woodsmen.

Luckily they were as tired as they were hungry and fell asleep as soon as they found a small grassed spot surrounded by underbrush.

In the morning light, Gisonne looked at Emil's sleeping face thinking how beautiful he was. The leaf-filtered sun warmed his brown skin to gold. His expression was serene, as soft and peaceful as a child's safe in his bed. It would be wonderful to be attracted to and wanted by a person like him. Yet she was relieved that it was impossible.

Then she remembered that he had ignored her order to jump out of the van. She should be angry with him but thanked pontus instead.

"Fish," he said, eyes still closed.

"Oh—but how? I don't—"

"I do," he said and his eyes snapped open. "On Double Neff we grew fish, caught fish, cooked fish, and ate fish."

"The smoke?"

"I can make a fire so that no smoke appears above the trees. We Double Neff groups outdid you High Garda lumps at everything. Let's just hope there are fish in that stream."

There were and they were delicious.

How long can one live in a forest—in a temperate climate—with a comfortable companion—eating fish and fruit? A lifetime. And a better life it would be than in the Procne or some corvi ship.

Gisonne and Emil talked about it, or rather joked about it. It was never a real possibility, not because the "predators" out there might enjoy human beings, as well as young corvi, for lunch, and not because both corvi and corvilla would proabably hunt them down, for different unspeakable purposes, but because there were things they'd rather do and things they ought to do.

Emil believed that the corvilla who flocked with Lichel stayed somewhere north of the central corvi lands. They had been travelling generally northward on the van. Fron surely knew that too and would—if he had not been caught—head north.

Gisonne and Emil followed the stream as long as it too headed north, which it did for several days, until Gisonne actually grew bored with the two kinds of fish it provided.

On the second day they felt the chill of the shadows of aircraft, none on the third day. On the fourth when the stream insisted on east and they continued north, the number of aircraft so increased that they could hear the sounds quite clearly.

That same day they crossed a road, which seemed to run east west. On its northern side the forest was less dense and a few miles farther rather sparse and later just about gone, replaced by a very large field with plantings in ordered lines. Gisonne recognized it as a giant version of the tiny vegetable gardens planted on terraces on z2.

They skirted the large rectangle, keeping close to the trees and bushes. Suddenly Gisonne saw something odd beyond the trees, something unnatural—square. It was a human-type building, a cube not a cylinder, and its entrance was on ground level.

"Good day."

Two men stood against the closest tree trunk, only a few feet away.

"Do you mean to stop?" the speaker, the younger man, added before either Gisonne or Emil could recover. His dialect was Stycian Octente.

"Do you . . . is this your place?"

"When I'm here it is," he laughed, "and it belongs to my grandson here when I'm not—unless he's not either." The two of them burst into laughter. Gisonne smiled with them though she didn't get the joke, unless it was that the grandson was at least fifty years older than the grandfather.

Both men wore the ubiquitous, voluminous black capes, the older—the grandson—had a patch over his right eye and a heavy scar on his left temple.

Gisonne and Emil accepted their invitation and followed them back to the house where they were made comfortable and fed as if they were guests in any relatively peaceful and stable human world. Until that moment Gisonne had not realized that there was such a thing as a human smell and a very good smell it was.

And later the grandfather talked with them while the old grandson looked on. Gisonne was delighted that at last a human being on this world was willing and able to hold a normal conversation.

They offered a liquid drug that Gisonne had never heard of—a Malaacan favorite, the grandfather said, that his widow had learned to make from plants. One of his widows. A few sips, a full stomach, not fish, a human physical environment, and Gisonne sat back to enjoy prying. And first, before saying anything about her crew's predicament, they had to find out their hosts' relationship to corvi, Ravel-centered corvi.

"You live far away from the Ravel centers, their village/house/flocks," she said.

"Not so far," the grandfather said.

Oh, oh, she thought.

"You are . . . connected to their flocks?"

"Speak slowly, please," he said. "My grandson's surgery slows understanding of words. He follows but he has to concentrate. It is difficult for him and he wants to hear your thoughts very much."

"Was he ill? I'm so sorry."

"No. No. You understand. It was the surgery to pilot. He was an excellent pilot. The surgery is easier now. The parts grow together quickly. One or two oe years."

Gisonne could think of no questions; you had to have something to begin with. And she was afraid to let him know her ignorance. Let him assume she and Emil were part of it all.

"And you?" she asked very, very slowly. "Your youth must be a story of great travels. Do you have wonder stories for us? Our friends Gape and Bram—"

Both men grinned. Gisonne had done exactly right.

"I flocked with Gape twice. And my grandson SPEEDED with Gape back and forth to Agnese. Time stuff that Rave was running—well, Rave's great grandfather it was then! And a human named Bram was there, on Agnese, between Octente missions for a couple of years."

"Wait, your grandson was a pilot—with corvi?" Emil did not see the need for caution.

"You can see he was," the young man said.

"And he navigated corvi space craft?"

The man seemed puzzled. "Of course. There is nothing wrong with my grandson! Why do you question his ability? He was much younger then—in his own life time."

Gisonne glanced a warning at Emil.

"We haven't been here as long as you," she said. "The Ravel corvi are training us now. We have been sent on this . . . this trek to learn—" Gisonne wondered if this were a preposterous explanation.

"You must have been chosen for flocking."

"But," Gisonne ad libbed, "I am afraid I won't be good enough."

"Once you have had the surgery—"

"They'll dissect our brains?" Emil asked.

"They don't dissect us! Unless we're dead, of course. Why did you leave Agnese?"

Gisonne sensed that she and Emil had gone too far. Certainly these people were in communication with the Ravel corvi.

"We are tired and somewhat confused," she said. "We believe we are close to corvilla territory but do not know. We thought that perhaps you—"

"No—this is corvi land! The whole world is corvi. The renegades steal territory, but it is temporary. Just be wary north of here."

"I'm afraid they'll smell us out," Gisonne said, smiling in case it should be a joke.

The grandfather laughed. "You know they have almost no sense of smell. But, seriously, remember all the lessons corvi taught. Their offspring can be ruthless. You must be cautious. Stealing you would be a fine crime for corvilla. And worse— they are young—one might look down at you with the left eye. Keep your capes always wrapped, especially when you travel on the ground."

Gisonne and Emil did not need the warning. Emil had his scars. They asked nothing else, thanked the men, praised Rave and Rave's flocks, and accepted amazingly comfortable beds.

In morning sunlight Emil and Gisonne left the human farm house and started across its "yard," the small partially-planted field, which fronted it.

Suddenly a blot of shadow flew over them and then another, and another until all became one. A small corvi air vehicle and individual corvi dropped from the air all around and they were trapped.

The last thing Gisonne saw before the door of the vehicle slid shut was the staring faces of the grandfather and grandson. Expressionless. Somehow that fact seemed important.

Right now she had to concentrate on her stomach, victim of instant odor and motion assault. The craft ascended vertically. It obviously was like the z2 island hoppers in function but entirely different in construction and operation. It had flapping wings with a shielded platform, just large enough for a corvi pilot, protruding like a head and beak from between them. The rest, engine casing and small goods and/or passenger cabin—no more than an enclosed poled platform—hung, and swung, below.

We're birds in a cage, prisoners again, Gisonne thought. Emil took her arm and, when her stomach let her, she turned her head.

"Perhaps they are corvilla," he said.

Yes, and if they were prisoners of the corvilla, they were being given fast transport to their destination! If these corvilla looked at them with only the right eye, if they were not already the objects of some great "criminal" act designed to horrify corvi parents, if they could meet this Dabwa right away, and if Dabwa were just mildly and not criminally insane.

Emil lay on his stomach squinting between the nasty poles at the ground.

"We're flying south," he said.

Their captors must be corvi and not corvilla.

The landing was gentler than the takeoff. It had to be if the baggage was not to be crushed. Gisonne edged through the door before a corvi could reach for her. She was prepared to be back on the plateau, perhaps on one of the landing roofs. But instead they were in a forest again, in a clearing. There were small cylinders in a straight line, like attached bungalows on some of the lower reaches of Nord islands.

The corvi led Gisonne and Emil to the roof of one of the squat, round structures and lowered them in on a riser. The roof swung shut and locked. The place had been designed neither as a prison nor a human habitat. There were the usual incidental windows in the walls. The floor was roled; the facilities minimal; water and corvi dry food plentiful.

"Are you sure we were traveling south?" Gisonne asked.

Emil nodded.

"But why this stopover? We surely couldn't have traveled far in the van or on foot. We'd have to be there already."

"If they're taking us back there," Emil said.

"Also most of them were flying by themselves. That's why we thought they were corvilla."

Gisonne knew the answer herself. Highly trained, athletic corvi could fly. These could be police or soldiers or worse— Ravel assassins.

Emil and Gisonne moved along the walls, nervously peering through windows at trees and more trees. Only one window gave a view of the raised courtyard/landing field but there was nothing to see there but the hopper that had brought them in and a corvi on a high watch station near it.

It was back to wait and see.

But not an hour later Gisonne saw another hopper land.

"Emil," she called, "they have three—no two—of them! And Jarl."

Jarl, Diana clutching her cloak against her chest, and Lonney climbed out and down from the cabin as the corvi pilot flew out of the "cockpit" and dropped to the ground. Another corvi waddled gracelessly across the open yard and the lookout dropped down and followed them all back toward the cylinders.

It seemed to Gisonne through the window that Jarl was talking at the corvi but they appeared to be paying no attention. Soon after, the roof opened and the three humans were lowered to the floor.

"Well, so much for this escape," Emil said.

"They caught Jarl right away and me second," Lonney said later. "We waited a long time while they searched for Diana and Fron. They discovered her just before dark. She had been close by the whole time; I knew exactly where she was—lying dead still next to a log wrapped up together with her little corvi in her cape." Lonney looked at Diana with admiration. "Then they stopped looking for Fron until morning. They only gave up in late afternoon and flew us here."

"Jarl, these are corvi, aren't they?" Gisonne asked.

Jarl looked like a prince who had become a pauper. Like Lonney he was disheveled and his clothes were torn and dusty. Only Diana was her immaculate self.

"Corvi?" he said. "Ravel corvi? Yes, but they won't listen to me. They don't live home much. They don't know me. When we get back—"

"What have they been saying?" Emil asked. "What will Rave do with us now?"

Jarl looked at Emil blankly. "They aren't saying anything about you. They're doing their work."

They sat around the edges of the room in silence. Since it was rarely occupied this cylinder didn't smell as bad as the Ravel village/house, but after the forest and the human dwelling it was newly unpleasant—and miserably uncomfortable: because of the completely poled floor, they had to sit up all night leaning against the wall.

It was still dark when the roof swung half way open. No lights came on. They could barely see the corvi that flew down and barely heard the lift being lowered at the same time. It stared only at Gisonne and Diana who happened to be sitting side by side, its eye reflecting faint light from the window behind them. Gisonne could not tell which eye it was—right or left.

It squawked—suddenly but almost soundlessly.

"Jarl, what does it want?" In her effort not to scream Gisonne whispered hoarsly.

There was no answer from the dark.

The corvi squawked again. Louder. It had moved closer; the eye was larger.

"Stop!" Emil shouted then. Gisonne could hear him struggling over the poles toward her. "Tell it to stop, Jarl. What does it want?"

Jarl blurted something unintelligible. He sounded terrified.

It moved even closer and clucked rapidly. Gisonne could smell it.

"It wants you," Jarl said, whispering but clearly this time. Jarl certainly believed it was a corvilla. "Go with it before it attacks us all."

"No, Gisonne, no," Emil shouted. He too was closer. Whether corvilla or corvi, Gisonne believed it would hurt Emil if he interfered. She rose to her feet and teetered dangerously on one of the cross poles. She realized then that she had pulled Diana up with her. They had been squeezing hands. The hatchling gave a little cry.

Gisonne tried to let go of Diana, to push her back, but Diana held on. She would go with Gisonne.

When Emil called to her again, Gisonne hurried to the lift platform, Diana stumbling along. They were raised above his reach, before Emil got to them.

The corvi flew to the roof and half pushed them with a foot/hand and a wing into a hopper cabin.

Chapter Twenty-Five

Dyad

7/19/40

It was broad daylight when the hopper dropped down in the center of a narrow road in the midst of dense forest. Gisonne, watching between poles as Emil had done, was sure they had been flying north.

The door slid open, and Diana and Gisonne climbed out to find two corvi standing close together, "muttering." Gisonne thought the larger was the one that had snatched them, especially since the smaller jerked its head quickly when they appeared, turned its right eye upon them, and stared for too long.

Almost immediately the larger leaped back up into the cockpit. Diana and Gisonne jumped out of the way as the hopper rose. The other corvi—corvilla, Gisonne was sure this time—stayed where it was, watching the hopper until it disappeared over the trees to the south. They saw then that it wore a patch on its left eye.

A few minutes later it turned its back to them and flew slowly, low, and straight, up the road. Without discussion Gisonne and Diana followed. It stopped several times to look back and wait until they caught up. The last time it stopped the dense woods on the side seemed to part and three more corvilla came out onto the road pulling and pushing another hopper.

Gisonne and Diana climbed into the cabin—on their own this time. They arrived at the corvilla city, home of Dabwa and Lichel, before nightfall.

"The most important thing, Louis Dubois said, "is the eyes—two directions, two views, views that do not overlap.

"They also hear from the two sides of the head but in a narrower range and it makes much less difference. And, of course, the senses of taste and smell are relatively weak."

The last information explained much about corvi living conditions. Gisonne nodded and waited for Dubois to go on. He smiled at her and then Diana, as if inviting questions and comments. In spite of his bald head, eye patch, scarred and wrinkled face, and bent body, Gisonne could still recognize the famous Professor Louis Dubois from early holos in the archives.

"It's smells better here," Diana said, looking up from smoothing the white down of the hatchling. It stood on one foot/hand on her right knee and watched Dubois with its left eye.

"Yes," he said, "I do insist on certain compromises. Please turn the infant the other way."

Gisonne was impatient with the interruptions. Were they prisoners or guests? The several human beings who greeted and cared for them had been polite and even talkative but had given no real information. They had been fed—food that had some taste—shown to large, humanly-enclosed rooms with separate cleansing cubicles of their own, and after a rest period, given fresh tunics and capes. And now, when finally they had been presented to the "Man" himself in his own apartments, he lectured on corvi physiology and ignored the vital question: could he and would he help them get off Parliament?

"Our SPEED ship," Gisonne began, "It has been brought down—"

Dubois smiled again but raised his hand to stop her.

"But do you know what has happened to Calib Lendari and . . . the ship's OS?"

"In time," he said. "I have friends—connections— among the Ravel corvi. I'll give you any information I get. Now corvi vision is—"

"What will they do to our shipmates?" Gisonne persisted."

"Do? In what sense?"

"Punishment? Or . . . send them out somewhere at SPEED before we have a chance to—"

"They are not criminals. And traveling is not considered a punishment but a favor, time travel, a kind of immortality. I'll let you know but let's get back to the subject.

"There are other differences in vision between humans and corvi than just the corvi's opposing points of view. The part of their brains for vision and balance are much larger in proportion than ours. Their eyes are sharper, far keener than ours, and focus more quickly. Distant objects have larger images on their retinas than on ours. And, because they are monocular and also can't move their eyeballs, they must turn their heads when—"

"Squawk," said the hatchling and turned and tilted its head in a single jerk to look up at Diana. Gisonne had to smile—with Dubois.

"And they need the balance to stand and tread on one hand/foot so that the other is free as well as—" he continued.

"But it seems these are only physiological differences," she said. "In intelligence, logic—"

"Do you believe that the nature of 'thinking' can be free of its organic base. There can never be such a thing as pure mind."

The words were like a sudden blow to the stomach. Trjol and his pontus-spewed theories! But Gisonne knew the underlying meaning here was entirely different and paid attention—as she had unfortunately not done back on z2.

"Corvi see in opposite directions simultaneously. So for them 'reality' has different divisions, different approaches, different speeds since preception and apprehension occur with different timing from ours. The object itself is different. The very experience of living differs."

Edel! Gisonne thought of its two "eyes." Opposite views— SPEED space ahead and ship interior behind.

"Their minds," Dubois was going on, "like primate, grew on a particular organic structure—intelligence in striatal areas— and that earlier structure determined the mind's shape. So even after they developed a neocortex and abstract intelligence increased, grew more and more abstract, their way of 'seeing,' the thinking, kept its original paradigm.

"The double vision and the corvi brain, the organic brain are the same! Yes, the brain is double, split into two hemispheres like ours—but more so. But here is the astounding difference: the hemispheres have almost no communication, no corpus callosum."

It had to be nonsense, this theory, Gisonne thought. No intelligent being could live with two minds. Yet it explained so much. Both the corvi and the edel. But she was determined to say nothing about the edel to this man—not yet.

"You are saying," she asked, "that there are two great, separate humps of intelligence? I mean are they duplicates? A repetition of the same material?"

"I don't know. Some of it probably. We—they and I—know that the two parts are far more differentiated than ours in function. For example, in us the language center is located mainly in the left hemisphere, but there are pockets of language in other places all over the brain, especially in females. In corvi the language center is only in the left hemisphere. Space, art, vision, the internal visual or graphic representation of an external object is right brain only. That is why they are careful to look at you with the right eye only—otherwise you are grub. Dinner."

"When we were taken by corvilla—your people! . . . " Gisonne started to say.

Dubois nodded corvi-fashion politely but did not explain or apologize.

" . . . one attacked us. Did it think we were . . . grub?"

There was a hum from above and a section of Dubois' ceiling swung open. A large corvi with a patch on its left eye dropped down to the solid human floor rather awkwardly and made a show of straightening itself and shaking its wings smooth. It reminded Gisonne of Riik; both corvi were unusually old.

"The left eye saw featherless, fleshy, live material crawling on the ground. Food," Dubois went on paying no attention to the newcomer. "Then when you opened your mouths and squawked you were nestlings and the others came to your rescue."

"But," said the corvi, waddling slowly across the room, "most of your rescuers were sensible corvilla who were careful to look at you only with the right eye and knew exactly what and who you were and were doing their jobs—bringing you to us. It was they—brilliant young ones—who diverted one of the Ravel corvi landing crafts."

"Lichel," said Dubois, "may I present our guests, Diana and Gisonne of the Arine Archipelago of Zalterius II."

Lichel nodded with more energy than mere politeness demanded.

"You speak human language perfectly!" Gisonne said.

"But, alas, not easily," Lichel said, "and I must admit to some enabling surgery. And I hear that Gisonne has learned song."

"You . . . you know this? How can . . . who—"

"Rave," Dubois said.

"When? How? My Rave?" Gisonne did not say Rave was supposed to be their prime enemy but they understood.

"How do you think you were rescued from the Ravel corvi and brought here?" Dubois said. "It was Rave who managed your escape."

"But it was Rave, the Ravel, who arrested us! It rescued us from itself?"

"It wants you to go home to your parent," Lichel said.

Fron had made his own way north and almost reached the stronghold before the corvilla discovered him. Gisonne was very proud.

It was a pleasure to give information to Fron for a change. She succumbed to temptation and drew everything she had learned out slowly and dramatically as they sat over their fifth human meal of the day; one adopted some alien habits more easily than others.

"And the cloaks the human beings all wear," Gisonne said, "are a kind of illusion. They trick the left eye. We look more like them, less edible."

"But I had thought it was an embarrassing example of the inferior imitating the superior, the prisoner dressing like and imitating the behaviors of the guards," Fron said as he tossed his head back and dropped a nugget of food into his mouth. "There is a long history of such—"

"They are proud to identify with the strong and beautiful," Diana said and that closed that part of the discussion.

"The double brain is interesting, fascinating. I have to learn more. It affects my theory of the two types of corvi; there are two types but two in one—one organism."

"Well, not quite two types but two minds. "

"But two types of minds, ways of perceiving, and . . . you know the two completely different communication systems we encountered? One for each hemisphere.

"But first how does any of this affect us?"

"I don't know. It may not at all. I tried to get them to talk about plans but Dubois refused."

"He said later," Diana said. "He's right. We can't go if you don't understand these things first."

"How do you know that?"

"It was obvious."

"Then do you understand the connection?"

"It's irrelevant for me to understand any of it."

Two of their human hosts gave Fron and Gisonne a tour of the corvilla city—really more strings of connected structures but including blocks as well as domless rotunda. A guide pointed out the "heavy" fortifications—electric fields above each roof. What good would that do against any type of weapon?

The guide frowned. Weapons? The question made no sense. Who would use a weapon against corvilla?

The land around was beautiful. The settlement lay—almost sprawled—along the gentle slopes of a foothill. Beyond and high above was a snow-covered moutain. In the opposite direction the land flattened gradually until it met a sea. Gisonne was certain she could see and hear the water though the guides said it was impossible. Later Lichel promised they would be flown to the shore.

They sauntered along the beach, Gisonne, Fron, Diana and the hatchling—sometimes walking on its own, Lichel, and two other corvi. Obviously Lichel wasn't the only "traitor."

Gisonne was delighted and heart-pained by the sight and sound of the ocean. The horizon was more distant, the waves less wild, and the shore breezes softer than on z2, but it called up longing and memory.

"In the right side of my brain," Gisonne said to Fron.

"Yours is a smaller, denser planet," Lichel said. "Almost as beautiful as this but so rough and wild. Those winds!"

"You've been there?" Gisonne asked. She sensed Fron's ears sharpen next to her. They all stopped and watched a skein of geese.

"More than once," Lichel said.

"Why is there no report of it? When?" Gisonne instantly suspected the OMB of withholding.

"Centuries ago and again more recently. Corvi avoid publicity."

"Diana, do you . . . do your people know of these 'secret' visits?"

"No," Diana said. "Of course, there are always stories. And the bas relief and drawings in our house."

"Yes," Fron said, "legends. History or myth? The giant birds of early Nord scupture? Ancient paintings in your Arine galleries."

"There was a time," Lichel said, "long ago, a thousand years before my time that our cultures and technologies borrowed from each other."

"I know that," Fron said.

"Of course you do. But perhaps we were too different. It was hard. And the winds of your planet made flying impossible."

You don't fly anyway, Gisonne thought.

"There was no way for us to have children."

"How is that?" Diana asked. Gisonne was surprised she had been listening.

"If it can't fly, how can a hatchling become a child? Perhaps you humans would say be 'born.' Emerge from the womb or nest?"

"It is not a person . . . it has no identity until the first flight," Fron paraphrased.

And so in the nest the smallest "growth" can starve—and often does, Gisonne thought. She glanced at Diana's hatchling. It stood on tiptoes, arched its neck, and flapped half-naked wings.

"Yes," Gisonne said. "Only when it flies, do you name it."

They had started strolling again and were approaching the strand. Gisonne took off her shoes and waded in. The lucid blue-green waves rolled around her feet, long and slow, stretching into the horizontal rather than breaking. And there were fish! Many fish. Schools of fish. Not farmed, pond fish but free, indigenous. There must be millions and millions in the oceans. The three Zalterians stared in wonder. An autonomous ecology. The thought of importing food from off world for these fish was ludicrous. Estuary seemed a pathetic, hopeless effort.

"Lichel," Gisonne said, "where is your marshland, your esturary?"

It didn't answer. Gisonne thought it was confused.

"There must be more than one," Fron said.

Lichel waved a wing in a wide arc. "Do you refer to the tidal inlets? Why do you mention them?"

"It is a serious enterprise on our world," Fron said. "Our geologists are attempting to restore a closed ecological circle."

Not quite right, Gisonne thought, but she didn't correct him.

"They are everywhere—all along the shores," Lichel said. "There is one on the other side of that cape. We can take the air car."

"Surely we can walk," Gisonne said.

"You can, but I—and that," it pointed at the hatchling, "—cannot."

Diana scooped the hatchling up and they returned to the air car that had brought them.

The estuary and marshes failed to create the claustrophobic response in Gisonne z2's that Estuary had. In fact, it was rather beautiful and its smells were pleasant.

"Parliament was a chosen world for us," Lichel said. "If you were corvi what kind of planet would you design or choose? One with strong air thermals, high safe places, plenty of food, indigenous prey and work animals and even some natural predators—I know that is a subject of debate among us right now—and all species avian, of saurian descent—except for fish."

"Why?" Fron asked.

"What about us?" Gisonne asked.

"You don't count. Past experience has taught us our weaknesses."

Gisonne knew they would learn no more at the moment.

"But," Lichel went on, "our smart corvi ancestors had one more requirement: rich and plentiful supplies of one important natural resource—a resource in short supply elsewhere, yet much needed by organized, technological peoples. We have a monopoly on bacterial protein, a special bacteriorhodopsin. The key element in all your Operating Systems originates in the salt marshes of Parliament, synthesized by a unique "salt-loving" bug—a particular variety of halobacterium salinarium."

"There is another element, more important," Diana said. "I own it."

Gisonne tried to give her a warning signal but it was impossible to get her attention. Fron jumped in to cover her words.

"How can this be true? We'd know about it. I am not an expert on interplanetary markets but everyone knows that the particular strain of bacteriorhohopsin that works with quiveron comes from a number of very different places. And also if you had a monopoly on it, your people would be one of the great powers?"

"No, it would be taken from us. We are relatively defenseless."

"I have learned that you are right!" Diana said with more passion than Gisonne had ever heard. "But we Zalterians are not hiding."

Gisonne couldn't tell if Lichel understood that Diana was talking about quiveron.

"And there are xenophobes, especially in your leagues," it went on. "We have been able to market our 'product' through our human citizens and intermediary worlds. You must appreciate that our very existence is hidden."

In spite of the humid warmth of the tidal flats, Gisonne had been growing colder and colder with dread as this discussion went on. They would never let her people go.

Dubois visited them in their block two days later. The latest news from his "connections" among the Ravel corvi was that Emil was back in the Nil house/flock and Lonney had been brought to the Procne and was living in it temporarily.

"No doubt they needed a human being familiar with the systems," he added. "It's hard to learn a strange technology in quarters too narrow for corvi bodies."

Lonney was the last person to be familiar with any systems. The edel must have asked for her, Gisonne thought.

"But what about Calib?" she asked.

"I didn't hear anything about him. But there is no reason you can't communicate with her."

They were familiar with a local version of the human horn, a subsystem of the corvi OS specially adapted for communication among the human inhabitants, but assumed it would be forbidden to them—especially by the Ravel corvi.

Lonney had already been told they were all right.

"Calib is very bad, sick," she said.

"Where is he now?"

"Corvi took him away," she said. "Edel and I tried to take care of him, to cure him."

Gisonne could only imagine Calib's reaction to that help.

"He screams all the time that he is Edel's brother."

"What?"

"Professor Treejal is their father."

Chapter Twenty-Six

Chain

7/24/40

"Look, Dubois," Gisonne said, "we—I haven't pushed you. What's going to happen—to us? Our crew."

Dubois leaned heavily on the low wall bordering one of the cylinder roofs, staring out toward the distant sea. His naked head gleamed, the unpatched eye squinted, and every wrinkle and scar was highlighted in the bright sunlight. He looked very old.

Gisonne had followed him by herself up to watch the corvilla flocking, but as yet there were no flocks in sight.

"The question is difficult," he said after a while, not turning to look at her. "It depends more on you than on us."

"I can't understand that answer," Gisonne said.

"Watch," Dubois said.

Without warning or the usual Ravel fanfare, a huge, sharp V of corvilla rose up from behind them and sailed over their heads. Then the two lines crooked simultaneously so there were three vertices instead of one. They had made a chain, one form of dyne, Gisonne thought. The analogy was strained; such perfection was mechanical next to the unpredictable chaos of a human group.

"Rave said there is no complex mechanism controlling the process of flocking—and no leader. But it seems impossible that a flock is what we, my ZD, call a decentralized system."

"But it is," Dubois said. "It's the vertices, not centers, that matter. Vertices create an illusion of a center. There is no center."

"I have a hard time with the concepts because they seem to conflict with everything I've learned about grouping," Gisonne said.

"Really?" Dubois asked. "I don't see why. I belonged to all kinds and sizes of dynes whenever I lived on z2 in the last four hundred years."

The corvilla chain reversed itself abruptly and flew back toward the building. And, equally suddenly, it formed a five point star and then eliminated the ten vertices and became a circle.

"Group behavior is flocking," he went on. "In both what 'seems to be complex global behavior can arise from interaction of simple local rules.' In a large flock each member 'has direct access to the whole scene's geometric description, but reacts only to flockmates within a certain small radius of itself.'"

"What are the 'local rules'?" Gisonne asked although at the moment she didn't care. How had he gotten her off the major topic?

"With actual flight patterns they call them 'steering behaviors.' The individual maintains a certain distance from local mates, steers in same direction as local mates, and moves toward the average position of local mates. That's it. Even though it can see the whole flock geometry, it interracts only with those in its immediate vicinity.

"And did you know that 'group alignment [is] not possible without motion'?"

Gisonne found that observation interesting but still didn't see how it applied to human dynes?

"A group is much more complicated than you understand, Dubois," she said. "It is an unbelievably complex interrelationship of energies. It is an energy field itself composed in turn of many centers of energy. In other words, each element, the single member, is not just a point in a three-dimensional field, but is a center of and source of its own energy—energy of different degrees, different speeds, different vectors—all bouncing off one another. Look how everything changes when a third person joins any two."

"Yes, right," Dubois said. "Each person is totally independent—and that creates the group. Without the individuality there could never be a flock. We agree completely."

Gisonne did not see at all.

"I think," Dubois added, "after this discussion, that it is likely you will go home."

Gisonne tried to report the conversation to her two remaining "flockmates."

"Either you are not reporting accurately or it makes no sense," Fron said, rudely Gisonne thought, but, though he seemed to be growing more and more cantankerous, he would never make CN.

A blast of crackling noise from the corvi communicator port in the wall of their human block further shattered nerves. The hatchling squawked back at it and Fron splayed his fingers mysteriously close to some part of it—without any effect that Gisonne could see. He had been trying to figure out corvi operating technology with some help from the human inhabitants of corvilla land.

"Or he doesn't want us to understand it yet. As you always say, we need more information before we're ready."

"And the rest of our 'crew'? How do they fit Dubois' plans for us?"

Gisonne shrugged.

"I don't trust him," Fron added.

And he was right.

Several days later Gisonne was summoned to Lichel's apartment—by herself.

It was a balcony in a cylinder, poled, stinking, outfitted with the familiar waterfall/fountain and food spreader. Lichel said nothing after the polite nod and a single squawk. It stood in profile to Gisonne on one foot/hand and fed itself constantly with the other, its right eye never leaving her face.

Another corvi flew up with food for Gisonne, put it before her and remained in attendence until Lichel squawked loudly. Gisonne was startled and realized that this behavior toward underlings had been much more common in the Ravel city/village/houses. The corvi seemed amazed too and froze. Lichel said something more to it, softly this time, and it nodded and leapt off the balcony.

"Our flocks are not pyramids here," Lichel said in Octente. Maybe, Gisonne thought. "Except of course for the corvilla who must be controlled." Maybe, Gisonne thought again.

"What is it that's so private that I had to come alone?" she asked.

"Before Dubois arrives I want to talk to you," it said and stopped tossing tidbits into its beak for a while. The eye nictated and then opened to stare again.

"It is not easy or polite to talk about human beings objectively in human company."

"I'm human," Gisonne said. Or was, she thought.

"But with you it is necessary. It is about you. About your human flocking crew. It is a poor, ineffective, self-destructive flock. Unbalanced."

Gisonne was angry. Emotional. "Our interrelationships worked! In impossible circumstances! Oh—it's too complex for you to comprehend in any way. Our rules are not so simple as those of your flocks. Difficulties are necessary for strength—"

"The nature of the human mind mandates the failure of collective behavior. Your hemispheres are a muddle. There is no clean division in function. The two sides of the primate brain 'excite each other,' engage in wild activity. You almost destroyed the hatchling in your ship's operating system."

"What! Who? How?"

"May I come in now?" Dubois asked from the human entrance of the riser. "Aren't we off the subject of Gisonne's homeward journey?"

"We were never on that subject!" Gisonne shouted. Maybe it was all some kind of crazy corvi test. Well, she was failing it.

Lichel said, "I was explaining to Gisonne why her crew/flock cannot operate the spacecraft for a return journey."

"That is not Lichel's real reason, Dubois," Gisonne said. "It won't let us go because we'll tell the worlds that Parliament exists."

"Whatever," Lichel said, "Your crew cannot go. Your ship has been dismantled. It would have been inoperable any way because of your behavior with the intelligence within it.

"But we will let you go, Gisonne—you alone. A corvi flock will take you directly and secretly to Zalterius II in a corvi SPEED ship."

Home. Arine. Laurel house. How soon? How fast? They had been at speed fourteen months, but had travelled two sides of a triangle. So say another year—ten oe years. Twenty years would have gone by altogether. Her mother. She might see her mother again. Her parent. Thank Rave.

"No," she said.

"You know there is no other way," Dubois said later as he and Gisonne walked along outside paths back to the human block.

"Why? We got here. We worked together in horrible circumstances for—"

"Really, Gisonne. You probably did as well as possible but . . . you were never able to control your own destination, the OS, or that mind growing in it, or finally your interrelationships."

"The last is not true. It was hard but I—"

"Who 'murdered' you? And who was the victim?"

"I . . . don't know."

"Might it have been one of the crew who fixed the route?"

"No. Yes. Yes, it might be. I don't believe it though."

"So any one of you could be a secret killer and suicidal and you don't know. And one of you must have been the intended object. And you don't know which."

It had to have been Diana, but she would say nothing about the mission to Quivera.

"Yes, but we're here aren't we? I'm not a prisoner of the Ravel corvi—"

"The strange mind of your OS, whatever it is, saved you by bringing you to Parliament, the corvi got you out of your SPEED ship in spite of yourselves, and it was not you but Rave who freed you from the Ravel corvi—just you."

They walked along in silence for a while. Dubois' pace slowed; his legs were stiff and cramped with age. Gisonne suspected that corvi had access to Malaacan medicine— unknown to Malaaca, of course—or had very similar healing technologies of their own, but Dubois had lived too long for any treatment to help much.

"You know," he said, very gently, "these heroics will be for nothing. How will it help the others if you stay or not? They'll remain with the corvi in either case. And some of them may prefer life on Parliament—as do many humans."

"There are many ways to be a hero," Gisonne said, "intentional or not. Why did Rave decide to let me go? To help me? I must have done something." Can emotional behavior be a kind of heroism? Diana would say no.

"What did you do?" Dubois asked. "Rave's a tough old bird. I have been curious."

"I sang a flight song."

When Dubois and Gisonne approached Gisonne's living block, Diana and the hatchling were sitting under a tree with "neighbors," a human mother and ten-year-old girl. It was a pretty scene: the woman had brown skin and large, oval golden-brown eyes fringed in thick black lashes. Like Diana she wore her tunic casually thrown back, revealing a full length of deep plum tunic, which contrasted vibrantly with Diana's white.

The two "children" played together. Gisonne could swear she heard the little girl squawk and cheep and the hatchling answer.

And the hatchling, standing by itself away from Diana, was obviously no longer an infant. It was still thin but quite tall and it had more feathers than down now. Its pale eyes and pink beak were odd after the sharp, total black of all other corvi. When was Diana going to name it? They couldn't keep calling it the hatchling or the "hatch."

After Dubois the woman and child left and Fron returned. Gisonne told him and Diana only that the meeting had held nothing new or helpful. Fron was distracted anyway with his own news. He had been learning from other humans in the block some of the issues dividing Lichel and Dubois' people from the rest of corvi society.

"The corvi are changing some old customs and mores and the corvilla leaders don't like it," he said. "The corvi want to eliminate the large predators—that is the ones that prey on them."

"That sounds sensible," Diana said, watching the hatchling.

"Well, it means that their death rituals are changing—a history gone. They have always left their dead to be reincorporated into the ecosystem."

"Oh," Gisonne said, "it's theological rather than political? I thought—"

"Ecological—maybe the same thing. Historically the dead were left where they fell. Vultures consumed the remains. Some of the predators were actually imported. But now it seems corvi have adopted sophisticated practices—maybe from indirect off-world influence. Bodies are placed in deep caves—to be 'safe.' It is said that some were actually sent off into space though the humans believe that may only be a rumor."

"And it's the corvi who are doing these things? It should be just the opposite. The corvi seem so conventional and reactionary. In fact, I thought the issues were political— feudalism versus democracy or vertical versus horizontal."

"One must not make assumptions based on human expectations—" Fron began.

"I heard they need some of the predators for their periodic song fests—to complete the choirs. You know the countrapuntal—"

Diana laughed, Fron was clearly affronted by the joke and interruption, and Gisonne wondered if she were reverting back to Tension Releaser. She had certainly failed as Task Leader—as Dubois seemed to be pointing out.

"You kept us alive," Diana said, watching Gisonne's face.

Astonishing Diana! She must have sensed bad news from some change in Gisonne. But also poor Diana. Gisonne would have to tell her the facts—soon. She'd never see either of her planets, the one she owned or the one that owned her. The quest of the daring hero to save her people had been unromantically aborted. And Gisonne felt twice a failure—once for herself and once for Diana.

She tried to tell herself that Diana's mission had been unrealistic. The Octente was using a technicality retroactively to steal Quivera and its quiveron from z2 and to humble the Zalterians. Power was above legalities. Even if Diana had made it to Quivera, Malaacans and Stycians would have found something else or just used force and later, if necessary, rewritten history. Only mariners would know the truth.

"Diana, do you remember what Lichel told us at the wetlands? About the bacteria something?"

"Bacteriorhodopsin," Fron said.

"Yes," Diana said, rising from her chair and gathering up the hatchling. The sun had set.

Fron and Gisonne followed her into their block. "Well, since that stuff is so important to most Octente technologies, quiveron is probably less valuable than it was. So your trip—"

"That's not valid," Fron said. "Neither component works without the other. The discovery of quiveron in 2883 oe would have been of no significance without the protein—Ow!"

Gisonne was pinching the back of his arm above the elbow through both cape and tunic sleeve—hard. She wanted to pinch herself even more for talking about it in front of him. What matter if it was true or even possible as long as Diana thought it might be?

"I mean," Gisonne said, giving another lighter pinch significantly, "that your not getting to reestablish your claim to Quivera will make very little difference to the fate of z2."

Diana turned in anger, eyes blazing. Gisonne had obviously said the wrong thing.

"Quiveron has been our blood," Diana said. "It courses through the great body that is the Octente. And we Zalterians are the heart that pumps the blood."

Oh, horrid pontus, Gisonne thought. I can't speak this language.

She tried: "And what's the salty bacterium then? Black bile?"

"No," Fron said. "Extending the metaphor, it would be the oxygen that the blood transports to every part of a living organism." He seemed pleased with himself. Fron was never poetic.

Gisonne woke him just before dawn.

"Was Lichel telling the truth about the bacterium?" she whispered.

"I don't know," Fron said—smoothly, as if he had not been sound asleep two minutes earlier. "I was sure it had many sources and that it was marketed and delivered by a variety of merchants and middle men. I think that was common knowledge. Commerce has never been of interest to me."

"Can we find out more? Can you use their OS?"

"I haven't been able to," he admitted.

"Well, what about our own?"

"On the Procne? How?"

"Edel."

Lonney and Gisonne chatted in the Zalterian dialect, speaking quickly, innocently, and at length, catching up and boring any listeners who understood modern Octente.

"How is your shipmate Edel?" Gisonne asked. "Have you been friendly?"

"Yes. He speaks corvi with the corvi almost all the time. He is not so angry any more. He treats me like a pet animal."

"Is he still . . . connected to the OS information stocks? Find out. Ask him. You know how. See if you can find out some things for us. I'll let Fron tell you what."

The records Lonney sent neither verified nor disproved Lichel's claims but they didn't reinforce Fron's "common knowledge" either. There were enough discrepancies, contradictions, inconsistencies, and duplications to arouse the suspicion of anyone who knew what she was looking for.

The clincher for Fron and Gisonne was another line of information from the Procne OS—microbiological. General bacteriorhodopsin was found on most worlds where saline water interfaced with land—z2 was the exception, unique because of its geological history. But certain strains were very rare. The one that combined with quiveron was most rare of all.

No matter how unpleasant to the senses Lichel's chambers were, it was important that they meet with it and Dubois there. Gisonne sent Fron up first to its balcony. Diana was next— without the hatchling. Gisonne waited out of sight until Dubois had arrived and ascended. Only then did she step on the rise herself.

She heard only two voices, Fron's and Dubois', polite, strained. Diana and Lichel were silent. Gisonne hoped it felt the tension and seriousness of the occasion

Lichel had separated itself physically from the humans— including Dubois. It was not looking at anyone and did not turn its head to see Gisonne as she entered. She got one polite cluck. Maybe she had gone too far and it expected unpleasant pleading and anger.

Wishing for a round table, Gisonne crossed over the awkward pole flooring to perch herself on a swing among the humans. Diana then walked, without teetering, to a bench next to Lichel. Wonderful Diana.

"Now look," Dubois began, "let's just—"

Gisonne raised a hand stopping him just as he had done when they met. She was in charge of this meeting and the first thing she did was squawk the corvi order call/greeting.

"Lichel, you own the only source of the bacterium," she said and waited for it to turn its head to see her. Only when it did, did she go on: "Diana owns the only source of quiveron."

Dubois shook his head. For once Gisonne had the pleasure of seeing the unflappable old man show surprise and confusion.

"All corvi own the bacterium; the Octente owns the quiveron," Lichel said.

"Zalterius II owns Quivera," Diana said, shifting her position slightly to look into Lichel's unpatched eye, as one monarch to another, lesser one, "and supplies quiveron to the other member states of the Octente. I am major stockholder and controller."

"That may be true," Lichel said. "However it is not relevant to Parliament's marketing."

"From my research," Fron said, "it is most relevant. Without quiveron the bacterium has no use and no markets."

Lichel strutted to an OS connector and stepped on and tread for a few seconds. They heard some squawks and beeps and then nothing for a few minutes.

Dubois' eyes moved from Gisonne to Fron to Diana and back with a new expression. No one spoke.

Lichel came all the way back to its original position and swallowed a tidbit of food before it spoke.

"It is true," it said. "Zalterius II owns Quivera and is the only supplier of quiveron to the industrial/technological combines of all the worlds. That this one individual owns the majority is not in our records but her family is the center of the dominant poltical organization."

"I have more than enough proof on the Procne," Diana said.

Gisonne trusted that Diana would not say why she had been given deeds to the Zalterian families' holdings on Quivera. Surely the corvi could not yet know that Malaaca and Styxx, in the name of the whole Octente, were even now wresting Quivera away from z2. She and Fron had worked out the timing and distances again and again before attempting this proposition. Even with the boomerang course the Procne had traveled at SPEED, they had not gone far enough out for intraOctente missions to catch up with information to most member worlds. And even then word would have to come back to Parliament on one of the corvi's own surreptitious return flights.

"Do you realize what it would mean to corvi security if you had influence over all quiveron supplies?" Gisonne asked.

She knew enough not to try to entice Lichel with the reward of power.

"Wait," Lichel said. "You may officially own this resource, and even if the whole of Zalterius II owns it, why will the other worlds of the Octente respect it?"

"Yes," Dubois said, "the OS records on your ship and information from you yourselves indicate you have been at SPEED for more than 14 oe months. There may be shifts of influence. Zalterius II has been a rich and politically powerful world, but it is small and as defenceless as Parliament."

Gisonne feared they were getting close to what was most likely the horrible truth.

"Together Parliament and Zalterius II can be the strongest, most secure worlds in this part of the Galaxy. Withhold the bacterium."

"It would mean making our existence known to—"

"No," Gisonne said. "For generations the deceptively large number of suppliers have assured the major Malaacan and Stycian buyers a safe and apparently inexhaustable redundancy of sources. When the supplies dry up here and there and everywhere within a short period, they will panic. It will be far more effective if they don't know who or where or what you are.

"Diana and her flocks will be your intermediary. She will have the power over quiveron and speak for those who control the bacterium. If they touch z2 or Quivera they lose the bacterium."

"And Parliament's safety and strength?" Lichel asked.

"We will be able to withhold the bacterium from z2 itself if they fail to protect us and represent our demands," Dubois said to Lichel.

The five persons were silent for a while.

"We'll think it over," Lichel said finally.

"Not acceptable," Gisonne said—and prayed to all the evil water gods that it didn't challenge her.

"What makes you think that I—an outlaw—can make such a decision? The Ravel corvi—"

"I know that your wars are theoretical, that you are CN, the negative wind that strengthens the flock, and that for all matters of importance for the wellfare of Parliament you and Rave will be as one."

"And what do you want?" Dubois asked.

"To go to Quivera," Diana said.

"To go home," Gisonne said.

Chapter Twenty-Seven

Callosotomy

9/15/40

They could not travel on a corvi SPEED ship. Corvi space technology could not be adapted to human use, nor could human beings be altered sufficiently mentally or physically to handle corvi technology. Corvi pilots and technicians could not appear on human worlds. It had to be the Procne and that meant Edel.

And Lonney said no.

"The whole existance of z2 depends on it," Gisonne said.

"I've been on long SPEED trips almost my whole life and I don't belong to z2," Lonney said. "And neither does Edel. We never lived there. And you Zalterians have hurt her."

"So you would rather stay here on a world of . . . "— Gisonne looked at Lichel, who was listening intently—"people so different from you—"

"But not so different from Edel. It is better for Edel here. She has me and now that she is on planet and connected to . . . teachers and scientists and just friends she can talk to, she learns all the time and plays games and even understands my speech a little."

"Can the edel . . . is Edel listening to us now?"

"No."

"Will you put it . . . her on?"

"No. You'll just confuse her and make her feel bad. Like you're trying to do to me."

Gisonne resisted an angry answer, or worse, the direct command of an autocratic TL. She looked at Lichel who gave the corvi version of a shrug. Fron started to speak but stopped when Gisonne frowned at him. One of his lengthy explanations would do more harm than good.

It had to be Diana—Diana in person.

It was ironic that the Procne was so unfamiliar from the outside, an oddness added to by its contrast with the winged corvi ships nearby. It seemed small, dull gray, and without definition—as if it had undergone some kind of amputation.

That made it more of a shock to come inside, especially to the center. It was charged with every pain, memory, fantasy, grief, and hope Gisonne had felt for over two years. Too full, drowning, breathless. So small, suffocating. Diana seemed not to notice but moved to her usual place.

Lichel, who had insisted on accompanying them, tried to ruffle its wings, seemed to snort, and backed out awkwardly. It stayed on a staging just outside the open port.   Lonney came out from navigation. She looked harried and worried. Although the temperature was comfortable, she kept her black, corvi cape wrapped, covering her yellow tunic completely. Next to her and the black bulk of Lichel, Diana and Gisonne looked like bright, misplaced flowers.

Diana began as they had planned: "I have to go to Quivera. I cannot go without the Procne and Procne cannot go without the . . . without Edel."

Not personal, Gisonne thought. She had urged, almost commanded, Diana to make an emotional plea, a private request—aimed at Lonney the caretaker, the TR.

But Lonney's expression moved slightly, softened. She smiled.

"I'm sorry, Diana," she said. "Calib always said your mission was a fantasy quest. There is no time left for you to make it. And even if there were, it can't work. You know big politicians from the Octente will just make up any rules they want. We all talked about it so much when— "

"But please, Lonney," Gisonne interrupted with her own emotional plea, "I cannot live away from home. I miss my—".

"They are all dead! Don't you know? You haven't SPEEDED like I have. Every time I came back to a place all the people were dead a long time and everything was different!"

"No, we've figured the time," Gisonne began. "Fron has—"

"Gisonne," the edel said, then continued in Corvi. Gisonne understood some of the words, especially when it said their names.

When it stopped, Lichel said, "It will go. It will take you—if Lonney will go too. And it says it is you—whatever that means."

Lonney shrugged. "And Diana? You still say you will go?"

Diana nodded.

"If she will go, I will."

Later Gisonne managed to be alone with Lonney.

"Why?" she asked. "Why Diana? She is so cold—most of all to you."

"To warm her," Lonney said. "She needs me to warm her."

The Procne became a hybrid, human and corvi. In essence it was its original OS base, without which there would be no edel. However, except for the exterior which had to look the same when it reappeared on human worlds, the rest was corvi—all replaced damaged parts and additional system hardware that made the operations more efficient in general and enabled the edel to function more completely and comfortably— with both its hemispheres. However, in order to use—and become part of—the equipment, the original human crew had also to adapt and be adapted.

Because corvi SPEED ships had always been structured after their flocking, flying, and physical patterns, i.e. vision and brain, the crew was a much more integrated part of the system than a human crew, but not cybernetically. Also, just as there were two of every corvi communication, operating, and entertainment system for the two distinct ways of interfacing with and managing reality, there were two, not duplicate, ship systems. These were not alternate or redundant modes of operation, nor was one a backup of the other. It was as though there were two space vehicles capable of SPEED, but each had been generated by a different species, species that had never met. Somehow the two ships had been combined into one.

Gisonne and Fron discovered, after some confusion, that these corvi flight technicians were somewhat analogous to human ZD dyne designers and to navigation system engineers at the same time.

Since it was in so many ways a corvi ship, neither Gisonne nor Fron could contribute to the design. They could only trust that the corvi engineers could engineer human beings into the configuration. Corvi claimed to have included humans in their crews for centuries but always as a minority. Now the crew was to be totally human—except for the edel.

Ironically the navigation/engineer flocks were made up of both Ravel corvi and Lichel/Dubois corvilla and corvi. So much again for the mortal enemies, Gisonne noted.

During a period of the work the edel had to lose its senses temporarily; sensory deprivation for at least two days was dangerous for humans and more for corvi. For the edel the outcome would be problematic.

However the edel understood and agreed.

Dubois laughed when he told Fron and Gisonne that some corvi systems technicians—not the navigation specialists— couldn't understand why the edel could not be duplicated, copied into their own machines. It is not technology but neuroscience that produced the edel, they were told.

"What was Lichel talking about when it said our crew damaged the edel? And the edel then damaged the ship?" Gisonne asked Dubois. "Surely its 'creator,' a certain Cres Trjol, bears responsibility for making a miserable monster?" Or perhaps two miserable monsters, she thought.

When Dubois looked at Gisonne curiously, she flushed. He had never seen her speak quite so venomously.

"If this Trjol designed the horn itself, he would be partially to blame, but human Navigational Operating Systems have long had the same sensory structure. Its 'scans' face two directions without overlap: one covers the interior of the ship; the other is part of the ship's skin, staring outward into space.

"So when the accelerated evolving began, naturally the mind itself was divided and—"

"Wait! Are you saying that edel developed double minds like the corvi's?" Gisonne asked. She had seen the connection herself in a flash once and rejected it.

"It can't be," Fron said. "Logically, abstract intelligence has no pattern. The very word 'abstract'—"

"I have explained all this," Dubois said. "It is a much more natural and logical way for intelligence—mind—to evolve. It takes the double vision to multiply the connections, to provide the conditions for the energy leap from one to the other that is consciousness."

"But corvi hemispheres are unconnected." Gisonne said.

"Relatively," Dubois went on, "True, they don't leak into each other or share functions and so weaken the separate activities of each—ending in the sloppy confusion that we humans must constantly struggle to control. For human beings the independence of the cerebral hemisphere is only potential— although the compartmentalization is far greater in the male than the female. The corvi' two minds remain independent and necessitate that grand leap—when they do connect."

"Do you mean like multiple personalities—one is forward and the other suppressed at any one time? Are they aware of each other?"

"Not at all," Dubois said. "It is not two people in one body! Or even in one head or brain. And it is not a combination but a deal that had to be made, the give and take that is the person, the ways of being one or the other. Let's say the person is the dialogue between the hemispheres."

"The edel has never learned to use Octente," Gisonne said.

"Language is part of a being's perceptions of reality," Dubois said. "Your speech made less sense the corvi. Also the right hemisphere seems to have dominated in all the early stages of the evolution of most intelligent species. Perhaps the edel's left wasn't mature enough yet on the first part of your voyage."

Often Gisonne argued, not only with Dubois and Lichel, but with the professional corvi "mission designers." She made some demands because she honestly believed them necessary; others were to ensure that power was balanced between the Zalterians and corvi. She wanted her original human crew, in its original role configuration. It had taken too long to evolve the group into a patterned flow of energy which multiplied rather than cancelled the collective power.

Bram had already gone off in another direction on another corvi ship with Gape and a corvi crew.

"They claim you don't need Calib," Dubois said.

"Calib is needed more than any other one of us—except perhaps me," Gisonne said.

"I don't think it's going to be possible, Gisonne."

"Why? What's the matter? Where is he?"

Dubois didn't answer.

"What happened to Calib?" Gisonne said loudly. "Is he dead?"

"I've gotten the impression that Calib was the least liked of your crew," Dubois said.

"He is CN. Without him we are wet corvi pap, inert, useless. I want to know where he is."

"I don't know. They told me he wasn't available. We didn't think you would make this demand."

"Find out."

Dubois spent minutes on his communicator.

"Calib is a patient—confined. When they pulled him out of the Procne, he was not sane."

"I want him. That's it."

"But, Gisonne, he must be dangerous. He could jeopardize the whole mission."

"He will be included."

Before she left the corvilla area for the last time, Lichel met Gisonne once more in Dubois' quarters. It wanted her to sing the flight song to it. She refused in such a way that it didn't repeat the request.

It nodded the polite corvi nod and presented her with an Octente translation of an ancient history/myth/sermon to read while she could still read.

"Corvi ancestors once lived on a perfect world of mountains and rivers and valleys. Then corvi committed an error against the land and the mountain tops roared and poured out their wrath onto the people and the sea waters rose. Corvi prayed to the sea gods and the waters rested for many generations but again the corvi damaged the land and again mountains spewed out their vomit and angered the sea gods. The sea threw itself onto the land and tried to break the mountains apart. Once more corvi were given a chance and they changed their ways and the waters rested.

"When corvi erred one more time, they were most sorely punished. The wind god grew so powerful and so fierce that corvi could no longer have children. The earth god was kind and gave ease but the wind god made the sea god drown the earth god.

"Then barbarous primate tribes invaded and settled the mountain islands. The winds were not as terrible as these new animals.

"But corvi and the primates shared, stole and learned from each other. Corvi would soon die out. So scouts were sent to find a new home."

Later Gisonne asked Dubois if he believed there was any historical truth behind this story. If corvi or humans had sophisticated SPEED capabilities, how could it have been prehistory?

Dubois shrugged. "Wars might have wiped out everything. Or it didn't happen or it didn't happen the way they believe. It is true that they are not indigenous to this planet."

10/1/40

A human translator—one who had traveled with corvi at SPEED—explained to Gisonne and Emil: "We, corvi and humans, find that the time is sometimes boring without the right eye to read, and to listen to talk and oral entertainments—yes, and to study—especially for those who are accustomed to such things. We have devised other forms of entertainment, picture stories, dance visuals, flocking parades and contests for corvi, manual games, models to destroy and reconstruct. Also those who begin to excercise and develop the potentials of the left mind for the first time are tired and sleep for longer times. In addition there is medication for the inactive periods. The eight and a half SPEED months will be subjectively shortened."

1/1/32 oe

Gisonne's head didn't hurt. (She couldn't remember the word "head"—or "hurt" either.) In fact, it was numb, not there at all. But how could something that didn't exist feel so large?

These were not thoughts—if thoughts require words. They were sensations and pictures. Memory seemed intact. There were no missing places in time that she could locate. It was just that there were no words to go with the images.

She heard a muffled groan and turned her eyes. There was a woman she knew on a human bed on the other side of the room beneath strange headgear. She couldn't think of the woman's name.

Gisonne remembered clearly that she and the woman were to have surgery performed on their brains so that they would be able to travel in a corvi space ship at SPEED and be navigators.

So even though she couldn't remember the word "mind," she knew there was nothing wrong with hers. She knew what had happened, what she had agreed to, and what was going to happen. She knew the tall man from the other side of the home planet, too, when he came into the room but she didn't know his name. He came close, looked down at her, and sounds came from his mouth but they had no meaning.

This man with his flat features, and others—she brought up the faces in her right mind's eye: one brown and strong—a good feeling; the other dark browed—frightening. Faces without names. She remembered the edel. (This memory was without a label or image. The only picture that could arise was the outside of the machinery that contained it.) Was this how it had been for it all those months? Mute.

Chapter Twenty-Eight

Steering

3 mo's SPEED
4/10/43 oe

Gisonne had never before seen so completely and so clearly—with a patch over her right eye! She couldn't remember the word for machine, yet she had begun to know how the corvi machines worked and learned to use them. She began to play/solve corvi space games. Purposes, interfunctioning, relationships of the part to the whole, all made sense immediately. She even understood the ship's engineering. How smart she was!

Yet when she looked across at the familiar woman-in-white and the talking-man from the other place at home—each wearing a left eye patch, she was totally stupid. Their actions, tools, and most of all, words were incomprehensible no matter how hard she looked and listened. The woman in white used to draw. Gisonne recollected the pictures in her right mind's eye and wished she would make more so that they might understand each other. But the woman couldn't. She talked and talked to the man and studied noisy, illegible, unintelligible screens. Yet the woman seemed unable to move about without stumbling or weaving. She often reached out with her hand before her to measure distance between objects.

The other man, the one with the golden-brown skin and good face, was different. Gisonne didn't know his name either, but she understood his behavior and knew the "meaning" of his expressions and gestures. He too wore a patch on his right eye like hers and had a scar on his left temple. They worked perfectly together. She sometimes led and he followed and sometimes he led, but neither was quite true. It depended on the eye.

Gisonne knew the other human beings in the far back, sometimes front, of their common cabin/navigation area. She understood them better than the woman-in-white and her partner, with their left eye patches, but still not completely. They wore no eye patches and functioned with both hemispheres but weakly, just as the surgeon/healer/engineers had told them, just as Gisonne herself had done—before surgery.

The mad-man-in-manacles had frightened Gisonne as she had known he would, but she was also glad of him. Although at first he didn't speak or move, she could feel the strength he caused. Because of him their separate energies were multiplying. She had no words but saw the picture of the moving pattern they made.

The emotions of the third woman were clear to Gisonne because of the expressiveness of her face and body and the vivid tones of her voice. She related to everyone, including edel, with both hemispheres—as she always had. But during sleep cycle, she shared the q of the woman-in-white.

The other persons in that part of the cabin were difficult for Gisonne. The edel had no face and she couldn't understand its words, whether in its male or female voice, or whether it talked to the tall-talking-man, either of the two women, or squawked and sang to the corvi child. The charts, drawings, and graphs it presented to Gisonne and her partner were clear but impersonal and not so helpful as the OS direct navigation information.

When they had to send or request information from the talking ones they used the edel, giving it pictures to change into words.

The hatchling made no sense at all to Gisonne. It produced more and more sound, but she couldn't tell what languages it was learning—if the sounds were any language at all.

6 mo's SPEED
12/20/45 oe

Gisonne knew she was not in another state of consciousness. Nor was she half conscious. She was one part of herself that had always been there but was now growing. In a sense she was more lucidly aware than ever before. She had become fascinted with the physical world, all its parts from the subatomic to the astronomical. Subjectively time passed quickly when she learned new things or navigated.

Now Gisonne realized that the hatchling could speak human language and Gisonne could not. It was very funny.

The man-in-manacles was connected to the OS in many different ways. The attachments were not the same as for navigation. He had gone from silent to loud and angry. He shouted at everyone but mostly the expressive woman, who always answered him softly. Then one day when he was especially loud, she turned and screamed at him. Gisonne, of course, did not understand her words but she knew what she meant. The man said nothing for a few days and then he began to talk in normal tones to the woman.

And now for the last month the two had been talking together much of the time. His face was not angry as Gisonne remembered it on the route to Waldseemuller or as distorted as it had been when they took him back from the corvi care.

7 mo's SPEED
9/28/46 oe

The hatchling very suddenly flew through the cabin, in and out and around them, and then in an endless circle around the walls. The tall-talking-man said something and the woman-in-white said something hard back to him and the hatchling kept flying around and around. Gisonne's warm silent partner and the expressive woman were laughing. That woman clapped her hands.

Later the woman-in-white said something to her partner, the tall-talker, and to the hatchling. No. Gisonne knew it was now a fledge, no longer a hatchling—even though she couldn't remember either word.

The expressive woman nodded and the man-in-manacles started to laugh. The woman-in-white came over to Gisonne and made some sounds. Gisonne shook her head. It was hopeless. The woman took a screen and typed large letters and held it up to Gisonne. It was big, bold marks, and she understood that they meant the fledgling's name, but she couldn't read it.

8 mo's SPEED
7/10/47 oe

Something was loosening or growing. Gisonne could almost feel it physically in her head. Once in a while she remembered the name of something or someone, and sometimes a sound the speaking persons made had a meaning. But then it was gone again almost immediately. The surgeons had said it would come back, perhaps, some of it anyway.

The-Man-in-Manacles was no longer in manacles. Lonney has healed him, or Lonney and Edel. Gisonne remembered that his name was Calib.

She turned her attention to navigation. They were nearing the place they had to visit on the way home. The woman-in-white had to complete her mission. Her name was . . . Diana.

Chapter Twenty-Nine

Quivera

9 1/2 mo's SPEED
9/20/48 oe

The Procne did not seem to drop because the left eye alone saw no depth. Rather the geometry of the planet's surface zoomed, fast, spreading wide and wider until it was all there was. A small piece of the quilt, a crude yellow triangle, grew until it filled the port and the eye, and then, without a jolt, they were on it, the yellow island made of quiveron.

Gisonne pictured Diana stepping out and planting a Zalterian flag? Would she ask the OS for fanfare?

But, of course, she and Fron would be more cautious than that. It was frustrating to Gisonne not to know if there had been any change in their original plans and she resented it bitterly. Fron and Diana had been in communication with Quivera as soon as they were within range, but Gisonne could only trust that there had been no give-away information, no warnings of exactly who was arriving and with what purpose—just in case the Malaacans or Stycians were already in possession.

They could not see through the ports because of the intensity and angle of the sunlight, but the OS screens displayed images of a number of persons—human—approaching the landing flat.

Fron and Diana had been listening, reading, and discussing verbal information from Quivera before landing and now they stared, frowning, at these pictures. They asked Lonney something and she pointed to details in the scene outside. Gisonne knew Lonney was trying to tell them what they were looking at.

Then Diana spoke to the crowd outside through the ship

speakers. She and Fron listened in turn to answering speech. And again they spoke to each other. Gisonne's frustration grew excruciating.

Diana did go out first when the port was opened, though she needed help from Emil. She had had trouble with balance and judging distances since her surgery. Fron followed and then Gisonne. The fledge, Calib, manacled, and, of course, the edel remained within the Procne.

The glare was painful and blinding, disconnecting Gisonne completely. She heard voices, familiar—her dynemates—and others unknown. She reached out a hand to touch something—anything, and someone took it. A stranger was speaking to her and attempting to put something over her head. She felt again the smothering corvi hood and her panic erupted in a cry.

Diana spoke to her then, calmly. And a moment later Gisonne could see again. She saw a blue world around her—through goggles. They had put goggles on her to cut the blinding reflection on the arpartite crystal surface from the extraordinary brilliance of the primary. Gisonne remembered that this unusual sun had created quiveron. The memory, of course, consisted of images in her mind; a child's drawing of a sun and a small planet orbiting it and then a complex solar chart—no words.

Several people had come close enough to stand in a circle around them, or rather around Diana—if centers counted for anything. The configuration was ambiguous; were they captives or gods? To be worshipped or imprisoned?

Diana was speaking but her face, cool and expressionless as always, told Gisonne nothing. Fron too was enigmatic. Lonney's smile said there was no enemy here. But how could they be sure? Lonney was always too trusting.

The people wore outer garments cut like the familiar Zalterian cloak but made of a light, heloid material, protecting the wearer from sun rather than wind. Hair styles and inner clothing were out-dated, of course, but definitely Zalterian in intent.

The circle of people wheeled about and Diana led and was led toward a structure lighter blue than the ground beneath their feet but darker than the ocean in the distance. The horizon was closer than Parliament's, more like z2's. In spite of that, the whole place was strange—perhaps because of the mica-like material beneath their feet and forming small hills in the distance, stubby flat-topped mounds, or because of the deception of total blue the goggles created.

The circle of human beings, known and unknown, walked toward the largest—or perhaps closest—mound, others trailing loosely behind. Even though Lonney held her hand, Diana moved cautiously, testing each step, but bearing herself nobly at the same time. She carried a physical packet—credentials carved in metal—appropriately dramatic.

Emil had somehow fitted himself into the outer circle. Fron took Gisonne's elbow and followed her lead unsteadily until they stopped on a wide, crystal platform before an open door in the side of the mound. Through the goggles the interior appeared to be a dense, deep blue with a sparkle of mica here and there where the light touched. Gisonne pulled the goggles down, looked in for a moment, and put them back. The glisten of gold within the mound was bearable, not blinding as it was outside, but uncomfortable. Her eyes had begun to burn and itch. And it was not worth it. Walls, floor, and thick, simple furniture were all molded of the same material, mica-like, the stuff of the island itself—stuff that contained the quiveron but was not the quiveron.

Both sides had begun the expected, tiresome, unintelligible, public orating, speeches Gisonne didn't mind missing. She listened to the style and formality in Diana's voice and inspected the planet's inhabitants, made up of Allain and other Zalterian connections: partners, employees, agents. Some were supposedly distant relatives. She knew from the records that many had been born on z2 or had lived there in past generations and most of these would retire there in the future on high bonuses, as most Zalterian off-world workers had done in the past.

As another member of the welcoming circle cleared her throat to begin a speech, and the entire company turned toward her, Gisonne continued her study of the rest.

Something wasn't right. People, beyond the closer circles, seemed to be hanging behind other stragglers and differed from those in the foreground. There were a dozen, no, two dozen. Their cloaks hung awkwardly. And their faces were wrong— narrower, sallower than most Zalterian. They were too tall. They were Stycian!

But how? We must have been betrayed, Gisonne decided. But that was impossible. No one could know that the Procne was not still on its way to Waldseemuller with Quivera's erstwhile owner on board. Only the corvi . . . ! But the Procne was as fast as the fastest of the corvi ships. Perhaps earlier, before, way before, when the Procne first arrived at Parliament, some ship might have gone from there to . . . somewhere . . . to Styxx?

In the seconds that these pictured thoughts flew through her right mind, Gisonne noticed something else. There were at most thirty Stycians, no more than two of their typically large crews. And they were not smiling, not gloating. And they were being cautious. They were obviously as surprised at the Zalterians' arrival as Gisonne was at seeing them. That meant they had already been here taking over the planet when the Procne was detected approaching. So the cloaks were not an attempt at disguise; they were worn by everyone against the sun. The hiding had been a last minute decision.

Gisonne signaled Emil, the only one who would understand her. He saw immediately.

At the same moment a few of the Stycians farthest away from the mound were backing toward the Procne, one by one, slowly and silently.

Gisonne hoped Lonney or Fron would not see and let out an alarm. There were too many Stycians, and the Quiverans obviously would not help since they had not revealed the occupation. Not openly that is, Gisonne saw, when she looked at Diana, who had just begun a formal response to the last "welcoming" speech. Diana knew. One of the Allain people must have whispered.

No one in or near the circle moved. Diana kept talking. Slowly Gisonne shifted her eyes back to the Procne. Two Stycians were pointing hand controls at the port while another was prying at a seam with some kind of metal tool. So far they hadn't been able to get in.

They must have realized the Zalterians were defenseless after all since they were no longer trying to hide themselves. It became impossible to pretend not to notice, yet Diana continued to talk.

Gisonne reached for Lonney's arm, leaned as if for support, mouth close to her ear. She moved her lips but no words came. When Lonney glanced, startled, Gisonne shook her head and put finger to lips.

Diana talked on, and Fron seemed to be listening to her.

One of the older Quiverans moved closer to Diana and reached for her wrist. Emil jumped at him but Fron blocked Emil. Gisonne shook her head at Emil as the old man attempted to pull Diana through the door into the mound. Their only choice was to follow.

Two or three other Quiverans broke out of their circle, moved closer and urged them toward the door, while the majority did nothing. Meanwhile the Stycians moved up from the rear, passing around and between Quiverans, breaking at last into a run. The first of them reached the mound just as the door slid shut.

Wrong move. Useless, useless, Gisonne thought. The loyal old man had bravely tried to rescue "The Allain," but for what? The Stycians would dissolve the mound if they couldn't break in. In fact it would suit them better. Dissolve the mound and the Procne and delete the Zalterian landing and claim. The Allain had long ago disappeared. Or had the worlds ever learned that the mission had been reprogrammed for Waldseemuller? It depended on who had done it. What did these Stycians know or think they knew?

Low lighting had come on inside the mound as the portal closed. Their rescuers—only four—were removing their goggles. Emil, Lonney, and Gisonne did the same but Diana and Fron couldn't seem to figure it out until helped.

Then Diana pushed the small OS terminal at Gisonne and said something. Only Gisonne could see how to turn it on and adjust the range. As soon as a test beep sounded, she, reluctantly, handed it back and Diana began to speak to the edel. But it was Calib, not edel, who answered—and then both of them. But Gisonne did not know what they said. At least the Procne hadn't been dissolved—yet.

There were sounds outside, growing louder.

The Quivera OS system design was mainly for the mining and processing of quiveron but it had a complete enough communication system that the Quiverans could aim audio and video ports onto most areas of the exterior island. Gisonne could understand the sounds: human shouts, obvious orders or curses, the noise of demolition equipment, frighteningly like the explosions on Estuary. The scanners verified the hopelessness of their plight. The Procne was amorphous, enlarged with scaffolding and crawling with Stycians. So Gisonne had been wrong. They would not be dissolved, at least not yet. The Stycians were obviously determined to learn all they could about the Zalterians and their ship. After the speech making, they knew Diana's purpose, but, again, did they know exactly who she was, where she had really been, or where she was supposed to be for the next two hundred Octente years?

Suddenly there seemed to be a sudden pulse or twitch of the Procne and the living cloak dropped away, leaving empty scaffolding around the ship and bodies on the ground below...

Diana talked into the OS terminal, listened, said something

to Fron and Lonney. Lonney, in turn, mimed sending and getting some kind of shock, perhaps electric, and Gisonne and Emil understood. The edel had charged the Procne hull.

Hours later a reverse scan showed that the very mound they were in had begun to lose what little shape it had. The Stycians, with all their machinery and tools, had moved to it from the Procne and now seemed to be attacking its shell with the same concentration. Several individuals raced back and forth from one hump to the other, like insects with purpose, but they never climbed onto or touched the Procne again.

Gisonne listened to Diana and Fron talking and talking to their four Quiverian rescuers and yearned to understand and to ask her own questions. Was Fron asking how much life support there was in the mound? How long could they hold out if the Stycians failed to break in? Were there weapons they could retaliate or defend themselves with? When was the next SPEED ship expected from Zalterius II? From any other world? There was to be one meal anyway. The old man and a boy dialed for some food and fetched more from inner rooms. Gisonne found herself eating half consciously as she watched the screens. Everything was in motion but nothing seemed to change. Her skin itched as she watched the Stycians, still crawling over the mound above their heads.

It seemed to be taking a long time for them to break through the mica material although they had the Quiverians' mining tools as well as their own weapons. Every once in a while a small fountain of mica seemed to erupt by itself from the surface, and one or two of the attackers would leap away or simply drop in place. Lonney smiled and pointed to the tiny explosions, but Diana and Fron shook their heads blindly and jabbered away. Gisonne, who could see action on screens, could not understand what they were saying or know what was happening.

When it grew dark—Gisonne realized she had not learned the speed of Quivera's revolution—lights flooded the plain and landing field, but were soon destroyed by the Stycians. Then only the Stycians' smaller lights dimly illuminated their activity.

Gisonne did not sleep that long night—fourteen oe hours it turned out—and thought the others didn't either though Diana, Fron, and the old man stopped talking for a long time. The outside noises grew louder for a few hours, stopped for a while, and then started again.

Dawn, when it finally came, was so bright that even through the scanners, the glare couldn't be comfortably dimmed without the lose of images altogether.

They ate, almost enjoyed one of three very large human lavatories, and walked through the rooms and halls dug out of the mound. Now Gisonne saw herself as an insect inside a hive. Insects outside were trying to devour insects inside—their own species, cannibals?

It was too much. In the middle of the long day, she actually fell asleep for an hour.

Day, too slowly and too quickly, became night and day again. The "miners" had moved to the far side of the mound and were less visible. Nothing else seemed to change except the loss of sound when the Stycians finally found and destroyed the audio port. The video stayed on, whether because they had not detected it or because they wanted the Zalterians to see them, Gisonne didn't know. She wondered what Fron thought.

As close as she had grown to Emil in their new similarity, she had never shared with him the passion for information and intellectual speculation that she had with Fron—not only because they could not talk. Gisonne and Emil had acted together, understood nameless things together, recognized a history and values together before any surgery—much more than she and Fron. But words had been extraneous to their relationship. Gisonne was hungry for words.

Even if she had been able to understand speech, she would not have known how Diana thought or felt. Diana knew how to keep separate matters separate.

All along Lonney had patiently touched and loved and

never let frustration turn to anger when Gisonne and Emil were dumb. Now, locked in this den, she kept at it but couldn't hide her own fear. Whenever edel's voice, male or female, came over the hand OS terminal, there were tears in her eyes.

On the fifth day most of the outside activity came to a halt except for the few individual Stycians who always seemed to be moving back and forth from ship to mound.

On the bright dawn of the sixth day loud words boomed into the mound through a new attachment mounted on the outside of its door. The Stycians were making an announcement and Gisonne couldn't understand it. She looked desperately from one to the other of her people but each was preoccupied, locked into listening.

When the voice stopped, Fron, Lonney, and the old man burst into speech. Diana seemed physically bent, as if holding something to her chest.

Something horrible! What?

Gisonne stared at the video screen, but there was little to see, the tiny explosions here and there, no movement at all now from the Stycians, not even the individual gophers on their errands.

And then she saw the machines. It would be dissolution after all.

Fron was shouting now. Diana was looking away from him. The old Quiverian was saying something.

The ultimatum.

"Wh . . . wh . . . what?" Gisonne shouted. She grabbed at Diana.

"Sur-ren-der!" Diana said, shook her head no, and added something else. Gisonne scrunched her forehead and then understood that word and headed for the door.

Fron came fast behind to stop her or to join her. She didn't know. But Diana screamed and shook her head again and threw herself toward them.

The door wouldn't open but Gisonne had studied it and

would open it soon. To stop her Diana pushed them all against it.

Lonney was pointing at the video and shouting. There on the screen the Stycians were setting their machines on the platform just outside the door. There was a large metal shield behind it.

Gisonne shoved Diana down and her left hand knew how the door mechanism worked and opened it and she tumbled out onto the Stycian machine.

Fron was behind her with Diana trying to drag him back but Emil was jumping ahead to put himself between all of them and the machine.

A young Stycian raised a tool above his head and a female Quiverian, somewhat older, stopped his swing, shouting something. And more Stycians surrounded them then.

Suddenly they, enemies and friends alike, were drowned in black. Huge black shapes with glinting, piercing swords had fallen upon them and darkened the field. Punishment from the depths of the ocean's evil gods. No. Gisonne saw that these shapes were only shadows, shadows of even blacker bodies, familiar bodies in the air above. Flapping wings, slashing beaks. Corvi.

The corvi had followed them. They were going to take Quivera for themselves! They would control the known part of the galaxy with both the bacterium and quiveron.

Fron was shouting, cursing, waving fists as he never had before. Only Diana seemed pleased.

A Stycian lay bleeding and others were scattering; the largest rout was to the other side of the mound where their ships must be. Didn't they see that they would be destroyed before they could leave the ground? The Procne too would be obliterated. There would be no evidence of Parliament or corvi existence. Unseen, with total power, they would be as gods to human beings.

Gisonne wanted to shout to the running Stycians, to tell them to wait, to unite, human against corvi. The Zalterians knew how the corvi operated. But Gisonne couldn't speak, and if she had, no one would listen.

The two older male Stycians, who had been about to run the machine, were still there, pressed with Fron, the Quiverian boy, the older woman, Diana, and Gisonne against the front of the mound—all trying to shield themselves from diving beaks. As Gisonne turned, as if to speak, the shorter Stycian grabbed her and dragged her with him back through the open door. Diana was pulling Gisonne as hard as she could the other way and shouting, when the other Stycian pushed her in after Gisonne and pulled the door shut—locked—behind the four of them.

Seeing that Diana and Gisonne had no weapons, the two Stycians ignored them and watched the screen, which had never been turned off, gaping widely at the things still flying above the field. Gisonne imagined their terror meeting corvi this way for the first time.

Later the men talked to each other as if their prisoners could not understand Octente or as if it didn't matter.

Gisonne couldn't understand why Diana didn't talk to them, reason with them, tell them about the corvi; after all they were all citizens of the Octente—all human. She looked at Diana and pointed at her own mouth and nodded toward the men. Diana shook her head.

And once again Gisonne could only wait and see. She stood and walked around the room, approaching the screen for a better look. The tall Stycian half turned and, without looking at her, swung his arm back, smashing the back of his fist against her forehead, knocking her backward against the sharp edge of a crystal bench.

When she regained consciousness, the mound's interior lighting was on. The tall Stycian was still, or again, staring at the screen. He was eating and drinking quietly. The other, the shorter one, was kneeling over Diana on the bench just above Gisonne's head. She could just see the hem of Diana's white tunic and his feet a few inches from her face. Diana started saying something, when Gisonne heard two loud slaps and Diana was still.

There was something on the floor close by. Slowly Gisonne turned her head, soaking her cheek in her own blood, smelling the blood. The object was Diana's small but heavy metal plaque, the credentials, also wet with blood—Gisonne's or someone's.

The man on the bench made some kind of guttural sound or laugh but Diana was still silent.

As slowly and silently as possible Gisonne crept her hand toward the plaque. She willed the tall man to stay fixed to the screen in permanent deaf stupidity. When she finally felt the metal edge just at her fingertip, she had to control the impulse to grab and hurl it at the back of his head. Instead she slowly shifted her weight to the side and moved her knees, inch by inch, closer to her torso. Only then did she curl her fingers around the plaque, still quietly, slowly, until it was firmly in her grasp.

And then she sprang—a single leap from prone to standing, a childhood coup practiced on the rock ledges of High Garda— and, in the same motion, twisted to face the bench and smashed the plaque onto the back of the shorter man's head. She hit him again and again and had broken his skull before the other one turned around.

He hesitated, staring dumbly at his companion's brain tissue oozing down the side of his neck and onto Diana's tunic. Now Gisonne did hurl the plaque at him, but at his face; he ducked as he lunged at her so it struck his temple. It hurt enough that he cried out but completed the lunge, tackling her so hard that both of them fell onto the bench on top of the dead man and Diana.

For seconds they lay, he heavy on Gisonne, panting, and she very still, not knowing if he was unconscious or only taking time to regain his strength. When he moved, she jammed him in the groin with her knee. As he twisted in pain, she slid out from under him, skidded in her own blood, recovered her balance, ran for the door, opened the lock, and plunged out.

A large corvi, black wings spread wide, stood on the

dissolution machine before her and reached one clawed foot/hand out in greeting.

Chapter Thirty

Reconfiguration

9/23/48 oe

There were her people, her dynemates, standing freely around this one corvi; they were not captives. Calib was there, too. He came forward, raised his right hand, and said, "Michalis."

"Di . . . Diana," Gisonne said and pointed back to the mound door.

Lonney and Calib ran into the mound and Gisonne heard Lonney's cry when she saw what was there. Gisonne wanted to warn her that one of the men was alive but she found no word but "no" and then Emil and Fron were inside too, making their own noises.

Outside there was one wounded Stycian propped against the mound wall and another, dead, next to the machine the corvi sat/stood on. The field beyond seemed empty but even late in the day, without goggles, the sunlight was blinding. Gisonne squinted at the Procne at the far end of the field and thought she saw corvi or corvilla near it.

Where were the Quiverians? Killed with the Stycians? And if all those human beings had been destroyed, why had Gisonne's people been allowed to live? Even if she could speak to ask, this corvi could not understand or answer.

The old Quiverian man came around the corner, followed by the boy and several others. At the same time Calib and Emil emerged from the mound. Emil's face was drawn tight, but he smiled weakly at Gisonne. Diana was, or would be, all right.

When Fron came out, all the human beings seemed to talk at once and Gisonne held her ears. Better to hear no sound at all than endure the frustration.

It was only hours later, when they had all moved to meet close outside the Procne, that she was able to learn anything. With help from Lonney's miming, the edel became translator for a three-way communication: a bit of Fron's human language, various corvi languages, and Emil and Gisonne's right brain functions.

The corvi had followed the Procne to Quivera closely in a SPEED ship—to support the Zalterians, to protect them if necessary, they claimed. More likely Lichel had not really trusted them, Gisonne thought. But it didn't matter. They had remained in orbit while the Zalterians landed.

The edel had signaled them and while waiting, impeded the progress of the Stycians with the only weapons it had, laser beams.

The terrified Quiverians slowly began to reappear in small groups from the mounds, but keep at a distance from the corvi. The Stycians had run toward their SPEED ships, but the corvilla had blocked their way and driven them into one of the empty mounds.

Corvi and corvilla don't kill one another. Do they kill other species? Yes. There were two Stycian bodies lying right there in the open—unburied.

But—the corvi speaker argued through the edel—corvi hate to kill; it is against their nature. They had killed only to protect the Zalterians and had to look with the left eye only to do it. And now that they had showed themselves, there was no choice but to kill the rest of these Stycian warriors to prevent their reporting the existence of corvi. Their news would be believed—unlike the odd tales of one or two old returnees, stray and strange-minded mariners.

And finally, the corvi said, since it had all been done for the Procne crew, that crew must destroy the Stycians. It would be easy: they had only to turn the Stycians' own dissolution machine against the mound they were in. There would be nothing heinous to witness and remember in years to come.

If Gisonne held onto the image of the two Stycians in the mound with her and Diana, it might be an agreeable act—she had deliberately killed one of them herself. And if she pictured life on z2 being preserved from the Octente, the act became a duty.

She looked at Emil, who would do whatever was decided, at Calib, whose face was fierce but appeared more rational than it had for the last nine months in SPEED, at Fron and Lonney, who had first tended the mess that was Diana in the mound. Their faces were contorted with anguish. And last, Diana's face itself, cut, bruised, and swollen, as it had looked when they carried her on a stretcher into the Procne for more care—OS medical and life support. Gisonne also saw that face—in her clear right mind's eye—as it had been, proud and beautiful as Diana watched the corvi flights, or, 28 oe years ago, as she rebuked the off-world envoy at Allaincroft. There was no question what Diana would do.

"No," Gisonne said and sought for words to explain another plan.

Her dynemates looked at her with anger and a little relief, trying to understand what she was saying. The corvi spokesperson jerked its head from side to side, almost turned its left eye to her.

"No Wal . . . Waldsee . . but far. Set . . . course. SPEED . . . ."

Only Fron showed he understood—still with more expression than usual. He started to question Gisonne but he spoke too quickly for her to follow. She resorted again to communicating through the edel.

Edel conveyed her idea to the others and sent her an old picture of herself smiling.

And they did it—again with the edel's help. The navigation OS in each of the two Stycian ships was set for a distant place—human-friendly, partially-settled. One was a world on the emptiest fringe of the Octente and the other, which lay in the opposite direction, was outside the Octente, five years SPEED, fifty oe—a hundred if they returned.

They made a variety of records of Diana's presence on Quivera from the holos and other vids taken when they had first arrived. There were also the OS copies of her speech and of the Quiverans' greetings and welcome acceptance. Some of this evidence was hidden in the Stycian OS's, some left on Quivera, and more put in the Procne and the corvi ship.

They knew all this certification and legalization would mean nothing; it would be good for historical argument in the distant future. The real struggle lay with the double control of Parliament's bacteriorhodopsin and Zalterius' quiveron.

"It is already happening," the corvi told edel who told Gisonne and Fron, in each of their ways of communicating. "Lichel keeps its word. Unless it shouldn't."

Not only had no more bacteria been shipped from Parliament but orders to intermediary merchants had gone in several directions when the Procne and the corvi ship left Parliament. It should have taken five years to reach the closest storage manager. If he had held back delivery of the supplies he had on hand, it would be two more years for that bacterium <u>not</u> to show up on Malaaca. A year later for Ipag and Anu to miss theirs. Word should have gotten to Corynn, and from there it was only six months oe to Styxx.

Things are already beginning to change on z2.

1/2 mo's SPEED
5/14/49 oe

Lonney and Calib were laughing—together. Gisonne did not know what about. Although she could now understand and use words better, she still could not read or follow the talk of the others unless it was directed at her slowly and clearly.

Lonney looked at Gisonne, said something to Calib, and Calib shook his head, then shrugged and laughed again.

　　"Calib and Edel have a plan for their father," Lonney said.
　　"Brothers," Calib said.

9/23/48 oe

　　The shuttle from Agricula landed at Nordport with
foodstuffs.

Chapter Thirty-One

Atonement on a Windy Planet

Gisonne
2/22/50 oe
The Plateau, Arine Archipelago
Zalterius II

Gisonne presses the knife against Trjol's throat, and with the palm of her left hand, pushes his head hard back onto the tabletop. She looks down into his gaping face and at the darting, terrified, ignorant eyes. For a while she doesn't move and then, suddenly, releases him.

He sags forward and she grasps his collar before he slips from his chair and looks at the face again. He is the same man though he looks so different. But she, though she looks the same, is not the same at all.

As she lets go, Trjol trembles and attempts to sit upright on his own. He coughs violently and strokes his swollen throat.

Gisonne turns and without looking back, passes out through the outer office and into the corridor. Behind her the off-worlder is shouting at the help people.

"Hurry! Hurry! The woman is crazy."

Telem

Telem looks around the room—HIS room. All the years of his adult life, through every miserable, humiliating deal he had to make for the family's comfort and very survival, the terms from the off-worlders he had to accept, all were carried on from here. It has been his private lair for fifteen years. Now even though she lies unconscious in the solarium at the other end of the house, it is hers. As soon as she was carried in, everything became hers. No, it has always been hers.

He hates her.

He becomes aware of the others: Dorey frightened, Troi confused, Pen fascinated, all watching him, and old Jev in his wheeler staring in through the doorway. What do they want from him? Reasons. Reasons for his anger.

"Pontus!" he curses, "just when things begin to change, this happens. Struggle for years to please those Pentente ocean scum—to appease, to scrape—"

"Tel, she is . . . was . . . your own mother."

Telem waves his arm at Dorey, dismissing her and her comments.

"The Malaacan ship in Nordport hasn't been unloaded yet. It holds more goods for the Arines than we've seen in twenty years. We—this family dyne alone!—is supposed to get quod enough for twenty years power—and a whole new generator. Heat, lifts, an OS that works. Pen's teeth. Pontus knows why the Pentente changed its policy but certainly now they'll change it back again. Perl—that pontus kisser—says we can't afford to harbor enemies of the Pentente!"

"Gisonne, an enemy of the Pentente!" Jevry snorts.

"Who?" Telem turns and stares at Jevry as though he never saw him before and continues as if he'd never spoken: "And they'll take back the floaters, and the new medical people who came in last year. What about Pen's teeth?"

Pen frowns and rubs his tongue across his front teeth. Better for him if the ship doesn't get unloaded.

"Well, this floater did crash," Dorey says. "There must be a defect—"

"Defect? You're defective. You don't understand anything, do you? You think that was an accident? They're trying to get her again."

Jevry moves the wheeler into the office, passes in front of Telem, and skins on a horn connection to Laurel House.

"She's not there. She didn't come home," he says. "Gisonne."

Telem can't understand who in Pontus he's talking about. Irrelevant. Jev's always been a crank. Out of touch.

Dyll Breff
Nordport
Archipelago Nord

"Perl," Breff horns. "You know what this means, this return ship. Make sure your people keep them away from everyone. Don't let them talk."

"I just heard," Perl says. "I'm talking to The Plateau now." As he nods, strings of his thin gray hair move over his pale gray face.

In ten minutes, ten long minutes, Perl calls back. His face now is almost white.

"Sir, I'm afraid it's too late. For a couple—"

"How too late?" Breff's sharp Stycian features are narrowed further, his lidded eyes squeezed, leaving only a glint of iris for Perl to see.

"They followed the usual procedures for returnees. They obeyed PMD regulations to the letter. If the ship had landed here at Nordport, we would have—"

"Never mind all that." Breff's tone is low and steady, more dangerous, Perl knows, than his shouting. "Tell me. Who? Where?"

"The Allain has been sent to—"

"The what?"

"Diana Allain is now with her family on High Garda, and so is a Norder, a Fron—"

"I know. Maces. Get on with it."

"The Michalis woman and Emil delaCour are still on The Plateau. In hospital. She claimed some kind of illness. Throat. Wanted treatment before going to her family. And he did too, I believe." Perl looks hopeful but is disappointed. Breff says nothing. Glowers.

"And the other two—"

"Two! Weren't there seven?"

Perl shrugs. "There are two still on the ship. But there's something else. Something's wrong about the ship. I don't quite follow but the technicians say it's completely different inside. Not like any ship they've ever seen."

"What? Same ID?" Breff looks over at his earlier report. "Procne. Seems like an ordinary small SPEED ship of that period—shuttles mostly. Many still in use now. Only difference was some pontus-fool experiment of old Trjol on the OS of this one."

"I only know what they told me . . . Sir. I'll have The Allain . . . woman and Maces picked up and—"

"No, no. Leave them for now. We don't want attention drawn until we find out more. And keep the others where they are. Isolate the two in the hospital. We'll see about the ship. Tell the buros and your people to keep quiet—no official reports to me. The whole ocean-damned thing makes no sense. They should not, could not have returned."

Gisonne
High Garda

Before hopping over to Double Neff with Emil, the island hopper pilot drops Gisonne to High Garda, landing on the orchard field above Allaincroft just as Perl's orders are coming in to the University Hospital on The Plateau.

The trees encircling the empty field are graceful, moving silhouettes against the early evening sky. Gisonne did not call ahead to her family. She doesn't want an escort buffer between her and her world, and there is still enough light to see the way, light which she doesn't need. She knows all the ways—high and low, long and easy, or short and rough—from this side of the mountain to Laurel House.

At first things seem exactly as she remembered, even or especially, with the new, vastly clearer and more precise imaging abilities of her right mind's eye and her physical left eye. Then she slowly becomes aware of subtle differences. A certain favorite view is altered because some of the cliff has broken away; the large grandfather tree they used to climb is gone; the plank bridge a long-gone uncle lay over the stream has rotted away and Gisonne must leap across.

And some things seem smaller than she remembered—that very stream and the jagged rock above it must have been inflated in her dreams of home. Other things, the sound of the sea below, its smell and the smell of the non-deciduous trees are stronger. And the wind! It too is stronger, both stronger and gentler, more loving, each gust a caress.

She is running home. She mustn't think of what she'll find. Just for now, just until she gets there, it is the home she left, with the people she left all just as they were.

And it must be so! There in the growing dark, below, are the roofs of Laurel House. An outside light comes on in the rear court yard where some of the small children are playing, and coming through the door to call them in, as she always does at this hour, is her mother!

Gisonne races now, leaping and sliding downward, and runs, a strange figure flying out of the dark, into her mother's arms.

They stand holding each other while the children watch in quiet wonder.

Gisonne has lost all her recovering ability to talk and to understand. But she does notice that something is odd. Her mother's voice. She pulls away and looks. It is not her mother. Who . . . ?

"Nimee."

"Of course, Gisonne," Nimee says, stroking Gisonne's hair back from her face, looking at the scar on the left temple. "You are so young! More beautiful. You look like my daughters. But you've been hurt."

Yes, of course, of course it is Nimee. Logic. Gisonne sees that it must be Nimee. She manages to smile at her.

"Mother? Where? Is she . . . ?"

"Not well. In her bed."

Gisonne stops at the bedroom door, afraid. Glad that Nimee has kept the children back on the lower level.

The old woman in the bed is her mother, alive, smiling at her, waiting. Gisonne crosses the room slowly, kneels, and lays her head on the soft chest.

"My parent," she says.

Jevry
2/23/50
High Garda

Jevry keys a shift in his wheeler to ease the ache in his bad leg. The early morning clouds have blown away leaving sun so bright that the glare from the water is almost blinding. Jevry considers dimming his goggles when he hears someone above him hurrying down over the lawns toward the beach.

Dorey, he thinks. Needing support. Needing to defend Telem. She should leave him. Walk out. She can walk.

Jevry pulls his worn wind wrap tighter and hunches his shoulders. He shrugs to let her know that he has been content in his reverie alone.

"Jevry?" she asks.

It's Gisonne. He doesn't turn around.

"It is you, Jevry," she says.

He won't answer, won't look. Yes, he will. He'll be defiant so she dare not pity him. He turns and looks up at her. "Yes. It's me."

But it isn't Gisonne! It's her face, her features, only slightly older, but its expression isn't hers There is no one-sided little shrug, half-apologetic, tentative. This person won't pity him.

Jevry knows all about SPEED, time distortion, returnees. Everyone does. But it's all theory—remote; this is up close. Gisonne is Jevry's history, his lost youth and lost soul.

She takes his hand and moves closer to the wheeler. He removes his sun goggles and they squint into each other's face silently.

Let her have a good look then. Look at the leftover, defective man in a leftover, defective wheeler. Better to have died with Denny on Estuary—in the Pontus-cursed estuary, under the tons of mud and muck!

"Denny," she says, as if hearing his thought as she so often seemed to. "They . . . told me about Denny and Hentor . . . and you this morning."

Her speech is odd, slow, Jevry notices. It may be emotion— there are tears in her eyes.

"It's been a long time for me," he says.

"For me . . . today." She sobs for a few seconds, swallows. They stare out at the sea in silence, and then she asks: "Who did it?"

Jevry shrugs. "We all had theories. Political first—the ones we couldn't say aloud. Persons against z2 autonomy, not just off-worlders. But sometimes privately one wondered." He looks away so she can't see his face.

"You . . . suspected someone," she says.

"For a while I suspected everyone. Everywhere I looked I saw the killer. Some were absurd, impossible. It was better to put it away. Call it an accident."

"Who?"

"All right. It's that he was there just before . . . Tel. That shows how irrational I—"

"Tel? But how old—?"

Jevry laughs. "He wasn't yet fifteen. That's just it. Young people do foolish things."

"Why?"

"Hentor," Jevry says. "Without him Tel became The Allain. Also he blamed Denny for Estuary, for bringing Pentente punishments—"

"It must have been . . . bad. I see the . . . signs all . . . all around," Gisonne says.

Troi

There is a horn call and then a horn message. Someone wants the grandmother and, when she is not available, asks for the Norder. Dorey turns this way and that, then sends a house/helper up the stairs to tell the Norder to skin the terminal in his room and she tells Troi to find a Gisonne, while she herself goes off looking for his father.

Just then a stern-faced woman with a white streak in her straight black hair comes off the lift from the beach. You can tell she's one of the Michalises but Troi has never seen her before.

Troi is glad his father isn't there to see them using up the precious power. Telem has been angry enough lately with the grandmother back. Troi has tried to stay out of his way but still has overheard enough to know that there are serious troubles, not the usual sarcasm and criticizing over nothing.

The Michalis woman turns out to be the Gisonne they are looking for. When she figures out what Troi is talking about, she runs off to the nearest horn—she seems to know their house very well—and listens for a while. Then she tries to ask questions but somehow she can't talk. Her face gets weird. She spots Troi and says: "Listen for me. Talk."

"The gov people are bringing OS technicians to study our OS," a woman is saying.

"I'm Troi," he says. "Tell me."

"Is Gisonne there? Or Fron?

"Gisonne," Troi says.

"Tell her they are planning to dismantle the Procne OS."

Troi, curious, skins the visual, but nothing appears.

"She says the gov—is 'gov' the viceroy?—the gov is going to take your ship horn apart," Troi tells Gisonne very slowly. "What shall I tell her?"

"Lonney, how . . . ," Gisonne shouts at the horn. "What right—"

Troi is amazed at this Gisonne. It must be something wrong with her mind, not just her speech. No one asks what right the Viceroy has about anything.

"Lonney, it's me Fron. Can edel override their orders?" The new speaker is the Norder upstairs. He's the only one on visual. Everybody else is making faces and shouting, but this man has no expression in his face or voice.

"He says perhaps," Lonney answers. "He can hold them off for a while the way he did the Stycians."

"No," Gisonne shouts. "They will . . . hurt . . . destroy . . . "

"Right," the Norder says. "Tell edel to do something to delay them but nothing that could be labeled attack. Unless they do something to threaten its life."

Gisonne turns away without another word and races through the great hall to the wing where the grandmother is in the solarium. Troi follows, trying to be inconspicuous. When they get to the solarium, he is annoyed to find his little brother Pen outside the door, openly listening.

"Father's in there too," Pen says in a loud whisper.

Troi doesn't need to be told. Tel's voice is loud and angrier than ever. Dorey is pleading with all of them in general. All as usual.

Troi hopes his father won't notice him. He moves deftly but Pen stumbles along noisily after him. It doesn't matter; only Dorey glances their way and she doesn't count.

The Michalis woman bends over the bed, touching the grandmother's face. Her eyes are open. Suddenly Troi hopes she'll be all right. It would be great to impress his friends and dynemates with a grandmother who looks like that.

"You have no right to be here," Tel is saying. "Don't you understand? My . . . Diana alone will call down misery on this house. That cursed Norder and now you, Michalis. Get out of here. Ruin your own people."

The Michalis woman pays no attention. She questions the house/helper, who has been sitting by the bed, and then says some words in a low voice to Troi's grandmother. Grandmother's eyes are open and her lips begin to move but Troi can't tell if she has actually spoken.

"Diana," Gisonne says. "You must . . . " She shakes her head, discovers Troi, and nods at the horn. "Fron," she says, pointing at the ceiling. "Fron. The Norder."

Troi knows who Fron is now and makes the connection for her. "She wants you to talk to my grandmother," he says to Fron.

"Who?" Fron asks.

"Diana!" Gisonne shouts. "Tell Diana."

Troi puts on visual both ways as the Norder repeats what the ship people said.

Grandmother Diana tries to pull herself up in the bed. The help person holds her down and speaks crossly to Troi and Gisonne.

"All of you, get out of here," Tel shouts now. "Troi, stay out of this."

"Only you can do it," Fron continues, ignoring all the noise. "Stop them. The viceroy."

"Viceroy?"

"Breff," Gisonne says.

"Pontus! Dyll Breff. Viceroy?" Diana's voice grows stronger as she speaks. She looks at Gisonne and then at the people around her. "I'll tell Breff. Horn him. Horn that Stycian sea scum."

"No!" Tel cries. Then he stops, takes a breath and lowers his voice, speaking calmly and slowly. Troi knows what effort it takes him. "Maybe you don't understand, mo . . . Diana. No, of course you can't. Listen. Things have changed. After you . . . left. They took over. Viceroy Breff and Perl, for the PMD, they own z2. We lost everything. They are the law."

"That's all over," Diana says. "It's been taken care of. Who are you?"

Gisonne

But do they, Breff, Perl, the O . . . no, PMD buros, know that "it's been taken care of," Gisonne wonders. She understood Tel saying there is an unloaded Malaacan SPEED ship on Nordport. When did it come in? How far had it traveled? Does it carry information about Zalterius II's repossession of Quivera, its odd control of most sources of bacteriorhodopsin, and thus its re-establishment as a "center of influence"? Gisonne again tries to figure and compare travel time from world to world. It is easy for her to understand and visualize the time and space relationships, but many of the words still escape her.

That Diana could not reach Breff on Nordport showed little. If he is deliberately not responding that means he doesn't yet know her new position in his reality. Or that his underlings don't know. Or it might well be that he isn't there. Perhaps on his way to The Plateau. He is not the kind to trust his own people, never mind native Zalterians.

Another message comes from Lonney to Allaincroft. They have taken Calib off and she has been instructed to remain —as a provider of information. Off-world OS specialists and professional navigators, and an eminent Zalterian physicist and linguist, Cres Trjol, have been assigned to investigate the Procne phenomenon. She has also been informed to expect another person, a "soft scientist" claiming professional interest in the Quivera mission, the Task Leader of ZD.

Gisonne wonders how such a crowd will fit into the ship. Even though the corvi combined navigation and the center into a much larger area, it will be impossible. And that might be helpful. Confusion, competition, opposition will all add time.

What will edel think of Trjol?

2/24/50 oe

Troi helps a weak and limping Fron out of the tractor van and into the island hopper. Gisonne follows. Except for Troi there has been no escort in this direction either.

The pilot drops down at the shuttle end of The Plateau's long landing field, but even from so far Gisonne can see there is little activity around the Procne, no living layer of Stycians, just a couple of helpers standing guard.

Fron and Gisonne are not stopped until they are within a few yards of the ship. Fron tells the buro exactly who they are, and after some upward horn consulting, another buro and some field personnel appear, and conduct them, not to the ship, but to the PMD office building. The first person Gisonne sees is a tiny, elderly woman with sharp eyes—Braitt Jones. Across from her is Trjol, eyeing Gisonne warily. A grim-faced man in lab dress glares at Trjol, ignoring the newcomers. And behind the room's only desk sits Persol Perl. Gisonne recognizes him only because she has been hearing his name often lately, assistant to the viceroy.

"I've examined my records," Trjol says, "and recall better . . . and have concrete evidence of the work I did on this OS. I have every right to the results of my experiment before the subsystems and hardware supporting it are contaminated by ordinary OS technicians."

Gisonne understands enough to laugh—and actually to agree. Better Trjol trying to study edel, living edel, than others dissecting the body and killing the soul.

But someone else does not agree. "I," says the lab man, "am not an 'ordinary technician,' but a navigation engineer and a specialist in OS astronomical programs. The nature of this SPEED ship requires the attention only of a person who—"

"Now, doctors . . . professors, the Viceroy wishes only that—"

"You know that I have always respected Viceroy Breff and devoted all my work to the good of the Pentente," Trjol says, pushing back the shock of pure white hair that falls over the intense eyes. "My original work on this OS is essential to our understanding of everything else. Once I have discerned the nature of what has evolved here, the rest will be clear. However, if we allow only external—"

"Nonsense," the lab man shouts. "This is fantasy. Pardon, I know your reputation, Professor Trjol, but at your age perhaps—"

Trjol's eyes seem to protrude from a face grown paler than ever. The only sound is a grunt or gurgle from his throat as he rises to his feet. Gisonne finds herself studying him with detached curiosity.

Perl's nervousness peaks and he too rises from behind the desk. "Now this can be worked out. We need all of you. I'm sure . . . "

"And us?" Fron asks.

"Information," Perl says to the IP.

And Fron gives the information. Much information. Enough to show that the neuroevolution theory has held up, just enough to give reinforce Trjol's argument.

Perl turns his back and talks quietly into the horn, and then gives his decision: Professor Trjol gets to work on the OS first—for a limited time and under the watchful eye of the navigation expert's assistant. Only after that can the OS specialists study the entire workings of the Procne.

Trjol
2/25-30/50 oe

Calib, Lonney, and Gisonne are house-arrested in PMD helpers' apartments. Gisonne is obviously speech-impaired and useless; Calib and Lonney spend much of their time answering OS navigation specialists' questions. Their ignorance overwhelms the interrogators.

Fron and edel "help" Trjol with his research, though, of course, communication with edel is incomplete without either Gisonne or Emil's right hemisphere. Trjol does not know this.

But he does learn enough to see that his germ of an idea has lived and grown. He was right all those years ago. He is overjoyed.

However it wounds him to see how badly the ZD-picked crew has done. The thing can not speak! It croaks! It seems not to be the single, complex, conscious, brilliant intelligence he envisioned but a deformed personality—or two.

But now he knows what can be done and he will do it.

Gisonne

"Gisonne!"
The voice is familiar. The face isn't.
Gisonne closes her horn, somewhat relieved. It is difficult catching up on thirty years of history when language is still so difficult. Visuals can be more confusing, sometimes totally misleading, without words to explain them.

Gisonne rises and politely offers the room's only chair to this elderly person—she must be in her mid sixties. Without Malaacan surgery, people show their ages quite obviously, Gisonne has noticed. It is not so much the permanent smile and frown lines but the slight limp, the stiffness as the woman lowers herself carefully into the chair.

"You've changed," the woman says.

She is the first person to say such a thing since Gisonne's return. She laughs at the irony and so does the woman. And with the sound of the laugh, Gisonne knows who it is.

"Aj!"

Aj laughs again and raises her arms for a hug, the way a grandmother greets a child, Gisonne thinks, and immediately regrets it. Persons are who they are at any age, aren't they? No.

"I remember . . . the . . . the returnees on—" Gisonne begins.

"Remember the two young men on Corse?" Aj asks at the same time. They laugh once more, but not for long. There is a strained silence.

"Are you all right?" Aj asks finally. "It is odd to worry about someone for thirty years. No, I won't say 'I told you so.'"

"When . . . did you know?" Gisonne asks.

"That you were headed far away forever? Not until we got back to The Plateau. It was so long ago now I forget the details."

"Three . . . years," Gisonne says. "What did people . . . think? Who did it?"

"Everyone thought the OMD off-worlders subverted the mission, of course," Aj said in almost a whisper. "We never said it aloud."

"But . . . but you were with me on . . . on—"

"What's the matter? Your speech? That scar? Some kind of accident?"

"No. I will tell you all about . . . it. Later. After it's all . . . finished," Gisonne lies. Not all. Not about the corvi, not ever, not even to Aj.

Aj purses her lips—an elderly expression, Gisonne thinks. She seems offended.

"ZD? Evan?" Gisonne asks.

"Evan dead. ZD almost dead, but coming alive again. With your help? One reason I came—besides wanting to see you, of course—was to ask for help. With your experience we can—"

"That day . . . Evan was with Braitt Jones. What was—"

"I don't remember a specific day. It was so long ago. And even IP's lose some memory with age. But I think they had some kind of deal. We all thought he subverted ZD himself, subtly." Aj lowers her voice. "His family was one of the few that suffered very little at the hands of the off-worlders."

"Cly?"

"He's with us again. Meaner than ever. And you?"

"Yes," Gisonne says. With this she will gladly help. When she can talk again.

Dyll Breff

A simple message has come to Breff from Diana Allain—a command. He ignored it. Then the Malaacan SPEED ship that is docked at Nordport begins to download its freight, and at the same time, it releases tentative reports from Styxx, economic assessments from Corynn, and copies of cries of help from lesser worlds, along with carefully-worded warnings and guarded cautions, none quite definitive.

It is enough to worry Breff, but not clear or final enough to change his present course—until the shuttle comes in from Agricula with more recent information. Breff receives the news on The Plateau, Diana on High Garda, families in the Arines and the Nord islands, all simulataneously. The statement from Corynn says in official, formal Pentente language—several times and in several different ways—that Quivera is, and always has been without interruption, a possession of Zalterius II. The league title Pentente was an error. The organization of worlds is obviously a Sextente.

Telem
3/4/50

Diana, Tel, and Troi stand on the steps of the landing field office. Breff, Braitt Jones, Persol Perl, and a small entourage of minor officials, approach across the open field in a small land vehicle.

Tel notices that his son is gaping and he tries hard to appear casual. No one should think he is provincial—especially his mother. Does she realize that neither he or Troi has been allowed to travel since z2 lost its independence? Tel, The Allain for fifteen years, has never been farther than here on The Plateau, and that only twice before.

Tel stares at the Viceroy, the person who has caused all the misery, all his family's pain and humiliation. He has seen the face all to often on OS. Yet he recognizes the man himself from something long ago. He was much younger, narrower, did not fill his space as strongly, but where? When?

Breff bows low to Diana and says: "We will work together quite agreeably, Mistress Allain." At the words Tel remembers.

"You have in all your years among us not learned Zalterian manners," Diana says.

"Oh no, I admire Zalterian ways. I think it would be presumptuous of me to—"

"Perhaps it would," Diana says and Tel is proud of her and then angry at himself.

"I shall be pleased to work with Diana Allain, The Allain, for the welfare of Zalterius II and the Sextente. Together—"

"Surely you must know The Allain is Telem, my son." Diana turns with gracious deference to Tel and holds the position just long enough to imprint. "And since Zalterius II does not require a viceroy, the Sextente officials in Corynn will send your replacement."

Telem has until now not noticed the little gray man who has shifted his place from Breff's side closer to Diana and dares to speak next.

"Diana," he says. "I want to thank you." Telem finds the address polite, the tone offensive. The man glances his way, almost a plea. The face is not familiar.

"I cannot express adequately my appreciation for your hospitality. Living with your family in my youth provided the experience, the indirect training without which I never would have earned the office I have held this last—"

"Yes," Diana says. "Our former viceroy will surely welcome your company on his trip back to Styxx. The SPEED ship is being readied even now. You will depart as soon as Professor Trjol has completed certain additions to its OS."

Gisonne

The day that Trjol is to leave Procne for his new ship Gisonne makes sure to be there—with others including Calib who has communicated with edel only from outside until now. Lonney has been there all along. Fron comes over from the field office. Gisonne wants a gathering

"Your sons," she says. "Cres, here are your sons."

Trjol glares at Calib. "Yes," he says. "Calib. Of course. My eyes and memory are weak. How are you?"

"Wonderful," Calib says. "Father! And how is my mother?"

"Your mother? I . . . I suppose—"

"Is she alive? Has our family survived?"

"Why—"

"Yes, father, she is alive. The little trip you sent me on helped them financially. Of course, it didn't come close to what you stole from them."

"I never stole—"

"No, you encouraged me to take everything from her and hand it over to you."

"But it was yours. And you are my son."

"I adored you. I would have done anything."

"I had to go to Malaaca. You were too young to understand the importance of my work."

"I was young too," Gisonne says.

"You killed my grandfather, starved our family, broke my mother—and I helped! And then you were gone. But why did you need to kill me? I was harmless." Then Calib laughs again. "But you failed. I'm back," he says. "You are not rid of me!"

"Son," Trjol says, "rid of you? I gave you my position on that mission."

"And made sure I and my position would go far!" Calib continues to laugh but this time it is more forced.

Then another voice echoes the sound and changes it to a musical note, repeats and strings the repetitions into an old tune, doubles the tune and times it like a madrigal, and plays the whole thing against itself like counterpoint. It is edel's laughter.

Lonney has learned not to try to pet the edel physically but she makes the gesture that both of them recognize and the edel is stroked.

"Your . other . . . ." Gisonne can't think of the word "child." " . . . son . . . laughs too."

Trjol shakes his head, simply puzzled.

"Edel," she adds.

"My sibling rival," Calib says.

"Your son, reared by Lonney and . . . some birds, educated by a Nord IP,. . . an Allain artist, a SPEEDship OS, and some ancient musicians, and di . . . disciplined by a fool—me."

It is the longest speech Gisonne has made since her surgery on Parliament, but it is wasted. Trjol shrugs it off as nonsense, further evidence, in fact, of their incompetence. Giving personality, personhood to this malformed mind and illogically blaming him. He tries to tell them that it is a kind of reverse anthropomorphism—ascribing animal emotions to pure intelligence.

"But I am not judging you," he adds. "It is amazing that you have accomplished anything at all. If you could do what you have done, I know what can be done. By me. And from your errors, I have learned to improve the methods and change the variables of the project. The Allain has offered me the perfect opportunity and conditions for success on this trip to Styxx. The edel I will conceive—"

"One request," Lonney says. "Name him something else."

Trjol shakes his head. Everything they say reinforces his opinions.

"Did you reset our course for Waldseemuller as Calib believes?" Gisonne asks.

"Course?" Trjol looks from one to the other of them.

"This ship," Gisonne says. "Procne. I was on it and you weren't."

"Oh, yes," Trjol says. "The new work going on on Malaaca. I couldn't miss the developments when the next ship arrived. When I realized how much more I could contribute by pursuing and correcting their findings, I knew I had to stay within reach. Of course, it turned out to be only a minor—"

"And why didn't you tell me?" Gisonne asks.

"Tell you? Oh, yes, yes. I don't remember now. . . . I had so much to do at the time. The material promised to be one of the most important—"

Gisonne's laughter drowns him out.

"You can see he didn't do it," Fron says.

After Trjol is gone, Calib tells Gisonne that he and edel will need her help for a particular project. They must understand each other very clearly, which they cannot do without her right brain. Gison puts on her eye patch but cannot see in the same way. The female corpus callosum has been regrowing.

They horn for Emil who arrives in a few days, carrying Jean's youngest grandchild on his shoulder. He seems completely happy. The returnee who has adjusted best and soonest, Gisonne thinks. Testing indicates his brain hemispheres are still separate enough for their purposes. And when Diana arrives on The Plateau with Troi and L'hirondelle, the corvi flies into the cabin, talking and squawking, and seems to join the work.

Gisonne and Diana leave them to that work, whatever it is; Gisonne is very happy to get out of Procne for the last time.

Troi

Troi loves Procne. It looks ordinary on the outside, but the inside is weird. The shape of the cabin is all wrong, round, confusing; one part seems to be the front, navigation, but then another part looks like it has to be for steering the whole thing. Like a prow or cockpit. They can't both be the front. And the furnishing is just as strange. You can't tell if it's equipment or machines or maybe furniture, seats and beds. It depends on which way you look at it, literally, by moving your head.

His grandmother's L'hirondelle is also happy. It actually says so and flies around until the weird man called Calib tells it to stop and help them instead. No one tells Troi to leave so he stays. It would be wonderful to travel in this ship, he thinks. Other worlds. Far stars. The ship fits all his very adolescent unZalterian dreams. Perhaps because the Pentente has so restricted movement on z2, his urge to travel is great.

And he would love to talk to this edel thing his grandmother told him so much about at Allaincroft and all the way over on the island hopper.

He is amazed when edel, female voice, asks, "Who?" A large cartoon-like question mark appears on a wall screen.

"Troi," L'hirondelle squawks and then repeats the name as a chirped melody.

"Troi," the edel says, male voice.

Gisonne
3/22/50 oe

Diana had hardly been out of the solarium on Allaincroft when she left for The Plateau. Now that she's back, she's looking around. Gisonne at least supposes she is and that she

must now be going through the shocks Gisonne herself
expeienced when she first returned to High Garda. But Diana
shows no delight, no amazement, no horror. She has not
mentioned her father, not asked to see Blake. She knows that
Hentor is dead but makes no mention of it. The only people she
shows any interest in are Troi—who does look more like Hentor
than his father, Tel—and L'hirondelle.

Gisonne and Lonney sit together on the short stone wall,
watching two white figures, Diana and L'hirondelle, in the
Allaincroft kitchen garden.

"Finally I have to ask. Why? Your relationship with Diana
makes no sense. No sense to me, anyway," Gisonne says.

"I had to warm her," Lonney says.

"And did you?"

Lonney shrugs and turns to smile at Gisonne. "No. Not in
the way I meant to. But maybe I freed her. And I will go with her
when she leaves."

"I still can't understand that decision; she seems to belong
here . . . to fit . . . and the power and appreciation—"

"She refuses to be an historical anachronism, or antique, or
curiosity and, as we have learned, control is possible only in
person."

"I know," Gisonne says, "she has to make sure the deal is
kept. But that still isn't enough."

"I think she wanted to leave Telem in place as The Allain to
. . . as a kind of reparation for her earlier crimes," Lonney says.
"And what would happen to edel if he stayed here? And
L'hirondelle must expose the existence of corvi."

"I'll miss all of you—even Troi whom I hardly know,"
Gisonne says. "And my dyne is broken—you, Diana, edel, and
Emil. He seemed so happy back with his family."

"He'll be back. That's the part he enjoys. Coming back."

Jevry approaches almost gracefully. His wheeler risers have
been replaced. He stops next to Gisonne and listens to their talk.

All three watch L'hirondelle wing/dance around the herb beds like a giant white butterfly.

"In twenty years when she comes back, she still won't be an anachronism or an antique!" Gisonne says. "We will."

"And will she give the properties back next time?" Jevry asks.

"Probably not!" Gisonne says. "She needs them to take care of all of us."

There is a bell sound and Diana turns to the garden horn. They cannot hear the message or her answer. In a few minutes she walks slowly over to them and says, "Breff's ship to Styxx left only an hour ago and now we discover that it is not bound for Styxx at all. Someone has reset the program—for a planet called Ruysch."

They can only stare.

"Ruysch? Where—" Lonney asks.

"I don't know. Fron says far outside Octente . . . I mean Sextente space."

"Breff and Perl are not young and . . . Trjol is old. They won't live to get there," Gisonne says.

"That's true," Diana says. "And it is Trjol's two sons who changed the course."

For the third and last time Diana and Gisonne laugh together.

Diana seems to notice Jevry for the first time. "Are you . . . ?"

"Jevry, Aunt Diana," he says.

She stares at him for a few seconds and then shuts her eyes.

L'hirondelle runs toward them, head lowered, wings back, and then springs onto the wall, creating a gentle tempest with its flapping.

"And still we will never know who changed our course," Gisonne says.

"Yes, you will," Jevry says. " And yes it was Breff, in a way. He knew about it—Braitt Jones saw the charts—and they did nothing—let you go. That's the same as doing it themselves."

"Denny knew how to do it or thought he did."

The three women look down at Jev in his wheeler.

"We believed he, Trjol, was going, never you, and we both thought he was bad for you. We were saving you. We almost thought it was a great joke. Just the name of the place. We didn't understand."

"Denny paid with his life. I . . . have only done partial penance."

"I don't . . . understand," Gisonne says.

"Don't you see? I did it. Denny and I changed the course."

The End

About the Author

Helen Collins was born in New London, Connecticut, attended the Universityof Connecticut, and, as an undergraduate, spent a year in Bavaria, Germany studying language, drawing and sculpting.

Ms. Collins earned an M.A. in English at the University of Conneticut, took advanced courses at the University of Rhode Island, lived in Manhattan, and taught English at Brooklyn College. As a professor in the English department at Nassau Community College, Ms. Collins taught courses in women writers and science fiction. Her first novel, Mutagenesis, was nominated for a Nebula.

In addition to her avid interest in science fiction, Ms. Collins is strongly committed to animals, to Svaroope yoga, to old houses (she continues to Restore her 1740's house in Niantic, CT), and to the preservation of the natural environment (her house overlooks a threatened tidal marsh).

Acknowledgements

Thanks to Nancy Tooney for many hours of help with scientific issues and for her critical readings of the text. I also thank Joan Gordon, Marian Parish, David Hartwell, and Kate Collins for detailed criticism and guidance, and Joan Sevick, Myrna Nachman, Patti Tana, Carol Gill, and Aileen Grumbach for many helpful suggestions.

www.ingramcontent.com/pod-product-compliance
Lightning Source LLC
Chambersburg PA
CBHW070552260626
47161CB00002B/581